LHG

HUNGRY GENERATIONS

HUNGRY GENERATIONS

JOHN WAIN

HUTCHINSON
LONDON

2 4 6 8 9 7 5 3 1

This edition first published in 1994 by
Hutchinson

Random House UK Ltd
20 Vauxhall Bridge Road, London SW1V 2SA

Random House Australia (Pty) Ltd
20 Alfred Street, Milsons Point, Sydney, NSW 2061, Australia

Random House New Zealand Ltd
18 Poland Road, Glenfield, Auckland 10, New Zealand

Random House South Africa (Pty) Ltd
PO Box 337, Bergvlei, 2012, South Africa

A CIP catalogue record for this book is available from the British Library

ISBN: 0 09 1741858

Set in Bembo by Pure Tech Corporation, Pondicherry, India
Printed and bound in Great Britain by Clays Ltd, St Ives plc

PAT'S

PREFACE

This novel completes the 'Oxford trilogy' on which I have been working for ten years. Its purpose is to describe and dramatize the Oxford that has been sinking out of sight, and fading from memory, for over thirty years. I can tell how far it has become lost in the mists whenever I read, or more often begin to read, a biography of some well-known figure from the Oxford of my youth; of C. S. Lewis, for example. As a rule these books (and articles, and plays, and films, and passages in books dealing with other subjects but with digressions about Oxford) are totally false to the reality they aim to convey – not because of this or that blunder that one could lay one's finger on in a review, but because the author was born too late, and has too little imaginative sympathy, to have any idea of the *feel* of Oxford in those days. And what you have no idea of, you can't convey to others.

Each of the three volumes has, obviously, its individual name, but I think of the triad collectively under the title of the first one, *Where the Rivers Meet*. Not only is Oxford built at the confluence of two actual rivers – the Cherwell comes flowing down to join the Thames at the corner of Christ Church Meadow, and from that point on the Thames becomes a major river – but it has a dual nature, both an international centre of learning and ideas and a hub of business and industry for the English Midlands. This double focus was always there, for medieval Oxford was an important town before the first student appeared in its streets, but for centuries the non-academic town was conspicuous as a market for agricultural produce, set in a wide area of countryside whose interests, on the whole, were Oxford's interests. In the late 1920s one man, W. R. Morris, later Lord Nuffield, began undermining this balance by the introduction of large-scale industry. In the ensuing sixty years, this industry laid waste the rural setting and disrupted the intellectual forum. Once hailed as ushering in a glorious future, Nuffield's empire has now collapsed, leaving a grimy detritus which forms the setting of our lives.

I mention these matters only because they concern the time-scheme of my trilogy. It is not, strictly, a work of memory. Of the two central characters, the brothers Peter and Brian Leonard, Peter is 13 years older than I am and Brian 15. This is because I had to site their adolescence at the hinge of the historical scenery, the point where the industrial development of East Oxford began to alter every aspect of Oxford life whether of town or gown. Peter, in fact, has to be a Sixth-Former at about the time when I myself was at kindergarten. The earlier treatment of college life, then, is based on what I know from talking to people, reading, and using my imagination. When the story gets to wartime it links up with my own memories. It is not, therefore, a thinly disguised memoir. Nor is it a guidebook. Nor is it a collection of anecdotes. Nor a history of Oxford in this century. But it has elements of all these, because it has need of them all.

Ending in the mid-fifties enables me to draw the curtain while the story is still 'historical' and concerned with *autres temps, autres moeurs.* After all, anyone who was 21 at the time of the Soviet invasion of Hungary is now round about 60. Inevitably, such a reader sees both before and after the story told here. A novel is a story about human life, which is to say that it generally contains some loose ends. The nature of life is to be ongoing; in any given year, or on any given day for that matter, many human lives are beginning, many are ending, and many are in mid-career. Likewise with projects, actions, ambitions, schemes for fulfilment or revenge. In a short, tightly organized novel it is possible to convey the sense of a completed action, a rounded whole. But when you cast your net wider, that unity is necessarily sacrificed. The breadth and diversity that are life-giving in one way are life-denying in the other, the way of pure aesthetic completeness. *Pride and Prejudice* and *A Passage to India* are perfectly organized, with the diamond-like perfection of a dewdrop. *War and Peace* and *Huckleberry Finn* are not. If they were, they wouldn't succeed in capturing as they do the struggling vitality of their respective historical epochs. Freedom is slavery. Loss is gain.

In this book, and its two companions, I am aiming at breadth, not the miniaturist's perfection. I yield to no one in my respect for the short, contained kind of fiction and, in my writing life, have several times attempted it. Some of those attempts may have been successful; other people must decide that. All I want now is not to be judged as if I had aimed at it here, and failed to reach it. There are loose ends; there are seeds planted which germinate but don't have time to grow; there are hints of a future that is not shown. There are small mysteries, like the crash Peter Leonard hears coming from Molly Whitworth's house a little before the headlong retreat of Hunt. (I have my own theory about this crash, but shall offer it to the reader as a guessing-game, not important to the essential story.) There are characters (Mairead's brother Dermot, for example) who existed in the mid-1950s but were taken to be simply irrelevant to the way things were going, and have since moved to centre stage.

Moreover, in telling a story that chooses to halt some forty years ago, I have of course to describe many attitudes and situations that are no longer in place. I have likewise to depict many things that time has turned into ironies. When the characters visit Binsey Church-yard, for instance, and are struck not only by its visual beauty but by the calm and healing silence that envelops the place ('a serious house on serious earth it is', and the seriousness flourished in the silence), this is an irony expressed not on the page but in the changed circumstances that resulted from the completion of the Northern Bypass in the early 1960s. Try hearing yourself speak in Binsey Churchyard today!

In the same vein, I put myself to the trouble of inventing a specimen of the work of the youthful pseudo-poet Pettifer, who doesn't even appear as a character, to point up the irony that this was the drivel that young pseudo-poets were producing before the last change but one: before, that is, the switch to four-letter, Vietnam-targeted protest drivel, which was ultimately supplanted by 'perform-ance' drivel. In all these cases, the irony has been provided by subsequent developments outside the pages of this story or any story.

Enough said. Human life is not simple, and history is a great tragi-comic novel continually writing itself, unstoppable and, to the superficial eye, indecipherable. All the professional novelist can do is to break off a chunk and offer it to the reader.

This I have done. If the work brings some enjoyment, and some illumination, to readers I shall never meet, in places I shall never go to, I shall be well satisfied.

J.W.
December 1993

PART ONE

It was the month of May, when all Nature seems young, and in that year of 1947 there was a special flavour of newness, of beginning again, afloat in the air. True, that spirit had plenty to fight against. The world, and Europe in particular, was only just beginning to recover from five years of war. Shortages were grim and all-pervading; very few people had quite enough to eat, enough fuel to keep warm by, enough clothes to wear. Wounds were still not fully healed, and the deaths — the long, sad, sour lists of deaths — were still fresh in memory, not yet tidily layered away in past experience. The winter that had come in at the beginning of that year had been the worst in living English memory, bringing Siberian cold and then, when it thawed, floods that had drowned green acres and trim gardens for mile after mile. Here at Oxford we were still in the middle of a colossal struggle to recover from the greatest disruption the place had undergone in all its eight hundred years of life. A structure complicated enough at best, that had slowly grown and accreted bit by bit over the centuries, never being planned as a whole and including many irrational elements that were there simply because they had been shown in practice to work better than more logical methods, had suddenly been booted sky-high and the fragments were still pattering to the ground. In addition there was the human problem of trying to oversee and encourage a student body made up of such contrasting elements. Fresh-faced schoolboys, with nothing behind them but eighteen years of a rather narrow middle-class life made all the narrower by the restrictions of wartime, which meant that they could never travel abroad and take a look at the wider world, shared lecture halls and common rooms with men who had fought in the desert or battled their way ashore from landing-craft on to beaches swept by storms of mortar and machine-gun fire. Never was there a greater test that Oxford, in common with the Universities generally, faced than that of holding in some kind of unity the untried young and the returned warriors.

If, that is, they did return. Many there were who left their bodies in the desert, on the beaches, in the cold depths of the salt water, or who blew away as ashes after the living cremation of a ball of flame at fifteen thousand feet. And they, too, were among us and made their presence known. We heard their voices in the silences of our lives.

So we struggled on, as so many people in so many places struggled on in that year of 1947, and we did what we could with such materials as came to hand: odds and ends that had seen their best days in the old world that ended at Dunkirk, plus the green, untried, unseasoned material of new growth, ideas and attitudes that seemed to belong to a world that was struggling to take shape but had, beyond that, no settled character.

No wonder the world was very different in 1947 from what it has since become. There was, for instance, no feminist movement. The notion that the boys get all the fat opportunities and the good times, while the girls are neglected and pushed into a corner, is not one that is very likely to rise into your mind when you are confronted by an R.A.F. pilot with half his face burnt away, or an infantryman who has jumped on to a mine and lost both his legs. In those years, being a girl did not seem such a hard fate, nor equality quite such a glittering prize.

To me personally, it had seemed like sheer good luck to be just too old for the youngest age-group of candidates for call-up, those who were called up automatically whoever they were and whatever skills they had, unless they belonged to one of the very few trades that were exempt from military serice. I – because I was highly trained and highly qualified and had some experience of administration – had spent the war behind an office desk. I could have joined one of the fighting services if I had actually volunteered, but surprise, surprise, I didn't actually volunteer. I don't know whether I have any good qualities, but if I do, physical courage is not one of them. I have a bare minimum of that, and you needed more than a bare minimum to volunteer as a fighting man in the years that spanned Dunkirk, El Alamein and Arnhem. I had told myself, as did most men who were in my kind of situation, that I was 'more use where I am', and perhaps I was right.

Right or not, I had survived the war and come back to my duties at Episcopus College. And to the outward eye, on that fine May morning, I was simply one of the younger Fellows of this venerable institution, stepping decorously across the front quadrangle on his way to call on its almost equally venerable President, Dr Salterton.

To me, it was the middle of a working morning; I had already driven in from our house at Chinnor and given an hour's tutorial to two first-year men, neither of whom had seemed fully awake; for old Salterton, I surmised that the appointment I had made to see him was his first job of the day. One couldn't really expect the old man to get into gear until he had completed his little rituals. One of them, I knew, was to read a chapter of the Bible, with a commentary to hand so that he could ponder on difficult passages; another was to eat some toast and honey. It was largely honey, he said, that had kept him alive so long.

Episcopus clock, lagging slightly behind some of the other clocks in the neighbourhood chorus, had just finished striking eleven as I arrived at the great polished door and lifted the brass knocker. Waiting for the maid to answer my knock, I thought briefly of Salterton's immense age and felt glad of it. The iron rule that heads of colleges must accept a retiring age had not yet been universally adopted in Oxford, though it was clearly making its way from self-governing college to college. There were still patriarchs enthroned in colleges up and down the University who connected us by their memories with a totally different England and a totally different world.

Salterton's mature, weatherbeaten female domestic, more a housekeeper type than a maid, had by now opened the door in the time it took me to formulate these thoughts, and indicated the inner room where I should find the old man. I entered. He was sitting in an upright wooden chair beside a densely smoking coal fire, obviously only just lit. Opposite him, on the other side of the fireplace, was another such chair; it was not his habit to receive his colleagues sitting behind a desk.

After the usual greetings I plunged in straight away. 'I shan't keep you long, President, I simply want to give you formal notification of a decision I've come to. A decision and request'.

'You have my attention, Leonard,' he said gently.

'During this summer, some time between now and October, my wife and I will be making arrangements to live apart, and I wish to apply for accommodation in College.' The words were out. I had rehearsed them in my mind a thousand times and now, finally, they were out.

As Salterton had grown older his face had become rounder. Pink and smooth, surmounted by that border of pure white hair, it looked cherubic. But the innocence he radiated had in it no hint of *naïveté*. He always made me think of that scriptural tag about being as wise as serpents and as harmless as doves.

'I don't need to ask you, Leonard, whether you have considered this matter carefully.'

'Yes, I have.'

'And discussed it carefully with your wife?'

'Yes.'

'The marriage tie is not one to put aside lightly. It must have cost you an effort, to reach the position in which you find yourself.'

'President, it has cost me effort, travail, reflection and suffering.'

The old man was silent for a moment. The sunlight beamed steadily across the room from the diamond panes of the windows, while in the grate the fire smoked densely and silently.

'You have, of course, the right to apply for living accommodation in the College; you hold a teaching Fellowship and you are one of the governing body. In these crowded times, though, it may be difficult to give you much choice of rooms, or perhaps to find you a room at all just at present.'

'That's why I'm giving plenty of notice.'

Salterton nodded. 'Those aspects of the matter you will of course be discussing with the Domestic Bursar. But perhaps you have already seen him?

'No, President. You are the first member of Episcopus to hear of my decision and my request.'

He looked at me mildly and seriously. 'You did well, Leonard. Not that I would have expected anything else. A college is a family. Like every family it is vulnerable to rifts and quarrels and jealousies. But when we elected you a Fellow here, we were doing more than making you an offer of employment: we were offering you a relationship – membership of a family. Not all the men understand that, but you have always understood it.'

'I have drawn strength from it. More than ever now.'

'And your wife?' he suddenly shot at me. 'Has she a source of strength?'

'She will have our family home, and the companionship of our son. And because I shall be able to live economically in College, she'll virtually have the disposal of my income.'

'Does that amount to strength?' he asked me with that piercing innocence.

'It amounts to survival – even to a margin of comfort. The strength she'll get from within her.'

'One hopes so, Leonard,' he said, looking at me steadily. 'And of course you have done, and are doing, your best to prepare her for the change.'

'Yes', I lied. I had not yet told my wife Heather that I did not intend to continue living with her.

'Is she – may I ask? – reconciled to your decision?'

'It is a joint decision, President,' I lied again. I saw myself, now, as simply playing a formalized game like chess. Salterton had his roots in an epoch when the Oxford colleges were very specifically Christian institutions and when, moreover, the Christian Church had regarded marriage as a sacrament rather than what, by 1947, it was already fast becoming: a legal and social bargain. I knew he had to make these moves, and the best thing I could do was to make the most obvious counter-moves, smoothly and as far as possible without thinking or feeling anything. It was a matter of moving a pawn, a rook, a castle.

'Go, Leonard,' he said, leaning back in his chair. 'Talk to the Domestic Bursar. As you know, until we can find a suitable person with professional training to attend to the complexities of College domesticity, McLennan is being so good as to undertake the duties. I know it is his goodness of heart that makes him agree to it. In my young days, the Domestic Bursar had not much to do except confer with the chef once a week, sign the accounts brought to him by the College accountant, and assign living-quarters to the Fellows – of whom there were at that time no more than a dozen, and over half of them married men with families.'

Yes, I thought, living in spacious houses owned and maintained by the College, paying peppercorn rents, and thinking themselves ill-used if the house they were allotted was more than ten minutes' walk away. But that was in the happy days when Billy Morris was still pumping up bike tyres.

I took my leave of Salterton and went out into the sunlit quad. McLennan, eh? I didn't swallow all that stuff about his acting as Domestic Bursar out of goodness of heart. I knew him better than that. The boring little troglodyte loved that kind of paper-work. Admin. was what he thought his life was for. I grinned as I recalled how McLennan had been the first person I had talked to after Salterton had told me, all those years ago, that the College had made me a Junior Fellow. I had gone over to look at the rooms I should occupy, or supposedly occupy, as a real live don, even a baby don. McLennan, who shared that staircase, had been hanging about, already a Fellow of one year's standing. My grin was caused by the memory of how he said he was looking forward to some good talks with me. He said that as an economist he was looking forward to discussing history with me, seeing how these economic questions looked from an historian's angle. I felt a glow of self-congratulation at the thought that I had shared a landing with him for the best part of three years and never had a single one of those good talks. He was a perfectly harmless man, yet if I had spent even one hour talking earnestly to him, instead of sitting in the pub with Harry Good-enough, or playing with Michael and telling him stories, or getting Heather into bed and satisfying her youthful needs – and my own too, bejesus – I would have felt cheated. I would have gone to unusual lengths to avoid that contingency, even if it meant having to escape by sliding down knotted sheets.

That afternoon, as it happened, there was a College meeting. These were heavily serious affairs, which started at 2.30 p.m.; a break for tea was allowed at 4.15, but there was no guarantee that it was all over with tea. We might all have to troop back into the committee room, and breathe that stale air and take up our seats again at those long tables, if there was still anything to discuss. All the Fellows had to be present, barring illness or some other weighty reason.

Usually, I went through these meetings in a dogged spirit of doing something that was a duty and good for my soul. But this afternoon I felt curiously distanced from it: as if, though everything I saw and heard was taking place in my presence, I was dislocated, jarred away from it by a huge displacement of my inner landscape. The men, their words and expressions and gestures, their thoughts and attitudes, the tables, the tall windows, the bundles of papers, the occasional sounds from the quad outside – all seemed to be coming to me through a gauze, or perhaps (save that it did nothing to cut off sound) a thick sheet of plate glass.

Obviously this, in turn, was caused by the numbing, disabling current of anxiety that was pumping through me. Having made public my situation *vis-à-vis* Heather, having formally conveyed to the President of Episcopus my request to be re-admitted as one of that bachelor community, a brother in that order of untonsured lay monks, I had started myself moving downhill on a ski-run. The College meeting had to be got through. I wasn't ill, at least in the sense that I could move my limbs, walk about, perform normal actions; to stay away in the absence of illness would have been bad for my relationship with the College community at the very moment when I most needed it to be sound. So here I was at the meeting. It was about to begin, and already I had that sense of the phantasma-goric, of absence-in-presence. As I settled myself into my chair and got out my copy of the agenda, those nearest me were just winding up their individual conversations, ready to give their attention to the business. The one immediately on my left was saying, 'Perkins baffles me. He spent the whole of last term on restricted molecular mapping of yeast chromosomes.' The other shook his head and pursed his lips, doubtless to indicate that he shared this bafflement, but the time for words was past and they both turned their eyes in the direction of Salterton, who was now opening the meeting.

I determinedly gave my full attention to concentrating on the business in hand, and got as far as hearing him say that the meeting had now begun and he would direct our attention to the first item. After that, my failure was total. If I had been promised a sum of money guaranteed to make me independent for life as a reward for following the discussion for ten minutes, I could not have done it. My anxiety, my apprehension and tension at the thought of what I had to do before this day's ending rose up in me, perfectly nurtured by the quiet room, the drowsy afternoon hum of the voices, and the prohibition against getting up from one's chair and walking about. I was trapped, and being trapped was like being alone except for the presence of my anxiety, which was like having to share a stall with a large and dangerous animal. Sometimes this anxiety made itself manifest in a purely physical way, a tightness that penetrated through all the interior of my body till I felt that my gullet, my throat, my stomach, my intestines and every vital organ were being strapped ever more tightly into some contraption designed to squeeze the life out of me. I remembered reading somewhere about the method used by the soldiers of the barbarian king Odoacer to execute the philosopher Boethius. They wound a length of iron chain round his head and went on winding more and more tightly till his eyeballs burst out; then they finished him off with clubs. It was their way of enjoying themselves, and if any of them had sufficient glimmer of near-literacy to know that Boethius had written a book called *The Consolations of Philosophy* it must have given them an extra relish to bring the club down on the helpless form and say, 'Let Philosophy console you for that one then.' I felt close enough to it to reach a kind of insight into what Boethius must have suffered, and I tried to claw up some consolation by thinking that there, at least, lay a few grains of understanding that had come out of this experience. But it was largely a vain effort. Feeling that one has something in common with other people who have been tortured is not, in practice, much help when one's own torture starts.

When at last, with infinite gratitude, I became aware that tea was over, the meeting was over and I was free to go to my room by myself, walk through the College to the Fellows' car park by myself, get into my car and drive back to Chinnor by myself, I did all these things with a feeling, almost, of happiness. Whatever was to come would not, at least, contain that particular torment, the torment of being the only person in a fairly crowded space who knew that I was about to commit a desperate action, a crime, an act of demolition – murder, almost; certainly a killing, of a kind, and yet not a killing I could refuse to carry out.

The effect of the familiar road in which the house stood, then the garden fence, then the garden, then the house, was every bit as crippling as I had feared. The normality of the family home seemed as solid as a medieval castle: thousands of tons of granite, carefully shaped and placed according to a master design, century after century, the work leisured, unhurried, expected to last for unnumbered ages. And I knew I had the job of dynamiting it single-handed, now, this evening.

I had known all along that Michael would present the chief problem. He had to be encouraged to tackle his homework and make a reasonable job of it. Then family supper, and during it he mentioned that there was a radio programme he wanted to hear, about smugglers. (This was in the pre-television era, when radio was still a powerful magnet of attention.) Would I listen with him? He always liked to involve me, to listen with him to anything special.

In the ordinary way it would have been no trouble to listen with Michael to a programme about smuggling. It was always a pleasure to share any interest with him; his face, which at thirteen had not quite emerged from childhood, took on a particularly rapt expression when a subject really absorbed him. Sitting up now in bed, his dressing-gown thrown loosely around his shoulders against the chill evening air, the radio on his bedside table (already carefully tuned and with the volume exactly right, checked and re-checked, well before the programme began), he was listening with that seraphic attention that seemed to shine out of him with the intensity of light. It was, normally, a joy to be part of such an experience, and I knew that he loved sharing it with me too; the radio was the more obsessionally tuned, the preparations the more meticulous, when I had agreed to join him. But tonight, though I sat still, it was nothing but an agony: an interruption: the interruption of an action I was desperately set on carrying through: the sickening fear in the pit of the stomach as I reached the end of the swing from one trapeze and was forbidden, yet, to grab for the ring and trust my weight to the next – out there in nothingness, over a dark silent pit.

The programme finished at nine-thirty. I knew Michael wanted to know what I thought of it, to prolong the pleasure of listening to it together as we always did. But I couldn't join in because I couldn't have repeated one fact from what we had heard; it had simply rebounded from my hard, dry, clenched mind. I told Michael it was late now and we would discuss it in the morning. He lay down in bed. I tucked him up and he looked slightly surprised. Surprised at what? Tucking him up in bed was something I used to do when he was much younger. Did I still do it? Had I, or hadn't I, already given up tucking Michael up when I left him at bedtime? I honestly couldn't remember. I wasn't usually in his bedroom when he went to sleep. Or was I? I couldn't remember that either. Could I remember my own name? Or where I lived? Yes, I was Peter Leonard and I lived here. But for how much longer? I said good-night to Michael shortly, almost gruffly, though I loved him so much. Then I hurried, almost ran, from the room. I had to get downstairs, I had to talk to Heather and get this over.

She was sitting at the kitchen table idly reading the *Oxford Times*. I sat down opposite her. She looked up and made some remark like, 'Has he settled down?' and I said, I suppose, 'Yes.' Then I stopped.

There was a bottle of whisky, about half full, on the dresser within reach of where I was sitting. I had intended, firmly intended, to go through this ordeal cold turkey, in a state of utter clear-headed, desperate, icy calm. But the sight of the golden liquid in the bottle was too much for me. I stood up and reached down a glass from the shelf, tore the cork from the bottle, sloshed a large amount into the glass and gulped half of it down.

Heather said, 'You needed that, didn't you?'

'Yes,' I replied.

'Any particular reason?'

'Yes, I've got something terribly painful to say to you.'

'Oh,' she said. Then she sat back, straightening her shoulders, coming out of the relaxed, easy attitude in which she had been browsing on the paper. 'Well, in that case you'd better let me have it.'

I pushed the bottle towards her.

'I mean let me have what you've got to say, not let me have the bloody whisky,' she said tensely.

'You may need the whisky. This is a bad one.'

'Well, *tell* me for God's sake! Have you committed a crime? Have you murdered somebody and are the police after you? Or, since I'm probably allowed three guesses, I'll come out with the strongest one. It's a woman?'

I drank the second half of my whisky, set down the glass and said, 'A woman certainly comes into it.'

'Well, tell me who she is and how she comes in. Are you getting ready to tell me you want to leave me for some floozie? Is it that bad?'

I looked straight at her, hating myself. Nothing could ever be so terrible as this again. 'I do want to leave you.'

'So it must be for a floozie. Where did you meet her? On the pavement? Or is she one of your students? That's a pretty standard thing to do, isn't it, among your wonderful holier-than-thou stuck-up set, your dons? I seem to be always hearing about it.'

'I don't want to go on with the marriage. It's become unworkable. I'll go on supporting you.'

'That's big of you. You don't suppose you've any choice in the matter, do you? We happen to be married.'

'Heather, there's a law that says I have to support you just as it says I have to support Michael, and it's a just law and a good law and I shan't make any bones about obeying it.'

'You just want to go and live with your floozie, whoever she is. Got money of her own, has she?'

I put my hands on the edges of the table and gripped hard, whitening the knuckles. 'Heather, I don't believe that when we got married you loved me. I think you were ready to become my wife rather than stay on in your parents' home, but I don't believe love entered into it.'

'So what? You're talking about fourteen years ago. If what I felt, or what you think I felt, didn't suit you, the time to say no was in August 1933, not now.'

'Some things that are clear to me now weren't clear to me then.'

'So? Have you gone mad or something? We got married fourteen years ago and I've done nothing in those fourteen years that gives you any right to divorce me. If you leave me for some floozie, everyone'll see your action for just what it is – a piece of cheap selfishness. Who is she, some young trollop who's fooled you into thinking you're twenty-one again? How long's that going to last? You'd better grow up and come to your—'

'Heather, I'm not leaving you for a young girl. It may be that I'm not leaving you for anybody.'

She gave me a look, now, of frowning concentration, as if I had suddenly turned a strange colour. '*May* be? What on God's earth can you be talking about?'

I found that I was still gripping the sides of the table as if I were bracing myself to lift it up and hurl it across the room. My whole body was one mass of hard, riveted knots; I felt my veins must be standing out. Slowly, breathing deeply, I forced myself to sit back in my chair and made myself relax. I sat in a natural position, comfortable but not sagging, back straight. This had to be gone through, and if possible survived.

'I want us to stop living together,' I said. 'I realize that in the eyes of the law there are just a few specific reasons that would make it permissible for me to want that, and I haven't got any of those reasons. All the same, I do want it. It's obviously expecting too much to ask you just to accept the fact that that's how I've come to feel, and that I'm not going to change my mind again.'

Heather looked at me steadily. I knew I was going to be the loser in this contest, if contest was what it was going to be. I had already lost. Heather was right; I was wrong. She was on the high ground; I was on the marshy low ground. When she spoke, her tone was of anger tinged with icy contempt. But as her words went on, they became more flooded with anger to the exclusion of everything else.

'Yes, Peter, you're right to think it would be too much to expect. You think any woman on earth is going to sit down under that treatment – to have her life thrown on the scrap-heap for the sake of a mood that's blown up out of nowhere, that isn't even to be explained to her?'

'It hasn't blown up out of nowhere.'

'Well, why don't you have the guts to come out with it then, and say straight out that you want to leave me for another woman?'

'That isn't exactly the case, but if I tell you precisely what the situation is, it's going to annoy you even more.'

She rolled her eyes to heaven, briefly, then said, 'If you think what I'm feeling is just annoyance, it shows you don't understand anything.'

'Perhaps I don't. Perhaps I'm numbed by the long inward struggle that's been going on in my mind.'

'Oh, it's been a long struggle, has it? Between what and what?'

By now, the whisky I had swallowed was beginning to settle into my system. Without actually making me feel any better about the way I was behaving, it was starting to burn away at my hesitations, making me steadier, less confused, more icily determined to do or die. I knew this effect wouldn't last: I knew that having lifted me up, the whisky would go on to drop me at least as far. In about half an hour I would become weak, undecided, cowed. Press on, Leonard. You know you have to do this.

'Here it is, Heather,' I said. 'When I was working in London during the war years I met a girl who worked in the Irish Diplomatic Service.'

'Very much the expected thing, wasn't it? Married Oxford don let off the leash falls for fascinating colleen. Did she sing folk songs to you? Did she play the harp?'

'I don't know whether it was the expected thing, but for the first three years I was on that war work I never looked at another woman and counted myself very lucky to be able to get home every week-end to you and Michael.'

'And I'm sure you thought we were lucky too. I was doing war work as well, you know. I suppose you never wondered whether I was up to anything, in the privacy of the hay-loft.'

'If you were, now's the time to tell me.'

'I'll damn well tell you what I like when I like.'

'All right, I'll go on with what I'm saying. I didn't fall for this girl straight away. Or if I did, I kept it hidden from myself because I didn't want to be an unfaithful husband.'

'That's big of you.'

'There were plenty of men in that situation during those years who made a perfectly deliberate decision to have a bit of adventure during that time when they had a perfectly convincing excuse for being away from home, and expected to drop it when they returned. I imagine it worked out pretty smoothly in the case of most of them.'

'Smooth, eh?' She gave me a cold, appraising look. 'I suppose that's what you'd have liked for yourself, isn't it? Everything *smooth*? You're a bit of a smooth character, aren't you?'

'I've never thought of myself like that.'

'No, you think of yourself as being fearless and honest and forthright. All that shows is that you like to be smooth with yourself as well.'

I took a gulp. But only of air: the time for whisky was past. 'Look, I'll give you all the time you need to tear my character into smaller and smaller shreds once I've finished this very short summary of what's happened and the present state of things. I met this girl. I fell in love with her. After quite a long time it became evident that she shared my feelings. She loved me too.'

'Did you tell her you were married?'

'Not at first. But I think she always knew.'

'She knew it but she carried on regardless. Cheap little bitch, isn't she?'

'When the war ended and my job folded up, we drew a line under our relationship and said, "Enough". I came back to Oxford, she applied for a transfer from London, and we set about forgetting one another and going back to our previous lives.'

'Was she married too?'

'No.'

'So it was just you who were a betrayer, an adulterer, telling a pack of lies . . . whose idea was it to call it a day?'

'We both had the same idea.'

She gave a short, scornful laugh, the kind that slashes across your face like a whip. 'I'm sorry, but I don't believe that. You've told me yourself you weren't truthful with me for years, so there's no reason why I should believe anything you say and I certainly don't believe *that*. You both had the same idea, at the same time – "Now the war's over, let's call off our affair"? Pull the other one, Peter. She dropped you or you dropped her, I don't know which and I don't bloody well care.'

'What actually happened was this,' I said, keeping my voice steady. 'We parted at the end of the war, on my initiative. We made ourselves pull apart though we both found it very painful.'

'Poor you.'

'For more than a year I settled down to a life divided equally between you and Michael and my work. A settled life. I thought that was the end of the story, that everything to come would be solid and settled and predictable.'

'Sounds as boring as hell. No wonder you've got middle-aged itch.'

'It was what I wanted, and since you never said anything to the contrary I assumed it was what you wanted too. What changed it was the night we went to that party in Merton or somewhere, and met that girl called Hazel.'

'Yes, I remember Hazel. Just about. A little slut if ever there was one.'

'She'd had a couple of drinks too many and she was recalling old Birmingham days.'

'And you listened to her sick fantasies.'

'I knew she was telling the truth, in broad outline at any rate. I didn't attach any importance to the detail of the story, but what it showed me clearly, in a sudden flood of light, was that at the time we got married you didn't love me.'

'Oh, don't start preaching away about love, for God's sake, just because you've decided it suits your convenience. Love! What do young people of that age know about love? They're young, they're full of energy, they're just going for what they want like hounds pulling on a leash. What did you feel when you were chasing me, all those months before we ever got round to being married? Was it love? As far as I could tell, you just wanted to get your prick into me.'

'I suppose love often does start like that.'

'Well, you got it in, so what are you grumbling about?'

'It landed me in a marriage with someone who'd married me not because she loved me, but because she hated being at home and was desperate to get away.'

'All right, so what? I never said I *liked* being at home, did I?'

I went on grimly, like a battered old tramp steamer butting her bow into the tremendous waves of a south-westerly gale, ploughing on, rising and falling, shipping green water over the wheel-house, shaking herself like a dog after each immersion, going on, on, on, towards the unimaginable haven.

'What happened after Hazel filled in that background was that I found an emptiness within myself. I no longer had the motivation to keep holding down the lid on my feelings about Mairead.'

'Mairead! What the hell kind of name is that?'

'It's an Irish name. I'd been keeping down, out of consciousness, the colossal effort it was taking to avoid thinking about her. I'd managed somehow to hypnotise myself into believing that I'd broken away from her and the wound was healing. I'd even shut my mind to the enormous effort of keeping it all at a distance. It was like . . . I don't know what, holding a door shut when someone on the other side is using a tractor to push it open.'

'So then,' Heather said, 'Hazel released you from all that and you let the door swing open and the tractor Mairead came chugging in. Happy ending. All you have to do now is get rid of me.'

'I'd lost touch with her. Deliberately . . . as part of the overall plan. But when I had to face the fact that I *hadn't* forgotten her, I knew I had at least to try to find her and see if I could get back with her. It was the only way I could imagine of having a happy life. If it couldn't be done, all right, it couldn't, but at least I'd have tried; I'd know where I was.'

'Yes, and you'd know where I was, too, wouldn't you? On the rubbish tip.'

'I hunted around till I picked up a trail that ultimately led me to Mairead. She agreed to meet me, in a public place, and we had a short conversation. She told me she'd found it very hard to get used to being without me, and had finally managed it by developing what amounted to a new self which she wasn't even going to try to dismantle so long as I was still married. She said if I was serious I could, if I really wanted to, get in touch with her again when I could produce evidence that our marriage was over and I was alone, and free.'

'And that's what you've decided you are now? Alone, and free? Well, I've got news for you, Herr Professor Doktor. You're not going to get rid of me that easily. You're not going to throw me away like a crumpled paper handkerchief just because you've decided your nose doesn't need blowing any more.'

'I know that, Heather. I never thought it was going to be easy. But I want to give myself a chance to put my life on the right foundation – a chance to be happy.'

'*You* want to be happy? That's fine for you, isn't it? What about the other people in the world, or haven't you noticed them? What about Michael, and me?'

'Michael's young enough to adapt. His parents moving apart may be a disturbance to him at first, but he'll adapt and go on living and growing. With regard to you, well, I hope you'll adapt too. After all, when you set our marriage up – and it *was* you who set it up – you did it to achieve an object – getting away from your family, setting up in your own home – and you've done it. You never had to go back to your family and now you never will have to.'

Heather did not speak for a long time. She just looked at me across the length of the table, as if she were watching me recede into an immense distance. When she finally spoke it was in a very low voice, hardly above a whisper. If the room had not been so quiet I probably wouldn't have heard her at all.

'And you think that's all?'

I said nothing. I didn't know what to say. After a moment she went on, still in that almost-whisper, 'You think that's all there is in it for me? That once I'd got away from my horrible home and horrible family, there was nothing else I wanted from you?'

I felt like dirt. I felt like a leprous cur. But even feeling like that didn't make me want to change my mind and throw the whole thing into reverse.

'Look, Heather, I know this isn't the outcome you ever wanted—'

'Outcome? Why do we have to talk about outcomes? We're still young, both of us, we have our lives ahead of us, there's so much we could do with those years together.'

The scalding agony inside me forced me upright, on to my feet. I stood up convulsively.

'It's no good, Heather. I can't discuss it any more. Everything you say is true and I still can't help myself. I'm in the grip of an absolute need. What I'm doing is wrong and yet it's what I have to do. I could never settle back into an existence with you when I know that if I were alone I might have a chance of real happiness, the kind that would irradiate my life and make me into a stronger and more positive person.'

Now she had another mood-change, becoming hard and challenging again. 'So you're not even leaving me for another woman; it's not even as positive as *that*. I can't even think, well, join the club, Heather. You've been robbed. Some young floozie has stepped in and stolen your husband from you, it happens all the time. Even *that* I can't comfort myself with. No, I have to think, my husband has given me the final insult. He's left me just to put himself in a position where he *might* have a chance of getting some girl who's turned his head. Is that how you'd put it? Is that a fair description?'

'I might not use those exact words, but I have to admit that's pretty much how it is.'

She looked at me for a long time. Since she was sitting and I was standing, she had to tilt her head back to look into my face, a position that showed off her beautiful firm throat. They say a woman is as old as her neck. Heather's neck, particularly when slightly stretched as it was now, was as young as a schoolgirl's. And the electric light shone down on her golden hair. At that moment, she didn't look like a woman that any man would wish to leave. Yet I wished to leave her, because of Mairead. No wonder that love, overwhelming sexual love, has so often been envisaged as a calamity, a devouring state of madness that people pray to be shielded from.

Now, not abruptly but decidedly, she pushed back her chair and stood up. 'All right, Peter. You want to go, go. Go now. Don't stay here any more. Not even tonight. Just go to the door and open it and go out. If I've got to be alone from now on, let me begin straight away, while I feel I can stand it. There's some of that whisky left. I'm going to drink it and then go upstairs while I'm drunk and lie down in bed. If I've got to be in it by myself, let me start out while I can't feel anything much.'

'Are you sure you're—'

She made a fierce gesture of dismissal. 'Go. Give me that much. It's little enough to ask, isn't it?'

I went out into the hallway, through the front door and into the deep dusk. It was not totally dark yet, and in any case there was a fat, confident half moon that would be enough to see by. I walked a little way down the road, turned off along the lane, got up on to the dark immensity of the chalk downs, with silence and solitude totally enveloping me. Then I walked. My mind wasn't working: it seemed to have stopped. I just lifted one foot after the other, moving ahead, following the giant curve of the chalk down, not thinking anything, not feeling anything.

The night was mild enough, but after an hour or so a breeze sprang up and the temperature dropped a little. Instinctively I put my hands into my jacket pockets and on the right-hand side I encountered a small multiform metal object: my key-ring. The knowledge that I had a key and could get into the house must have affected me subliminally, because I began to walk in a wide circle – two or three miles wide – that eventually brought me round to the road again, not far from the house. By that time a light rain had begun falling and it became heavier as I approached. I paused and tried to assess whether Heather was still up; there was a light burning, but it seemed to be the one on the staircase.

My clothes were wet by now, and I decided to go in and get some dry ones before following Heather's instruction to take myself off. I looked round; it was the staircase light that was on, all the others were off. The door of our bedroom – sorry, Heather's bedroom – was closed. I went to the bathroom, took off my wet clothes, towelled myself and then, without thinking what I was doing, went to the airing cupboard and got out a pair of pyjamas.

At that point, of course, I came back to the realization of what I was doing, and in that instant I knew that I was, after all, going to spend one more night in the house. I had been just about to get into the pyjamas and head towards bed, from sheer force of habit: well, I would get on with it. My wet clothes lay in a sodden heap beside the linen basket. I even went over to the wash-basin and cleaned my teeth, as if this were a night like any other. Then I went along to the spare room. On the way I paused for an instant and listened at Heather's door. There was no sound; perhaps she really was asleep. Or had she gone out? But where, if so?

Well, the hell with it. If she had gone out, leaving Michael alone in the house, all the better that I was there. I went to the spare room. It was dusty and the bed wasn't made up, but there was some bedding lying folded on it. This was before the age of the duvet, when people still had sheets and blankets, and when I got it spread out I saw there was only one sheet and one blanket, plus a bedspread. I tangled myself up in it somehow and lay there chilly and stiff. It didn't matter; I didn't want to sleep, just to lie there and close my eyes for a while.

In the end I must have fallen into some sort of slumber, because I went into a forest of wild dreams. My wakening and re-awakening finally culminated in my coming firmly back into consciousness at about six a.m., when the daylight was just about fully formed.

I got out of bed and hunted around for some clothes. They were all in the room Heather was in (or wasn't); unreachable anyway. I went to the bathroom and scooped up my wet clothes, then went downstairs, switched on the heating and hung them to dry while I made a pot of tea. My dressing-gown, fortunately, was in the bath-room, and with that on and a cup of tea inside me, and my clothes drying, I felt more confident. I even sneaked into the bathroom and shaved. Why was it sneaking, suddenly? Because I didn't want Heather to burst in on me. I wanted to get away from the house without seeing her.

When I came out on to the landing I found Michael just emerging from his bedroom. He was wearing his pyjamas, with no dressing-gown or slippers, and I told him to put them on before he came down; he was still young enough not to feel cold even at times when he *was* cold. When he had them on he came down to the kitchen and we had a cup of tea together and talked about smugglers. It was still not 7 o'clock.

I told Michael I had got up early because I had to go to London and I would be away two or three days.

'You didn't say anything about it last night,' he said; but he was not complaining, just making conversation.

'No,' I said. 'It came up unexpectedly. A bit of unfinished business. There was a phone call last night, after you'd gone to sleep.'

As I spoke I thought *lies, lies, lies*. But that will soon be over, I thought. Soon, very soon, there will be an end of lying. An end of that shame at least.

I made a fresh pot of tea, poured a cup and asked Michael to take it up to Heather. He took it and went up the stairs. I went to the front door and put my hand on the knob to open it, then waited until I heard him go into the room. He didn't come down again straight away, as he would have done if she hadn't been there . . . or if she had slashed her wrists or hanged herself or any such thing. She wasn't that type, anyway.

Silence. He must be in there with her; they would be chatting. I opened the door, stepped out, went to the car, got in and started the engine. Then I nosed her out into the roadway and accelerated away towards Oxford.

It wasn't until I had gone a mile or two that I remembered that according to our prearranged schedule this was a day when Heather was due to have the car. Never mind, I thought, driving on. I would leave it parked in Oxford and let Heather know where it was. She could come in on the bus and collect it; I knew she had the spare key. And after that she could have it for ever.

★

In between beating that sudden retreat from Chinnor, and a set of rooms falling vacant in Episcopus, I had no home. It was like going back into wartime again, especially as more or less everything was still rationed; we all had Ministry of Food ration-books – if you lost yours you just didn't eat – and you had to give them into the keeping of whoever did the catering at your official address. I clean forgot about my ration-book on the morning of my final panicky exit from the house at Chinnor, but mercifully Heather had for some reason left all our ration-books, held together by an elastic band, in the glove compartment of the car, and after switching off the engine for the last time, and leaving the car to its subsequent fate, I did a routine check in the compartment to see if I had left a bunch of keys or anything. Phew! A piece of luck there. I knew she would never have sent it on. As it was, not wanting to risk theft, I scooped up her book and Michael's and put them in the post.

It only took me a few hours, since I wasn't choosy, to find a room in a boarding-house down the Abingdon Road, which would do for the time being, as I was there as little as possible. I saw the place through a gauze of temporariness: the travelling salesmen who mostly made up the other inmates never really engaged my attention, which was focused on what had suddenly become the main business of my life: getting used to College existence all over again, adjusting, after years of marriage and years of wartime, to a single life in a monastic-style community. We were a mixed bag, but I imagine a fairly representative one. We numbered about twenty – a bump up from the fourteen or fifteen of pre-war days – but even so able to cope with the tidal wave of teaching that hit us with the sudden return of the servicemen only by drawing in an army of fringe labour, weird auxiliaries who either emerged shaky and somnolent from the depths of retirement or were very recent graduates who kept one jump ahead of their pupils from week to week and had no higher ambition.

Alongside these waifs and strays we had, of course, a layer of much more solidly established senior men. Forty years is, and was then, a by no means unusual length of time for an Oxford don to pursue his working life, which meant that in the years immediately after 1945

–24–

there were dons about who had been elected to their Fellowships in the years between 1905 and 1910. Salterton, of course, was even older, his beginnings shrouded in a legendary past, but even a humble sexagenarian could recall times – and indeed often lived by the assumptions that once governed times – very different from the age that was coming in. Coming in diffidently and waveringly, yes, but coming in. Since a new set of attitudes was abroad in England and the world generally, these were abroad in Oxford as well, and though it was to be years before the surface resistance cracked, some of the bastions of Edwardian Oxford were already frail. Chief among them was the notion, once rooted in the heart of Oxford and of the kind of England that Oxford in those days mirrored, that the chief object of University discipline must be to keep the young men and young women from physical contact. Having contact with a girl would inevitably lead to sexual misbehaviour, since there was no correct behaviour outside the circle of the tea-table. At best it could only lead to marriage, and marriage, though not a misdemeanour in the eyes of Society at large, was certainly such in the eyes of the University unless and until everyone concerned had graduated and gone down.

Among our ranks at Episcopus we still had a few veterans in whom this attitude lived on. They had absorbed it in their own youth, regulated their lives by it, and now could not give it up or even see round it. Our Senior Dean in particular, an elderly Pecksniff of a law don with a scrawny neck and the facial outline of a turkey, used to refer contemptuously to the young men's habit of 'going girling'. Reflecting on how many times I would have been only too glad to go girling if there had been the possibility of getting any results – had, indeed, taken Vinnie to that horrible Holyoake Hall, in my second term was it?, as an exercise in girling – I used to look at him with silent disapprobation and pray for patience. I was quite sure this dreadful old man would have been glad to send an undergraduate down for kissing a girl under the mistletoe. For that matter, he would probably have argued that the mistletoe, being a druidical survival, was tainted by paganism and therefore had no place among the mental furniture of students at a Christian University. He and his kind, though usually sceptical in religion, were great on the Christian foundations of the University. It was the punitive side of Christianity, obviously, that appealed to them; the moral sanction it gave them to make people's lives miserable for a few years, citing the example of a Creator who, as depicted in the Bible, had created a cosmic penitentiary named Hell for the express purpose of making the entire human race miserable if they failed to toe the line, and throughout eternity, what was more. Once you had grouped them on either side of this basic dividing-line, the Fellows of Episcopus were the usual human mixture. In some, I found much to admire, and there were individuals for whom my admiration was deep-rooted and long-standing. Tonson, the Arabic scholar, was one of these. The historian R.S.C. Bax, originally my tutor and still a key figure in my life, was another; but Bax had obviously withdrawn into himself a good deal in recent years. I was one of the few who knew why; few enough, perhaps, cared to ask. The thick lenses he wore had always given Bax a certain air of inscrutability – he looked out through those multi-layered discs as from a defensive position, and quizzically. But now one felt increasingly that the looking out was becoming a formality. He cared less and less what he would see out there. He was prepared for it to be disillusioning, disappointing; threatening, even; but he had no real curiosity about it.

I was achingly sympathetic with his life-problems. Homosexuality was, as I have said, tolerated readily enough in the Oxford of those days on the grounds that at least it kept the women out, and women, collectively, were Public Enemy Number One. On the other hand a homosexual, unless he wanted to become increasingly labelled as Public Enemy Number Two, had to pick his friends very largely from among his own kind, which was hampering and limiting. Bax, I am sure, disliked his own homosexuality. He regarded it as an ill-natured practical joke played on him by the blindfolded Cupid. His affair with the slender, boyishly built Geraldine, clearly, had been a desper-ate attempt to construct a flimsy bridge over the gulf between the gender he actually desired and the gender that represented 'norm-ality': an expedient that must have been tried many times, though whether it was ever successful I have no idea. In his case it had not been successful. Geraldine began by falling in love with him and ended, after a long series of unguessable disasters (but if only they were unguessable! If only one were not so continually drawn, by sympathy and the depth's of one's fondness for both of them, to guess at what must have happened, to imagine the humiliations and col-lapses!), she had ended by rejecting him, splitting away from him, abolishing their relationship. It had broken him: he, a proud, reticent man, had wept helplessly, there in front of her, sitting at the desk in his own study. And after that he had never recovered. Something in him, some kind of mainspring, had broken. I pitied him. I lay awake at nights imagining his sufferings and trying to contrive some cure for them. But I never could.

He solaced himself by different methods in turn. Sometimes he had determined, almost demented spells of intensive work. He plunged himself into the investigation of historical problems: but always, I noticed, technical problems, enigmas that surrounded the dating of an event or the nature of a blood-relationship, or the precise inter-pretation of a document drawn up by a medieval parliament. He seemed to lack the heart to plunge into large general questions, as if life in its wider perspectives had lost its appeal for him. At other times, relinquishing his grip even on this droughty material, he frankly hit the bottle, reaching for the oblivion that alcohol brings unfailingly and at a high price.

Knowing him as I did, I could usually tell at a glance, when he came into Common Room for a cup of coffee in the morning, whether he had been spending the previous evening (a term that for him usually included the hours up to 2 a.m.) relentlessly at work or joylessly emptying glass after glass, weaving unsteadily over to his bedroom at last to sink into a deep but troubled sleep – nothing restful, more in the nature of a coma. Both kinds of evening left him deeply tired, but the drinking evenings brought him down to a lower circle of hell than the working ones. They poisoned him as well as draining him of energy. His face sagged and his skin looked as yellow as a Malay's.

Tonson, whose scholarship I respected as deeply as Bax's, was by contrast a man who not only deserved to be all right but evidently was all right. His slight, erect form, his round innocent face which confronted the world so candidly and freshly, seemed matched by an uncomplicated life. He had, I knew, an amiable wife, an undistin-guished, comfortable home, and a daughter growing up in a tranquil North Oxford setting. The fact that his area of endeavour was despised by some people as a luxury, a frill, a marginal subject kept going because it had once started, evidently troubled him not a straw. Obviously he had long been aware of the foolishness of that kind of stock market quotation. If Arabic never became a mass school, he would continue to study it as an important subject; if by some quirk of history it did become a mass subject, he was ready for that too.

Then there were the usual run-of-the-mill types, some amiable, some less so, who laboured in their respective vineyards and did their respective jobs with, one supposed, satisfactory results. In an aca-demic community, a certain amount of tolerance, of taking one another's competence for granted, is called for, if only because so many academics are engaged in work that is totally unintelligible to everyone in the world except themselves and their colleagues. If I am sitting at lunch or dinner next to a metallurgist or a microbio-logist, how on earth am I to assess his competence? All I can do is form a general impression of whether he seems intelligent in general conversation – not always a reliable guide.

Actually, to be fair, not many of my colleagues at Episcopus struck me as talking foolishly, though some of them had basically foolish attitudes that made them take up positions I found deeply false:

Watson with his supercilious snobbery, for instance. Watson was still engaged in keenly relishing the presence of our new Fellow in English, Noël Arcady, who effortlessly exuded an air of old money and the Great World. Arcady, of course, was not a snob. His way of seeing the world, and of behaving, was perfectly natural and unselfconscious. He was even, I could perfectly well imagine, a useful addition to the English Faculty generally. After all, some notable English literary works have been written by members of the aristocracy who lived in stately houses set in beautiful parkland: Sir Philip Sidney, for one, or Herbert of Cherbury, or some of the courtiers of Charles II who wrote, at any rate, graceful verses, and were sufficiently numerous to form a 'school'. Arcady was a natural inhabitant of what was left of that world – he was always being invited to spend the vacations at this or that great house that appeared in all the guidebooks; and, going to these places as naturally as the rest of us might take a week at an inn in the Lake District, often made interesting remarks concerning the Grinling Gibbons carving here, or the manuscripts in a library there, or the grounds laid out by Capability Brown in some other place; and his being not awed by these things but taking them as the ordinary furniture of his life made his comments the more natural and sensible-sounding. I preferred his comments on English literature and civilization to those of some narrowly watchful, sharp-elbowed type who had hauled himself up from a council estate and never for a moment let anyone forget it. I knew what life looked like from a council estate: not so damned different from what it looked like through the windows of the side-street public house where I had grown up in Oseney Town. It was more interesting to learn something new. I would infinitely have preferred Garrity in the job – Garrity, profound scholar, lovable eccentric, lonely wanderer of the countryside, poet *manqué* who lavished such craftsmanship on his superb translations from the German. But it was not to be. The Fellows of Episcopus, collectively, were afraid of eccentrics and not immensely fond of profound scholars, unless they did what was called 'wearing their scholarship lightly', i.e. never allowing it to appear at all. But, I thought, having missed the chance of getting Garrity, they had been quite lucky to find themselves taking on Arcady, by whatever mixture of motives and pressures. And with it, he was quite a good work-horse, not shirking his part in the dull routine of academic life. A decent man, though seldom on my wavelength.

Among the veterans, survivors from the thirties, old Weatherby the physicist was still there, knighthood, Nobel Prize and all. He was beginning to be physically frail – after all, without rivalling the immense age of the patriarch Salterton, he was not merely a survivor of the thirties but actually of the early twenties – but above and beyond the frailty there was something else that one noticed. He – like Bax, though for very different reasons – had suffered a blow from which he found recovery impossible. His work on the Manhattan Project, resulting in the first atomic weapon in 1945 and its immediate use at Hiroshima and Nagasaki, appeared, like Bax's very different trauma, to have broken something in him. Courteous, gentle, he seemed to haunt the rooms and passages of Episcopus College like some loftily mournful ghost – the shade, perhaps, of a tragic hero, central figure in some ancient tale of a grievous wrong and large-scale disaster which still had power to move even a generation to whom the issues were no longer real. The issue of right or wrong over Hiroshima and Nagasaki was, of course, still much in everyone's mind, but for Weatherby it seemed no longer discussable. Attempts to draw him into talk on that issue were always met by vagueness, almost incomprehension, as if that part of his mind had been struck such a disabling blow that it had become insensible, paralysed with shock. There were times when I almost feared he would take refuge in a clinical amnesia.

To complete the picture I should add that every October the College took on a very few young men as Research Fellows, some of whom had only graduated the previous summer. Some were destined to spend the rest of their lives at Episcopus, others to move out as wider opportunities presented themselves and other grass, usually non-academic, looked greener. One could never tell, just from a surface acquaintance, which ones would go and which would stay; they often did not know themselves, which was as it should be. Though I was only in my mid-thirties, these lads already seemed to me incredibly young, like undergraduates. But then, the undergraduates looked like fifth-formers. In short, I was beginning to experience the effects of time on one's way of perceiving the world.

One sign of advancing years I had not begun to show, and I should hope not at thirty-five: I didn't, yet – nor did I for a good many years to come – find young people more or less automatically irritating. To the old, the young are annoying for the same kind of reason that xenophobes find foreigners irritating: they live by different assumptions, they use language differently, they have a different view of the world that strikes the stay-at-home as impossible to reconcile with his own. Since all these charges are perfectly true, I see no reason why old people should be advised to regard their irritation with the young as a fault, one of the deformities of age, and be kindly encouraged to 'fight against it'. That's like telling a houseproud woman to fight against her dislike of cockroaches. The best thing she can do is keep her immediate living-space clear of cockroaches and try not to worry about the fact that when she has passed away, the cockroaches are set to inherit the earth.

But that's by the way. I had not then foreseen what would become my normal, standard reaction to young people as life went on. For that matter, as the nuclear weapons began to be manufactured on a wider scale year by year and the future of the world increasingly lay in the chances of accord between Congress and the Politburo, I was far from confident that life – my own life or anybody else's – would 'go on' at all.

I didn't, then, feel any dislike of our very new intake of Fellows merely because they were young. Young people, on the other hand, under their blanket similarity, are like people of any kind in that some are nice and some are nasty. Only one of ours struck me as definitely nasty, and I couldn't with certainty have said why. I just didn't trust him – didn't like the cut of his jib. He seemed to me the type who sooner or later reveals a bad streak: mean, self-seeking, or simply impercipient, doing damage of which he can't understand the extent.

This was a recent graduate named Manciple – Luke Manciple – who came to us glowing with recommendations from the people who had taught him. These people in their turn I had no love for. They represented the kind of Oxford don who is always looking over his shoulder at the great world of business, political intrigue, power and influence: in other words, the World. If Noel Arcady in his suave way represented the World in the sense of the *beau monde*, young Manciple with his hungry and slightly shifty eyes represented the world of men in business suits doing deals in the backs of chauffeur-driven cars. His subject was Politics, in itself a subject perfectly worthy of academic study, but which one felt he had chosen because it brought him as close as Oxford offered to the smell of the Real World. He was the kind of person who was always saying that Billy Morris had done Oxford a good turn by turning it into an industrial city because that had 'brought it into the modern world'. And when I once said to him that that was a purely abstract statement, very easy to repeat as a slogan and tempting to repeat because it was an easy popular line, but I had never seen any real concrete evidence that Billy Morris's factories had done anything to sharpen the consciousness of the intellectual community in Oxford, he fenced with me and said that 'intellectual community' was an abstraction too. I made a mental note to watch him and if possible forestall any really obnoxious and destructive moves he might make in the future.

Meanwhile he was busily digging himself in. He lost no opportunity to build up a network of influential contacts, and indeed to curry favour with persons of consequence of any kind. He had a bouncing self-confidence and a loud voice which seemed to pursue one all over Episcopus. There were days when I felt that I was never out of the sound of it, that braying voice of Manciple's. He was never so happy as when some kind of big international news broke, as in those days of continuous upheaval it seemed to do every few months. Most of these big news stories were political and Manciple, who was professionally concerned with the official world of politics but also took an obsessional, prying interest in its gossip and scandal and inside news, always had some confidential whisper about last-minute bargains and betrayals and face-savers which he gleefully announced in high volume. Listening perforce to his non-stop commentary on world affairs, I noticed one connecting thread that bound together all his fragments: he never took the side that appeared likely to lose. It was the time when tottering democratic governments, mostly under-mined by the exhaustion of war, were being shoved over and smashed by Communist parties drilled and ready with their tech-niques of infiltration and sudden take-over, and I noticed that the gossip stories retailed by Manciple never made fun of the new breed of Stalinist leaders who bestrode the prostrate countries of Eastern and Central Europe in the late 1940s. Perhaps this was because, cannily weighing the probabilities, he thought they might soon be doing the same to the Western ones, in which case it might be very unhealthy to say anything satirical now. Repressive regimes have long memories.

I couldn't blame him, given his self-serving and cowardly nature. It really did seem, in those days, quite possible that everyone from Vladivostok to Cork might soon be living in a Communist world if the cat happened to jump that way, and the cat seemed more readily disposed to jump that way than any other. It had taken what looked like, and almost was, a long jump that way on 10 November 1946, when the French general election put the Communists at the head of the poll. In December of the following year it actually did take a jump when Rumania became a satellite of the U.S.S.R., followed a couple of months later by Czechoslovakia – East Germany and Poland being already safely in the bag. All this time Manciple kept his alert, shifty eyes on the scene and his ears and tongue busy with amusingly revealing anecdotes about the weaknesses of international politicians: except, of course, Stalinist and (after September 1949) Maoist politicians. I knew his type. If Britain did get a Communist government, Manciple would work hard to rise in the system and become a commissar, in which case he would probably send most of the other Episcopus dons to Siberia. But perhaps Britain would have its own gulag somewhere more conveniently situated. The Orkneys, maybe?

By contrast, politics played extraordinarily little part in the life that was lived in the boarding-house down the Abingdon Road. The clientèle seemed to consist almost entirely of middle-aged men; certainly of men. Whether it was a conscious policy on the landlady's part I don't know, but in the time I stayed there I never saw a female fellow-guest. The men who stayed there were all representatives of business firms of one kind and another. They had breakfast all together, dispersed about their occupations, and returned at six to a high tea, after which the evening was theirs; though I noticed that, like dons, they often had to go up to their rooms and prepare work against the next morning. I broke this pattern only by not turning up for the evening meal and very rarely being around in the evening at all; I only knew that some of my fellow-boarders worked late at their papers because I saw the line of light under their doors, often as late as midnight. This was, thank God, before the days when it was *de rigueur* for establishments like that to provide a television set in each room, so at least one was spared the jabbering and the bursts of mechanical laughter as one walked along the landings. All in all, I had no objection to my fellow inmates. They contained, I was sure, no higher a proportion of boring, egotistical or arrogant people than did Episcopus College. I was present at their conversations only at breakfast-time, but my impression that they had no interest in politics was not weakened by this fact, since I knew that men to whom political issues are important tend to talk about them in the morning just after looking at the day's headlines. They were, indeed, interested in a mild, general way in the question of whether England should be governed by the Conservative or Labour Party, but wider and more general issues of world politics did not exist for them. The question of whether Western Europe should come under Communist control evidently concerned them no more than if Western Europe had been some very remote part of the galaxy, visible only by radio-telescope. For the most part, being serious middle-aged men, they talked about trade, with motor-cars a close second. Several of them had fought in the war but, as with nearly all men who have served in armies, it was the army that was the reality to them, not the country it happened to be sited in.

*

Frank Penney would soon be coming up to retirement age. He had been Head Porter of Episcopus ever since I had known the place. When I first enrolled there, in 1930, he gave the impression, in his large, grave majesty, of having been there for uncounted years, though I dare say to a lad of eighteen ten or a dozen years would seem like long service. To my generation, it was difficult to imagine the place without Frank Penney. In an Oxford college, everything that goes through the lodge is handled by one or other of the porters, and the porters are led, guided and directed by the Head Porter. There is nothing he doesn't know, and nothing he can't intervene to help or hinder.

Frank Penney, then, was synonomous with Episcopus College; he had a heavy face, large in area and with large individual features. His eyebrows were dark and abundant, and thickly overhung his large eyes on either side of his large nose, so that when he turned his full attention on you it was enough to make you feel scrutinized by an entire bench of severe judges. On that distant day in 1930 I had formed an anticipatory mental picture of Frank Penney staring at me in just such a way as he informed me that the Dean wanted to see me, doubtless to listen for form's sake to my stuttering and totally non-credible denial of the obvious facts of the case – namely that I had brought into my room, assigned to me for the purposes of study and an ascetic life, a young person of female gender and had subsequently, on College property (one mattress) undertaken the action of sexual copulation with her, to the extent of causing two of her hairpins to become dislodged, doubtless by vibration or similar oscillation. Hanging my head, I had rehearsed that empty denial a hundred times during that far-off day, mercifully without need. Now, I could see in Frank Penney's judging eyes, some at least of my offences had found me out.

'Somebody's been trying to get through to you with a message, sir,' he said.

Inwardly faltering but trying to keep up a firm exterior, I said, 'A message? What kind of message?'

'Couldn't say, sir. He rang several times last night. And earlier this morning.'

'He?' So at least it wasn't Heather, on my trail.

'Yes, an American gentleman, sir.'

'American . . . ?' I was baffled. I had a number of American acquaintances, but none that I was particularly in touch with at that time, none whom I would expect to be telephoning me. 'He didn't say what . . . he wanted or anything, did he?'

'He just said he'd been ringing your home, sir.'

'Chinnor?'

'Yes, sir, that's the address we have for you. Unless you've moved . . . I take it you'd have let us know if you had.'

This in itself was significant. On moving into the Abingdon Road place, I had gone into the lodge one day for the purpose of giving them the telephone number there. Mail, I explained, need not be sent on; I would pick it up each day in College. This was a temporary

–33–

telephone number. Frank Penney was not on duty at the time, and I gave the message to one of the other two porters, a perfectly reliable man. But Frank Penney had either not received the information or, what was more likely, chosen to act as if he had not. Such casual dropping-in of telephone numbers was not his way; he would want a proper notification. If I had a different number, that must mean a different address. Where was this? And how long for? And after that, what? No one fed scraps to Frank Penney. He was the Head Porter of Episcopus College and what he didn't know wasn't knowledge. As far as he was concerned, my new telephone number wasn't knowledge. It didn't exist.

'That number I gave, Frank,' I said. 'I'll be there for . . . a little while. I'd be obliged if you'd make a note of it till I tell you I've no more need of it.'

'Number, sir?'

'Yes,' I said lightly and repeated the number. At least, I tried to say it lightly, but it came out with a dry, effortful creak like a lock that badly needs oil. Extraordinary, the gift the man had for making one feel in the wrong!

'I gave the gentleman your home number, of course,' Frank said, 'out at Chinnor. Then he rang back and said your wife didn't know where you were.'

His voice was flat, drained of expression: one hundred per cent accusatory.

This, of course, was the moment when I ought to have said to him, 'It's quite true, Frank, that my wife doesn't know exactly where I am. She knows I do a day's work in this College every day and that she can get me here by telephone or leave a message for me to ring her. For the rest, I haven't told her exactly where I am and I think that's all I need to say. I shall be moving into College as soon as they've got room for me, and until then anyone who's trying to get me should leave their number and I'll ring them back in my own good time.'

What I actually said was, 'Did the man leave a telephone number where I could get him?'

'No, sir.'

'Well, if he rings again would you please get him to leave his number? I can't take it any further just now. My arrangements are a bit fluid.'

In short, I fluffed. Instead of looking him straight in the face and saying, 'As Head Porter of this College, Mr Penney, it is best for you to know that my wife and I are separating and that all arrangements will be made accordingly,' I fobbed him off with stuff about leaving numbers and mumbled about arrangements being fluid. Fluid! I said to myself in bitter self-mockery as I moved away. You're quite right that they're fluid. They're horse-piss.

But then, Frank Penney had always been too much for me. There was something about his size, his weight, his air of unquestioned and unquestionable authority, the way he looked down on the world from a pinnacle of absolute rightness. And I, as a far less self-satisfied character, knowing myself to be often mistaken, often wrong, sometimes well-meaning but indisputably a misbehaver, an adulterer, a thinker of uncharitable thoughts, a disliker of Watsons, a denouncer of Carshaltons, intolerant and combative in my opinions, how could I stand up for a moment to the lofty scrutiny of a Frank Penney? I would be weighed in the balance and found wanting. *Woe unto you, scribes and Pharisees, hypocrites!* No wonder I wilted, and mumbled about fluid arrangements, and shambled away to my rooms and got ready to face the next student, to weave the same evanescent web of facts and conjectures and alternatives and consequences and call the result 'history' – for history can be nothing else – and congratulate myself on my usefulness in teaching it to the young.

Looking back over that brief period in the Abingdon Road, the one unequivocally good thing that happened to me during it was that I acquired my hobby: or, if you don't like that word, my recreation, my leisure interest, the only thing I do just because I like doing it. Obviously I like doing things like looking round medieval churches, but that can't be a pure recreation because if I happen to learn something from it about the medieval sensibility, what I've learnt will show up in my work. Similarly, during the later part of my adolescence, when I had devoted every grain of spare energy and every second of spare time to the obsessional pursuit of sexual fulfilment, first with Vinnie as the primary target, then with Heather, I wouldn't call that a hobby. Pleasure, to be sure, was what I was after, but only in the sense that a deep draught of cool water, to a man who has been tormented by thirst all the way across a stretch of desert, is among other things pleasurable. It is pleasurable, yes, but mainly it is release, rescue, survival. In the 1930s, when adolescents had to accept the fact that the entire grown-up world was massed, mobilized and organized to frustrate any possibility of escape from their years and years of sexual famine, the said adolescents hardly thought of their desperate escape plans as 'pleasure' or 'fun'. It was more a matter of trying to get some normal life before you finally went mad with frustration and started doing things like rolling about in the mud of a Rugby field, clutching at other people of the same sex.

This, however, was pure fun – mind-releasing, gentle, character-sweetening fun. I refer to my hobby, begun casually in Abingdon Road and never since relinquished, of ornithology, sometimes known by its humbler name of bird-watching. I remember the very moment when it began, though at that moment I had no idea that a great blessing was entering my life.

On about my second afternoon in the place, I stood looking out of my window, which faced towards the back garden. It was the usual lodging-house garden whose main aim is to avoid attracting comment and be no trouble to keep up: a tidy lawn bordered by tidy flower-beds with here and there a patch of tidy shrubbery. This being summer-time, there were flowers, but by one means or another they had been cowed into standing in tidy rows and even, it seemed to me, having tidy colours.

As I gazed abstractedly at this non-spectacle, not really looking at anything but absorbed in my own rather monochrome thoughts, about seven or eight small birds emerged from one of the patches of shrub and started moving about on the gravel path and the nearer bit of the lawn. Their restless, unceasing action caught my attention. They were small, dark-headed, pale grey on the breast and a streaky brown at the back; sparrows, I supposed. The first approach to a thought that came into my mind was that even the most commonplace bird, thoroughly ordinary in every way, not rare, not beautiful, not a songster, was in fact delightful to watch. It was something to do with the vitality that kept them in endless, eager mobility; a bird, whatever else, is first and foremost a little ball of life, the pure essence of life. We, and all other creatures, are half dead by comparison with a bird.

For the first time in my life, I looked attentively at these sparrows – for that, I decided, must be what they were. Even I knew the colouring of a sparrow. Then I thought, most of them are getting about by hopping but two or three are walking. Why is that? Do sparrows sometimes hop and sometimes walk? I focused for a few minutes on a hopper, to see if it modulated into a walk. It didn't seem to. Then I singled out a walker and kept my eye on it in case it took to hopping. I had only a few seconds to follow it and then it suddenly flew away. So I found another walker. Walk, walk was all it seemed to do. Back to another hopper. That didn't change its style either. Yet as far as I could see they were the same species. Gender? How did one tell? I vaguely remembered that one distinguished male from female birds by colour of plumage plus body size. These seemed to be all pretty uniform in size. Were they all of the same sex? If so, why was that? Was it a time of day when they performed different tasks, one lot going off food-gathering while their mates guarded the nests? But why would they be guarding the nest now, with the summer well along so that presumably there would be no fledglings there and certainly no eggs? A second brood perhaps? Did sparrows produce a second brood? If so, did they do it routinely or only if some disaster befell the first brood? What a hell of a lot I didn't know about sparrows. Hardly a day of my life can have been spent without seeing a sparrow, even if I didn't register that I had seen it, and yet I couldn't think of a single thing I knew about sparrows except that they were mostly urban and inhabited the eaves of houses, that they didn't have a song but went *cheep-cheep*, and that the male was supposed to be very highly sexed. And even that last fact I didn't know from observation but merely from common speech and from lines in English poetry like Chaucer's:

He was as hot and lecherous as a sparwe.

It wasn't good enough. I turned to the birds again. Or were they different birds by now? I must have been watching them for a quarter of an hour or so; had some come and some gone during that time, or was the group fairly stable? How could I tell?

I watched like mad, determined to find out something. Then I saw one of them take off in flight – one of the walkers, I was nearly sure. And as it flew up and away I distinctly saw that it had a white flash on the underside of the wing nearest to me. I suppose it was the underside, though the rapidity of the wing-beat made it impossible to be certain, but I inferred it from the fact that when the bird wasn't in flight I had seen no white flash. So. In describing the colouring of a sparrow I would have to say that it had a white flash on the underside of its wings. Both wings, presumably; it wouldn't have it just on one. Speculation already, you see. To be cast-iron certain, I would have to net a specimen, get hold of it and examine both wings. Well, I would take it for granted; after all . . . then another one whirred up and this time, so help me God, there was no white flash on the wing that I could see. Neither on the outer side nor the inner side. I had a good view of it and I was prepared to take my oath that there was no white flash.

By this time I was in the grip of the same fever of excitement that has always driven the naturalist ever since there have been naturalists, which must be about as long as there have been people, even though doubtless the earliest ones thought of themselves as serving some other activity such as hunting. Did the common English sparrow have a white wing-flash, or did it not?

With that question my career as an ornithologist – amateur, unpaid, unrecognized, but devoted – was born. I realized two things: first, that during the time it had taken me to watch those sparrows and come up against that question I had thought of absolutely nothing else, that nothing else in the world had existed for me; second, that an immense undiscovered territory lay at my feet. Starting here and now, with the very ordinary little birds I could see by looking out into that very ordinary little garden, there was a world of investigation and discovery and fulfilment. Naturally I started reading up on birds, but I always, through the years, did it that way round. I saw something that raised a question – and practically everything I saw did raise one of some kind – and then dug in a book for an answer. Of course as I grew in knowledge the questions didn't stay as simple as the first one. I soon found out that as far as the females are concerned, the urban sparrow and the chaffinch are very difficult to tell apart, and the white wing-flash on the lady chaffinch is the best indicator. Easy – but on that first afternoon, for me, an insoluble mystery. *C'est le premier pas qui coûte.*

The problem of Heather, meanwhile, remained. If people were telephoning me at Episcopus and being given my home number – which was routine unless a Fellow gave instructions to the contrary – and she was telling them she didn't know where I was, just like that, there was only one possible conclusion: she had no interest in drawing any tactful veil over anything. She was determined to expose the situation, with all its rough edges, to the gaze of the world. And so indeed it proved.

For many reasons, then, that little episode with Frank Penney jolted me out of a dreamy, unrealistic state and made me face a few issues head-on. Up to then, I had been relaxing and breathing deeply in relief, having got through the grisly business of actually parting with Heather and leaving home, and I hardly faced any concrete problems. There had been so many small-scale things to do: for example, since I had left home without the traditional suitcase, I had not, to begin with, had even a change of clothes, so once I had found the Abing-don Road digs I had been forced to go on a shopping trip, first of all buying a cheap suitcase (one of the two clasps went wrong, and kept flipping open, when I had had it about twelve hours) and laying in underwear, shirts, socks, pyjamas as if I were off to the Amazonian jungle or somewhere else where these things were not for sale. Even toothbrush and razor I had to buy, even a pair of slippers. All that took up the foreground of my thoughts and to some extent numbed the pain of leaving home – because it *was* pain, and I was doing it on the gamble of being, one day, really happy for the first time in my life.

What the short exchange with Frank Penney did for me was to bring me out of that state of fussing around with trivia and make me face the bigger, harder issues. Michael, for instance. It was of im-mense importance to me not to let go of him: not to forget, and not to let him forget, that I was his father. But this example of Heather's intransigence brought me flat up against the fact that she wasn't going to co-operate in any way. No scruples about using Mike as a weapon against me! She would use anything or anyone for that purpose, and if suffering to individuals was part of the result, well, that would be laid at my account, not hers. *She* hadn't done anything; it was I who had left home wasn't it? Well, then.

I brooded over this for some days. I brooded over it in my room at Episcopus. I brooded in the garden, then coming up to the resplendent height of its summer glory. I brooded over it as I walked down to Folly Bridge and along the Abingdon Road to go to bed at night. Three times I tried to telephone the house, choosing different points in the twenty-four hours, but each time I got Heather, with agonizing results. She had various ways of attacking me and was always ready to go into instant action with one or other of them. I couldn't really blame her.

Finally I decided to write to Michael. I did so, inviting him to come and see me in College, and to telephone ahead so that I could be sure to be there. He did not answer so I wrote again, repeating the request. This time he sent a picture postcard representing a railway engine, one of the celebrated express steam engines that had held records in the 1930s and had names like 'The Flying Scotsman' and 'Cock o' the North'. Whether he had any veiled symbolic intention in the choice of illustration or whether it was just the only card he had lying around, I had no means of knowing. The handwritten part of the card said simply:

Dad, I don't want to come to College. I don't like it down there. I rang but they say you aren't living there. Where are you living and I will come there? Not weekends. Very busy with cricket club. I play and am secretary. Michael.

I puzzled over this for a long time. Was it simply what it appeared on the surface? Or did it represent an attempt on Heather's part to find out where I was? Had he written it to her instructions? He would hardly have much choice if she were really determined.

In any case, if I told Michael where I was, she would know. What then? Would she descend? Would there be a free-for-all involving Heather, myself and the landlady, with the other boarders as a frieze of interested onlookers?

Of course, if Heather's ambitions reached no further than making a scene that would embarrass me, she could perfectly well do that at Episcopus, where she must know I spent the bulk of every day. On the other hand, at Episcopus there were restraining obstacles, porters for instance, and a general prejudice against hysterical scenes that disturbed the regular rhythm of life. Other people besides myself lived in Episcopus and had the power to make their wishes felt and their privacy respected; whereas in the Abingdon Road lodging-house she could easily raise a storm that would result in my being thrown out neck and crop.

On the other hand again, had Heather no such thoughts? Was it simply a genuine wish of Michael's to come and talk to me in whatever place I was living in? Did he really find the atmosphere of the College off-putting: too large perhaps, too impersonal?

It then occurred to me that the natural alternative, as a place for Michael and myself to meet, would be the Bargeman's Arms, the home of his grandparents and my own original family home. And immediately, of course, came the thought, *Not yet.*

I had still, and urgently, to go and see them and set out the situation for them in all its comfortless clarity. However unwelcome the news was, they must hear it, and hear it from me – or was it already too late for that?

Well, there was only one way to set about the problem. The very next Sunday morning, well before the pub was due to open at noon, I made my way the short distance along the Abingdon Road to Folly Bridge, got down on to the towpath, faced upstream and set out towards Oseney. It was a bright, cool day of sunshine and fresh breezes. Memories crowded every step of the way. Beneath the span of Folly Bridge was the landing-stage where Tupper Boardman's father had moored his fleet of punts for hire, summer after summer, and where I had worked for a season, becoming adept at handling the slow, calm craft. It was the time of my life when, apart from the compulsion to study history, I had had only one other object in life, viz. and to wit, to get inside Vinnie's little white knickers. The wage I earned from Boardman *père* was destined to be used strictly towards that end. Over to the north-west, a short distance away across a tangle of lines and waste ground, stood the railway station, where old Tarrant had first introduced me to Mairead on that bleak wartime winter night, and at one stroke altered my life for ever. All around me lay the scenes of my boyhood and youth. Nestling at the foot of that line of hills over to the left lay the village of Wytham, where Vinnie and I had had that blazing sexual encounter in her aunt's cottage. Up on the shadowy green above it was the stretch of woodland where I had sat with Geraldine on that day during the trembling interval between the Nazi-Soviet Pact and the outbreak of war, when, facing a decisive end of a chapter in her, my and everyone's life, she had told me of her long involvement with Bax and its sad, sad outcome. And she had wept, suddenly, convulsively, holding on to me.

Here was Oseney Lock. Already. I could have wished the walk longer. I wasn't prepared yet. I knew this was going to be difficult. On the other hand, I never would be prepared, not if I waited for ten years. All I could do was to go through it blindly, and somehow come out on the other side. I walked past the lock and paused for a moment, as I had so many thousands of times, to look down at the smoothly flowing cascade that poured over the lip of the sluice immediately up-river from the lock-gate. It was so beautiful. The water just before it passed over that sill was as smooth as a pane of glass. Immediately on beginning to fall, it arranged itself in a series of long, slender columns which gave the impression of standing perfectly still. That wall of falling water as stable as if it had been carved out of wood. At the bottom, where it made its impact, all was white and boiling with turbulence.

Standing still, looking down at this water as my custom had always been, I knew why I dreaded the next half-hour. It was because of something that I recognized as basically good, basically a strength to me – my attachment to home and roots. If I had moved away from my parents, lost touch with them, given up any attempt to see the world as they did, it would not hurt me that I was now putting the bond between us under a strain. But I had not moved away. My life no longer occupied the same territory as theirs in its simple needs and simple issues; I was acquainted with, and affected by, a far wider range of ideas than they were. But the roots of my being were still where they had been: intertwined closely with the roots of theirs.

I walked round by the side gate in South Street and went into the house by the kitchen door, which was open. My mother was standing at the sink. She saw me before I entered and gave me a quick little smile; it was a kind smile, but it came and went in a moment, and after it had passed her face was serious.

'Hello, Mum.' I kissed her cheek.

'Hello, Peter. We've been expecting you to come round.'

'I suppose you have.'

She straightened her back and dried her hands on a towel, looking at me soberly. 'We know your news.'

'Oh.'

'Yes. Michael cycled over.'

I said, 'How was he?'

'He seemed not much different from usual. He told us you weren't at home any more, and Dad telephoned Heather and she talked about it all.'

'How does she feel?'

'About how you'd expect her to feel,' my mother said.

I could imagine their conversation. At least, I supposed I could. I didn't try to reconstruct it in detail. I switched my mind off; it was too painful.

I stepped back and looked at my mother. The room was very bright with sunlight, and as she stood there in the full shaft of the window it was as if she were being picked out by brilliant stage lighting. It seemed a moment for her to say something memorable, decisive, something that had the power to change everything. But I knew that she would not, and so did she.

'Are you surprised, Mum,' I asked, 'at the way things have turned out?'

'Yes,' she said.

Stopped in my tracks, I could only look round helplessly and say, 'Is Dad in?'

'He's in the cellar.'

'I'll go and say hello to him,' I said and went towards the door at the top of the cellar steps. My words hung emptily in the air behind me like a party balloon when everyone has gone home. Hello? Why should I say hello? What would he want with a hello from me? I had evidently been struck by a strange mental disease that made me incapable of talking like a thirty-five-year-old Oxford don and made me stumble verbally like a victim of aphasia.

I started to go down the cellar steps. There was a sharp bend in them half-way down, so that when you first began the descent you couldn't tell who was there, except that if the light was on you naturally assumed that someone was. It was on now. I called, keeping my voice as light and casual as I could, 'Dad? You here?' There was no answer. I went on down and emerged on to the cold flagstone floor of the cellar. The row of barrels stood on their wooden racks, as ever. My father was at the far end, doing something to the end barrel. He had his back to me, and he did not turn round.

I stood at the foot of the steps looking across at him. The yellow light from the single electric bulb fell nakedly on his head, bringing out the reddish tint in his thinning hair, picking out the broadness of his shoulders. It was not a naked bulb, but the cheap white shade over it masked the light as it went up, not down, so that it might as well have been a bare bulb that stared down at my parent. Slowly, as I watched, he laid down whatever implement he was using – I think it was a small hammer – and turned to face me across the intervening space, twenty feet or so. At last, in the echo-dead air of the cellar, he spoke.

'Peter,' he said.

That was all. No 'Hello', no greeting of any kind, just the name. In the movements of his body, in the brevity of that one utterance, I knew the depth of his anger, and of his disappointment in me.

'Dad.' I stood there foolishly. Neither of us spoke. To break the roaring silence I said, 'Haven't seen you for a bit.'

'I'm not surprised,' he said. 'Didn't know what to say to me, I expect.'

Another batch of seconds ticked by and then I said, 'No, I didn't.'

'Well,' he said, turning back to his work again, 'I'd better get on with this. We'll be opening in an hour and I'll need at least one new barrel.'

He leaned over the barrel and started tapping. No doubt he was broaching it.

I stood there and looked at him. My brain seemed to have switched off. I noticed that some whitewash had smudged on to the sleeve of my jacket as I came down the cellar steps and that was all I seemed capable of registering.

I wanted so much to say something to Dad, but what? Everything I could think of seemed so predictable and so doomed. I could tell, before uttering it, not only what it would sound like in the dead atmosphere of the cellar, but the response it would get from him. Response? Repulse would have been a better word. Every proposition I put forward to try to make my action in leaving Heather seem more understandable and – even! – more justifiable seemed to dissolve into thin air as soon as it drew near the spot where he was standing. His attitude would be simple, straightforward, totally uncompromising. What possible reason had I for breaking up my home, for leaving my wife and son, that could conceivably seem like a reason to him?

Back in 1933, Heather had set the marriage up to suit her own ends. She had pulled me into a marriage not because she loved me but because it was the best way for her to get out of a difficult situation (pregnancy) and rebuild her life, which was at a claustrophobic dead end.

Point granted. But that was 1933. This was 1947. I could, and did, easily formulate in my head his questions and my lame answers.

Has she, in the meantime, been unfaithful to you?
— No, at least as far as I knew.
Has she ill-treated your child?
— No.
Has she failed in her wifely role? Is the house filthy, the larder empty? Is she a drunkard? Does she attack you with the carving knife?
— None of these things.
Then you are leaving her not because of what is happening now, or in the recent past, but because of what happened a long time ago, when you were different, the world was different, everything was different?
— Yes.
It is plain, therefore, that you ought to let the past take care of itself and settle down with your lawful wedded wife, Heather.
— Perhaps so, but it has become impossible.
Settling down is never impossible. These are sick fancies.
— I am in love.
Poppycock.
— I renounced my life with the girl I love, at the cost of a great deal of effort and suffering for me and for her. Some months later, information came to light that revealed to me the unsound

foundations of my marriage to Heather and left me feeling that
it was a cause not worth giving my life for.

Unsound foundations? Has the building fallen down?

— I have pulled it down because I no longer want to live in it.

Then you must bend your back and build it up again.

My father and I exchanged this dialogue in complete silence. Except
inside my head, we did not actually utter a word. Yet I am convinced
that I was reading his thoughts accurately. I knew him too well, and
I was picking up his vibrations too clearly, to admit of any doubt. He
did not need to say those things in words. They were his opinions,
and I had known before coming on this visit that they were his
opinions – why should I deceive myself?

With an effort I forced myself into speech. 'Dad,' I said, 'I think
I'll go back up and see something of Mother before the bar opens.
When it does open I'd like to come into the bar and have a pint, if
you've no objection.'

'I've no objection,' he said, his voice colourless.

'I mean,' I burst out, 'there's no point in my hanging about here if
you've nothing to say to me.'

He straightened up beside the row of barrels, looked over at me
and said, 'I have got something to say to you.'

'And that is . . .?'

'People ought to stick to each other.'

I nodded my head as a sign of acquiescence: acquiescence and
defeat. He was right to speak for the entrenched values of the world
he had grown up in and still inhabited. Whether I was right in acting
by the values I perceived as having come into the world since his day,
I had no idea. The difference between us was that he felt right, and I
(most of the time) felt not so much right or wrong as pulled along by
forces I was powerless to resist. At this moment, as I slowly went up
the cellar steps, I felt just plain wrong.

It wouldn't last. None of these certainties ever did last, with me.
That was because I was *homo modernus*, a man of the modern world,
the world from which all certainties had departed. My father had
been born in 1889, I in 1912. To get a true reading from either year
one should add twenty to it, since it is the state of the world when
one is twenty that actually determines the cast of one's mind. That
would put my father in 1909 and me in 1932. Enough said. As an
historian I should have found these reflections interesting, even
stimulating. I found them nothing of the kind. The contrast between
the solidity of his foundations and the shifting nature of mine seemed
to me, as I climbed up to the flat light of day, the sun suddenly
dimmed by a passing cloud, merely numbing.

But I knew that that, too, would change. The next time I looked into Mairead's eyes, it would move like everything else. Their deep blue, set against the glossy black of her hair, would have its usual effect of banishing numbness from the universe.

I went back up the cellar steps. The tap-tap of my father's patient hammering followed me, becoming fainter after I rounded the sharp bend. I pushed open the door and came out into the Sunday noon.

My mother was still in the kitchen. She had moved away from the sink and was sitting at the table, slicing green beans. The beans were on a newspaper and as she sliced each one she put it into a saucepan of water. She looked up as I approached and sat down opposite her.

'Dad's very closed against me,' I said. 'I can't get anywhere near him.'

'It's my turn to ask you what you asked me just now,' she said. 'Are you surprised?'

'Not really, I suppose. But I thought he might have been . . . well, more tolerant.'

'He thinks you've done wrong, Peter,' she said simply.

I swallowed. My mouth had gone very dry and my tongue felt hard. 'So do you, I expect.'

'Well . . . I'd always try to take your part, whatever you did. But it doesn't seem the right way of going on.'

'It isn't, Mum,' I said. 'The whole thing isn't, and never was, the right way of going on. When you think of the situation as it was then: neither Heather nor I really had a free choice in what we did. We both had desperate needs, and we had to try to satisfy them at one another's expense, so it was like a building on twisted foundations, lopsided from the first, bound to fall down sooner or later.'

'That's the part of it your father doesn't understand,' she said. 'Why it was good enough to last all that time and suddenly has to fall down now.'

'Oh . . . it's absolutely impossible to explain to anyone who doesn't feel instinctively how much everything's changed. It's something to do with the war being over and a new start beginning everywhere. The war went on far too long – for anybody under about forty, five years is a very big chunk of their life, and everything was disconnected and discontinued, and when it all started up again there was a part of everyone, at least everyone of my generation and younger, that said, "Do I really want to go back to the way things were, or would it be better to start again and deal the cards freshly?" The things that happened in the war taught everybody so much, about themselves and about the way the world is . . . . Well, not everybody of course. Some people did absolutely routine jobs and grumbled their way through the bombs and shortages and were just glad when they could go back to the same ways as they'd had in the thirties. But for others it was like 1919 all over again, the world had changed beyond recognition, and when they wanted to link up with what they felt and thought in 1939 they found it all didn't exist any more.'

'Well, I can't say anything to that, Peter, because it just didn't happen like that to me. In 1939 I lived with your father here at the Bargeman's and helped him to run it and make a living, and in 1945 we were still living here and I was still helping him, and I loved him in 1939 and I still loved him in 1945. And we had two sons and neither of them were killed in the war and we felt very lucky when we saw how people suffered who'd lost sons, and our house wasn't knocked down by bombs and we knew that thousands of people had been left without a roof, and we felt very thankful to be spared and very sorry for those that weren't. That's about as far as it went, and if the world has changed so that nobody would recognize it I have to take your word for it, because mine hasn't and as far as I can tell neither has Jack's. The only really big change we've seen is that both our sons got married, and we were glad they'd found themselves wives and settled down because that seemed to us a good and right thing to do, and now both their marriages are over. At least, Brian's wife left him and it doesn't seem possible that she'll ever come back, and now you've left your wife and from the way you're talking now it doesn't seem possible that you'll ever go back to her . . . and what's to come of it all I'm sure I don't know. And on top of it all you seem to be surprised that your father doesn't know what to say to you.'

'No, Mother, I'm not surprised. From his point of view it must simply seem that he's living in a madhouse. And I see no reason why he should rack his brains to find something to say about it. There are some situations there just isn't anything to say about. My own situation, as it happens, is an interim one. I've left Heather because I don't love her and I never have really loved her and I love someone else. The someone else won't have anything to do with me because I'm married to Heather, and she won't even consider the matter of whether to let me pay court to her until I'm a single man again.'

'What does she mean? You can't be a single man again, you're married and that's that.'

'Well, a dismarried man, then. One who was first single, then got married, then got unmarried again. I'm afraid that's one of the changes in people's thinking that have come about – you only have to look around you.'

'So,' she said, 'you're going to get dismarried, as you call it, and then go after this woman, whoever she is, and meanwhile Heather's got to wait.'

'I don't expect Heather to wait. What I expect Heather will do is simply take the biggest cash settlement her lawyer can get for her and put her life in a new shape and settle down to live in it.'

'You make it sound easy.'

'If I do, I'm not conveying my meaning at all well, because I know that it isn't going to be easy, I know it's going to be very, very difficult and painful, but unfortunately that's the course of action I'm forcing on her because I find myself unable to do anything else.'

'And if it comes to nothing, Peter? If you put away Heather and leave your son, and at the end of it all the woman you say you love doesn't want you, and you're left with nothing, what then?'

'What then, Mother, is simply that I shall be one of the millions of people walking the earth who have gambled and lost.'

'And Heather? And Michael? They'll have lost too and they didn't even gamble.'

'There are millions of those too,' I said flatly.

My mother got up from the table, took up the newspaper on which the beans had been lying, and which now contained only the tops and tails and the long stringy side-pieces. She folded the paper over so as to contain them neatly, carried it over to the kitchen waste-bin and dropped it in. Then she took the saucepan full of sliced-up beans, shook some salt into the water, put it on the stove and lit the gas. By these actions she signified that, for the present at least, she also had nothing to say to me.

I left the house by the side door, as I had entered. In a few minutes the pub would be opening, and normally I would have stayed to enjoy a sociable glass of beer and chat with my father. But it seemed impossible now. For the time being? Or for ever? How could I tell?

As an historian, I knew well enough that the story of humanity is full of breaking, destruction, demolition. Sometimes things – buildings, social systems, ways of thinking, people – are destroyed for ever and remain only as memories. At other times they are reassembled, using mainly the same components but in a different form. Sometimes the restored form survives better, as a broken limb can heal and be stronger in the broken place. No one can foresee these things. I knew, as I walked away, that I had inflicted a destructive shock on the loving, nourishing, unquestioned alliance between myself and my parents. What I did not know was whether it could be repaired. As I walked back down-river, past sluice and lock-gates, I looked across at the opposite bank. It hurt me, in my grief, to see that the sun was shining with cheerful indifference on the drab, cluttered waste ground which, once, had been home to the magnificent buildings, the stately gardens and orchards, the solemn and devout ceremonies of Oseney Abbey. If such a pinnacle of human achievement as that could disappear and leave nothing behind, why should the family bond of the Leonards, consisting of nothing more than the mutual affection and need of three or four short-lived humanoid primates, not blow away on the same wind?

I didn't know why. I just hoped, dumbly, inarticulately, with animal persistence, that it would not.

★

My *villegiatura* in the Abingdon Road ended with a highly visible disaster. I had been trying to get Heather to disgorge some of the personal belongings, mainly clothes and a few essential books, that I had abandoned on leaving. I knew I could borrow a car for a few hours if necessary, and at a pinch I could always hire one. My idea was to drive over and take away what I really needed, having first asked Heather the favour of being out for an hour or so. I knew the possibility that she might say yes and then lurk in the house to leap out at me and enjoy a free-for-all, but that was a risk I decided to take. It would be highly unpleasant, but it would not affect the course of our lives one way or another, and meanwhile I badly needed some of the books and could well do without the expense of duplicating clothes and shoes that were useless where they were.

I wrote to her with this suggestion; she didn't reply. I nerved myself and telephoned, but she hung up as soon as she recognized my voice, which was immediately.

I was just turning over in my mind what, if anything, I ought to do now to try to get hold of my few chattels when I received a terse telephone message one afternoon while sitting in my room in Episcopus: 'Will Mr Leonard kindly return to Number such-and-such Abingdon Road without delay.' Whoever sent the message – obviously the land-lady – could have been put through to my room and asked me in person, but the terse third-person directive sounded angry, unceremonious. I cut short what I was doing that day and got down as soon as I could. The landlady met me in a mood of trembling anger. She had had a furious row with Heather; she would not put up with scenes like this; they got the house a bad name; she must insist on my leaving immediately. She would never have a moment's peace with the possibility hanging over her that this kind of thing might happen again.

With the utmost difficulty I got her to let fly at me with the actual facts. Heather had turned up in the car, parked at the gate and hammered on the front door. When the landlady appeared, she had said that the husband who had deserted her had taken refuge in this house, that he had asked for certain items of his property, and that she had brought them. When the landlady said that she knew nothing of the matter and Heather should call when I was there, so that I could take charge of anything she had to deliver, Heather had retorted that this visit was the only one she intended to make and that she was leaving the things now. She had no intention of taking them away and the landlady would have to accept them. The landlady said she would do no such thing and slammed the door. Thereupon, Heather had gone back to the car, taken out some clothes – a couple of jackets, shirts, underwear, shoes – and chucked them over the fence into the garden. A small, interested gathering of spectators had appeared from nowhere, blocking the pavement and attracting the attention of a constable passing on a bicycle. Heather had topped up the job by producing from the boot of the car a burlap sack containing thirty or forty books and heaving it over the railings. It had landed on a flower-bed which unfortunately contained tulips, at least a dozen of which were snapped off. Heather had then explained to the constable, in ringing tones much appreciated by the rapidly swelling throng of witnesses, her version of the situation and why her errand was necessary. All this concluded, she had driven off, leaving the landlady, fuming, to gather up my belongings from the front garden and carry them round to the back, where at least they could not be seen from the road. They were there now. A light rain, which had begun to fall during the landlady's impassioned and circumstantial recital, was steadily soaking them. I carried them indoors, books first. There was not really room for all this lot in my little box of a room. I heaped them up in corners, and in a squashed pile on top of the wardrobe. Going downstairs, I formally accepted my marching orders and agreed to depart as soon as I could find somewhere to lay my head.

Fortunately, this happened in the last of the eight weeks of term. The man who was occupying what were to be my rooms explained, in response to my urgent telephone enquiry, that he was making arrangements to leave in about ten days' time. I spent those ten days in a larger and far more expensive hotel, where they could make available some storage space for my impedimenta, which I stowed in large cardboard cartons and took over by taxi, another grotesque expense. I even did this with a certain relish. After all, Heather and I were engaged in a game. She was playing it voluntarily, I involuntarily. The game was called, 'Make a Monkey Out of Peter'. Heather was playing it with fine, thorough-going relish. She had style and conviction. This latest master-stroke must have given her a great deal of satisfaction, and it even gave me some. I wondered what she would do next. Certainly the possibilities of pelting me with pig-shit were virtually infinite; there was scarcely any limit to the damage she could do me, if she chose to. I had heard, strictly on the grapevine of gossip, through people like Noël Arcady (it was only ten years later that such things hit the official biographies), that T. S. Eliot's first wife, after they parted, would turn up at his occasional literary lectures and walk about at the back of the hall wearing a placard that read, 'I AM THE WIFE HE ABANDONED'. Heather was quite capable of coming into my lectures in the History Faculty and displaying some such placard, or of leaping to her feet half-way through and appealing to the sympathies of the audience. I hoped she had not thought of it, but you never knew.

I knew that my stay in these new quarters would be a short one, but during that brief spell I had an idea for getting in contact with Michael. Heather had somehow or other sussed out where I was in Abingdon Road, but that had probably taken a little time, and it may be that if I acted promptly I might give Michael the information as to where I was and for a few days he might be able to keep it to himself. The next morning I telephoned his school. I got through to the school secretary and said I was the father of a pupil and wanted to get a brief message through to him.

'What is your son's name?' the woman asked, coolly.

'Michael Leonard. He's in Four A, or is it Four B? Anyway, he's thirteen.'

'Leonard, Leonard . . .' She seemed to be looking at a list. 'You say you're his father?'

'Yes.'

'Is it something urgent?'

'I just want to have a couple of words with him on the telephone.'

'I don't think we can bring him out of the classroom unless it's urgent.'

'It's not that urgent. I'd just like to get a message to him to ring me at lunch-time. I know he stays at school for lunch. I want him to ring me between having his meal and going back in to class. There's bound to be a space of a few minutes.'

'You don't want him to ring you before going to the refectory?'

'No. I know how hungry one gets at that age and it's not fair to send him off looking for a telephone and all that while his digestive juices are going at a mile a minute. Let him eat first and then get through to me. I'm at . . .' and I gave the Episcopus number.

The woman seemed to be saying something over her shoulder and then she came back to me and asked, 'Is it something like illness in the family?'

'Something like it, but not it,' I said.

There was more background talking and then a man's voice took over, firm and aggressive. 'Good morning,' it said. 'This is a parent wanting to have a telephone conversation with a pupil at the school, do I gather?'

'Just for a few minutes before he goes back into class for the afternoon,' I said. 'I don't want to disrupt the routine of the teaching day and I don't even want to disturb my son in the process of satisfying his natural hunger. A brief message is all I'm asking for.'

'Well, sir,' said the breezy fiend, 'it seems to me that if it's non-urgent enough to wait until the beginning of afternoon school it could equally wait another couple of hours and then he'll be coming home for the evening and you can talk to him there.'

'I'm not at home,' I said. 'I'm taking an aeroplane to Kuala Lumpur this afternoon and I shan't be at home when Michael gets back.'

'And you didn't know when he came to school this morning that you were going to Kuala Lumpur this afternoon? You couldn't have talked to him over breakfast?'

'I overslept,' I said. 'I didn't see him at breakfast. And I have something particularly important to say to him before I go to Kuala Lumpur. Are you going to give him my message or are you not?'

'You must forgive me, sir, for being careful. But this is a day school. We only have the pupils for seven and a half hours out of twenty-four. Teaching these boys and girls is a full-time job. If we went running round the school after them every time some parent wanted a chat—'

'I quite see that,' I said soothingly. You verminous rat-bag, I thought, you pig-faced git. 'I wouldn't expect you to waste school time on trivialities.' You syphilitic moron. 'It's just that – well, it would be particularly helpful if you could have someone pass him a message asking him to ring that number just before afternoon school begins.'

'If that's Michael Leonard who lives over at Chinnor, I happened to notice that his mother dropped him at school today. I've no doubt she could give him any message when he gets home. Unless she's going to Kuala Lumpur too,' he added, obviously to torment me.

In a flash my imagination had supplied a full scenario. This bloated tapir of a headmaster had his eye on Heather. He fancied her. He had gone to see her on some pretext about Michael. She had told him her troubles, and the wrongs she had suffered at my hands. He had responded by gratifying her with his flabby caresses. On the cinema screen of my mind I saw a flickering scene of their copulation. Then it was wiped and Donald Duck appeared, accompanied by Huey, Louie and Dewey. Clearly I was unhinged. My sense of reality was leaving me. The man was simply a fussy, bureaucratic pedant.

'I have to ask you again, Mr Leonard,' his voice came along the wire, 'is this message too urgent to wait till the end of school hours? We have a great deal to attend to without—'

'Drop dead,' I counselled him and replaced the receiver gently and courteously. Obviously it would have to be a matter of pure random chance whether or not I managed to get into contact with Michael. My bolt was shot.

At last, however, I was safely in Episcopus, in a smallish building, very elegant and rather tucked away round at the back of the place, overlooking a small garden not much frequented. It was an eight-eenth-century building; Episcopus, like most colleges, had been added to here and there through the centuries, but nothing much had been put up in that century, the one I liked best to study and where my professional work lay, so I felt it was a good omen. There were three floors, and my quarters were at the top, reached by a handsome spiral staircase with a most beautifully carved set of banisters, making it a pleasure to go up or down. I thought I would be peaceful there, once the immediate storms died away.

But meanwhile, what, what, *what* about Brian? I had at least formally notified my parents of the situation in my life; unnecessarily, yes, and with no progress at all towards reconciling them to it; but for all that I had notified them. I had not been silent. But no word had passed between me and my brother and this silence must be broken. He must, by this time, have heard. He must, one way or another, have an attitude. It was important to find out how things stood. On an impulse, on about my third evening in my new quarters, I swallowed a whisky and soda and dialled his number. He was at home.

'I hear news about you,' he said.

'I suppose there's no need to ask what kind of news.'

'Well, there wouldn't be, would there?'

'No, there wouldn't,' I said. 'And of course what I want to know is not whether you've heard my news but whether you've got an attitude towards it.'

'What kind of an attitude to it would I have? Why should I have an attitude especially? Apart from being just generally interested in what happens to you, brother. I don't want to give you the idea that as far as I'm concerned you're just noises off. But when it comes to attitudes, well . . .'

'I don't know,' I said. 'It's just that . . . Mother and Dad made me feel a bit of a pariah.'

'I suppose you mean Dad did.'

'Well, he was the one who actually bit me. But she didn't do much to salve the wound.'

'She just thinks she ought to stand by Dad, that's all.'

'Look, Brian, you must have an opinion and I'm not going to ask you what it is because you'll tell me if you feel like it and that's fair enough. I've left Heather, and that's the sort of action people always do have feelings about.'

That was as near to involving him personally as I felt able to get. What I meant, of course, was that because Brian's wife had left him and when I happened to drop by to see him just after he had read her goodbye letter . . . .

Correction. I had not just happened to drop by to visit Brian on that strange, eventful afternoon. I had gone there, unwillingly because it was far from convenient, at my mother's insistence. Behaving quite uncharacteristically, she had rung me up at Episcopus and more or less ordered me to go out and visit Brian in his house over on the far-flung edge of town. She had left me no alternative. Some kind of message had reached her from somewhere (What kind of message? From where? How transmitted?) to convince her that Brian needed an intervention that would save him from disaster. And, for once using direct moral pressure and maternal authority, she had got me out there in time to discover his unconscious but still living body slumped in the car, and switch off the ignition before myself being seized with giddiness and vomiting.

What message had that been? And the boy? That strange boy who had suddenly emerged out of the dusk when I was knocking on Brian's front door, and volunteered the information that he was in the garage at the end of the garden? I never saw that boy again. Had he a physical existence? Was he a manifestation gathered out of the air by the sheer dynamism of our mother's will? Of what unknown world had I, for a moment, teetered on the frontier? Or had it all been just chance, a fortunate accident that had saved Brian's life?

Conclusion of correction. To proceed with main-line account: when I had gone to see him after he had read the farewell note from his wife, I had found him in his car with a length of rubber hosepipe connected from the exhaust to the interior and all the windows wound up. I knew that the experience had put him into a state of mind, at least for the time being, in which he found existence unendurable. For all I knew this might have resulted in his hating anyone who walked out of a marriage without obtaining the prior agreement of his or her spouse. If that were so, he must hate me, however he concealed it under a layer of impassivity. I had a sudden wave of need for my brother. I didn't want him to hate me. Though at the same time I had to admit that if I couldn't go after Mairead on any other terms I would still go after Mairead. An obsession is an obsession, whichever way you look at it.

Did I mean that the love of man for woman was simply an obsession? I did not. What I meant was that sexual love must always have an element of the obsessive in it or it doesn't exist. The ancients knew this and it is why they invented that strange goddess, Até.

What a don I was. Incurably a don. Producing parallels, delving into analogies, even when I was talking to my own brother about leaving my own wife. Did I do nothing non-intellectually? Never act without a bookish frame of reference? Yes, of course I did. My entire life had been governed by irrational impulse. What was my embracing of the Muse of History herself, that silent declaration of a lifelong devotion when I was about sixteen, but a wave of irrationality? What had my mad, daemonic pursuit of Vinnie been, which had several times almost capsized my career and finished up by reducing me to a state of clinical sexual exhaustion on the very eve of my marriage to a splendid young woman? I, if any man, was in the grip of the irrational.

'Have you fainted?' came Brian's voice over the telephone.

'Yes,' I said. 'I was thinking how little control I've had over my life.'

'Well, I could say the same, but it's too late to start worrying about that now.'

'Would it ever have been any use worrying about it?'

'I don't know. Why did I want to be a racing driver? It was all I cared about. And I got pretty close to being one, too.'

'And at the same age I wanted to be an historian. And I've got pretty close to that, too. Not that it's anything to compare with being a racing driver.'

'Don't give me any bullshit. You know we all just do what we're made for.'

'Well, Brian, it doesn't look to me as if being married to Heather was what I was made for.'

As soon as the words were out I wished to God I could recall them. They were crass, foolish, irresponsible. The thought they would naturally set going in Brian's mind was just about the most painful he could have – the thought that if that line of thinking were true, then he, Brian, couldn't have been made to live with Primrose. And he loved Primrose. She had been to him totally beautiful and totally desirable. He had never loved anyone else. And she had left him for a nice young midget-car racer named Chet. No one could object to Chet; even Brian liked him. But I should not have said what I said. I felt like killing myself.

'I mean . . .' I said.

'Never mind what you mean,' he said. 'I get the gist.'

I sat there wanting to slash my wrists. Finally I said, 'Brian.'

'What?'

'Don't stop being my brother.'

'Why would I do that?'

'Because I'm a silly swine.'

'Oh,' he said. 'The world's full of them. You're no worse than most of them. And you're better than some.'

'Don't give up on me.'

'I wasn't going to.'

I thought about this, then said, 'Can you help me to get back into dialogue with Mother and Dad?'

'Time will do that.'

'Not without a bit of help.'

'Well, we'll give it a bit of help,' he said. 'I'll need to sound out the situation and see what seems to be the best line of approach, but I'll tell you one thing: I'll do it. Leave it to me.'

'Thanks, old Brian.'

'Any time.'

'I hope there won't be any more times. Not for this kind of thing.'

'There can be as many as it takes. Marriages come and marriages go, that's how I look at it.'

It was in the cynicism of that last remark that I saw the silent depths of his pain. I bowed my head in the wordless recognition of that tragic agony. We said good night and rang off. Then I had another whisky and soda. A big one, with the whisky coming almost up to the top of the glass. The way I sloshed it out, I might have been Bax.

★

Grandfatherly Salterton settled his aged bones into the Presidential chair at the first Episcopus meeting of the academic year 1947–48, swivelled his pink, round face, still so innocent and unlined after nearly eighty years of life, and included us all in a wide-angle stare of benign greeting. The fine-textured silvery hair still lay in a smooth carpet round the back and sides of his head; his manner and bearing still had that blend of the antique and the infantine.

'Gentlemen,' he said, 'I shall open our proceedings with a short announcement concerning my own position.' We stopped fidgeting and shuffling our papers.

'At my time of life, my dear colleagues, the pace of one's reactions and mental processes has become slow. So slow, in fact, that the surrounding current of life seems by contrast to have speeded up. The years, which in one's youth seemed to go by in slow and stately procession and still, into one's fifties and sixties, had a satisfying rhythm in which each succeeding year had its own pattern, now slip past like telegraph poles seen from a speeding train.

'To me, a year has come to seem a very short time. I therefore choose this moment to tell you formally that at the end of this academic year, that is in September 1948, I shall lay down my duties as President of this College.'

All present received this news with a slight inclination of the head, something that could be described as half-way to a bow, in acknowledgement that this was serious information. There were no cries of protest. It would have been absurd to pretend that a man of

Salterton's years ought to cling to any kind of office. But neither were there any 'not-before-it-was-time' side-glances, no wordless expressions of relief. The veteran had given his best, and his best had been good.

'For at least ten years past I have been ready, as far as my own devices and desires were concerned, to relinquish my duties. But I felt that it would create difficulties if I resigned during the war, when able men had many claims on their energies more urgent than the stewardship of a college, important though I take that to be. And when the fighting ceased at last, the upheaval caused by the war needed time to settle. That process is nowhere near complete; it will not be complete for years. But as an old man, it seems justifiable in me to lay down the reins, knowing that in your collective wisdom you will find a suitable pair of hands to take them up. I have perfect confidence, gentlemen, in your judgement. And now we will proceed to our business.'

I looked round the large, stark lecture-room which we always used for College meetings. It was rather like a school classroom; the bright but sunless autumn day stared in at the long windows. The Episcopus dons, ranged out at two long tables with an overspill on to a smaller one set at right angles, looked, at first sight, a strange gathering. What, I wondered, would an outside observer, suddenly parachuted into their presence, take them to be? Would they give him, unprompted, the impression of a roomful of distinguished scholars, men of learning and insight? But then, what sort of an impression would that be?

One element would have been common to all random guesses: these were not business men. There was hardly a smart, well-pressed suit among them, or a pair of shiny shoes, such as business men are compelled to wear in one another's company to avoid having it thought that they are slipping downward. Equally obviously they were not politicians (not sufficiently vulpine) nor civil servants (no collective impression of somnolent complacency). Authors, or literary people generally? Possibly, but they seemed to lack the rat-like cunning of the tribe. Clergymen in mufti? That might come nearer: as of men beset with many nagging responsibilities, yet with a vague expression of idealism, as if serving some half-forgotten ideal which they were continuously struggling to recall.

There were, of course, exceptions. Nobody could have mistaken Noel Arcady, with his elegant, perfectly chosen clothes and graceful, relaxed manner, for anything except what he was: a young man of wealth and good social position, who took an interest in the arts and had decided to spend some years in the academic teaching of one of them. (It wasn't possible, when you came right down to it, to

-56-

imagine Arcady as a lifetime don, slogging it out with examination papers and candidates for admission and Collections and all the rest of the carry-on.) Watson, for his part, I decided, could have been an out-of-work film actor who normally played minor parts in espionage dramas. Over the years since I had known him, the falsity that was so much a part of his character had eaten more and more deeply into the fabric of his nature and surfaced in his appearance. Had he been an actor, he would have been perfect as the greasy minor villain who sidles up to the hero in a grimy bar in Ostend or Penang with a bribe from some international agency that turns out to be a front for some nest of traitors, and that in turn a front for a counter-organization, till he himself has lost count of which side he is on, and the audience is supposed to find this psychologically subtle and profoundly interesting, though in fact it is as grey and boring as commonplace lying always is. Watson no doubt was reasonably competent at whatever kind of science he did for a living – it was some kind of biology, which at least was better than sociology or linguistics, depths from which he was probably saved by his purely social snobbery (one wouldn't be seen *dead*, would one?). But in his general dealings with the world he seemed to have become, in the fourteen years since I had first met him, steadily more predictable, stereotyped, standardized. He must have been aware of this ordinariness, because for a year or two now he had begun to cultivate touches of the *outré* in dress and appearance. During this last summer, for instance, he had compensated for his increasing baldness on top by allowing his hair to grow very long at the back. To walk behind him was to become aware of following this nondescript mouse-coloured curtain that flopped down almost to shoulder-level and looked shabby, even in a curious way dusty, as if he never washed or combed it, though I was sure he did both. And if his appearance had become unsatisfactory from the rear, it had not improved from the front, with that indentation just below the lower lip, as if a sculptor had made a model of his head in some soft material such as marzipan or industrial floor-soap and then, using a tea-spoon, scooped out a hollow just below the mouth. Below that again, the nasty little chin jutted out, thus saving his face from a porcine appearance at the cost of making it seem more malevolent than a pig's – an animal which, if one looks at it attentively, has in fact a rather benevolent cast of countenance.

I was in a state of nervous alertness, and therefore more sharply observant than usual, because at this meeting I intended to raise a motion, namely to suggest the election of Garrity as a member of the Senior Common Room. Garrity had, that term, quitted his anchorage in that industrial town and appeared in Oxford as a member of the English Faculty. The complex and slowly evolved organization of

Oxford University, which appears to be riddled with contradictions but in fact works remarkably well, means that every don works both for his college, where he usually has a teaching or research Fellowship and a salary to go with it, and for the University as embodied in his own particular Faculty, which pays him another salary and requires him to lecture, examine and deliberate on matters concerning the curriculum and so forth. If a man is elected to a college, the Faculty is obliged to take him on; but if the Faculty really wants him and no college can be found to elect him – the game of musical chairs having for some reason gone against him – the Faculty can, at a pinch, make up his salary from its general funds. He then becomes a stateless person, an employee of the University but with no social base, nowhere to meet friends or have his being except such accommodation as he can find for himself. If this happens, the man or woman concerned would do better to steer clear of Oxford, because to be without a college there is a miserable situation, like that of a lost dog on the pavement.

The current Merton Professor of English, himself a newcomer, admired Garrity and had offered him the post of Lecturer in the English Faculty. He probably did so in innocence, knowing that Episcopus, though not able to make him their Fellow in the subject (Arcady already had that job), would provide an anchorage for him – for a Member of Common Room has all the social privileges of any other don. My task this afternoon was to get this formality attended to. It ought to have been merely a rubber-stamp job; unfortunately I knew enough to feel far from confident that it would be. The vote, after all, was to be cast among exactly the same people who had already refused to take Garrity on board as a working Fellow. I knew they had refused him simply on personal grounds, because one or two of their number, irritated by his surface mannerisms and lack of small talk, had put it about that he would be a bore. And if they had feared him as a bore then, there was no reason why they should not fear him as a bore now. No one knew better than I that Garrity was not a bore. He was a delightful companion, other-wordly and self-forgetful, with a vast fund of knowledge which overflowed naturally into his talk from an innocent abundance of spirit. Exactly the kind of thing that cagey little men like Watson found boring. I knew I had a fight on my hands, and I was afraid I was going to lose it.

Still, I had to do my best, and I made a brief speech of nomination. I pointed out that Garrity, originally an Episcopus student, had risen through the years to a position of eminence in his scholarly field; that his edition of the Parnassus plays was acknowledged as authoritative; that in his leisure time, instead of merely relaxing on the golf course or growing roses, he had made immortal translations of great European

-58-

poetry; that he was a widely travelled, deeply cultivated man who knew the arts, particularly music, as he knew history and languages, which he seemed to have acquired almost by instinct; that he was a wonderful example and inspiration to all who knew him, and a kindly, approachable human being. I said we should be grateful to have the chance to know such a man on a personal level as a member of our own community. Then I made my one mistake. Perhaps it was fatal, perhaps it made no difference; it may be that the anti-Garrity movement was already so entrenched that my suggestion was certain of failure. I don't know. What I do know is that it was a mistake, purely and simply.

'Garrity has been appointed to a Faculty Lectureship,' I said, to finish with, 'and that, professionally, is recognition enough for any man. But he has, at present, no membership of a college. He lives alone, he's a bachelor with – as far as I know – no family circle, and it's my belief he's rather lonely.'

As soon as the words were out I knew I had made a king-size balls-up of the whole thing. Oxford – like many places but more so than most – is full of people who, if they think you need sympathy, will avoid you for that very reason. They think failure and bad luck are as catching as herpes.

I sat down and a silence followed. Into it Watson said silkily, 'It's to be hoped that our worthy colleague hasn't put a false interpretation on the fact that the College, for taxation purposes, is registered as a charity.'

'All the colleges are,' I said sullenly. I wasn't in the mood for his fooling. And I knew 'worthy' was one of his sneer words.

'So they should be. They spend fortunes maintaining beautiful old buildings and they educate the young. But I think we should guard against the assumption that because we're registered as a charity we have a duty to be charitable to every deserving case of every kind.'

I could see what was coming and so could everyone else, but Watson was like a cat that had a broken-winged bird at its mercy. Cats aren't programmed to feel mercy and neither was Watson.

'Naturally I'm affected by the touching account of Garrity's loneliness, his single state and his lack of a family circle. But I don't see that Episcopus College, in the persons of those of us gathered here, has a duty to compensate him for those misfortunes which must have reasons that are nothing to do with us.'

'He's lonely because he's just moved from another town,' I said. 'There's nothing surprising in that, and there's no need to imply that people avoid him because he smells bad or something. And if it comes to that, I think it could reasonably be called part of the duty of any academic institution to be considerate towards a man of learning, a man devoted to the same ideals that were in the mind of

the founder of this College and the generation that originally established it. One of its minor responsibilities, and I do know it's a minor
one but real all the same, might be to help such a man to live his life
cheerfully and in a friendly atmosphere.'

'Your sentiments do you credit,' Watson said derisively, meaning,
'We don't need your holier-than-thou preachifying. We're men of
the world even if you're not.'

'I don't think they do me any credit, I think they're just normal for
anyone involved in our kind of work and pursuing it in what ought
to be our kind of spirit.'

A square-cut man called Hodblat or Hogwash or something of that
kind, whose field was automated taxidermy or something equally
displeasing, now joined in and said brusquely, 'In my opinion the
point isn't whether Garrity's to be pitied or not but whether he's
Common Room material or not. And I don't think he is. He talks
shop. We don't want to encourage that.'

I wanted to say, 'Well, Todflap, old boy, talking shop about the
kind of thing Garrity knows about isn't quite the same thing as
talking shop about the kind of thing you know about.' But I knew
that such a remark would have seemed to most of the men present
merely offensive. Besides, I don't really approve of the notion that
some kinds of knowledge are intrinsically inferior to some other
kinds, though of course I drew a distinction between knowing things
(languages, history, the sciences) and playing at knowing things
(sociology, or talking about the 'methodology' of things rather than
the things themselves). Once you got into the realm of actually
knowing about things, which I recognized even Dogsplat did, I was
wedded to the belief that we all started fair. I wasn't recommending
Garrity because he knew the classics and the medieval and modern
literatures, and was steeped in what everyone recognized as Culture;
I was recommending him because he was a decent and friendly man
who welcomed open-minded discussion of just about anything, and
was totally free of envy and snobbery.

Watson, to whom absence of envy and snobbery was the perfect
recipe for boringness, obviously had a dislike of Garrity that was
genuine, possibly the most genuine thing in his character. People
who aren't snobbish or envious don't make spiteful conversation,
which was the only kind Watson liked.

I had to answer Hogsnatch, so I answered him directly. 'One of the
things I admire about Garrity is the spontaneity of his interest in
things. Before he makes a remark he doesn't pull himself up and ask,
"Just a minute – will this be regarded as shop?" It might be a remark
on a certain kind of wild flower that grows in the Harz mountains,
or a good cider in a Gloucestershire pub, or a feature he's noticed

-60-

about the paintings of Goya in the Black period. Or he might have been reading Aeschylus, or—'

'That's exactly what I mean,' the square-cut man said. (He left us soon afterwards, for a chair in Adelaide I think it was. I really only remember him on this one afternoon.) 'It seems to me that when you've had a hard day's work, just about the last thing you want is to find yourself sitting beside someone whose talk is always on such a relentlessly high plane.'

I wondered, silently, what his idea of a suitable plane would be and why he felt the need to spend his spare time in College at all. The free meals, I realized, might be an incentive, but why didn't he slurp them down and go out to some pub in the town and sit in the saloon bar where he could soon find a circle of cronies? They would be genial, relaxing evenings telling smutty stories and comparing how many miles to the gallon they got with their cars.

Trying to defend Garrity's case without driving still further away the goon element as represented by Codpat, who all had votes, I said soothingly, 'Well, there's not much ordinariness in Garrity's conversation, I grant, but I've never found him boring.'

Watson leaned forward in his chair; the hollow beneath his lower lip suddenly seemed like a little cauldron of poison. 'That, my dear colleague,' he said spitefully, 'is because you are a sobersides.'

I ought to have let that go, but counter-aggression swelled up inside me and burst its banks. 'I know Mr Watson's vocabulary well enough,' I said, 'to understand what he means by that remark – he's calling me a bore. Well, for the record, I'll tell you what bores me, Watson. In my opinion the most boring feature of Oxford life is the obligation to be amusing.'

Chubby, bouncy Ransom, who was always such a Good Fellow and hated acerbity at College meetings, put in uneasily, 'I say, d'you really think there's any point in getting into this kind of issue?'

'It's been raised,' I said, 'and it ought to be settled. The dominant atmosphere of any gathering in Oxford, particularly of a social nature but spreading into any kind, is the assumption that just before you arrived someone made a tremendously witty remark, and everyone's still sitting around grinning and smirking and ready to burst out giggling again. No one in fact does say anything witty, but it's in the surrounding air, this wonderful epigram, and it's such a pity you just missed it because if you'd heard it you could be simpering and tittering like everyone else.'

Bax, who had been studying his folded hands as if trying to detect symptoms of a fungoid outbreak on them, looked up and said, 'You really find that a characteristic of Oxford behaviour?'

'It doesn't affect the first-rate people,' I said, 'but the second-raters, of whom every institution has a majority, seem to be afflicted with it universally.'

I looked at Watson as I spoke. I was behaving badly, I knew, but if Watson was going to keep an honest man like Garrity, who intellectually and humanly would make ten of him, out of our Common Room by smearing him as a bore, it might be best to have the matter out in the open and let everyone see in broad daylight what people like Watson really thought was boring.

But the point was fluffed by decent, run-of-the-mill Ransom, who hadn't much humour himself and had never even tried to make a witty remark, and in consequence was rather over-impressed by someone like Watson who had a superior air and knew when to snigger knowingly. Ransom was one of those middle-aged men whom you can easily imagine as schoolboys, and indeed he looked at this moment as if he had just come in from an hour at the nets. He was embarrassed and troubled at the scene that was developing, and this caused a flush to spread over his open, artless features, but all the flush did was to suggest healthy exercise.

'I must say I do think, Mr President and gentlemen,' his words came tumbling out, 'that we ought not to go down any alleys, so to speak, this afternoon when we have a . . . well . . .' he tapped his bundle of papers, 'particularly heavy list of things to bring up for discussion. We have a lot of issues to make up our minds about – it might be a mistake to get, well, too involved in domestic matters . . .'

He floundered to a stop, but his intervention had done its work. Suddenly everyone wanted to drop the issue of Garrity and get on with business. Indeed, the only reason we had been speaking of it so near the beginning of the meeting was that it was our habit to get small domestic issues out of the way before we began to tangle on large questions involving money, property and future policy. As a rule there was no wrangling about matters such as who was, and who wasn't, to be a member of Common Room. They went through on the nod. That Watson should have opposed Garrity's membership, and organized others to oppose it, served to show the depth of his commitment to his own particular ideals – ideals of triviality, frivolity and empty superiority. We rapidly took a vote. There were thirty-seven Fellows present; twenty-eight said no to Garrity. I had lost, Garrity was out, and the dead-heads could breathe in peace. Noël Arcady, sitting perfectly still, abstained. I didn't resent that. I could see how he was placed.

Ransom was not in the Chair at this meeting; Salterton was that. He was not the Secretary, in charge of the minutes; the College secretary was there, her pencil scattering shorthand like confetti. There was actually no need for Ransom to nudge us on to the next item at all. But I don't think anyone resented it. The man was simply expressing his feelings. He valued College solidarity more than anything else. He wanted harmony, the papering-over of differences. If a struggle to import an original like Garrity would open rifts within the Fellowship, Ransom would prefer to forget the matter and keep the rifts closed. It was a point of view, and he had a right to it. And if the result was a victory for Watson and a defeat for me, I could live with that. In another twelve hours my annoyance would have cooled down; in a week it would be just something I lived with, like the weather and the income tax.

The only thing that would remain to give me uneasiness would be the thought of Garrity, alone in his lodgings or sitting, a book propped against the cruet, in some shabby restaurant. I hated that.

★

All this time the business with the lawyers was grinding on, as Heather and I slowly toiled our way towards a divorce. In those days, it was a business not only immensely protracted but totally adversarial. One partner or the other had to be innocent and the other guilty, and the guilty one had to give, or to have given, 'Grounds' to the innocent. These 'Grounds' were all the expected ones: cruelty (no thanks), desertion (h'm), non-consummation (too late for that by a long chalk) and, of course, adultery. The softer modern options, 'irretrievable breakdown of the relationship' and the like, had not then been invented. It took me no very long time to settle for adultery, which would not only be the quickest and the most straightforward, but which also was – if one wanted to put it in those terms – something I had actually done.

Then the question arose, how did one set it up? I couldn't get Mairead involved in it. If she had decided to live with me for the rest of her life, being cited as the cause of the divorce might well be something she would just take in her stride and put up with. But she had expressly said that I wasn't to get in touch with her at all, not even to approach her on tip-toe, until I could tell her I was no longer married to Heather. What then? I asked advice from a man who had been through all this, having got married before the war, then been away for years in far-off places, culminating in two years in a prison camp (a German one, fortunately, and therefore, however unpleasant, ultimately survivable). He had come back to be confronted with a strange young woman whom he hardly recognized but whose identity he had to accept as that of his wife. Fortunately her reactions were much the same as his and they went about the business of regaining their freedom in a businesslike spirit. This man told me of a solicitor somewhere in North London who could set up adultery cases on a kind of conveyor-belt principle. A booking was made at an hotel for Mr and Mrs Smith; you turned up, so did Mrs Smith, you were introduced, and you then retired to a bedroom which you duly shared, being observed at prearranged intervals by witnesses also laid on by the firm. He said the fee was a bit steep, but I replied philosophically that lawyers were of the opinion that if they didn't charge steep fees the client would think they couldn't be much good as lawyers, so I was ready for it.

He gave me a name and address and I duly sought out this firm in their lack-lustre office in a lack-lustre street on a foggy November afternoon. It was all immeasurably depressing. The member of the firm who interviewed me was a sallow-faced man in his thirties with a light grey suit and horn-rimmed glasses. He went through the details of the case as if his attention was elsewhere, which I must say I didn't blame him for, he must have been so bored with it. We settled everything and then, just when I had got up to go and was reaching for my overcoat, he shot me a look I couldn't quite read and said, 'There's just one thing, Mr Leonard, that I always mention to clients.'

'And that is . . .' I was feeling for the arm-hole of my coat.

'The lady doesn't like to be interfered with,' he said flatly.

Holy Christ! I thought. Does he think I look the type who would do that? Then I calmed down enough to reflect that, since human nature includes every type, some men must exist who, in this situation and having agreed to part with the aforesaid steep fee, might think it a good idea to get as much return for it as they could, including a supplementary fuck. I looked at the grey-suited solicitor, trying to work out whether he looked the type who, had he found himself in this situation, would react like that.

'You don't have to worry,' I said.

'It's not me that's worrying, sir.'

'No,' I said, speaking clearly. 'It's the lady who has to be careful. I'm sure she meets all sorts in this business.'

He stood up to indicate that the interview was over. For my part, I couldn't get out fast enough. Although the events of my life and the pressures of society had put me into a position where I needed his services, I felt that there was something grubby about the atmosphere of his office. Even after I got well away, it seemed to hang about me, in my hair and clothes. I felt, illogically enough, as if I had been put off sex for life. The feeling, as I say, was irrational, but it lasted for a long time.

When the appointed evening came and I had to report at the hotel and meet Mrs Smith, I went through it like a zombie. I kept hearing the man's flat voice. 'The lady doesn't like to be interfered with.' I'll say this for the lady, she didn't look the type who *does* like to be interfered with. If I'd seen her walking along the street and been asked to make a guess at what she did for a living, I'd have said she was probably the manageress of a dry-cleaning establishment. The room we had to spend the night in contained two beds, of course, and I kept so clear of her, gave her such a wide berth from first to last, that she must have wondered whether she had bad breath or something. I had nothing against her, naturally. I just lay awake nearly the whole night wishing that the grisly farce were unnecessary. I suppose it *is* unnecessary, these days, and women like her can give all their working time to managing dry-cleaning establishments. So some things, after all, do improve.

★

Dispirited as I was at my failure to have Garrity elected a member of the Common Room at Episcopus and thus make a dent in the loneliness of his life, I decided to see as much of him as I could, not only for my own sake — for I genuinely delighted in his company — but because, by having him to dine pretty often, I could see to it that he was a familiar presence about the place. The initial impression he made on people was, obviously, odd, because he had spent so much time isolated among his own thoughts, marooned for years in a densely populated area within which no one had shared his interests and intuitions; but I was confident that if I invited him to dine fairly steadily — a couple of times a month, say — the more open-minded Fellows of Episcopus, who after all were in the majority, would very soon realize that he was not a bore. Garrity was so approachable, so companionable, that it was a mystery that he should have become so solitary, even in a Philistine *milieu*; at least, it was a mystery *prima facie*, but you soon came to see the roots of the matter when you got to know him. A good deal of it arose from his celibacy. If he had had a wife she would, in the ordinary processes of living, have done much to interweave him with life. Bachelors (especially what are called 'confirmed' bachelors, as if they had been through some kind of ceremony to restate and reinforce their bachelorhood) necessarily spend much time alone and, if they carry themselves courageously, sometimes give an impression of preferring loneliness, of having chosen it. Also, in our time which places such enormous emphasis on the act of coitus, single status in a man is often thought to imply homosexuality. It is more often the case, in fact — and certainly this was true of Garrity – that some men, through a combination of shyness, lack of opportunity during the right years of their life, and assorted pieces of mischance, simply miss out on marriage. During the years – the mid-twenties up to about thirty – when they would normally be selecting their mates and settling down they fail to do so, and they find themselves in a position where it is every year less and less expected of them: they are in the condition that girls used to call 'being on the shelf', an expression that has died out now that girls have no use for shelves. In the late forties and early fifties, both men and girls could end up on the shelf. Garrity, from the point of view of matrimony, had been on the shelf for years. He had become accustomed to bachelorhood, accustomed to celibacy, accustomed to having his domestic arrangements made for him by a landlady or perhaps, as he advanced a little in prosperity, by a housekeeper; and if he wanted a special-occasion meal, on a birthday for instance, going out to a restaurant. This had been his life in the unpleasing industrial town at whose university he had put in so many years of conscientious work. When he was at last bidden to Oxford, the prospect had moved closer that he might find an anchorage in a college, with pleasant rooms, good food and an untroubled daily routine, tested throughout centuries and found reasonably workable by studious men who liked the right blend of company and solitude. Closer, but not close enough. The years of loneliness had bred in him oddities of manner, harmless eccentricities, very seldom found in a lifelong Oxford don polished by the daily contact with his peers.

Garrity's oddities were so superficial, such a thin covering over the warmth, the generosity, the affection that radiated from his nature, that it amazed me that I could see straight to those qualities while the Fellows of Episcopus, collectively, tended to be put off by the outward coating. Why was this? Was I more intelligent, more perceptive, than they? In some ways, undeniably yes; I had had the inestimable advantage of growing up in a riverside pub in West Oxford rather than being incarcerated in a public school during my adolescence, mixing with only one social type, which at that date was still true of so many of them. My experience at eighteen may have been no deeper than theirs, but it was broader. I had learnt about life from Old Trundle, from my father and Brian, from Tupper Boardman, my mother and Bessie Warmley, from Vinnie, at the thought of whom I still shuddered uncontrollably with longing, with anxiety, with excitement and with dread. This was bound to be a richer mixture of experiences, leading to faster growth, than the single-class, single-sex atmosphere of the cloistered and exclusive public schools in the phase of their development that coincided with my schooldays. If as a result I grew up less blinkered, more adaptable, than most of my colleagues, that would account for the fact that I delighted in Garrity, relished his personality, while most of them kept a wary distance from what they considered his 'oddities' in case they should turn out to be (the worst possible Oxford stigma) 'boring'.

I did not despair, with the aid of patience and good humour, of being able to turn this situation round. I was determined to keep Garrity before the attention of the Episcopus Common Room, and I had no great fear of failing in my ambition of one day getting him accepted in our midst – though Watson's spoiling tactics, admittedly, might prove a cause of delay. Still, Garrity could wait; he had a reasonably pleasant dwelling in North Oxford, a large sunny flat someone had helped him to find and whose rent was within his means. And he had a kindly woman who 'did' for him and usually cooked his lunch before she left for the afternoon. For the time being, he was all right. And of course, like most lonely people in that line of work, he took with immense seriousness his relationship with his students, to whom he always referred, in old-fashioned Oxford wise, as 'my men'.

'I set aside an evening a week for my men,' he told me. 'I canvassed their opinions and found that most of them preferred Thursday, so Thursday it is. I'm always to be found at home after dinner on Thursday, and all my men have a standing invitation to come in. And anyone else too, who feels like a wide-ranging discussion. The talk just goes anywhere.'

I muttered something in reply to this, but I never joined him and his 'men'. I had no objection to giving part of my leisure time to my own students, but I never had an invariable open evening. In my experience that kind of thing turns into a ritual, and rituals in the end go soggy. Or perhaps it is just in my hands that they go soggy. At any rate, I preferred to ask individual students round to my rooms with invitations addressed to them by name and left in their pigeon-hole, and if some of them thought of the invitation as a summons, I didn't care. When they got there they never found it a heavy occasion, we just talked generally, but I wasn't going to leave it to them whether they came or not. I was for a tighter rein than that or no rein at all. Only lonely men like Garrity had open evenings.

One of the evenings when I had him in to dine has remained very clearly in my memory because on that occasion he happened to coincide with Molly Whitworth, busily maintaining her usual high standard of assertiveness. The monastic stonework of Oxford had at least begun to crack to the extent that every college, by this time, put on a weekly or bi-weekly 'ladies' night', when the presence of the female of the species could be tolerated, given firmness and a sense of vocation, for a few hours. It seems inconceivable that they could have kept Molly Whitworth out under any circumstances, with or without a ladies' night, but I suppose at that time they might have just managed it; after all, the 1960s were then in the undreamt-of future, and even the sixties saw only the first steps. Fortunately there was no need of a trial of strength. The philosophy don we had at that time had invited her and she was snugly ensconced on the right hand of the President, whose smooth diplomatic efficiency was well up to handling her.

No one else's was. As soon as I went into Common Room, where we were assembling, and saw her familiar profile – the alert, slightly out-thrust head, the frizzy, dark blonde poll, the rimless glasses through which she unblinkingly took stock of a new acquaintance – I knew it would take a blend of hard work and skilful evasive action to prevent the evening from being ruined. Above all, I must keep her at a distance from Garrity, both at dinner and at dessert. If she sat next to him and cut him dead as having nothing to contribute that interested her, that would be depressing for him; if for some reason she took it into her head to scold and harangue him, his innocent unprepared-ness would leave him no defence and he would be left wondering if he had done something wrong. Fortunately she did not waste more than a perfunctory glance on him before decisively turning her attention back towards people who could be more use in the great game of life, which to her meant personal prestige and advantage.

'The Faculty Board won't stand for that,' she was saying as we took our places. 'They won't scratch round for the funds and personally I wouldn't expect them to.' Her tone unmistakeably conveyed that if the Faculty Board did stand for this project, whatever it was, and did raise funds for it, they would have her to reckon with. Her philos-opher-escort grinned sheepish support; Mowbray, the new President of Episcopus, inclined his head gravely and non-committally.

In those days and for about ten years afterwards – the 'Post-War Period' – philosophy was very much the key subject at Oxford, the cutting edge where the progress was made and the news happened. Ayer, Ryle, Austin; the Logical Positivists and the general movement to empty philosophy of metaphysics; the 'ordinary language' philo-sophers; Wittengenstein sending galvanic impulses over from Cambridge – it was all go, all alliances and buddings-off and confron-tations, and the women were in it as much as the men, with Elizabeth Anscombe and the young Iris Murdoch in the thick of everything. There seemed to be no comparable stir of life in any other field. Historians got on with their work all right, but no radical issues seemed to be coming up for discussion; in literary criticism there were some faint rumblings of dissent from the old fact-based tradition of scholarship, but nothing comparable with the avalanche that was virtually to sweep the subject away thirty years later when the

Marxists and the feminists got going on it. In the pure sciences, it seemed to be a period of lull. Such colossal efforts had been made over the previous twenty years in nuclear physics that the people who worked in it were consolidating rather than pushing ahead. Astronomy was throwing out interesting theories, but they didn't affect anyone's thinking in general. A real, over-turning revolution was just over the horizon in electronic engineering, but none of the people who were wandering about Oxford arguing their heads off about language and logic had any suspicion that the invention of the transistor in 1948 would lead them straight into the 'Brave New World' of information technology and deliver them, in another twenty years, bound and gagged into the pitiless claws of the computer.

No, only the philosophers were visible, in the Oxford of those post-war years, and Molly Whitworth, predictably, had elected herself to the position of a combined *gauleiter* and strategist of Oxford philosophy. Without making any contribution to the subject herself, she was maniacally active in seeing that it was taught, discussed, disseminated, marshalled and directed. Her husband had taken up a position in a Scottish university and was in Oxford only during vacations, thus sparing her the problems of trying to marshall and direct *him*, which would probably have been very difficult in view of his stubborn grain of individuality and his gift of switching off his attention while thinking his own thoughts. It also left her with a wider field for amatatory adventure which she had no difficulty, at least in the early days, in combining with the philosophic life; but more of that in its right place. This evening she was acting in her capacity of commissar, making sure that incorrect opinions did not spread beyond the narrow limits allowed by 'free discussion'. Which turned out to be not very far.

At that time, the big name to flourish in conversation was Sartre's: a purveyor of ideas and coiner of slogans with a huge following, mostly in France but spreading out world-wide. The man was rapidly becoming an idol. That squat figure topped by the curious frog-face, with one eye looking out to the side, attracted crowds wherever it appeared, and his most ordinary observations were immediately given the status of philosophical aphorisms. (Example: 'Other people are hell,' a perfectly natural response to the wear and tear of proximity and abrasion, seemed to the disciples mysterious and important when inverted into '*L'enfer, c'est les autres*' and pronounced with sufficient portentousness.) Existentialism, which was in fact destined to be short-lived, looked at one time capable of changing the world, though scarcely for the better, since its major effect seemed to be to justify a particularly corrosive brand of selfishness. My own attitude to Sartre had always been that while I was willing to pay some attention to him as a novelist and playwright – he had a bleak materialism of outlook that at least gave his work the thrust of consistency, and he had a gift of expression – as a social-cum-political philosopher I had always thought him a windbag and, in view of the instability of European opinion at the time, a dangerous windbag. The gas he was filled with might turn out, I thought, to be actually poisonous, made up as it was of stale Marxism and marsh gas.

On this particular evening I managed to get the pair of us seated sufficiently far away from Molly Whitworth not to hear anything she said at the dinner-table, but when the rump of the assembly went into Common Room for dessert there was no escaping the sound of her voice. She was laying down the law about Sartre and his doctrines, and the law was very much *Thou shalt hear, and obey*.

Since she was obviously not going to ask me my opinion, the only thing to do was to confront her in sudden opposition like one footballer unexpectedly taking the ball away from another. So, waiting for a moment when she paused to take a breath and let some point sink in, I said abrasively, 'Sartre's obviously quite adept at constructing arguments in defence of fanciful positions, but I don't find myself in agreement with what I take to be his values, do you?'

The rimless lenses turned momentarily towards me and their owner shot me a look of surprise, as if the furniture had suddenly addressed a remark to her.

'You can't abstract something you call his "values" and talk about them in isolation,' she said with a cold patience that suggested she was dealing with a particularly backward schoolchild who was at the same time unusually dislikeable. 'You have to take them as part of the *gestalt* of his position.'

'I suppose I'd have to agree with you,' I said, 'if the *gestalt* of his position is made up of all that junk he absorbed in the thirties from Kojève and Heidegger.'

'Is that what *their* thinking seems to you – junk?' She made the word sound undignified, trivial, ridiculous.

'Yes,' I said. 'You have a better word for it? Stale, parasitical, particularly ready to be parasitical on power, whatever the nature of that power, the means by which it came into being, the ends it pursues. Lacking in dignity, in decision, in anything one can admire morally. Founded on a willingness to break human bonds and betray human trust.'

The person on my right now drew my attention to the fact that the decanters, on their second journey round the table, had been standing for a while at my elbow. People further down the table were showing signs of impatience and I ought to move the wine along. I sloshed out some port, saw that Garrity on my left was looked after, and resumed the offensive, but the pause had given Molly Whitworth time to prepare her defences.

'I believe you're an historian,' she said. 'Do you read history in that spirit – looking for things you can admire?'

'Not just like that. But when I find an historical figure who seems to me to have no admirable qualities I don't mind saying so rather than beating about the bush. I don't think people who've been dead for a certain length of time should be treated by different standards from those that apply in everyday life.'

'Still less are you going to take your values from French philosophers,' she said, broadening her counter-attack to bring in the implication that I was Philistine and insular.

'Their nationality is irrelevant. Sartre produces arguments to justify tyranny and torture. He worships Stalin, who employs those things as means, and I'm pretty sure if Nazism had become seriously established in France he'd have found arguments for approving of Hitler too, and cheering on the Gestapo.'

'Dear me, I hope you're not writing a history of France.'

'Let me merely say that I hope whoever does write it sees things in the same way that I do.'

'You want to impose uniformity?' (Too clever to miss that one.)

'Not as much as Sartre does.' (Got you there, dearie.)

At this point someone started talking about De Gaulle, doubtless to cool the atmosphere. Before long Watson had intervened and directed the conversation towards his favourite topic: his own exquisite sensibility and how it particularly manifested itself on his travels in delectable places.

'I can't think how many times I've been to Avignon,' he informed us, 'but there's always something one hadn't noticed – something first-rate, I mean.'

'Has anything particularly drawn your attention recently?' – Tonson's polite enquiry, obviously submitting to the inevitable.

'Yes, the painted wooden statues in the Church of St Symphorien. It's so easy to walk past that fifteenth-century facade and conclude that the interior must be quite ordinary. But something prompted me to go in and there are these three wooden statues of about a hundred years later. Superbly done, and though of course the colours have had to be restored, they struck me as having been done very sensitively.'

'Conventional subjects, I suppose?' Tonson asked, still politely feeding the monologue.

'Yes, Christ, the Virgin and St John. A great impression of freshness and energy.'

You sound like a Sunday newspaper critic, I thought. One of the things that infuriated me about Watson was the way he trivialized the arts, always treating them as special effects arranged to give pleasure to people like him rather than as ways of perceiving human experience. Perceiving experience to him was Serious, and the Serious equalled the Solemn, and to be Solemn equalled being a Bore. To be thought of as a Bore would have been, for Watson, the lowest circle of the Inferno. I would willingly have consigned him to it.

Molly Whitworth's championing of St Jean-Paul seemed to have started a sombre train of thought in Garrity, who, after a period of being silent, opened up when he and I were sitting somewhat apart from the rest, drinking coffee in the Common Room after both stages of the dinner were over. He took out his ancient and faintly appalling briar pipe ('I've smoked this pipe every day since 1927'), lit it with a furious doggedness, drawing the tall flame of his lighter deeply into the bowl as he always did, till his voice emerged from the centre of a blue cloud, and said thoughtfully, 'On the question of Sartre and his value or otherwise, I must confess to not being, temperamentally, a real philosopher, though I try to take an interest. I'm incurably pragmatic – ideas on their own don't engage me very deeply until I begin to consider the consequences of carrying them over into action. And I have to add to that the fact that I've seen enough of political oppression to make me deeply suspicious of any body of theory that might seem to underpin or countenance it.'

'Political oppression, yes,' I said. 'You've seen it in its German form, of course.'

Garrity's normally mild face became set hard. He clenched his teeth on his fuming pipe in a way that made the boniness of his long jaw seem, suddenly, capable of stubbornness, even aggression.

'My fondness for the imaginative depth of the German vision, on its artistic side, has always led me to spend time there and to keep up with my German friends, who, naturally, have come from the section of the population that understands and values these things – a minority, as it is everywhere, but a not inconsiderable minority. As the Nazis dug in more and more securely, and tightened their hold on the country more and more every year, I still took the decision to keep visiting Germany, to maintain contact with my friends, and to seek out that true German imaginative spirit wherever I found it, never to lose personal contact unless and until something happened that actually forced me to.'

'The something you envisaged being a war, I suppose?'

'That was always a possibility, though of course until the moment when it actually broke out, war was a very unknown quantity, England being so pacifist, so anti-militarist by tradition, and with a populace so indifferent to anything that went on beyond their own shores. As we know, it did finally come, but right up to that moment I kept in touch with Germany and with German friends. I used to take my bicycle across the North Sea every summer, and enter Germany through Holland. Or sometimes go across the Channel and enter via Belgium. I knew all the roads and all the frontiers. I often think I must have been a familiar figure to all the border guards and Customs officials. I wonder they didn't examine my panniers more rigorously.'

It would have been a complex double or triple bluff, I reflected, to use Garrity as a spy. But certainly such things had happened.

'One of my friends,' he continued, puffing, 'was particularly isolated. I felt his situation with a special keenness. He was an art historian, with a wonderful understanding of painting in all its aspects, including its historical relationships. For a living he was a museum curator – not an important collection, just the local art gallery in a town in Bavaria. He told me, not by letter – that soon became impossible – but on my annual visits, how things became more strained and difficult for him year after year. Already in 1934 the local Party officials were inviting him, with some edge of insistence, to join the Nazi movement. When I saw him in 1935 he had continued to ignore their suggestions. By 1936 their visits had become more frequent and their tone more pressing. Why didn't he want to join the Party? Was there something wrong with him that he felt no wish to join this great new movement that was revitalizing Germany? Or was it perhaps something wrong he saw in *them*? Had he any criticisms to make of the Führer and the movement? If so, it might be safer to make them *now*, while he was still at liberty and could speak voluntarily.'

Garrity's face was no longer just grim. It had been invaded by sorrow, and underneath the sorrow lay a deep anger. He was living through the agony of his German friend, the art historian. He was looking back on that still bleeding historical wound with the eyes of a man who had been close to its merciless gash. Close? Perhaps his friend had been more than merely close to it. Perhaps he had been destroyed by it. I waited in silence for him to resume. There seemed to be nothing that I could say – nothing that I had the stature to say.

'The last time I saw him,' Garrity went on quietly, 'was in 1938. How he hung on so long, and still without becoming a Party member, I shall never know. It was heroism – not the kind of heroism that has epic poems written about it or statues erected, but heroism for certain. He simply could not endure the thought of attending Party rallies, applauding those dreadful speeches, giving that odious salute, chanting the slogans full of hate and aggression. It would have killed him.'

I was silent, thinking of the courage of this unknown man. And of the reasons Sartre would have thought up for calling him a fool.

'When I was preparing that 1938 visit, I wrote ahead and told him of my arrangements. I planned to put my bicycle on an express train, get off at the nearest main-line station to where he lived – it was an outlying village – and take the little local train the last few miles, arriving at a time I told him. He lived in a building that was rather like a lighthouse or Martello tower. I don't know what purpose it originally served, but in form it was a tower and on this particular day he was sitting at an upper window, looking across the fields towards where the railway line ran; I think it was a single track. As my train came clanking along he saw it, ran down the stairs and started along the field path to the station. I got off the train, put my bicycle on to the path and began moving towards his house. But before I had gone more than a couple of hundred yards he had run towards me and we met, in the middle of the field. He had a reason for that, I dare say. I shall never forget how he caught hold of the handlebars as I stopped, as if he were taking both me and the machine into one great rapturous embrace, and burst out, 'Oh, Garrity, I'm glad you've come! It's like living in a mad-house!'

Garrity had lowered his pipe during this last sentence or two, and now sat staring fixedly at me. His brown eyes were full of the intensity of that recollection of his persecuted friend and of those strife-torn days. It was one of those moments when, in spite of the general comicality of his appearance, with that centre-parted hair and thoughtlessly selected clothes, he took on the dignity of a man of stature; a perceiver; a witness to the truth; almost, in his unassertive way, of a prophet.

'You say that was in 1938,' I said. 'Did you go to Germany in 1939?'

'Yes. I went at Easter.'

'And visited your friend?'

'I tried to visit him. I didn't write ahead because by that time I felt certain that it would be dangerous for him to receive letters from England, and particularly from someone like me who was not going to influence him towards being a good Nazi. I simply arrived unannounced. I got off the express as before, put my bicycle on the little branch-line train as before, got off at his village halt as before, and pedalled towards his tower as it stood, seeming to await me, staring out over the acres of grass.'

'And did he come to meet you?'

'He wasn't there. The building was occupied by other people – a rather hard-eyed couple with a brood of fair-haired, very Aryan children. When I mentioned my friend's name, they said he had moved and they had no idea where he had gone. They were by no means friendly with me. When I left, which I did straight away, the man came a few yards down the path with me and asked me, when we were out of earshot of the others, what my business with the Herr Doktor was. I said he was an old friend and that my business was simply to keep up our acquaintanceship. He made no reply to that – just stood and watched me out of sight.'

'And since the war? Have the two of you got back into touch?'

Garrity took up his pipe. Being so full of accumulated gunge, it had gone out immediately when he stopped drawing on it, and he now re-lit it vigorously. From the centre of the noisome cloud his voice reached me so quietly as to be hardly audible. 'I have not yet succeeded in locating him.'

★

Some time in the New Year of 1949, I happened to learn from casual gossip that Otto Nussbaum had been taken ill and was in the Radcliffe Infirmary. I learnt this by pure chance, not being in close touch with him, and it made me wonder, uneasily and rather guiltily, who actually was in close touch with him. Katz was, of course, but Katz, in my mind and I'm sure many people's, hardly had an existence as a separate person; he was one half of a strange bipartite creature, a kind of amphisboema, called Katzannussbaum. You could hardly imagine Katz coping with life on behalf of the two of them, if Nussbaum became incapacitated, any more than you could imagine one half of a pair of Siamese twins hastening off for help if the other half were confined to bed. Katz must know Nussbaum's news, but who else knew it? And oughtn't someone else to know it? It was now a quarter of a century since the pair of them had arrived in Oxford, escaped from the murderous malice of the Nazis with nothing but the clothes they stood up in, leaving behind their books, their savings, their precious box-files and card-indexes, their friends and for all practical purposes even the reputation that gave them their employment, except among a minority of classical scholars scattered thinly about the world. Many of the Central European Jewish savants who had arrived in a similar condition had managed by now to find permanent posts and more or less rebuilt their careers, but these two still seemed, though as highly esteemed as anyone, to be living the same hole-and-corner life they had lived when I first met them. In earlier days, though, when they were much younger and still breathing out gratitude to the blessed country that had given them shelter, there seemed nothing odd or unfair about shabby lodgings in Jericho, humble jobs at the Press, pub meals, threadbare overcoats that did little to keep out the biting cold of an Oxford January. Now, it was beginning to be more serious.

Oxford, in my opinion, ought to do more for these men. But then Oxford ought to do more for Garrity. What was the reason for this withdrawal, this silent passing-over of major scholars with a touch of oddity, perhaps a spark of creative madness that leavened the years of painstaking acquisition of knowledge? Why were such men passed over for positions they would have held with superb distinction, while smoother and more sinuous creatures, rat-like some of them, tabby-cat-like others, slid past all barriers?

I was being unfair, of course. Many distinguished men, and increasingly women, gave their lives and their gifts to Oxford in those years, as in all years since the end of the twelfth century. The standard had never been seriously let down. But my worry remained. The ones who were not fully accepted, not given places in the inner circle, whose natures contained elements too angular, irregular, perhaps just too individual, to fit smoothly in with the close weave of the place – these were held at a distance and, because I loved Oxford and admired her achievements, that distance worried me. It also caused me moments of self-accusation. What was lacking in me, that the system had managed to absorb me? Was I conciliatory, average, predictable? Was I (as Heather had bitterly flung at me) *smooth*, even? Not that, surely!

Such thoughts lay uneasily in my mind as I walked over to the Radcliffe Infirmary that afternoon. Nussbaum had had a stone removed from a kidney, an operation serious enough but not usually threatening to life if the patient is sound in other respects. He looked thin, but then he always looked thin. His face was spare, his eyes a trifle sunken, but I saw no reason to suppose that he would not make a full recovery. I had taken him some grapes and an eighteenth-century edition of Perseus which I had picked up at a second-hand bookstall in a country town. He looked at the book before sampling the grapes.

'I have heard of this edition without ever actually seeing a copy,' he remarked. 'The commentary obviously owes a good deal to Pierre d'Holbach,' or some such name I did not quite catch. 'He was a Genevese who gave most of the later part of his life to a detailed commentary on Perseus. This editor, I think I shall find, has read him with profit. Thank you, my friend, for this most thoughtful gift. It will make my convalescence seem less tedious.'

'Where will you be spending your convalescence? They won't keep you here, I suppose?'

'No, this is not a convalescent hospital. They are sending me to some place on the coast of Hampshire. I think they said Hampshire. I have to accept what the authorities give me out of their charity, as I have no money of my own. As soon as I feel strong enough – in a very few days, I hope – I shall escape and come back to Walton Street.'

'Couldn't you go back there straight away? You must have someone who'd look after you – call in and give you your meals and that kind of thing.'

'Who would do that?'

I was too realistic to offer to do it myself; I had far too much work to do and my domestic skills were poor. God pity any invalid who had to depend on being looked after in the spare time of *my* life. 'Well . . .' I said, a trifle desperately, 'what about Hans Katz?'

'Leonard, Leonard,' he said gently, 'you are behind with the news.'

'What news?'

'Your ordinary neighbourhood news. It is to be expected. You are too absorbed in the detail of events that took place two centuries ago to have any attention to spare for the trivia of life in your vicinity.'

'College life consists ninety per cent of trivia,' I said. 'It's being immersed in that that clogs up my mind, not historical study. More's the—'

'You do not know that Hans Katz is almost at the end of his preparations for departure?'

'Departure?' I was thunderstruck. For some reason it had never struck me as a possibility that either one of them would move from Oxford. That one should go without the other had seemed a compound impossibility, entirely unthinkable. *One* Siamese twin? Castor without Pollux?

'He has accepted an offer of employment at Berkeley,' Nussbaum said. 'By next May he will be a citizen of California.'

'Well, a resident,' I said. 'I mean, he can hardly be a citizen of California until he's a citizen of the United States.' By making this kind of niggling point I was frankly playing for time, trying to give my mind a moment or two to get back on balance. Katz going! Leaving Oxford! Leaving Europe! Leaving Nussbaum!

We talked over the matter a little longer, but neither of us had any appetite for it. Katz had a perfect right to live anywhere he chose, and of course we both understood that it was better to be employed at a well-funded University on the Pacific Coast than to try to carry out his work in a tiny cramped office, hardly bigger than a boot-cupboard, at the end of a long corridor on the top floor of the Oxford University Press.

After a little more mechanical talk, I wished Nussbaum a successful convalescence, hoped he would not be too bored at wherever they were sending him – a hope we both recognized as totally forlorn – and emerged into the cold, gritty wind. Needing to make some small purchases, I decided to leave the hospital by the back entrance, down in Walton Street, rather than by the main entrance in Woodstock Road. I chose a convenient door that would let me out not far from that point. If I had gone out the normal way, I would have missed one of the most distressing sights it was ever my fortune to see. It was a sight that has come back to my mind over and over again in the years that have passed, the single sight I would choose if I were given the privilege of blotting out just one from all those I have seen.

Coming up the slope towards me from the Walton Street gate, labouring doggedly onward in the chill wind and under the bleak white sky, was a wheel-chair pushed by a woman and containing a man. The man was old, heavy, thick-set. He had a pork-pie hat jammed down on his head and a bulky overcoat buttoned tightly up to his chin. His head was canted to one side, and indeed his whole body had a tilt that suggested helplessness, conveying that if he slipped over from the perpendicular he had no way of righting himself and if no one heaved him up he would continue to go down until he slumped far enough to overturn the chair and lie on his side on the ground. His eyes were fixed straight ahead but did not seem to be looking at anything. They did not look like blind eyes, but there was no light of recognition in them; scarcely even any consciousness. The lines of his face were taut and rigid, the more noticeably since it had obviously once been a round, ruddy face; one side was grappled into particularly tight lines.

The woman who was pushing the chair was giving her energy to the task as if it were a penance imposed on her from hell. Her expression, the set of her shoulders, the vehement way she shoved the chair along against the wind and against the slight gradient, all proclaimed that she was doing it because she could not think of a way of getting out of doing it.

The man in the wheel-chair was Old Burrell. The woman pushing his helpless bulk up that slope was his wife Alice Burrell: my mother-in-law that was.

As she drew level I opened my mouth to say something, but with no idea what. I think I kept it open for an instant, still expecting to speak, but nothing came out. As she passed me Mrs Burrell's eyes rested for an instant on my eyes with a concentrated rage and hatred that almost burnt them out of her sockets. If ever I knew myself hated, if ever I heard myself surrounded by unspoken curses, 'curses not loud but deep', that was the moment.

My mother-in-law did not break her stride; I did not break my stride. The wheel-chair continued to labour its way up the slope, towards whatever department it was where Old Burrell was going to be looked after by some specialist. Specialist in what? It hardly mattered. All of us needed to be looked at by specialists in something. Specialists in hatred, specialists in sadness, in loneliness, in disappointment, in wasted lives.

The Fellows of Episcopus, fretting, fussing, scurrying to and fro with confidential messages, holding breakaway meetings behind closed doors, finally managed to elect a new President and Salterton made his slow, dignified exit to join his two aged sisters in Bournemouth or wherever it was they lived. But before his turn came to die he made one more visit to the College, and it happens to be riveted in my memory.

The time was late September 1949, just a year after his departure. I had seen him about for a couple of days, staying no doubt in the President's Lodgings as the guest of his successor, an ex-diplomat by the name of Jocelyn Mowbray. Perhaps he was making a last round of visits, or perhaps gathering up some odds and ends of his belongings. I had exchanged a few words with him and found him in good form, rested by a year in the sea air and not yet a prey to the absent-mindedness that comes with having nothing to do.

It was one of those lulls that occur naturally in the academic year; the last days of the summer vacation were trickling away, and there was a general air of expectancy; the sense of space, of having leisure to ponder wider issues and distant horizons, was the more precious because it would so soon be lost. Ahead lay two months of lecturing, teaching and pell-mell involvement, with hardly time to read an article; after that, with no break, the business of admissions – reading the entrance papers of the young who wanted to come up to Episcopus the following autumn and then interviewing those who seemed promising. It was a time for tying up loose ends in one's research before putting it to one side to face the demands of teaching and administration. It was, I expect, on some such tying-up business that I was going into the College Library after dinner. This in itself was no casual business, involving as it did climbing a flight of stairs, unlocking an ancient oak door, remembering to lock it behind you again unless you were going to sit just inside it, switching on the requisite lights from among a complicated system, and then moving down the long L-shape formed by the two galleries lined with alcoves. There must have been something, I forget what, that I needed to consult, and my busy day had given me no time to do it until now.

As soon as I got in, I saw that there was a table-lamp glowing softly a little way down the long passage. Salterton was sitting in a chair, one of the light, comfortable wooden chairs with arm-rests that were good both for reading and thinking. A large calf-bound folio lay on the table beside him, as if he had originally come in to consult it. But what he was doing now was thinking.

I wondered for a moment whether to leave him to his thoughts and just duck out. But he had seen me. He was looking in my direction, and something in his look had the power to draw me towards him.

'Ah, President,' I said. I had always called him 'President'. Never 'Salterton'. And never in my most grotesque dreams would I have addressed him by his Christian name, as even the youngest Junior Fellows have since become accustomed to addressing the heads of their colleges. He had three Christian names, and I didn't even know which he was called by, supposing that anyone called him by any of them.

'Leonard,' he said. 'You're pursuing your studies?'

'Well,' I said deprecatingly, 'just trying to tidy up a few details . . . a date here, an exact legal term there . . . shavings of the workshop.' I never gave myself the airs of an important scholar when talking to Salterton; indeed, since getting to know a few people who actually were major scholars, I had never been tempted to give myself such airs at all.

Salterton sat erect in his wooden chair, the great folio open beside him in the circle of lamplight, and all around him the shadowy presence of the Library, storehouse of knowledge and disputation, crammed with thought, speculation, accumulated fact, the garnered sheaves of so many lives. His eyes, which had always seemed to me merely benign, had taken on a different quality as he gazed straight in front of him: visionary? Would that be too much to say? At any rate, deeply penetrating.

'Leonard, I took over the helm of this College at a troubled time, though I did not, at that moment, see how troubled it was. I relinquish it now at a time that anyone, the shallowest and least reflective, can see is deeply, radically, fundamentally troubled, when everything is disturbed as far as the eye can see.' He spoke slowly, in perfectly formed sentences, but there was no rehearsed feeling to his words, no impression of something repeated from stock; it came from the pressure of the moment. 'And in particular, anything that we, you and I, would regard as civilization is under attack.'

'I fear so, President.'

'Not merely simple attack, not sporadic and unplanned hostility, but sustained, ruthless attack from powers that have sworn to root it out from the earth. And such powers, Leonard! Confronting us at a time when we are drained and exhausted, such powers!'

I knew what must be uppermost in his mind.

'Twice in my lifetime, Leonard – twice in your lifetime, for the matter of that, for even at the time of the first conflagration you were on this earth – the able-bodied men of this country have been called on to shed their blood in defence of the things we believe in as a nation. Freedom of thought and action. Equality under the law. Tolerance of various races and religions. The right of a man and his family to live their lives without interference, as long as they behaved peaceably to others.'

The tall alcoves of the Library, reaching up into the darkness above his venerable head, seemed like attentive listeners in the silence that surrounded him. As for me, I could only nod wordlessly. I didn't know whether he was conscious of my presence or not, by now.

'Some there are who say that the first conflict was unnecessary, a tragic farce. They say that the German Empire presided over by the Kaiser was peaceful, just and equitable to its citizens, willing to co-operate with the outside world. For myself I have never believed that. When Bismarck united the German states in 1870 he influenced them to take their prevailing tone from Prussia, the German state with the military tradition, the one that had stood out against Napoleon, the state where a soldier felt himself a natural aristocrat. The German Army was Prussian in spirit, and if Germany had won that war, Europe, and therefore the world, would have been ruled by Prussian militarism. I believe we were right to resist that.'

'So do I,' I said. For some strange reason of association I thought of the Royal Flying Corps with their flimsy 'put-putting' aeroplanes taking off from Port Meadow: I thought of Bettington and Hotchkiss being killed in 1912, and Uncle Ernest going out to Wolvercote to gaze in awe at the prophetic wreckage.

'But if Germany had evil in its nature, the Germany that grew from its ruin was all evil. All hatred, all vengefulness and cruelty, fuelling its hatred with absurd theories of racial hegemony with no shred of scientific evidence, making of that great country one enormous weapon and, behind it, a torture chamber. Our young men had to go out again, Leonard. The young, the healthy, the resilient, those with their lives in front of them like an unopened book. You saw it, Leonard. So many of them never opened that book. We helped to put it into their hands, here at Oxford, here at Episcopus, and then it was taken out of their hands again and consumed in the fire of war.'

In which again, I reflected silently, we managed to avoid defeat. Exactly as if he could read my thoughts, Salterton went on: 'I am as grateful as anyone for the Allied victory in that second war. But "victory", in modern warfare, is a highly relative term. Even the victor could more aptly be described as a survivor. So, we have survived. Bloodied, depleted, and in tatters. Hungry. Surrounded by worn-out and broken objects. Essential tasks perforce neglected for years. And now, at this moment as we draw breath from those years of stress and sacrifice, we find ourselves having to face the sworn, implacable hostility of two powers who were lately our allies. The two largest states in the world, taking in between them virtually the entire eastern half of the globe, populated with teeming millions and constantly on the increase. And both those states, and all those millions, united by a single fighting creed. They hate us, Leonard. They have been taught to hate us, and well they have learnt their lesson!'

Salterton relapsed into silence. His gaze remained fixed straight ahead, but now I saw clearly what he was looking at. He was looking at the ruin of his hopes, the crumbling to the ground of everything he had spent his life trying to build up. Or at least the threat of that ruin, that crumbling. He was a spent old man and he was not going to live long enough to see what would actually happen. On the evidence he had, his view was the sensible, rational one. That alliance against us, the hate-filled slogans yelled out from behind the forests of levelled bayonets, did look like the finish for us and our way of life. If Salterton saw it that way, so also did I. I could see nothing to do about it except hang on as long as I could and sell my life dearly when the time came. But what could Salterton do? How could he sell his life dearly, the few faltering months, at most two or three years, that remained to him? Who would buy them?

Salterton was speaking. 'I shall go back to the Lodgings now, Leonard. I have only three more nights there. Perhaps you will be so kind, when you have finished what you came to do, as to lock up the Library.'

I said I would, we wished each other good night, and he walked away down the long gallery with his slow but still firm tread. The great oak door swung open to admit his thin form, shrunken with age but still with a dignity I now saw as tragic. Then he was gone.

Lock up the Library! Could he, at this fateful moment in history, have said any other four words with quite that reverberation? For that matter, was the reverberation lost on him, or did he know perfectly well what he was saying?

Deep in thought, almost bemused, I saw to it that all lights were out, locked up, and went down the long stone curve of the steps and out. Only later did I remember that I had not, in fact, done what I came to do. I was crossing the windy autumnal quadrangle when the recollection came to me, and I smiled grimly and shrugged my shoulders as I walked on. With so many people wanting to kill me, I thought, why should I fill my head with knowledge?

In this manner, and to the accompaniment of these thoughts, did Salterton and I greet the news, released earlier on that day of 21 September 1949, that General Mao Tse-Tung had proclaimed the foundation of the People's Republic of China and its intentions for the future.

PART TWO

I liked my rooms at Episcopus. I enjoyed being in that stylish little bit of eighteenth-century infill, so obviously put there to use up some empty space and seal a draughty gap where the winds could whistle round the side of the College. Pure utility, and yet so elegant. It bore the name of 'Pearce's Building', one Pearce having put up the money to build it in about 1770. Oxford is full of rooms, staircases, buildings, accretions, yards and spaces generally which have been gratefully named after some benefactor to commemorate his or her name, and that is exactly what they do and no more: preserve the name, though what manner of person bore the name, no one knows or cares. Being an historian and having one day a passing fit of curiosity, I looked up this Pearce and found that he was one of those ecclesiastical pluralists who abounded in the eighteenth-century Church, an Englishman who held an Irish bishopric and collected an income from it without ever setting eyes on it. I could imagine what Mairead would have said if such a bishop had been mentioned in her presence. But to think that made me think of Mairead, and I headed off the thought abruptly. It was too painful to think of her during this period when I was under sentence of complete separation from her. So I went back to thinking about the building itself.

It was a perfect home for a single man. The rooms were lofty and dignified though not large, and a sense of spaciousness came to it from that wonderful central stairway, with the graceful oak banister winging and winding its way to the top. I found the place conducive to meditation, particularly of course for a *dix-huitièmiste* like myself. My own room, in furniture and decoration, was harmless. It couldn't help being a bit institutional, a bit college-y, with its off-white paint and its sensible shelves and cupboards, but it hadn't cost me anything to set up. There were times when I sat by the gas fire (for coal burning in open grates was relentlessly going out year by year) and looked about me and thought I was well-off.

There were other times when it all seemed a little bleak and monastic. I wasn't, I knew, cut out for celibacy. To be blunter and more precise, I wasn't cut out for chastity. Ever since I had been an impulsive adolescent cooped up in this same College, my sexual needs had always made themselves very distinctly present in my consciousness. I could not, as more placid natures could, say to myself philosophically, 'Ah, well – simpler to put off all that side of life for a few years and then attend to it in a regular, above-board fashion.' I had a robust, well-grown weapon and I wanted to use it – soon, repeatedly and with maximum enjoyment.

Well, I was now living the life of a bachelor, more or less, and there was nothing, on the face of it, to stop me from going out hunting. All around me lay a terrain that promised to be reasonably full of game. Of course there was the factor of Mairead. I was, and I had no doubt of it, in love with Mairead. After that two-year stagnation, caused by a very natural and indeed laudable wish to pick up my life after the chaos of wartime and go back to my wife and son, I had become completely clear that it was Mairead I loved, Mairead I wanted, both in and out of bed. I wanted both a horizontal relation-ship and a vertical relationship with her. I wanted us to share every kind of pleasure: both the urgent, obsessive, unreflecting pleasure that we shared with the animals, and also the pleasures that were predominantly human, the pleasures of listening to music and talking to each other and sharing ideas and pooling knowledge, and reading books and discussing them together, and looking at pictures and buildings, and walking about amid landscapes, of travelling the world and seeing rivers and mountains and seas. I wanted us to share a vast range of experience and be constantly at work on the fascinating pursuit of widening our common horizons. I wanted us to enjoy being civilized beings, not out of some priggish notion that civilized beings are superior to lumpish ordinary beings, but because of the simple observable truth that people who are civilized have a wider range of experiences than those who are not, and the wider your range the more chance you have of finding life interesting and fulfilling. I wanted Mairead and myself, as a couple, to have it all. I wanted ours to be the deepest partnership, the strongest marriage, in the world. And if the deal turned out to involve parenthood, I was ready for that too. Being Michael's father had already proved deeply rewarding, and I knew it would be even more so if it were grounded in a stable family life. I was ripe for that now, whereas in 1933, when Michael had first made his presence known inside Heather's bur-geoning young body, I could hardly imagine such a thing.

And if I relieved my pent-up longings and needs with some not-Mairead during this long dusty time without her, wouldn't that all just fly away in a shower of fragments when the real thing came? Wouldn't it, however enjoyable and however much a solace now, just go like a puff of smoke on the wind when that happened? And then a small, stubborn voice of fear would say from some unreachable place inside me, You mean *if* it happens. No, No! I would feel like shouting. I mean when! I mean when, when, *when*, damn your cowardice!

I thought back, often, to the promise I had made to her during that last fateful conversation before the onset of this long, frozen pause. There, on 18 March 1947, in the downstairs bar of the Great Western Hotel, Paddington Station (would I ever go there again?), I had undertaken not to obtrude myself upon her notice, to leave her to her own life, until I could truthfully tell her that I was no longer married. Foreseeing that this process would take years, I had had just enough self-protective instinct left – even at that moment when I was clutching at her as a drowning man clutches at a rope that trails past in the water – to ask for an address so that I might write to her with any crucial, situation-altering information. And even at that moment when her own self-protection dictated a complete withdrawal from me, she had written down a telephone number that would reach her 'if it became plainly essential'.

But had we agreed on what exactly we meant by 'essential'? Had I – and this is what I strove, fruitlessly, to reconstruct – actually undertaken not to speak to her *at all* unless I had some concrete information to impart? – something, that is, more concrete than 'I love you, I miss you, being without you is like being shut up in a coffin and I'm afraid I may not be able to breathe much longer'?

What finally made the situation unendurable was that torturing, ineradicable doubt as to whether I was, to put it in simple terms, trying to stretch a clothes-line from post A to post B, and had begun by attaching it firmly to post A without first making sure that post B still existed and still stood where it used to stand. I had secured one end of the line – and in truth it was a lifeline, not a clothes-line – and now I didn't know in which direction to throw the other end. There was dense fog all round me; was post B in that somewhere?

Did I still have a place in Mairead's memory? Worse – insidiously, agonizingly worse – was her image still safe, undamaged by time, in my own memory? Much as I adored her, desperately as I needed her, could I be absolutely certain that I remembered her in every detail exactly as she was? For hour after hour, I thought back over every memory I had of the times when we had been together: walking in streets, sitting in pubs and restaurants, encountering each other in rooms and corridors, being alone together, making love . . . sleeping, waking . . . I even strove to recall exactly what she looked like when chewing her food. I lingered, in a delirious blend of agony and joy, over certain memories of how, when we were making love, her expression would change as she moved towards her orgasm, finally, as she was gathered up into the fullness of it, becoming totally blank . . . It always brought me off when I saw her face become expressionless, as if she were compelling me to join her in some all-engulfing Nirvana. I re-ran these memories over and over in my mind – but that was just the trouble; were they really memories? Had I not constructed them, produced and edited and directed them as films in my interior cinema, casting myself and Mairead in the two leading fantasy-roles? Were they really memories any more?

The mixture needed an injection of reality, a few crumbs of the real Mairead, the actual young woman as she lived and breathed. As she spoke and moved and sat down and stood up. As she gestured and laughed and brushed away her hair with the back of her hand and crossed one ankle over the other, and how she buttoned up her coat when she was going out in cold weather. I needed her identity, her presence, her objective self. If I didn't get it, or some approach to it, I now knew beyond doubt that I would actually go insane. My intelligence would break down to the point at which it would no longer perform the tasks I habitually demanded of it, and at the same time I would become incapable of normal self-control. I would become a madman, Crazy Peter of Episcopus, but in my case there would be none of the visionary quality attaching to the Dostoievskian visionary madman. I would just be a poor devil to be bundled into an institution somewhere and left to spitball in a corner and stare vacantly in front of him.

I shall never forget the occasion on which I felt the actual onset of this condition. It was a sleeting February day and at five o'clock in the afternoon, just as the light drained away, I had begun a tutorial with two Episcopus undergraduates, history students, whose names were Morley and Arbuthnot. When I had first paired them up, I had liked the ring of their names in combination. It sounded like a staid old-fashioned firm of solicitors in a country town: Morley and Arbuthnot – rooted, English, comforting, accustomed. Not that anything in my experience was comforting in my present state. English they might be, and so was I, but Mairead wasn't, and what did it all mean anyway?

This was in the transition period between the old leisurely days when Oxford seemed able to lavish unlimited resources of time and thought on teaching, and the newer production-oriented world of statistics and results. We had largely given up the old one-to-one tutorials, where the undergraduate had his tutor's undivided attention for an hour every week, and were taking them on in pairs. Each week one of the pair read out his essay, while the other had to 'open the discussion' and, at the end of the hour, leave his own essay for me to read. It didn't work too badly, and it meant that I could handle my thirty pupils, that term's stint, in fifteen hours, leaving me some time for work that I found more stimulating. On this occasion, I remember, Arbuthnot was reading his essay. He was a strongly-built youth with a mop of hair, fresh-complexioned, looking a little like a country landowner or someone who might grow up into a country landowner. I believe in fact that his family did own a few acres in the West Country somewhere. With his broad build and tousled head, he looked not unlike the way Harry Goodenough had looked at the same age, but without the dream-haunted eyes of the visionary.

I tried to keep my mind off these irrelevancies and concentrate on what Arbuthnot was reading out, but it was as boring as hell and in any case when I did get my mind off him and the West Country and Harry Goodenough it only flipped, as if by elastic, to Mairead. And not even to Mairead but to a dark red skirt of hers, hanging over the back of a chair. Yes, bejesus, I was wrapped in a trance-like vision, not even of Mairead but of that dark red skirt she had had in about 1944. One afternoon we had been lying in bed, having somehow snatched a couple of hours' assignation in the middle of a day when we were supposed to be doing other things, and in the course of undressing she had hung her skirt over the back of a chair that stood beside the bed. I had looked at it keenly at certain crucial moments, it had burnt itself into my memory, and here it was rising in my mind now, irresistibly, in the quiet of this winter afternoon in my room in Pearce's Building, with the gas fire comfortably roaring and hissing to itself, the sleety dusk outside the window, and Arbuthnot's voice maundering on just outside my attention. A deep red suits dark-haired people, not that I ever remember Mairead wearing any colour that *didn't* suit her – she had an impeccable instinct about those things. Of course the colour that suited her best of all was her own pearl-pale skin; technically I suppose you would have had to call her skin white, but it wasn't actually white at all any more than a pearl is white; in each case there is a luminosity that seems to be coming from inside, though with a human body one knows that can't be literally true; there can't be a myriad subcutaneous microscopic light bulbs that someone switches on at the right time, whatever may be the case with a tumour or callous produced in an oyster by the action of an irritant grain of sand. Enough, enough! I struggled to get my thoughts away from Mairead's skin, and succeeded perfectly, but only to the extent of getting the skirt again . . . the dark red skirt with its rich folds over the simple wooden chair. It seemed to me, suddenly, that I would never come again unless there was a red skirt hanging over the back of a chair beside me. As I considered this new element in my experience, I became aware of another new element that had entered the room. It was thick and creamy and very powerful and its name was Silence. Arbuthnot had stopped speaking; he was looking at me with an air of expectancy, but the expectancy had already begun to be tinged with surprise. Morley, too, was looking surprised. Morley had a fleshy but clever face, with small, keen eyes. He was the kind of student who goes on to become Chancellor of the Exchequer and that kind of thing. He was boring but efficient, and you never had to tell him anything twice.

Evidently Arbuthnot had stopped for a reason. What was this reason? I looked at my watch. Fifteen minutes had gone by. That didn't help me. Sometimes an undergraduate wrote an essay that didn't take more than fifteen minutes to read out, but that was a little shorter than average. Had Arbuthnot come to an end? Or had he stopped to interpolate some query? What had he been saying? How was I to avoid revealing that I had no idea what words had passed his lips for the last quarter of an hour?

I settled myself back in my armchair and said judicially, 'Well, let's hear your reaction to that, Morley. Suppose you go ahead and open the discussion.'

'Without hearing the rest of Arbuthnot's essay, you mean, sir?' Morley asked me, his voice silky and wreathed in irony. Just so, in another ten years, he would be demolishing his opponents at the dispatch box or whatever they call it.

'Yes, I think we've heard enough,' I said bluffly. This was a lie. I, for one, had not heard enough; I had not heard anything.

The essay I had set them was on a straighforward topic: 'To what extent could George III control the electoral system?' They ought to have found plenty to say about it. Perhaps they *had* found plenty to say about it. For all I knew, the essay that Arbuthnot had just finished reading – if he *had* finished and not stopped for some other reason – had been a very interesting essay, persuasively argued and aptly illustrated. I simply had no means of knowing.

They were both looking at me now. Morley, I felt sure, had rumbled me. He knew I hadn't heard what Arbuthnot was reading out, even if he didn't know the reason. Probably he didn't care about the reason. If, as I surmised, the little bastard was going to grow up to be a politician, it would be quite enough for him to see a chance to get past my defences and put the leather in. He would do it quite impersonally; just for practice, so to speak.

Still, there was no retreat now. I had to confront him boldly. 'Well,' I said, brisk and businesslike, 'let's begin by getting Morley's reaction to that, shall we? Will you open the discussion, then, Morley?'

'You mean now, sir?' Morley asked, his expression telling me that he knew he had me wrong-footed and with one shove he could land me flat on my back. The knowledge brought out all his killer-instinct. With something bordering on open insolence, his little eyes held mine; I could sense the enjoyment behind them.

'Why not now?' I said. 'A tutorial is sixty minutes, and we haven't got all day.'

'I thought,' he said maliciously, 'Arbuthnot had paused to ask advice.'

'The middle of an essay isn't the best time to ask advice, Arbuthnot,' I said, seizing on the lifeline.

'It isn't the middle,' Arbuthnot said. 'I just explained that I've said the bulk of what I had to say and the part I hadn't read yet was given to developing a private theory of my own that you might find irrelevant.'

'About Rockingham, you remember, sir,' Morley put in maliciously. I felt like jumping up and shouting, 'Yes, you self-serving little prig, I'd wandered away into my own thoughts because I'm in love, which is a state you'll probably never know in all your stuffy little life. I'm thinking about Mairead, Mairead, Mairead, and the thought of her comes over me in great waves and blots everything else out! Remember that when you're Prime Minister, damn you!'

Actually I said, 'Arbuthnot, if it would help you to read the rest of your essay, go ahead and we'll take account of your views on the Rockingham ministry along with all your other views. I don't see how they can be completely *off* the point.'

'They're – they're pretty speculative,' Arbuthnot said, colouring. Obviously he was in the grip of that feeling that comes over one in tutorials – the feeling that the next bit is rubbish and to read it out will be a humiliation. Actually this is one of the strengths of the tutorial system. Only the slightly better student, the type who has begun to see the difference between sense and nonsense, ever gets this feeling. I felt quite benevolent towards Arbuthnot. 'Do go on, Arbuthnot,' I said encouragingly, 'and then I shall get Morley to initiate a discussion on your views on Rockingham and all your other ideas.' Whatever they are, I finished inwardly.

I don't remember what Arbuthnot had cooked up about the Marquis of Rockingham, *alias* Charles Watson-Wentworth (1730–1782), whose political career was largely one of opposition though he finally attained the office of Prime Minister while a few weeks of breath remained in his body; the man's complex political life might well deserve the speculations of any student, even a beginner like Arbuthnot. I remember that tutorial chiefly as a blank, interspersed with flashes, mostly of dismay and vexation.

That evening, the business of the day over, I knew beyond doubt that the time had come to speak to Mairead. No more hesitation. I had reached the decision; there was no reason why the action should not follow, and every reason why it should. The time was 8.45; there was, at any rate, a chance that Mairead would be in if I telephoned. If I rang during the day she would probably be out. Today was a Thursday; to ring on a weekend would involve the high risk of missing her. I was moving towards the telephone as these thoughts shaped themselves in my head. Resolutely, I interrupted the shaping process. I opened my telephone notebook at the well-remembered page, I checked the well-remembered number, and I dialled it.

Almost at once, she answered. She said, 'Hello?' The way one does it in answering the telephone: slightly interrogative; slightly lilting, if one happens to have a lilting voice.

At first I couldn't say anything, my vocal cords seemed paralysed. I just sat there perfectly still, and of course I expected every second to hear her say 'Hello?' again, more sharply, with an edge of impatience. I was making a balls of it already. I was a failure. I didn't deserve the good luck of finding her at home and ready to answer the telephone at my ring. My fear of annoying her became a panic, and I said, much more loudly than I meant to, 'Mairead, it's me, Peter.'

'Peter,' she said. She spoke unemphatically, as if making a statement in response to a not very precise question. But at least, thank God, she didn't say, 'Peter who?' She knew it was me all right.

'I just . . .' I said.

'Just what?' she said after waiting a bit for me to go on.

'Just wanted to speak to you.'

'What about?' Mairead asked.

'Not about anything, really,' I said and then the words came out with a rush. 'I just felt such a need to hear your voice. I mean just to hear your voice tells me so many things I want to know.'

'I don't see how it does that.' She sounded a trifle cool now. 'As far as I can see it only tells you I'm answering the telephone.'

'For God's sake, darling, it tells me that you still exist, and I didn't even know *that* until I heard your voice.'

'Well, I suppose that's true enough.'

'I just had to hear you. I just had to.'

'All right, Peter, point taken.'

'You're very cool.'

'I have to be.'

'Have to be?'

'Yes,' she said, annoyed now, 'And if you don't understand what I mean by that, you'd better sit and think about it till you do understand it. Dons are supposed to be clever at thinking things out, aren't they? Or aren't you a don any more?'

'Yes, I'm still a don. In fact I'm pretty much the same as I was in early 1947, when we . . .' I hesitated for the right form of words.

'Yes,' she said crisply. 'I know what we did in early 1947.'

'Well,' I said, speaking quickly, trying to get in my essential message before she forced me to ring off. 'I'm keeping up my side of it.'

'And just remind me,' she said, evidently now feeling a need to hurt me, 'what was the part of it I was supposed to keep up?'

'Nothing, you must know that, except to give me the same chance as anyone else when the time came that I wasn't married any longer. You surely remember that.'

'Yes, I remember it.'

'Well, that's all. That's all there is to it.'

'Oh, I see. And what you're doing now is just keeping in touch. Checking up that I still exist?'

'Well, I wouldn't exactly put it like that.'

'I know you wouldn't. It's I who am putting it like that.'

'I rang you because all of a sudden I knew I couldn't go on without hearing your voice say a few words. I've gone two years without any contact with you of any kind and I don't even know anyone who knows you, that I could ask for news. It's impossible, humanly impossible. So of course I rang your number because the moment came when I just couldn't help it. And if that's something I should be ashamed of, I'll be ashamed of it.' When hell freezes over, I thought.

There was a pause and then she said, 'I understand, Peter, of course.'

'Oh,' I breathed out.

'And I'm glad.'

'Glad?'

'Yes. I'm glad you're behaving like a human being.'

'It's no trouble,' I said. 'If one happens to be a human being, that is.'

'Look, Peter, I don't know what's going to happen when all this waiting's over. There's probably a lot more of that still to go.'

'Oh, don't say that,' I groaned. 'Two solid years already – how much longer can the bloody thing be spun out?'

'Oh, they take simply ages. It's set up like that on purpose.'

'Well,' I said, 'I'll stick it, I know that.'

'You know I'm not giving any commitments. But I don't mind you ringing to exchange a few words. I don't even mind having my existence checked up on. It's logical enough. Two years is a long time and I suppose anything might have happened. I don't mind that you rang. I'm glad you did, as a matter of fact. I always knew you as a human being and I'm glad you still are one.'

'I've always been one. Which, in view of the general character of our species and the things human beings do to one another, isn't much of a boast.'

'No, it isn't,' Mairead said, 'but I prefer that to your being an animal because animals can't use telephones. And I think you ought to ring up every now and then. Every few months, that kind of thing. Not too often or it'll get to be a habit and you'll find it hard to handle. And of course you must ring when you know the outcome of your . . . legal proceedings.'

'No fear of my not doing that,' I said.

'And then we can . . . turn our attention to the matter.' She wasn't giving anything away.

Yes, I thought. Do turn your attention to it.

'Thank you, Mairead,' I said.

'You're welcome,' she said, like an American. Had she been there?

'I appreciate it,' I said.

'I'm glad,' she said. 'Goodbye now.'

'Goodbye.' I rang off and sat looking round the room. It had changed.

No, it was I who had changed.

Correction. Everything had changed. The entire world had changed. What had been slowly happening over the last two years, too slowly for me to notice its gradations, too slowly for its total effect to be perceptible, was simply that the colour had been draining out of my life. Everything I was, everything I looked at and thought about, seemd to exist in a thick, lack-lustre, yellowish light that admitted no glitter, no exhilaration. When I remembered Mairead's voice I remembered that I loved her – remembered it, that is, not simply as an intellectual entity but as a rich, complex, many-layered living experience to be remembered, equipped all over again with its limbs and members and all the parts that belonged to it. Even the fact that her voice had not lost its Irish quality – the softness that clings about the consonants and tunes the vowels into cadences, bringing to the language a quality that only the English – who brought the language into being and then very largely betrayed and debased it – would dare to insult with a hard, external word like 'brogue' – even that small fact, I say, brought back everything about her, all the qualities of her mind and body, till I fell into a half-swoon of longing from which I could only, in the end, emerge to the extent of rising slowly from my chair, turning off my gas fire and moving like a somnambulist towards my bed; where I fell immediately into a deep unconsciousness that was broken only when, at first light the next morning, I was awakened by the penetrating sound of a mistle thrush, otherwise known as the stormcock, uttering its monotonous but poignant cry from the top of the tree somewhere near my bedroom window, on and on, never changing, never stopping, against the bleak February dawn, the perfect symbol of the longing within me.

Hearing Mairead's voice on the telephone, though it gave a sharper edge to my suffering, also came as a tremendous liberation. I felt that I had been rescued from a tomb of ice and set back among living, breathing humanity. And with that feeling came the knowledge that it wouldn't really make any difference if a sexual *divertissement* offered itself for my enjoyment along the way. If it helped me to survive the long, dragging time that must still go by while the lawyers spun their infinitely complex and (to them) profitable webs, it would be of great benefit. All I could do was to avoid embarking on an escapade with someone vulnerable who might end up getting hurt.

Small wonder that when I finally met Cynthia, which didn't happen till the early summer of that year of 1949, and got encouraging signals from her, my hesitations vanished as fast as hailstones on warm ground (*very* warm ground).

She worked in a clinical department in one of the first of the big research hospitals in Headington, mostly built with money heaped up by Billy Morris to stifle his conscience after smothering with cheap rubbish the beautiful town he was born in. He had to smother the one and then the other, first the city and then his conscience, and in either case you could still see the corpse of the victim under the avalanche of grot. Cynthia was a dedicated medic. She was all brain-power and will-power. You knew, as soon as you looked at her, that she would make important contributions to medical science with her brain-power, and after that she would be borne on a tide of her will-power to become some kind of supremely important figurehead. She would be Minister of Health, or speak on health-care matters in the House of Lords while also being the first woman President of the B.M.A., all the while carrying on crucial research in a shed in her back garden on Sunday afternoons. 'I can do *anything*,' her expression and bearing said. 'Just show me any job, and if I think it's something worth doing I'll do it, probably with one hand and certainly in double-quick time.'

In appearance she was a commanding figure, tall for a woman (when we were both barefoot I often noticed that we were exactly the same height) and with bright red hair, almost orange in hue, which she wore coiled up elaborately at the back of her shapely head. At least, she wore it like that when she was being disciplined and managing, which was 95 per cent of the time. The other five per cent, when she was being carefree and irresponsible and playful and very, very feminine, she gave this bright orange coil its freedom and let it spread out in savage abandon all over the immediate space, which at such times usually meant the bed. I revelled in her. The only thing about Cynthia that I found less than attractive was her manner of speaking, which she had been drilled into and couldn't help. She was a real daughter of the governing classes, and had been given, too young to be aware that she was being given anything, the speech mannerisms of her caste. She clipped her words, flattened all her cadences, barked out her sentences like commands. In the days when England had a large overseas empire her kind were much in demand as memsahibs, and indeed that was an excellent manner in which to issue instructions to servants, especially those over whom one has total authority. For normal everyday purposes within one's own national boundaries it was of less utility, and indeed after about 1945, with the steady increase in the number of English people who were actually antagonized by this manner, I would say it increasingly became a disadvantage to anyone unlucky enough to be saddled with it. In this respect, though, Cynthia was in the right profession. An accent like hers presupposes an interlocutor, or more frequently a simple listener, who is humbled beforehand, very ready to tolerate or even welcome a note of command from above. And of course as a doctor she was dealing with people who, before they came into her presence, had been well and truly humbled, by pain and suffering or by the fear of pain and suffering. If you are ill, and have hopes that a doctor might restore you to health, you put up with much more loftiness from him or her than you ever would from a clergyman offering to care for your immortal soul, or a don offering to improve your mind. Souls and minds can wait! Their doctors must behave themselves! Doctors for the body are the real masters.

And mistresses. Cynthia was bursting with energy in every direction and the general pattern of her life, plus the creative interest of her work, was well suited to absorb and direct this energy in all its forms save one. Her sexual needs were double-strength and an adequate cavalier service did not automatically come with the job. She looked around, and she found me.

I met Cynthia almost by accident, at a party in Episcopus given by a man who wasn't particularly a friend of mine, but neither was he an enemy and I supposed he wanted a few people to make up the numbers for a drinks party one Friday evening. I expect I was subconsciously on the *qui vive*, but Cynthia's tall figure, bright woven hair and fine intelligent features (they were what used to be called 'chiselled', and particularly beautiful about the mouth and eyes) would have drawn me across the room in any case. I don't think I had been at the party more than two minutes before I was making for her with a very obvious triangular fin sticking up out of the water.

She hadn't come to the party alone, but on the other hand she wasn't specifically *with* anyone – the four or five people she was with were a random loose-knit group who just happened to work in the same place. And in any case, once I had listened to a few sentences in her energy-charged voice and stood for a few minutes within close range of her splendid eyes, even if she had been with another man I would have been perfectly ready for a knife-fight in the middle of the front quad. I had put down for dinner in Hall that evening, but I'm afraid that was one evening in my Episcopus life when I was catered for and didn't show up. By the time everyone else sat down to the plain honest High Table dinner, I was sitting with Cynthia in an Indian restaurant in St Clements about which I now remember nothing. I can't remember what we had to eat, nor what the restaurant was called, nor even − since it didn't last long before being replaced by another business − exactly where it was. What I do remember is what we did when we got back to Cynthia's flat in Headington afterwards. I know what that was called all right.

Afterwards, back in my own bed shortly before dawn, I tried to summon up some guilt, some self-accusation, some sense of being the base betrayer of an ideal. But it was no good. I felt too happy, too relieved, too full of uncomplicated, straightforward gratitude for what she had given me.

The autumn of 1949 was a season of almost-peace, thanks to Cynthia. Thanks likewise to her, the spring of 1950 was a slow fever, illuminated by the coloured stars of rockets going off.

The summer that followed was a good one, or so my memory reports it. When I think of that year, I think of blue skies and warmth. I realize, though, that there may be a subjective element in all this. Fine summer weather has a way of seeming all the more brilliant when one observes it longingly through glass. Not many of us, after all, have the privilege of going out of doors whenever we happen to feel like it. Work claims the bulk of our waking hours, and work, for most of us, is something that goes on indoors. This was true for me, and to a particularly irksome extent, in that summer of 1950. To begin with, I was examining, the first time this quasi-compulsory ordeal had fallen to my lot. This meant that once the heavy sheaves of scripts began to come in, starting at the beginning of June, until the vivas in mid-July, I was doing nothing but reading, judging, re-reading, re-judging, attending meetings formal and informal, and waking up in the middle of the night to worry over whether I had devoted enough finesse of judgement, and enough vigour of imagination, to identifying the elusive line that divided $\beta -$ from $\gamma +$ in a paper from a shaky candidate. On such distinctions would depend whether the student emerged with a lower Second or a Third; this in turn might affect his chances of getting some job he was planning to go after, and from there the consequences might knock on and on and on. Perhaps it wouldn't make that much difference in the end, because most people ultimately settle down at a career level that roughly represents their level of ability; still, the beginning of one's twenties can be a very important decision-making time, and a stagger at that point is to be avoided if possible; certainly not something one wants to inflict on any young person.

To make it all worse, before ever the river of desperately scrawled scripts began to flow towards me, I had an unusually heavy load of ordinary teaching. Unobtrusively – at least I hope it was unobtrusive, because I genuinely didn't want people to notice – I began to take over more and more of Bax's work-load. The man was visibly wilting; month by month, it seemed to me, he was losing energy and motivation. It didn't take any penetration to know that the trouble lay in the desperate bleakness and loneliness of his inner life. He was, in that respect, a normal person. It is simply ordinary, middle-of-the-road human psychology to base one's character on the satisfaction of two needs in the same way as one's body stands up on two legs. One leg is the intimate life of personal relationships, the life that centres on sex and sleep and warmth and the need for closeness and sharing, the life in which the small details of domestic life seem not trivial and boring but as comfortable and reassuring as the fluff that birds use to line their nests; the nest would be useless to the bird if it were made solely of fluff, but comfortless and unwelcoming if fluff were absent altogether. The other leg is the outward, public life of work and achievement, lived in the broad light of day and in full view of others, including perfect strangers. Even the most outwardly successful people need their intimate lives of contact and familiarity, woven round with the close mesh of domestic continuity, everything that is summed up in the expression 'hearth and home'. Bax had wanted these things. Perhaps in his youth he had nurtured dreams of finding some kind of relationship with another man that might have given the two of them something permanent and helped them to live more or less in the same way as a male-female couple who happen to be childless. For whatever reasons – for I knew nothing of them, apart from Geraldine's one brief mention of a major scandal that had blown up early in his life at Episcopus – this solution to his problems had never materialized. In falling under the spell of Geraldine, he may have been drawn initially by the hope that by mustering some thrust of physical desire for her boyish prettiness he might get safely to that first base from which a deeper relationship could begin to get itself together. What precisely had gone wrong with that plan and in what way, I never knew nor enquired. But gone wrong it had, Geraldine had escaped and with her had gone one of the two pillars on which Bax's life, like most lives, needed to rest. On a single pillar, the pillar of his professional work as scholar and teacher, his existence found no stability. It swayed. It teetered. It seemed, at every moment, likely to crash down and lie in broken pieces.

Partly because I genuinely cared about him, and partly just because I saw so much of him, Bax's sufferings were very real to me. Outwardly, it would have seemed that our two lives were very much the same: both historians, both living singly, one the former tutor of the other and therefore well acquainted with the landscape of each other's minds, a somewhat older Tweedledum to a somewhat younger Tweedledee. But inwardly the difference was total. I had hope. I cherished the ambition of a very specific happiness, an ambition focused on one specific individual, a raven-haired young Irishwoman with vivid blue eyes, a body almost as slender as Geraldine's but more feminine in its flowing movements (she would never attract a Bax!), and a mind as quick as Geraldine's but less programmatic, more geared to take account of the unexpected and the paradoxical.

This young woman was withdrawn from me at this present time; concealed, by mutual agreement, in the huge opaque cloud of gas called 'London'. At one time I had been desperately afraid that she would recede so far into this cloud that I would never see her, never be aware of her living essence, again – that I would begin to find her actually unimaginable and that that in itself would rob me of the courage to get back into contact with her when I finally had the all-important thing to say. But since that blessed occasion when, giving way to an overmastering impulse, I had beaten down the barriers and forced myself to speak to her on the telephone, even though the time of authorization was still far distant, that fear had gone. I knew Mairead was there all right. I even felt her vibrations. I felt her breath on my cheek, felt her heartbeat under my hand, though it was years since we had met. That was the difference between me and Bax. He was really alone.

On top of all the other things I was doing that term, I had to lecture twice a week, and after about half-way point I had run out of my prepared material and was improvising, hastily bundling together week by week the facts and arguments I needed to keep talking for another hour on my chosen theme. Driven as usual by some invisible demon, I had chosen a subject I had never tackled before, where a more canny person might have dug out some tattered old notes and re-run them. No, I had to struggle with 'Constitutional Precedent and the Evolution of the Office of Prime Minister before 1783', and its complexities were growing week by week.

One Saturday, when the sunshine was particularly glorious and the sky a particularly soft blue, I was indoors the whole day, taking pupils till lunch-time (this was before the five-day week became *de rigueur* for the nation as a whole, including the Universities) and preparing Monday's lecture in the afternoon. Sunday, come what may, I was determined to spend in the open air, reading nothing and thinking as little as possible, hoping by that means to ward off the nervous collapse I could see coming towards me. At about six o'clock, having made enough progress to be secure against utterly disgracing myself before the few obstinate limpets who were still turning up for the weekly monologue (some students can become addicted to listening as some lecturers can become addicted to talking), I closed up my books and wandered out into the balmy air. One great blessing attended life at Episcopus; when not actually working or otherwise immured, you were only a few steps from the matchless, the magical, the inexhaustible beauty of that garden, planned with so much care and so much intelligence, known and loved all over the world, celebrated for hundreds of years as one of the chief glories of Oxford; and never more than two or three minutes away from where one was sitting.

My eyrie looked down on a small plot of cultivation, not quite a garden and yet not quite not one, occupying the space between the outer wall of the second quad at Episcopus and the boundary wall of the next college. This, no more than a strip of breathing-space that kept the buildings from being too jammed together, was used for growing a jumble of plants, some that I conjectured were being tried out as candidates for introduction into the main garden. It was closed off at the far end of the strip by the stone wall that surrounded 'the garden' itself, the official garden, so to speak. There was a door in this wall and to this door I had a key, so it was my usual way into the garden, which I therefore entered at the south-western corner, and took in its full majesty at first glance.

On this particular early evening, however, when I stepped out through the door in the wall, I found myself looking at the back view of a scout in a white jacket who was serving drinks from a table. Someone was giving a drinks party in the garden, a frequent enough occurrence at this time of year. I came up to the scout and asked who was the host; it turned out to be Watson.

I could see Watson standing in the middle of the lawn, glass in hand, talking to a girl in a flowered dress. From a distance, it was a pleasant, civilized prospect, and I determined to keep it like that. To approach and be recognized would not be a wise move. Looking in close-up at Watson's porcine face, hearing what kind of deftly ill-natured remark he would come out with, were beyond my tolerance just then.

Thinking quickly, I decided to walk down the length of the garden – slowly, so that I could savour its beauty – and then, once I got to the wall at the far end, let myself out through another door similar to the one I had just come from and answering the same key. That would put me in Parks Road, a few steps from the King's Arms, where I could drink a leisurely pint of draught beer and forget the Watsons of this world.

As I neared the end of the garden the chatter from the party reached me more faintly, and I began to congratulate myself on having made an easy escape. I had in any case managed to steer sufficiently clear to avoid being able to catch anything that was said, keeping it comfortably within the harmless category of 'Noises Off', except that at one point I heard Watson's voice raised in a high, nasal drawl that carried across the lawn. I made out the word 'extraordinary', pronounced in such a way as to give exactly equal emphasis to each syllable. That pronunciation, coupled with the drawling utterance, managed to convey, even within the compass of one word, the impression that Watson was talking about something, or more probably someone, who had done, or said, or permitted, or revealed, or confessed to, something that Watson found foolish, or discreditable, or disadvantageous, to the point of being 'ex-tra-or-din-ary'. I was glad I could hear nothing more. I was nearly at the exit gate now.

Near the end was a screen of thick shrubs, planted no doubt at least partly to form a barrier against the traffic sounds from the road outside. Anyone standing among these bushes was totally invisible from a few yards away. As I approached them, a figure stepped out on to the path, thereby barring my way. It was Hunt.

What Hunt had been doing among the bushes I neither knew nor cared. Perhaps he had been emptying his bladder. Or perhaps he had had to remove his clothing in order to apply ointment to a rash on some intimate part of his body. Or perhaps he belonged to a religious sect that enjoined silent prayer and meditation for a specified number of minutes at that hour of each day. No, probably not that; Hunt would not have any religion.

He now addressed me, using the same slightly ironic, slightly mocking tone that he had used every time he had ever addressed me, since about 1930 or 1931 when we had first met. It conveyed, as it was meant to, that even though I might not have done anything amusingly *gauche* in the last few minutes, I was the kind of person who was very likely to do so in the *next* few minutes.

'Off already, Leonard? Is the party so boring?'

'I don't know what the party's like,' I said. 'I'm just on my way through the garden.'

'Oh? You weren't invited?'

I ignored that one. What the hell business of his was it whether I'd been invited or not? 'See you around,' I said, moving forward.

But he still barred my way. 'Unsociable beggar, aren't you, Leonard?'

I'd had enough of him already; he was someone I easily had enough of. 'I don't know, and I'm not interested enough to know, your definition of unsociability,' I said, 'but if it means not having time just now to stand and chatter to you, I don't mind if you apply it to me.'

Hunt gave a slight shrug. 'Have it your own way. I had no great desire to talk to you for your own sake, anyway. It's just that I'm feeling pleased with myself, things are going my way, and I'm in a mood to enjoy telling people about it.' 'Even you,' his expression conveyed.

'Well, there are plenty of people at the party. You can tell them about your good luck.'

'I didn't say it was good luck. I said things are going my way, and they're going my way because I've played my cards right. There's no luck in it – I'm rising in my profession, that's all.'

'In your profession, isn't rising generally a matter of sinking?' I said. I knew I was being spiteful, but in my opinion Hunt deserved it. 'Isn't the big money down at the bottom, in the gutter?'

Hunt was a little taller than I was, which gave him the advantage of being able to look slightly downwards at me when we faced each other. He did so now, quite successfully. 'You're very predictable, aren't you, Leonard?'

'Yes,' I said.

'It so happens that I've been given a very responsible assignment which, except in the case of someone like you who is just prejudiced, most people with an interest in ideas would see as serious and respect-worthy.'

'What on earth can that be?' I said, really wanting to know by now.

'I'm on my way to California. Just dropping in at Watson's party for a cheerful glass on the way to the airport. I fly tonight. My paper's sending me to do a big interview.'

'Well, go on, who with?' I fed him his cue.

Hunt paused impressively for a second, then said with quiet pride, 'Wilhelm Reich.'

I felt a strong sense of anti-climax. Wilhelm Reich? I had the impression that I had heard the name before; yes, surely I had . . . Reich, Reich . . . Wilhelm Reich . . . But I couldn't run it to earth.

Hunt said contemptuously, 'You look for all the world as if you'd never heard of him.'

'I can't tell you whether I have or not. But I certainly have to confess that if I have heard of him, I can't remember in what connection.'

'Well, well. Of course I can't really say I'm surprised. Your head's probably crammed with all sorts of information about nonentities in the Middle Ages that I've never heard of and wouldn't want to.'

'I study the eighteenth century,' I said. 'I don't know a lot about the Middle Ages.'

'Still, I expect you know a lot more about them than I do. It's the present day you obviously don't take any interest in. That's the Oxford tradition, isn't it?'

'I'm not going to be drawn, Hunt,' I said. 'Tell me who Wilhelm Reich is or shut up and let me get on with my evening.'

'I can't really believe this,' Hunt said, still savouring his advantage. 'I suppose it'll turn out next that you've never read *The Function of the Orgasm*.'

To my astonishment, because she had not haunted my conscious mind for many months, I had a sudden vision of Vinnie's pale, intent face. Vinnie! Go away and leave me to my life!

'Not only have I not read it,' I said, 'but I'm damned sure that the person of my acquaintance who knew most about orgasms, how to have them herself and how to give them to other people, had never read it either.'

'Now that Reich has come out of prison,' Hunt said, ignoring my digression, 'I'm going to spend some time with him and research a big piece on the man, his life and his opinions. I'll write it when I get back and the paper'll run it in August. That's always the best month for that kind of stuff.'

'What kind of stuff?'

'Human interest,' Hunt said. He looked at me mockingly. 'By the time I've finished, even people like you will know something about Wilhelm Reich.'

'I misjudged you,' I said. 'I hadn't realized your motive was purely idealistic. See you at the British Academy.' And I took myself off, fishing around in my pocket for my bunch of keys to get out into the street. I wanted the peace of the King's Arms and the coolness of draught beer. Hunt! I groaned inwardly. Why did Watson keep inviting him, thus increasing my chances of running into him unawares? The question was self-answering as soon as it was formulated. To see the problem was to see the solution. A few millimetres down, Watson was a Hunt. And Hunt was a Watson. They needed each other, and the fact that I needed neither of them was a problem I had to solve for myself on each occasion when it cropped up. *Sauve qui peut!*

'A pint of bitter, please,' I said, settling on to my stool.

★

Cynthia was a B.A., a circumstance she ascribed to 'an Oxford shibboleth', such being her impatient way of describing the Oxford practice of calling the first degree the 'B.A.' no matter what field of knowledge it concerned; though to me, it had always seemed a harmless survival of medieval nomenclature. After her graduation she had spent the required amount of time as a house doctor in a London hospital, a process she succinctly described by saying, 'I spent two years being made to eat shit on toast.' She had then returned to Oxford to take up research work at her clinical department in Headington.

Something else she did at Headington was to invite me round to her pleasant, brightly decorated flat whenever she felt she had a need for me. I always let her make the running. I knew well enough that it was a case of 'Theirs not to reason why'. I was more than happy to do or die; indeed, in the seventeenth-century sense of the verb, to do *and* die. Our relationship, though firmly enough based on that shared taste, never struck me as likely to last very long. I was a guest in her life and I was determined not to outstay my welcome; consequently, I was always at least half-packed to leave. With some women, this would have been a very stressful and finely balanced relationship, but not with Cynthia. She was too practical and down-to-earth, too clear about her objectives and candid about her needs. 'You're here to keep me from flying off the spindle,' she said more than once. 'It's all too easy to build up a centrifugal force.' I generally responded with the words of Jeeves to Bertie Wooster, 'I endeavour to give satisfaction, sir.' I left out the 'sir', of course, but the rest of it seemed pretty apposite.

Usually our trysting-place was her pad, but now and again she would visit me in College for what she called 'a change of décor and bed-springs'. Her tall, rangy figure climbing effortlessly up the spiral staircase always seemed to me a strange and wonderful sight in the handsome but slightly prim setting of Pearce's Building. It might even have occurred to me to wonder what Bishop Pearce might have made of it all, had I not known that he was an eighteenth-century cleric and therefore no doubt well able to see these matters in a tolerant light.

One person who was, I think, rather disconcerted was the other long-term resident of the Building, McLennan. At the time when I had first known him, I had had my own sufficient personal reasons for wanting to spend as little time in College as possible. And even if I had envisioned being in College, it would not have been McLennan I wanted to talk to. He was inoffensive, but he was flavourless and a bore. His views were worthy, but totally unoriginal. His knowledge was systematic and diligently obtained, but it was not illuminated by any personal vision. His dough had very little yeast. I felt certain he would develop into an excellent college tutor – for second- and third-class men.

Now, by an irony, after fifteen years I had again ended up living cheek by jowl with McLennan. All kinds of things had happened to me in the interim, but very little seemed to have happened to McLennan. He had steadily pursued academic economics (the only remark I can ever recall him making was 'I'm not one of those economists who are afraid of mathematics') except for a few equally uneventful years doing something in Army Education during the war. As a result his appearance had, it seemed to me, not changed at all, though perhaps he had bulked out a little. For the rest, when I first saw him he had had sandy-coloured hair and had worn steel-rimmed spectacles. He still had hair of the same colour and wore glasses rimmed with the same material. Perhaps they were the same glasses, as, in a sense, the eyes that looked through them were the same. One's whole body is said to replace all its constituent atoms over every seven-year period, which would mean that McLennan was now on the third pair of eyes since our first acquaintance, but essentially they were the same – they were McLennan's eyes, guileless, uninteresting, observant but only in the pursuit of routine judgements.

He saw Cynthia often enough, of course, but usually only the whisk of her disappearing round a curve or into a doorway. One afternoon, though, the three of us came abruptly face to face on the stairs: she and I were going up and he was coming down. McLennan looked confused, I think he actually blushed. He evidently didn't know whether the right thing to do was to pause and be introduced, or pass by with the minimum polite acknowledgement of our presence; for two pins, I thought, he would have turned and gone back upstairs, except that now we had seen him.

'Hello, McLennan,' I said from my position at the rear of the cortège.

He seemed thrown by this greeting. He knew, of course, who Cynthia was because my acquaintance with her was a common topic of conversation both behind my back and in my presence. Watson, in particular, enjoyed the sport of varying the tone of his references to her according to whether I were present or absent, though their content remained substantially the same. I could well imagine the ones I didn't hear.

'I don't think you've met Cynthia,' I pressed on. 'This is my colleague McLennan,' I said to her. 'We share this staircase.'

Since this was not a remark of the slightest interest, Cynthia, in characteristic fashion, showed not the slightest interest in it. McLennan ducked his head nervously at the mention of his name, made a short convulsive movement as if to hold out his hand, then spasmodically withdrew it. Like every Englishman, he knew it was socially incorrect to shake hands on being introduced and yet sometimes had an impulse to do so. 'Ah,' he said. 'Good to meet you. I hope you . . .' Having no idea what he hoped, he fell silent again.

I felt a sudden urge to shock McLennan. There was no reason at all why I should want to hurt him; I didn't *want* to hurt him. But I felt something ought to happen to him. He was so clockwork, so standardized; everything he did and said was so ordinary and accustomed. For a mad instant I wondered what would happen if I said to him, 'I'm just going to take Cynthia up to my bedroom and fuck her till the pictures fall off the walls.' And whether the impulse that kept me silent was one of pure benevolence, not wanting to administer a rude shock to an entirely harmless person, or whether it was a blend of cowardice and conventionality, I was never afterwards able to decide.

★

My father's birthday was in early September. As one looks back across the years, September tends to merge into September – always the same softness and stillness, the same sense, even after one of our less good summers, of ripeness and fulfilment, the wave hanging for an instant before creaming forward into autumn and winter – but as it happens I remember the September of 1950 with some distinctness because it was the year when I resumed regular visits to the Continent. I say 'remember', partly because my age group of academics, people who could remember the world before September 1939, had all been in the habit of spending the summer vacation months on the European land-mass as a matter of course, and for them it was the resumption of a normal life-nourishing habit. I, with Heather and Michael to support on a Junior Fellow's salary, had managed only short and sporadic visits even to France, while Italy, Germany, Holland, Switzerland, the Iberian peninsula – places where so many crucial events in European history had taken place – I had never even set eyes on. In October 1946, 1947, 1948, 1949, autumn after autumn, the mealtime conversation at Episcopus, as at every college in Oxford, had turned unfailingly on 'Where did you get to this summer?' My answer, year after year, was boring and predictable. In such leisure as I had and with what funds I could spare, I had invariably sought out some part of the British Isles still new to me: and in retrospect, how glad I am! Simply by being alive and mobile at the right time, I was able to travel England and Wales, even venture into Scotland, before the age of ruthless disfigurement – before the disappearance of little friendly railway lines between country towns, the widening of lanes that used to be overhung with whispering trees, the savage slashing of agricultural land into motorways, the invasion of village high streets by chain stores and fast-food outlets, and perhaps most of all the taking hostage, and ultimate murder, of the traditional English wayside inn. None of this had happened in the later 1940s, though the forces that were going to make it happen were flexing their muscles and sharpening their fangs; with the result that I got to know a lot of wonderful places while they were still wonderful; as, for that matter, Oxford still was for a few years longer, in spite of Billy Morris.

Still, for a patchwork of reasons, I was confined within Albion's shores until the summer of 1950 and even then I had to get the chore of examining off my hands. (I couldn't turn it down because it earned me some extra income, and for that I would have peeled potatoes in Episcopus kitchen, if I could have got away with it.) So, for the first time, I was abroad at the time of my father's birthday, which my mother had always brought very strictly to the attention of both of us, Brian and myself. She didn't insist on anything else much, but she had hammered it into us that 'Dad likes a card and a visit' on his birthday. In 1950 I didn't manage the visit, and to my shame I didn't even remember the card. Cynthia, who couldn't (or at any rate wouldn't) accompany me consistently throughout the whole trip, had managed to snatch a week to be with me in Corfu, which was the furthest point I wandered to. And a week in Corfu with Cynthia wasn't the kind of experience that leaves you thinking of birthday cards. During that whole week, the only thing that took my attention away from her was the sudden sight of a golden oriole, one of the most splendid of all Mediterranean birds, a bird I had read about, heard about, talked about, even dreamed about, but never seen until one suddenly paraded nonchalantly along the top of a wall, near to where we were sitting at a café table. I didn't stop talking about that bird for twenty minutes, until Cynthia became sufficiently irritated to threaten to catch the next plane home. I took prompt measures to deal with her discontent, but I never forgot the golden oriole. To paraphrase Sam Johnson on London, people who don't get excited about birds don't get excited about life.

And between the golden oriole and golden Cynthia, I totally forgot my father's birthday; and, though birthday cards were not the kind of thing my mind tended to run on when I was with Cynthia, I ought at least to have remembered to send him one. These annual cards had become all the more important in recent years since the jolt of my divorce from Heather. My father had never shown any signs of approving of this decision and had never since admitted me to the old easygoing geniality. He had, it was true, ceased to ostracize me.

After a period of a few weeks in which I had not been able to muster the courage to show my face at the Bargeman's Arms, Brian had telephoned me one evening and made a date to meet me down there for a drink at lunch-time on the following Saturday. We had a drink together and Dad, who was serving, had talked mainly to Brian but had not actually cut me out of the conversation. Those of his remarks that were general were addressed more or less to both of us. We left before the afternoon closing time, deliberately, so as not to present our parents with the problem of whether to invite us to join them in the kitchen after they came off duty, as we had always done; the issue might have been that Brian would have been invited and I would not. We didn't want to drive it that far and neither, we suspected, did Dad. He just wanted, so far as we could divine his wishes, not to feel manipulated, to be left free to make his own choices. We went to the Holly Bush, just round the corner in Bridge Street, and had one for the road, and I asked Brian, 'You've been working on my behalf, I think?'

'With Dad? Yes, I pegged away at him one evening.'

'Any support from Mum?'

'Well, she didn't say anything for the first half-hour, wanted to keep right out of it, but at last I got her in on my side. I didn't use any subtle arguments, just told him he didn't have to approve of everything his family did, they were still his family. I said no family would ever stick together if they all had to approve of everything the others did, all along the line.'

'What did he say to that?'

'He said that was all very well but there were standards. He said if a member of the family did something really beyond the limits they should be made to realize it – not just have family approval switched on again like an electric light. They should take a bit of time to earn it.'

'So I'm in Coventry?'

He laughed. 'Well, the suburbs of Coventry. Solihull, let's say.'

'All right, Solihull.'

I stayed in Solihull for three whole years; that's how serious it was. My father was really very wounded and disappointed at the way I had acted, and I acknowledged inwardly that he had every right to be. During this period he spoke to me in a perfectly friendly fashion if I entered the pub for a drink, but never invited me backstage and very, very rarely gave me my drink on the house. He mostly let me pay for it like any other customer. Nor was I invited, during the whole of this time, to one of the sacred Sunday dinners. I felt like a wild animal that prowls the dark tundra just beyond the circle of firelight, able to see the comfortable ring of companionship and smell the delicious waft of roasting meat, but can get no closer. And if that is an exaggeration it is not a very big one.

During this long stretch I could tell that my mother was hoping, and probably working quietly, for a reconciliation. She didn't agree with what I had done any more than Dad did, but her attitude was that to break the family into chunks would not put anything right and would only produce two tragedies where there had been one. Michael was fond of his grandparents and liked to visit the Bargeman's, and even Heather dropped in now and again, and my mother evidently felt that this was common ground that everyone shared and was an advantage that ought not to be thrown away. She resolutely welcomed everyone who turned up, and if the Sunday-dinner invitations had dried up, that was obviously Dad putting his foot down.

I also knew that Brian was in there somewhere, batting for me, and I had hopes that old custom would prevail in the end when my father judged that his point had been made with sufficient amplitude. And it all happened, but it took a long time. The September of 1950 had come, and almost gone, before Brian gave me a telephone call and suggested meeting at the Bargeman's for a drink on the following Sunday morning.

'Sunday morning?' I said dubiously. 'What about when it gets to lunch-time?'

'It's a family affair. Sunday dinner. The works.'

'Am I invited?' As I asked the question, I tried not to let it matter too much. As I had been for three years I could, if I had to, go on.

'Yes.'

I felt my breath escaping in a great gush, though I hadn't been conscious of holding it in.

'Brian,' I said slowly, 'what's happened?'

'Time flows on, brother. See you Sunday.' And he rang off.

Sunday came, a calm, misty morning that steadily brightened; dank and limp at eight o'clock, hopeful at nine, already resplendent at ten. Knowing that this was to be an important occasion, however the Leonard family might choose to underplay it, I walked down from Episcopus, taking a longish way round so as to have peace and quiet, to prepare my mind and nerves in tranquillity. First I went nearly a mile in the opposite direction: over to Walton Well Road, across the neck end of Port Meadow to the river, then down the towpath, passing on my left the reed-bed where on the very night before my wedding to Heather, I had so suddenly and so totally abandoned myself to the lustful enchantment of the vixen Vinnie. Why had I done that? But I knew the answer: best not to think about it, look straight ahead as I walked, think of matters that concerned today and tomorrow, not the yesterday that the pale, slender, brown-haired succubus had so ruthlessly devoured. I walked on: I crossed the Botley Road at the point where the road itself crossed the Thames; I reached the Bargeman's Arms. The lunch-time session had not long begun; the bar was filling up with customers, but slowly. Brian was there, a half-pint glass of bitter in his hand (he always drank in halves; he said it slowed him down), chatting casually with our father, who was serving as usual. No, that word doesn't quite get it. What he was doing, what he always did through all the years, was a combination of serving and presiding.

They both greeted me exactly as they had always done, exactly as they had greeted me ever since I first went away to College in 1930. I could see at a glance that Dad intended to handle my re-admission to the family circle with no ceremony, no extra words, no outward and visible sign, just by the fact of re-admitting me. Well, that was fine with me.

After a moment he moved away to attend to a knot of customers. Brian drank up his half-pint and said, 'There's something I want to show you upstairs.'

I indicated my almost full pint glass, but he said, 'You can bring that with you.'

Something in his tone suggested that it was important to him, so I took the pint and went with him out of the side door into the yard, in again through the kitchen door and, after greeting Mother and asking her permission, up the stairs. Here it all was, so much a part of my boyhood and adolescence, so little visited since: a passage going past the bathroom (installed some time in the 1920s by getting rid of a spare room), running slap into a dead end at the far end but, before it did so, opening into two rooms of equal size, one on either side. Brian's room on the right, mine on the left, as they had been. My room looked down into the quiet garden, and over the wall the gardens of the houses that faced on to South Street. Brian's looked out on to East Street and the river. By grown-up standards mine was the better room because the gardens were quieter than the street; from Brian's room you could hear such motor-traffic as we had – not very much, in our time – and also any loud discussion that happened to break out between citizens who had just left the Bargeman's Arms with unresolved disputes still occupying their minds. In boyhood, of course, Brian's room was unequivocally preferable; that was why it was Brian's room. He was much more tuned in to life, much more involved with people and activities, than dreamy, bookish younger-brother me, and it was right that he was the one who could open his window at any time and hold urgent dialogues with friends in the street who, from the pavement, could address him with their faces only about six feet below his own.

Brian, purposefully leading the way, opened both bedroom doors. The one that had been his was nowadays a box room, full of suitcases, cardboard cartons, baskets and what appeared to be bundles of newspaper, though they probably contained something. The one that had been mine contained a small neat bed and a couple of chairs: the guest room.

'Pretty cramped, aren't they?' he said dismissively.

'We got along all right in them.'

'Of course,' he said. 'A boy doesn't know any different. But you wouldn't like to live in one of them now, would you?'

'Well, we didn't *live* in them then,' I said. 'Mostly we just slept in them.'

'You've forgotten,' he said, still dismissively. 'You used to spend hours in yours, reading. I never understood how you could stick it, just reading away. It could get pretty cold in there, in the winter months.'

'Oh,' I said, remembering, 'I used to get into bed then.' I had sat with my knees drawn up and my dressing-gown draped round my shoulders, reading *The Cambridge Modern History*, trying not to think about girls.

'Anyway, not being a kid,' Brian said, 'I'm proposing to knock the two into one.'

For an instant this remark lay on the surface of my mind, not being absorbed. Then I understood. Brian was going to take up residence in our two bedrooms, having first made one room of them. Was that why he had brought me up here? To get my approval? Why should he think he needed my approval? But what was he doing? What was his master plan?

Brian now took a tape-measure from his jacket pocket and measured the end wall of the room that had been mine. He muttered figures to himself under his breath. Then he measured the width of the passage. 'H'm,' he said, sounding reassured. 'That gives us fourteen feet. Should be plenty.'

'Are you asking me, or telling me?' I said.

He stopped and looked at me. 'Both, in a way, Peter. The fact is, I'm planning to move in here, knock the two bedrooms into one and make a nice little studio of it. Quite enough for my needs.'

'You're coming back to live at the Bargeman's?'

'Yes, if no one has any objection.'

'Well,' I said, 'the only people I can imagine having any objection are Mother and Dad, and—'

'They're all right about it,' he said quickly.

'Well, there you are then. I know of no one else whose business it is.'

'Yourself?' he said, as if tentatively.

'It's God knows how many years since I lived here and I can't imagine why I should want to move back, fond of the place as I am. You must know that as far as I'm concerned it's all yours, and that includes knocking our two rooms into one. If it gives you enough space, that sounds like a good idea. But now that I've got this far, let me ask you a question that I might hesitate to ask just out of the blue. Why are you doing this? I mean, are you fed up with living on your own?'

What I actually meant was, 'Have you given up the idea of either getting Primrose back, or finding a replacement for her?' But I put it in a slightly indirect way, knowing Brian's answer would tell me what I wanted to know one way or another.

'The full reasons behind it all,' Brian said, facing me in that so familiar upstairs passage between our two bedroom doors of long ago, 'are part of why we're all having lunch together today.'

'Do stop being mysterious,' I said. 'Are you saying that you managed to get me invited because it's some kind of special occasion?'

'I'm not being mysterious, at least I don't want to be. I just don't want to steal the old man's thunder. He's got a special announcement to make.'

'Well, surely it can only be a special announcement to me,' I said impatiently. 'Obviously it's something you know about – and don't tell me Mother doesn't; she knows his thoughts before he does himself.'

'Look, Buster,' he said, 'if Dad wants to make an announcement to the family when he has us all together, and he wants you here for that reason, my advice would be to take it for what it is, a gesture towards you. If you don't want him to make gestures towards you, just say so.'

I felt fittingly squashed, and we went down to the bar again. The time passed reasonably smoothly until 2 o'clock; Dad cleared the customers out, as usual having to get a few laggards over the doorstep by something approaching strong-arm methods; and then we locked the doors and went into the kitchen. I helped to lay the table while my mother put the finishing touches to our meal, the usual Sunday roast. Brian fetched in bottled beer. Dad just sat down. I remembered him from years ago as utterly tireless but now, I could see, two hours in charge of a bar that grew steadily more crowded and whose decibel level rose in a relentless curve had been enough for him. What he wanted now was to sit with his family, and talk, and eat, and rest his limbs. That inexhaustible energy was at last on the ebb-tide.

Not that the general atmosphere round the table was of weariness. On the contrary, and allowing for our father's natural readiness to sink into a chair, it was one of expectation and buoyancy. No one said anything about its being a special occasion, or referred to my being back at the ritual Sunday table after so long a gap. Those thoughts were expressed, but not in words: it was more a matter of what the world came in another decade or so to call 'body language'. My mother, in particular, looked bright-eyed. As always at the Sunday meal, her face was flushed by the heat that wafted up from the oven, but I noticed that as the meal progressed and the oven-scorched look faded out, she still had more colour than usual. Her blood was activated, not by the heat of burning gas but by happiness, interest in what was going on, enjoyment of the situation. Her family was back in one piece, and around her. Unfortunate, sorrowful, regrettable things had been done. But at least we were still here. Her nature, like every feminine nature, had a strong element of the same impulse that governs the world of plants: the unquenchable need to reach out, to bind, to put down roots, to knit up and connect. And here she was, having survived an uprooting, a tearing-out, a cutting. The plant had lived, and its leaves and stems were about her.

All this was consistent with the fact that my parents, as I saw clearly now – the first time for some years that I had sat down with both of them together and looked at them unhurriedly – were beginning to show their age. My father's sandy hair was at last predominantly grey; my mother's, being fair, did not show the change of colour so clearly, but she was greying too. Their faces had become thinner and more lined, their movements stiffer. How old *were* they? Dad – I fished up the date of 1889. That would make him . . . let me see. . . .

Uncannily, as if I had been speaking aloud, he turned to me at that moment, rested his knife and fork on the plate as if to signify a gear-change in the pace of his eating, and said meditatively, 'Peter, when I had my birthday a few weeks ago, you were away.'

'In Italy,' I said.

'An interesting trip, I hope,' he remarked with indifferent politeness.

'Very interesting, thanks . . . and long overdue. It was the first time I'd crossed the Alps and seen that part of Europe, and of course there are all sorts of things you can't really—'

'I was sixty-one,' Dad said, interrupting me not rudely but with the abstracted air of a man wrapped up in his own thoughts.

'Oh.' I wasn't sure what to say but wanted to sound interested, eager to hear more. What did it mean, in his life, to be sixty-one?

'I'd always expected to carry on as licensee here till I was sixty-five. It's when a man generally stops work and I always thought I'd go the distance. My health's always been all right, and I wasn't sure what kind of pension I'd get if I stopped working full-time. There's the "Old Age" of course; your mother'll qualify for that in a couple of years because it's sixty for women, but she won't be able to get it because the wife has to wait till the husband starts getting it, and that's at sixty-five. So it's a pension for single women and widows. They must save themselves quite a lot of money that way, the government. But it's only fair really, if a woman has an earning husband. Anyway. Like I was saying, I'd always thought to go on to sixty-five, but just lately they've started to talk about younger men coming in to run the pubs. Keep going on about changed times . . . things being different in the licensed trade . . . changing this, changing that. They seem to think that once you've turned sixty you can't tell a change when you see it.'

I didn't need to be told who 'they' were: the brewers. When my father had first kept a pub, landlords generally owned their own premises, and were attached to a brewery whose products they bought in at a preferential rate. But in the Depression, when so many businesses went to the wall, pubs included, the breweries took advantage of bankrupteies to buy up a great many properties and put in landlords as managers. Those who remained as independent landlords had that independence steadily whittled away. By the time the post-war era got into its stride, a landlord essentially took his orders from the brewery. Relations might be cordial on the surface, but money talked, and both sides knew what it said.

'They're putting in younger men wherever you look, Peter,' my father continued. 'Ex-servicemen, a lot of them, and good luck to them. I was ex-service myself in my day. They specially like that N.C.O. type who got used to dealing with officers and with other ranks. Knew how to speak to 'em both, see? You find 'em in half the pubs you go into. Specially those Raff* types with the handlebar moustache. After a year or two they pick up the general Raff manner and you can't tell whether the chap was a Flying-Officer or a fitter doing repairs. Well, as I say, good luck to 'em. But a bloke like that, he could have served five years in the war and come out still on the right side of thirty. Young and energetic, and not hindered by much in the way of experience of how things used to be.'

'And with a young and energetic wife,' my mother put in, 'to back him up with the catering.'

'There wasn't a one of them that had a wife as good as the wife you've been to me, Katie,' my father responded firmly, 'but certainly that's another change that's come in and it hasn't stopped coming in yet. Food — proper cooked meals. They won't stay with the old

---

* This was how my father always referred to the Royal Air Force.

sandwiches no more, like Peter and Brian used to cut before they went off to school.'

'So,' I said.

'So, they're after me,' Dad said, 'wanting to know my retirement plans. That's the thin end of the wedge. What it means is that they want to know when I'm going.'

'Couldn't have made it plainer,' Brian put in.

'So I thought,' Dad said, 'I'd better make the running. I went to see Mr Bladderwrack' – or some such name; I gathered the man was the Managing Director – 'and put to him a little project that Brian and I had been talking over for a few months past.'

He paused and I said, 'Well, surely you're not going to stop there?'

'Over to you, Brian,' he said.

Brian, who was just finishing what was on his plate, ate in silence for a few seconds before laying down his knife and fork in a way that indicated he was about to take the floor. Then he said to me, 'Now you know what all that was about upstairs.'

'The alterations, yes. You getting ready to move in.'

'I'm going to learn the trade,' he said.

I didn't know what I was supposed to say, so I just looked from face to face. As I did so I thought, for the ten thousandth time, what extraordinarily powerful stuff the seminal fluid must be. Here was Brian looking at me with our father's eyes and speaking with the *timbre* of our father's voice. 'It's a big change in my life, but not too big for me to be ready for it. Not that you have to sit around and wait for change, these days. Change comes to you. It's come to the licensed trade, as Dad says, but not only there. My job at M.G.'s due for a shake-up too, and I just haven't got the patience to hang around and wait for it. Enough is enough. I went to work for Morris Motors after I left school, then I managed to slip through the fence into M.G. because that was the only interesting part of Morris Motors, the part where I could be mixed up with racing. Then Billy Morris stepped in and put his foot down on it, and a flat heavy foot it was. "No more racing!" Just like that. All that work wasted, all that experience. The good ideas chaps'd had and the risks they'd taken. And now, all these years later, because he sees a chance of even bigger money-bags. he's giving up on his original firm. We're not even going to be Morris Motors any more.'

'Aren't you?' I was startled. 'What's happened? Is he moving out of making cars altogether?'

'You haven't heard, then?'

'No. I've been very busy lately, and a lot of things in the news have passed me by.'

'Well, he's still going to make cars, but not as Morris. He's always been deadly rivals with Herbert Austin – well, now they're going to merge Austin and Morris into something called the British Motor Corporation.'

'What will the cars be known as?'

'Hardly matters, does it? The Mortin, I expect, or the Austis. If I'm to believe the rumours I hear, they're going to buy up a lot of small firms that have a good reputation from years ago, firms like Riley and Wolseley, and stick their radiator badges on 'em. A new breed of mass-produced tin cars. I expect M.G.'ll be one of them. Well, it's not for me and I'm off.'

'Oh,' I said. 'Well, that's news.'

'I've never had any heart for it,' Brian said, 'ever since Billy Morris stabbed us in the back just when we were doing so brilliantly. I ought to have left then. But there was nowhere to go, in . . . when was it? Thirty-four?'

'Thirty-five,' Dad said. 'It's not like you to forget the year.'

'I try not to think back to it, tell you the truth.'

'Ah, that's understandable. I never saw anybody as disappointed as you were then, lad.'

Mother unexpectedly put in, 'I remember hating Lord Nuffield.'

'Lord Nuff— oh, you mean Billy Morris.' That was how we referred to him in the Leonard family. It was an iron convention, at least among the male element.

'Yes, but Lord Nuffield was his proper name already by then, wasn't it?'

'He was Sir William at least,' Dad said. 'He was knighted and then he was made a lord. But he was always Billy Morris to them that remembered him starting out. Your Uncle Ernest used to go to school with him.'

'Well, whatever his name was, he was nobody to us at M.G. after the way he let us down.'

'I don't see that *you* need have any feelings about him one way or the other, Katie,' Dad said to Mother, as if anxious to shield her from the atmosphere of remembered acrimony that had suddenly blown up. He wanted her to have womanly neutrality, to leave all these dust-ups to the men.

'He spoilt Brian's twenty-fifth birthday,' she said simply. 'A person ought to be happy at twenty-five.'

'Well, that's as may be,' Brian said. 'I think I could have forgiven him if he'd just told us we weren't to go racing any more and that was the end of it. We'd put everything into it for four years and sweated blood and never had a thought for ourselves, it'd been M.G., M.G., M.G. all the time, and then he pulled the rug out without warning and if that'd been all I'd have said, "Fair enough." But he went on making money out of the M.G. reputation, and he's making

-116-

money out of it today. We made him that reputation and what did we get? A boot in the face. And what did Kim get? The sack. And then killed by a bloody railway train, of all things, when he was off on a journey trying to earn a crust.'

Brian's face had gone dark red. There was a silence and my mother got up and started clearing away the dishes from the meat course. I, too, got out of my chair and helped her. We put out some bowls and tinned fruit. I fetched spoons. Calm descended. Billy Morris was put away in his box of sharp memories, not to be handled without gloves.

When we were looking at our next course but had not yet begun to eat it, Brian resumed. 'Now's about the last time I could make a change as big as this. And even that's only because the licensed trade isn't really a new world to me. Growing up here, I picked up a lot just through my pores. I know a lot about keeping a pub, if I just rummage around in my mind for it.'

'Ah,' said my father, 'they all say that. They all think it's just common sense and being used to the place. But there's a lot of specialized knowledge, Brian. It'll surprise you, when you get into it.'

'No, it won't, Dad. It'd only surprise me if I expected it to be easy. And I'm sure it's a job that takes everything a man's got.'

'And a woman,' my mother said. 'Everything a woman's got too.'

'Especially now,' Dad said.

Just to keep him talking and to encourage him to open up, I decided to play the role of the wide-eyed know-nothing and put in, as I took up my dessert spoon, 'So things are changing fast, are they, Dad? You expect the next, say, five years to be different from the last five?'

'Well, I can't look into the future,' he said, 'but one of 'em's started already. They've told us to get ready for the women's trade.'

'They?'

'The brewers,' Brian said laconically.

I nodded.

'So it's *Get the saloon bars ready for the women*, and that's an order.'

'What does that mean in detail?'

'Spending money, mostly. Carpets. Armchairs that are something like the ones they sit in at home. Their idea is that when a woman comes out of her house in the evening, she doesn't want to go somewhere that's not as nice as her own home. Furnished to the same standard.'

'Quite right too,' said my mother.

'Well, yes, Katie, it is right, but she ought to allow something for the fact that there isn't a bar in her own house where she can order any kind of drink she wants, that it has to be laid in and transported from a distance, and stored and looked after properly . . .'

'We've had all this,' my mother said. 'It's only the draught beer that takes any looking after, and it isn't one woman in a hundred that drinks draught beer, Jack. You know what women drink – bottled light ale, sometimes a port and lemon or a sweet sherry, stuff that just stands on the shelf till you want it.'

'So to sell a few bottles of light ale and a bit of port and sweet sherry,' Dad said, 'we've got to have carpets on the floor, armchairs, curtains in fancy patterns, make it just like their living-room at home. Don't they want a change when they come out?'

'Not that kind of a change. And they don't call 'em living-rooms now, they call 'em lounges.'

'Not that I'm against it, mind,' Dad said with his judicial air. 'The women ought to have what they want. They done a good job all through the war, and if they want a bit of carpet—'

'That's just it,' Mother said. 'It's the war that's made the difference. You'll never get them to go back to the days when the woman slaved in the house all day and then had to twiddle her thumbs while the man went down to the pub with his mates all evening. The younger ones, and the ones with more to say for themselves, were already getting fed up with that before the war, but what with five years when they were working in factories and on the land and keeping the country going while the men were away – they're just not going to have the old life.'

'A war always does that,' Brian contributed. 'The first one got women the vote, and the second got 'em into the pubs – and everywhere else they want to go, come to that.'

'Yes, and there's another change coming,' said Mother, her jaw setting in that firm line it took when she intended to assert rather than discuss. 'This last war'll *be* the last. Now that women are getting their hands on a bit of the power, they won't stand for it. There'll be no more wars. I've told you before and I'll tell you again, the future belongs as much to the women as to the men, and the women are for *peace*.'

'Well, I hope you're—'

'It's not a question of hoping. I'm a woman myself and I know I'm right. The world's full of women like dear, brave Bessie Warmley, who had her husband taken away from her in one war and her son in the next, and both in the same part of the world too, not that it makes any difference what part of the world it was, only it seems to underline it – they couldn't sort things out by fighting the first time, and they don't seem to have sorted it out by fighting the second time, and each time it cost her the person she loved best, the dear good soul.'

'You think there won't be any Joan of Arcs?' I asked her.

'Joan of Arc?' Mother wrinkled her brow. 'She heard voices, didn't she? Voices from heaven telling her what to do? There won't be any need for that in the world that's coming in. Women'll have a voice telling them what to do all right, but it won't have to come from heaven, it'll be their own voice coming out of their own lives. And they won't let men pull them down into all their stupidities and crimes and murders. Can you imagine women making wars? Can you imagine women digging trenches and getting down into them with helmets on, and spending years there, shooting at one another and every now and again coming out and having battles? Wicked, stupid battles where they kill each other by the trainload? Can you see *women* doing that? They've got too much sense.'

She fell silent, looking from face to face of her menfolk. The afternoon sun lit up the windows and fell with a gentle late September radiance on the white tablecloth, the stacked dishes, the composed, attentive faces. No one felt inclined to answer back. For myself, I saw no reason to doubt that women were just as capable as men of cruelty, ruthlessness and aggression, though they might be motivated by somewhat different goals; but I certainly agreed with my mother that they would be unlikely to demonstrate these qualities by taking part in trench warfare.

Sitting at the opposite end of the table from my father, she stared at us, her three men, in that sudden glow of sunlight, and after a moment her face softened, the fierceness dimmed from her eyes and she said, 'It's not myself I'm thinking about. It's when I think about women like Bessie that I get angry.'

I knew that was true. She was angry about the way men and their wars and their battles had plunged the life of Bessie Warmley into a terrible cold shadow where the sun could never reach her. She was angry for Bessie, and for her husband of long ago, and her son Ivan, Brian's friend, drowned in the dark, breath-stopping Arctic waters. She trusted the world's women to reshape the world so that such things could never happen any more. Or she yearned to trust them.

When the meal was finished we sat at the table rounding off our family conference until that too was finished. Then I helped my mother to wash the dishes and put them away, while Brian and Dad went down to the cellar on some weighty, mysterious professional business.

Mother and I talked as we worked, and of course our conversation turned to Michael.

'He's a fine well-grown lad, isn't he? Sixteen now, he was telling me the other day.'

'Yes, sixteen.'

'Is he clever?' she suddenly asked out of the blue.

'Well, you see him quite often. Doesn't he seem clever to you?'

'Oh, yes, he does, in ordinary talk. But young people have to be clever at such strange things nowadays. Strange and out of reach. A person like me couldn't tell whether they were clever in that way.'

'What way, Mum? Is there really such a different way of being clever?'

'Of course there is, with all this special education they have to have now and the strange things they have to know about. I can't talk to them about that kind of thing. When you were doing all that reading for your scholarships and papers and stuff, I couldn't have talked to you about all that.'

'No, but surely you could tell whether I had a normal head on my shoulders when it came to ordinary matters, which after all take up most people's attention most of the time.'

'All I can say is that you never seemed to have your mind on ordinary things when you were Michael's age. Your head was always in the clouds. I had to speak to you three or four times, often, to get an answer out of you.'

'I was probably sulking.'

'No, you were quite good-humoured. Your mind was just away somewhere.'

I was probably thinking, I reflected, about the girl who used to serve behind the counter at week-ends at our local tobacconist and sweetshop. I admired her, in a manner quite untinged by any idealism; my notions were all strictly practical. I used to go into the shop quite often and buy a box of matches, purely for the brief companionship with her that the purchase afforded. And while she handed me the matches and gave me my change, I would stare at her and try to work out my chances of being in a position, one day, to pull her knickers down.

'Does Michael's mind often seem to be away?' I asked my mother.

'No, he generally seems quite wide awake and he talks like a normal person. It's just that with the kind of thing young people have to know about today, being a normal person and being clever could be quite different things.'

As they obviously were in my case, I reflected. Well, things turned out all right in the end. Or as nearly so as one has any right to hope for, anyway.

At this moment Dad and Brian came up from the cellar. Dad was yawning and clearly intended to take a Sunday afternoon siesta. Brian asked me if I intended to go back to Episcopus straight away.

'Not straight away,' I said. 'It's such a pleasant afternoon, I thought I'd take a stroll.'

'I'm glad you're not in a rush,' he said. 'I've got something to show you.'

'Fine. I'm all attention.'

'I'll be ready right away. I left my tape-measure upstairs.' He disappeared to the upper floor and for a moment I was left alone again with Mother.

'Tell me about Heather,' she said quietly, obviously not wanting her voice to ring through the house.

'What in particular?'

'D'you see her?'

'Not a lot.' We had had two or three short, businesslike meetings on neutral ground, mostly to discuss matters concerning Michael.

'How is she?'

'So-so. Her wants are taken care of, as far as money goes, and I think she's found things to do that interest her. I really don't know much.'

About the only thing I knew was something I didn't care to pass on to my mother. Heather had smelt of gin each time I had been with her; the last time you could smell it at five yards. The lines of her face were hardening into rigidity, and the whites of her eyes were tarnished with yellow. Otherwise she still looked well and strong. Her country-bred constitution would take a long time to break down, even by the gin bottle.

'Doesn't she drop in here sometimes?' I asked.

'She came about half a dozen times in the first year you . . . weren't together. Then it tailed off, you might say. We haven't seen her for about six months now.'

I believed I knew a possible reason for this. Our interminable divorce process had reached the stage at which our respective lawyers had sternly ordered us to have nothing whatsoever to do with each other. Apparently, if the King's Proctor got to know that we had exchanged a friendly word in the street, or if I had held a door open for Heather to go through, the fact would immediately have been noticed and the entire expensive fabric would have collapsed like a house of cards. 'Collusion', it would have been called. If Heather was avoiding the Bargeman's because it was a place where she might run into me, that at least meant that she wanted the divorce to go through, which was what I also wanted. This, in itself, I recognized as a good thing; though, in the perverse and contradictory way of the human heart, I also found it a sad thing, painful to think about. Who was the philosopher who said, 'Out of the crooked timber of humanity, no straight thing was ever made'?

Brian now came down the stairs. 'Ready, Peter?'

'All ready. Thanks for the meal, Mum. See you very soon.'

I kissed her cheek. As I moved away she gave me a glance that told me she was glad of this drawing together of the family. I was glad of it too; our smiles signalled this mutuality. Then I was outside and the door was closing, but gently.

It was now about half-past four on a calm, sunny afternoon, the kind of day when Oxford always looks at its best. Brian's car was parked across the road from the pub and it had a trailer hitched behind it. The trailer looked a solid job, ready to take quite serious loads; it had two pairs of wheels set near the middle of the generous platform, and looked capable of carrying a medium-sized boat or car. It was, however, empty at the moment.

Brian ignored the car; evidently the place we were going to was near enough for us not to need it. He led the way along South Street, into West Street, then turned left and went over the little footbridge that crossed the Bullstake Stream. This brought us to what was then the end of the Ferry Hinksey Road. This road, paved and lined on both sides with terrace houses, ended abruptly and became a foot-path, the immemorial route by which the villagers of North and South Hinksey walked into Oxford, pulling themselves across one of the little branches of the varicose Thames by a wooden punt fixed to an endless wire. In those days, just before universal car ownership got going, people still walked along these paths and still pulled themselves over in these punts; there was another similar one over the Cherwell on the Marston Ferry Road, which likewise ran out into a footpath. Simpler, better days!

Instead of taking the footpath, however, Brian turned aside to a patch of waste ground where stood a row of three or four lock-up garages, simple wooden buildings but safe enough to leave a car in, with concrete floors and sound roofs. He approached one of these, proprietorially.

'Good move, getting hold of this,' I said. 'Looking ahead to when you're living at the Bargeman's, I suppose?'

'No,' he said. 'It's not for my ordinary car; I'll keep that in the pub yard. It's . . .' His voice took on an almost hushed tone of reverence. 'It's for this beauty.'

He had been unlocking the door as he spoke but I believe, looking back, that something in his tone had already told me what I would see in the garage. A silvery-grey snout – that off-silver colour that one can only call 'aluminium' – two stark front wheels, a streamlined radiator with the octagonal M.G. emblem. Of course! The K3 M.G., Brian's goddess, his fetish-object, the one substantial treasure he had salvaged from the wreck of his early, golden life as a member of the hand-picked *équipe*, glamour-encircled chevaliers of speed.

We entered the garage. Brian took a soft cloth from a shelf and passed it lovingly over the sleek body of his idol.

'I keep plenty of insurance on her,' he said. 'Not that I'm really afraid she'll be nicked; she'd be too recognizable. Every one of these beauties is known, individually known. The engine numbers are known, and the chassis frame numbers, and the history – whose hands they've passed through.'

'Of course in this case you don't need to be told any of that.'

'Course not. I've looked after her ever since we put her together at Abingdon. And when Fergus Kingswood bought her – that was when he was a student at the same time as you – I was given the job of easing him into knowing her.'

'Of course I remember.' I saw again that sunlit morning at Magdalen when, coming away from a lecture or something, I had suddenly run into Brian.

'He picked it up pretty fast. Of course, now that I remember, it was a C-type we started him with. The K-type wasn't developed yet. But he was ready when it was. You had to be ready. They were the fastest single-seater we ever did. But Fergus measured up.'

I was amused, but gently and sympathetically, at the way the Honourable Fergus Kingswood – dead so long ago, killed even before Dunkirk, killed as a member of the British Expeditionary Force in the spring of 1940 – still lived for Brian. Even I could still see him clearly: tall, with curly brown hair and that lopsided grin. He had become one of Brian's family: not his physical family, but the emotional and imaginative family of those who loved the racing cars that Cecil Kimber and his team at M.G. had produced during the brief years when they could get away with it: loved them, cared for them, raced in them.

Which brought me to the only question I could think of asking: 'Does she get any exercise?'

'I race her,' said Brian, but sadly and with reluctance.

'Really? At her age? Isn't she . . . well . . . fifteen years old at least?'

Brian smiled at my *naïveté*. 'I race her at meetings of the V.S.R.C.C. Often she's the youngest car in the event.'

'The V.S. . . . ?'

'The Vintage Sports and Racing Car Club. They have race meetings twice a year at Silverstone.'

'Oh.'

'There are a lot of owners who go in for these races because it gives them a chance to bring out their cars, show them to the present-day public, and have a good fast drive, which of course they'd never be allowed to do otherwise. If they put them on the road and drove them ten yards they'd be prosecuted for not having them in road trim. They haven't got mudguards and lights and silencers. They'd never go at all if it wasn't for these Vintage races. But even so most of the cars don't get any chance to show their paces because, well, the drivers aren't as fast as the cars. Frankly, most of them are just touring round.'

'And is that what you're doing? Touring?'

'I'm afraid so,' he said resignedly. 'Even when I take her up over the ton I know I'm nowhere near pushing her. If you saw her go round with a real racing driver handling her, you'd see why the K3 was one of the great milestones. Why, the power she develops—'

Heading him off gently, I said, 'Don't you know, among your wide acquaintance, a real racing driver who'd take her out now and again?'

Brian shook his head despondently. 'No, it has to be me. The first-rate drivers have a very full programme, and I don't want a second-rate one. I'm second-rate myself, dropping down to third.'

'Oh, come, with all your experience—'

'I'm just having fun. But having fun isn't enough. I tour round all right, and give the crowd a good look at a K3, let 'em know what she looks and sounds like. And what it does for me! To see the track ahead of me, to feel that kick in the back when I put my foot down, to have other blokes around me who are getting the same feeling from their cars, ready to give me a race . . . But most of us are getting a bit old for it, and nearly all of us were nothing much to start with, as competition drivers go. She needs a younger man, don't you, sweetheart?'

My interest kindled again, after all these years, in the machine that could arouse the same emotions as a beautiful woman. I took a step or two into the garage to look attentively at Brian's sweetheart. I readily admitted that as a piece of single-minded design, everything narrowed down to the one purpose, the car was a magnificent achievement. Squat, hugging the ground, she was also sleek, pan-therine, suggesting a will to hurtle forward at unbelievable speed even as she stood there in silence and shadow. The afternoon sun was very bright, everything lit up in that dramatic, almost surprising way that seems to occur on certain afternoons in early autumn, and as Brian made no move to wheel the K3 into the open I had to let my eyes become used to the gloom inside the garage, with its one tiny window heavily smeared, to get an impression of her. The tiny oval windscreen jutted just above the steering wheel – racing drivers in those days sat high up, where they could see all four wheels – and behind the single seat was a projection, coming up to about the height of the driver's head, which tapered backwards over the long, saurian tail. The exhaust pipe, running along the outside of the car and fed by six little inlets, one from each cylinder inside that firmly strapped-down bonnet, was of a matt black colour that seemed stern and purposeful beside the muted sheen of the aluminium body. In designing this storming little invader, Cecil Kimber's skill had not failed him. And his reward? Denial of funds, isolation, the hostility of his fellow directors, dismissal, shortly followed by death in a meaningless train accident at a main-line station. A lesson to the Brians of this world: follow the beaten path of convention and routine, or suffer. It was at the time of Cecil Kimber's dismissal, I recalled suddenly, that Brian's mouth had taken on those hard lines at the corners that had now become deeply etched. Would anything soften them? Would the Bargeman's Arms? That depended, I thought, on whether the brewers took up the role of Billy Morris.

Cutting into my reverie, I heard from the sunlight outside a voice I recognized saying, 'Somebody having a look at the projectile?' And Brian's voice answering, 'Yes, your Dad.'

Good God! Michael! I hadn't known he was in Oxford. I had imagined him spending the usual kind of Sunday out at Chinnor, keeping Heather company.

But then, I realized quickly, I didn't actually know what Michael's usual Sunday was, or his usual any day for that matter. I didn't really know anything about him, at this stage of his life.

I came out of the garage, blinking a little.

Michael made a striking picture standing next to Brian. You would hardly have guessed that they were related. To begin with, Michael had, like me, taken after our mother rather than our father, inheriting through me her pale hair and slighter build, in contrast to Brian's chunky limbs, reddish hair and broad face. On top of that, Michael showed a contribution from Heather. He was taller than I was, holding himself very straight, his eyes a pure blue. He had my thoughtful cast of features, together with what I liked to think of as a certain delicacy of facial structure (or was it just weakness?), but he also had a dash, stirred into the mixture, of Heather's beauty, her classic regular features and large eyes.

Altogether he was, as my mother said, a fine well-grown lad. An intelligent, healthy, energetic, impulsive, lovable young animal. And he was mine. Or at least some of him was mine. Or at least a part of him was partly mine. At any rate, I hoped so.

'Hello, Dad.'

'Hello, Mike, how's everything?'

'Spot on,' he grinned.

'Mum all right?'

'Never better. Been looking at the projectile, have you?' Evidently this was his name for the K3. I never in fact heard him refer to it in any other way.

'Mike's a great help in all the little jobs to do with keeping her in trim,' Brian said.

'Is there much work to do on her?' I asked. I must have sounded sceptical, since I couldn't for the life of me imagine what jobs there could be in maintaining a car that never went anywhere except to blast round a racing circuit a few times on a couple of occasions a year. There was a defensive note in Brian's voice as he replied shortly, 'You'd be surprised how much there is to keep an eye on.'

'Only this morning,' Michael put in, 'we were busy for two or three hours just getting the timing right.'

'Timing?' It sounded like something to do with eggs.

'Yes. Two of her cylinders were firing a bit raggedly. To be fair I don't think I'd have known that myself, just from listening to her, but of course Brian picked it up, and after we'd got it right I could tell the difference.'

'You must be learning a lot.'

'Well, I am, but of course I started from a long way back.'

It struck me that he was just about the age Brian had been when he went up to Cowley to get his first job at Morris Motors, after messing about for a couple of years in dead-end jobs. It hadn't taken him long to realize that he would die of boredom if he just stayed on the assembly line making Morris cars, and that the place for him was M.G. And once he knew that, it hadn't taken him long to worm his way somehow into the M.G. set-up, starting with the humblest of tasks. Singleness of purpose had served Brian well – at least, till it had come into collision with Billy Morris's singleness of purpose, which was to cut costs. Singleness of purpose, for that matter, had carried me through the Sixth Form, to Episcopus College, and thence into academic life. What of Michael? Was he showing singleness of purpose? It didn't altogether look like it. But then, a boy needed hobbies. And perhaps a designer of racing cars was what he was destined to become. Why did I know so little about him?

'Let's have an evening, Mike,' I said. 'You tell me an evening when you're free and we'll go and have a meal somewhere.'

'All right,' he said. Friendly but hardly enthusiastic. I understood. Sitting with your father in some boring restaurant, chewing your way through a boring meal, discussing the sort of things your father thought it important to discuss. I could tell how unexciting I must seem in his eyes, though I felt confident that he was not altogether without fondness for me. Deep down. But how deep down?

'You were working on . . . the projectile this morning, then,' I said, trying to join in and share something with him. 'Well, you had the weather for it. I suppose you had to wheel her out to get at her properly.'

They both laughed and Brian said, 'Oh, we don't work on her here.'

'No?'

'I should think not. Of course you've never heard the note of her engine, have you? We're far enough away from the nearest house to get away with it for a few minutes, I expect, but not starting her up again and again like we had to do this morning. But that's not the real problem. It's the kids that make it out of the question. Once that engine note sounded out, they'd hear it up to half a mile away and they'd come running. All the time we were working on her they'd be round us like a swarm of minnows, wanting to look at this and handle that, wanting to sit in the driving seat, trying to pull bits off her for souvenirs, the lot. It's the chief trouble you have when you're in charge of a racing car. I should know; I've had it in England, I've had it in France, I've had it in Germany.'

'So where d'you take her?'

'Over to Abingdon. There's a shed in a corner of the factory area. They don't mind me working on her there, because nobody uses that shed on Sunday and anyway they've got a certain amount of goodwill because after all she's an M.G.' He laughed shortly. 'Not that she's anything like any M.G. *they'll* ever work on. Sometimes the young apprentices crowd round just the way the boys'd do here, and when I lift the bonnet I see sheer amazement on their faces. They've never seen a real car before.'

'Makes me feel privileged, Dad, I can tell you,' Michael said contentedly.

I turned away, pretending to look into the interior of the garage. I didn't want a disapproving or sulky look to come into my face. But I was beginning to find the situation unpalatable, difficult to handle. Brian shared something so important with Michael. What did I share with him? Nothing. Just my blood. Blood is supposed to be thicker than water. But it didn't, at that moment, seem to me as good a bonding agent as motor oil.

Then another thought struck me, and I turned back to Michael. 'We had lunch at the Bargeman's today, with Gran and Grandad,' I said. 'If you'd been working with Brian at Abingdon, I suppose you were somewhere around, not out at Chinnor.'

'Yes, I was around. Brian usually gives me a lift back to Chinnor in the evening, when we've been working.'

'Least I can do,' said Brian.

'Yes, but what I mean is . . . what did you do at lunch-time?'

'Oh, I had some lunch. Some sandwiches.'

'Just on your own? That can't have been much—'

'No, I was with a friend. I was over at Medley Boat Station; that's where I've just come from.'

'Oh.' My one syllable dropped into a pool of silence.

'I was helping to clean a sailing dinghy,' Michael said, 'and lay it up for the winter. A fibreglass job. It's a bit of a nasty assignment. The fibreglass tends to get into the skin of your fingers. The chap who owned the boat needed a bit of help.'

'So,' I said encouragingly, 'you're friendly with a man who belongs to the sailing club at Medley. D'you go out with him?'

'Well,' Michael said, 'not actually with *him*.' He faced me with a look that said, 'Let's put a stop to any misunderstanding before it develops,' and went on, 'It's not actually him I go sailing with. It's his daughter.'

'Oh,' I said. 'Well, that sounds fine.'

Of course it was fine. Two young people, appropriately partitioned as to gender, going out sailing together on that broad, tranquil stretch of the Thames just where the village of Binsey looks across Port Meadow. Innocence, youth, eagerness and a touch of adventure, all in beautiful surroundings. I ought to have been pleased.

So why was I not pleased? Because I was a bad loser. I was, plainly, losing in some kind of hidden contest. I wanted – needed – to have a fruitful relationship with my son. And here was this same son, grown tall and good-looking, self-possessed, a son to be proud of, standing in the clear sunshine looking at me with what seemed a wary benevolence. He spent Sundays of absorbed, dedicated leisure work with his uncle, my brother. He had a girl-friend with whom he went sailing. Whether she was technically his girl-friend or not (that term was just coming into its modern use to mean 'lover'), I had no means of knowing, but at any rate he had reached the threshold of that period of his life and she was obviously the front runner. I remembered, with a sudden red-hot stab of agony, how at his age plus a couple of years I had eagerly punted Vinnie up the Cherwell as far as its secluded reaches, with picnic supplies aboard, for one motive only, and how I had been at the very flash-point of fulfilment when those yobbos had suddenly dived into the water and showered us with spray and raucous laughter. Times were changing: things would be better for Michael. But would I be near enough to him to be in any sense part of his life – as Heather was because for good or ill he lived with her, as Brian was because they shared an obsession, as this girl, whoever she might be, was? A cast of characters was assembling to play out the story of Michael's life and I was wondering, as I stood there, whether I could count on even a walk-on part.

Brian, now shutting the door of the garage, said to Michael, 'When d'you want to get back to Chinnor?'

'I should be there about seven. More or less.'

'Well, that gives you,' Brian looked at his watch, 'nearly a couple of hours before you have to set out. I'll run you out there, of course.'

'It's very good of you, Brian.'

'No, it isn't, it's part of our deal when you work on the car with me on Sundays. You free next Sunday, by the way?'

'You bet I am!'

Standing by, wondering if either of them was aware of my presence, I was thinking, 'If Michael has two hours free now, why doesn't he spend them with me? He's seen his girl-friend, he's worked on the racing car, now he could surely . . . he could surely . . .'

'Mike,' I said with a casualness that I tried to keep from sounding dreadfully hollow, 'if you're free for a while just now, could I offer you some tea and toast by my fireside at College? I'm sure Brian wouldn't mind picking you up there.'

'Course not. Anywhere.'

'It's kind of you, Dad, and I'd like to do it some time, but—'

'I know it's not very exciting, but I think it's a good thing for us to . . . chat now and then,' I finished lamely.

'Oh, yes, I think so too. It's just that today . . .'

'You've arranged something?'

'Well, yes, really. I mean I just nipped over to see Brian and fix up about going back this evening. I went to the Bargeman's but they said you'd left, so I knew this was the place to try.'

'How did you get here?' Brian asked.

'I borrowed that.' With a grin, Michael pointed to a female bicycle leaning against a nearby tree. 'It's Sophy's.'

'So of course you've got to take it back,' I said flatly.

'Well, yes, and then we kind of had the idea we'd play some records for a while. She's got a better record-player than I have.'

And even if it was a much worse one, it would *sound* better, wouldn't it, Mike? I was sixteen myself once. I watched him as he swung the bike round and mounted it, glad to be away, glad to have his duty visit over.

'I'll come for you at Sophy's, then,' Brian said. 'About six- thirty.'

'Well . . . six-forty-five. I'll be ready, I promise. 'Bye, Dad.' And he had whirled off. He could almost straighten his legs on Sophy's pedals. Was she a long-legged girl, or had he adjusted the saddle? What was she like? Would I ever meet her?

'You know where this Sophy lives, then,' I said to Brian.

'Oh, yes,' he said casually. 'When he comes into town he's gener- ally with her when he isn't with me.'

'Where does she live?'

'Hinksey Hill.'

That didn't tell me much. There are all kinds of houses scattered on Hinksey Hill.

'She lives on Hinksey Hill, she's called Sophy and her father's got a boat at Medley. Sounds pretty middle-class to me.'

'Oh, she's that all right. Her father's a plastic surgeon or something like that. Works at the Radcliffe.'

'Oh,' I said. I could see that was all I was going to get.

Brian put the key of the garage into his pocket and asked, 'What are you going to do now?'

'Sit around and talk to you,' I said. 'Let's go back to the Barg- eman's.'

'All right. Only you mustn't pump me about Mike.'

At first we walked in silence, but it was a silence I found myself impelled to break. After we crossed over the Bullstake Stream and were walking down the short length, hardly more than a space between the houses, that bears the name of Swan Street, I broke my even step and faced him and said, 'Why don't you want me to pump you about Mike?'

'Oh, no special reason, only I'm afraid you might get a bit obsessional about it.'

'Obsessional?'

'Well,' he said, 'you're worried about him, aren't you?'

'How do you know that?'

'I saw your face.'

We walked on and after another moment I asked him, 'What in particular did you read in my face?'

'Sadness. You feel that you've lost Mike and can't find a way back to him.'

'Well,' I said, 'that's just about how I do feel.'

'It's normal enough, you know. He's at the age when you don't bother much about your father. How much time did you spend with Dad when you were sixteen? Voluntary time, I mean – time when you went looking for him, tried to make him see that you wanted his company?'

'None at all, to be honest, but then it never entered my head that I needed to. We lived in the same small house, so of course I saw him a good many times a day whether I wanted to or not.'

'You caught sight of him, you mean.'

'That's true enough, but on the other hand I wasn't a rebellious boy. You hear in some families, absolutely as a matter of routine, of colossal rows developing between a father and son. Even fights sometimes. We never had anything like that.'

'Yes, you respected him, but in the year you were sixteen I don't suppose you engaged him in conversation much.'

'No, but it was different for him. He had me under his eye all the time, he didn't lie awake wondering how my life was getting along.'

'Yes, he lived with you and you don't live with Michael. That's what's giving you the anxiety. It's really your own life that's worrying you, not his.'

We had reached the Bargeman's Arms by now, but I didn't want to go inside. Suddenly I had changed my mind about wanting to sit about and talk with Brian. I wanted to go off by myself and think. It seemed to me that Brian was right: my life needed to be thought about. I stood on the pavement and said, 'Brian, give me a piece of advice.'

'I may not be able to.'

'Well, try. Give me your thoughts on just one matter.'

'What one matter?'

'Is there anything I could do to get into more of a dialogue with Mike?'

He smiled. 'As a matter of fact that's a very easy one. Do what I do. Share an interest with him.'

The jealousy hidden in my breast bit me again and I asked, 'Is that why you do it?'

'Why I do what?'

'All this business with the car.'

'No. In this case the egg came before the chicken. Mike came to see me one day, without any invitation or anything. I mean, he knew he was always welcome to drop round, we've always got along, but he wasn't in my thoughts at all. I was getting the K3 ready for a race meeting and he just turned up one Sunday morning. He seemed to get fascinated straight away and we just accepted that he was going to come round the next Sunday, and the next. The next, as it happened, was the day of the Silverstone event and it seemed natural for him to come along. After that we really were partners. Co-owners, you might say. It was as if it just happened.'

'Well,' I said, 'how the hell am I going to share an interest with him when your racing car is the only one he's got and it fills his entire mind?' Except the part that Sophy fills up, I thought wordlessly.

'Easy,' Brian said again. 'It isn't just the K3 he thinks about. She's the chief one, but it so happens he spends a lot of time day-dreaming about cars in general. Just any car interests him. Just the idea of owning a car, any kind of car, and driving it about.'

'How ridiculous! A boy at school can't afford a car.'

'That's true, but Mike isn't the only sixteen-year-old who day-dreams about having a car.'

'He hasn't even got a licence yet; he can't even take a test yet.'

'There's no need to swell up like a turkey-cock. Kids of that age aren't models of common sense and realism. He's crossing off the days till his seventeenth birthday and then he's going to take his test.'

'He can't take it on his seventeenth birthday; he'll have to have a period as a learner first.'

'Oh, stop splitting hairs. You know what I mean. He can drive pretty well, as a matter of fact. I've let him sit in my car a good few times, and start it, and run it around a bit in the factory yard when it's closed at week-ends. He's even taken it out on the Silverstone circuit when the officials happened to be away at lunch. He can drive it all right.'

'Good Lord! You've let him go howling round a *race*-track?'

'I was with him, for God's sake. Do relax. He's a safer driver than some of these old dodderers who learn to drive late in life. Or these young girls just out of the schoolroom who drive big heavy cars belonging to their fathers and wouldn't have a clue what to do if the thing skidded on a wet road. I'd back Mike to be one of the safest drivers around.'

'That's good, because he can drive Heather around when he gets his licence. She's got the car, after all.'

He looked at me thoughtfully. 'You haven't bought yourself one then?'

'Not yet. I might do one of these days. I want to see how things pan out financially. I part with a lot of money to Heather, and God knows when the divorce is completed it might be more.'

'Well,' Brian said, 'you asked me for advice and for what it's worth I'll give you some. Buy yourself a car and appoint Mike as your guide in the business. Don't buy a new car; get something second-hand and let him choose it and investigate what needs to be done to it. He likes tinkering around, and to be truthful there isn't always much to do to the K3. I often invent jobs just to give him a chance to get his hands on her. It's no trouble, I enjoy his company. But if he was doing the same sort of thing for you, and doing it for a real reason, I'd be glad. And you'd see plenty of him and have something to talk about.'

'Thanks, Brian,' I said. 'Good thinking. Thanks.' I gripped his arm briefly, then stood smiling at him in the now slanting sunshine.

'No trouble,' he said. 'Give me a real puzzler next time.' He put his hand on the door handle. 'You going to change your mind and come in?'

'No, thanks,' I said. 'I need to walk, and think.'

'O.K. See you around.'

'See you around.'

He went into the house and I walked along the river bank, facing upstream.

★

The next thing I did – the next decisive, significant action, I mean, not just things like shaving and giving tutorials and buying a pair of slippers – I did for reasons I can't explain to myself or to anyone else. Perhaps all our actions that arise from deep internal impulses are beyond rational explanation; they are, as the poet Larkin has it, 'what something hidden from us chose'. I can only say that it concerned Cynthia. Or rather, that it didn't. Not to speak in riddles (but how can we relate our experience without sometimes speaking in riddles, since our actions are so often inexplicable in the light of reason?), it concerned everything that my Cynthia was not and could not be.

It is the nature of a man's relationship with a woman to become all-pervading and all-involving. The sexual relationship is like a weed that invades one corner of a garden and ultimately takes over the whole demesne. You can halt it at this or that demarcation line, but only by killing it altogether, killing it stone dead.

That was the trouble with my relationship with Cynthia. We both willed it, from the start, to halt at an acquired demarcation line. Neither of us wanted it to become something that would grow into a force capable of directing our lives. I knew that for all her blazing attractiveness she was not a woman I deeply wanted. I must be careful here not to fall into absurdity. Obviously in some ways I wanted her very passionately; or perhaps it would be more honest to say in one way: I wanted to fuck her. Once that was accomplished, and I had rested sufficiently for my sexual energies to be renewed, I wanted to do it again, and then again and then again. The variations I introduced into the performance – and it soon reached a pitch at which where the Karma Sutra left off, we began – were that and nothing more. They were variations, and a variation is not a change. Still less is it a development. It can't lead anywhere, it does not change the personalities involved in it. Love changes the personalities of those who are involved in it. So, unfortunately, does hatred, which is why hatred can be used as readily as love to fuel a human life, though only to terrible purposes.

Cynthia and I were both intelligent people and we both realized these things. I would have been no use to her as a permanent life-partner. I had in fact no difficulty in imagining the man who, if he were ever to come along, would be an ideal life-partner for Cynthia. He would be a scientist like herself, a medical scientist; he would have the same driving energy in pursuit of his goals, and these goals would be of the kind that can be called 'humanitarian' and 'idealistic'. And indeed, objectively, they would be such. But I have been behind the scenes too often, spending my life in Oxford, to accept these simple surface definitions. Minds attracted by medical research can claim to be working for the love of humanity, minds attracted by research into pure mathematics or astronomy or Slavonic philology or Egyptology can't – that's too simple. It's the research, the fever of the quest, the original bright vision of knowledge for its own sake, that attracts them. I forget which colossus of modern science it was, which twentieth-century Copernicus or Bacon or Darwin or Pasteur, who said that if any scientist, in any field, told him he undertook his labours (and labours are what they are, by God) for love of humanity, he would not believe him.

The man who ultimately captured Cynthia's heart, as opposed to her pyrotechnic vagina, would have to have the edge on her intellectually. This would be difficult to do, but not altogether impossible, because purely scientific curiosity was not her sole motivation. She also had an administrative, a political, side. As I divined from the beginning, she could have headed a Ministry. But, woman-like, she had the need to give admiration, to accept a lead from the stronger vessel. If she were to fall in love with some purely intellectual genius, some Einstein of the medical world, she would be fiercely protective of him and it would express her nature.

She would never feel that kind of admiration for an historian because the historian's kind of knowledge did not touch her responses in the same way. She could see, in the abstract, that it had its place in the world, but that place was not part of her terrain. For me she would never feel admiration, nor submission. Therefore, never love. And if never love, then never any important emotion; only the attraction of the surface. She might acknowledge, freely enough, that I was capable of giving her the kind of attentions that brought on a record-breaking orgasm; but records, after all, are designed to be broken.

All this became deadeningly clear to me on the very week-end following that Sunday ritual gathering at the Bargeman's. Looking back afterwards on the wide-ranging talk we had had, on the momentous news that Brian was giving up the motor business and going back into the paternal occupation, on the disconcerting jolt of being brought face to face with Michael's growing-up and of the off-stage presence of the fair Sophy, I suddenly realized one thing: I had not, during that whole day, had one thought that concerned Cynthia. She simply inhabited a different sphere from my family, my offspring, my fears and hopes generally. She existed simply as a runaway embodiment of the pleasure principle.

Which was why I could enjoy myself so uninhibitedly with her without any painful thoughts of Mairead, who of course did belong in the world of truth and actuality along with my parents and Brian and Michael. Yes, and Heather. All of it, all the whole awkward, unmanageable bundle, because that bundle was life.

All of this came very clearly before my mental vision as I sat in my room in Pearce's Building on the Sunday night. I had spent all Saturday with Cynthia, and all Saturday night, and all Sunday, and she had worked me to a standstill. Finally, at about 8 p.m., she had cooked a scratch meal of scrambled eggs or something of the kind, because we were both in dire need of nourishment, and then said she had to work to get ready for the next week's programme.

That was Cynthia. Always had her priorities in order. Get rid of one need, then another – a man, then food – then she was ready for work. After that she would be ready for sleep. And so she would go on until the right man came into her life, the Albert Einstein whose pulsating power would sweep her gladly off her feet as Napoleon swept Josephine. Short of that consummation, no man would get inside the stainless-steel box in which her spirit moved.

So I found myself sitting by my gas fire in Pearce's Building, Episcopus College, at ten o'clock on a Sunday evening, too worked-out to do anything, not quite ready to sleep, with a glass of red wine beside me but no great inclination to drink it. And suddenly I knew that there was a sickness in my soul that could be healed by only one thing: another instalment of that life-saving contact with Mairead. With Mairead whom I really loved, really needed, really missed, really saw in the same perspective as I saw all the other real actors in my life. Mairead who was part of the real world – the realest part of the real world, the part where it attained its highest pitch and concentration of reality.

Eighteen months had gone by, more or less, since I had found the courage to make that first telephone call to her. That I had managed it, and that I had found her sympathetic to my urgent need for her, willing to enter into an occasional dialogue and thereby give me the occasional oasis in this desert journey, had kept me going till now. But now I needed another shot of energy. Cynthia had done me good; but the disillusioned quality of the thoughts I was now having about her showed me that as a source of energy she was wearing thin. I needed my true source. I needed to be reminded of a love that was made of something more lasting than the kind of high-spirited and benevolent but, at its centre, bargaining and selfish relationship that Cynthia and I had together. I needed, in short, to be reassured that one day my real life would begin again.

To realize that was to act. Again I was at the telephone. Again the distant ringing, the tight throat, the dry mouth – though not so tight nor so dry as the first time. Not quite so much was at stake; some ground, after all, had been won. I just needed a few words.

Ring, ring . . .

A man's voice answered. At the sound, a red mist rose behind my eyes. 'Who are you, you scum?' I wanted to yell down the telephone. In fact, of course, I merely said stiffly, 'Miss Hoey, please,' as if this were an inter-office call.

'I'll just call her,' he said. I could tell from the sound that reached me that he called the next words more loudly and with his head turned away from the telephone. 'Mairead! It's someone for you!'

In the background I heard a woman's voice, giggling. It didn't sound like Mairead's. It was higher in pitch, for one thing; and for another, Mairead didn't giggle.

Then her voice came on, unmistakeable: not laughing, but light and humorous, as if she were having a good time. 'Hello, somebody for me,' she said.

'Yes, I'm somebody for you,' I said.

'Peter!' Her voice was high, sociable, a party-going voice.

'You sound jolly,' I said.

'I'm reasonably jolly, yes. Some friends have come round for dinner and we've been drinking Spanish wine. Cueva de Solaña. Have you ever had that?'

'No, did you have much?'

'You don't need much, it's got quite high alcohol. But you didn't ring me to talk about wine.'

'No,' I said, forcing myself into calm. 'I'm just doing what we agreed. Ringing up just now and again when it all gets too much.'

'Not terrifically too much, I hope? You're all right?'

'Yes, I'm all right, are you?'

'There was a tiny pause and then she said, 'I'm living along. Trying to do it as well as I can.'

'You're having a sociable time, are you? Guests, and all that?'

'I don't live in a lighthouse, Peter,' she said quietly.

'Of course not,' I said apologetically. After all, it was I who was behaving badly. What did I expect the girl to do, go into a convent? And even if she had, I'd have been jealous of the other nuns and the Mother Superior. I'd have been jealous of anyone who could rely on seeing her regularly. The situation was an impossible one; the only answer was to stick it out and force the time to go by, as with a prison sentence. 'I'm very glad, of course, that you've got friends. Not that I'd expect you not to have any. I mean, I'm sure that your friends must like you very much and must want to see a lot of you. I'd like to see a lot of you myself, come to that, if only I had the . . .' I was babbling now, I knew that. But what was there to do except babble? It was such a sick, insane situation. 'What I mean is . . .' I started again. But Mairead, back in her party-going manner, interrupted decisively.

'I'm ringing off now, Peter, because I have two guests here and their names are Belinda and Evan and I've kept them waiting a terribly long time for anything to eat. I'm trying to cook noisettes of lamb, and it's the first time I've ever done them, and when you rang I was just looking in the oven to see if they were cooked. And I think they just about were cooked and I'm going to serve them.'

'Please do,' I said. 'Belinda and Evan ought to eat. Good night, Mairead.'

'Good night, Peter,' she said evenly and I heard the receiver go down.

I don't know what thoughts came into my mind as I sat there with the telephone still in my hand. I don't think any did. I mean that they didn't attain to the status of thoughts. They were just impressions, stimuli; they were *disjecta membra*. About the only thing I remember thinking was, noisettes of lamb, eh?

But the worst of the pain had ceased.

★

'Are you certain of this?' I asked Garrity.

'Unfortunately I'm all too certain. There were official notices in the local press. And the other day I was going past the station on my bicycle and I saw that there was a notice up on the wall, just at the top of the steps. I couldn't read it at that distance, so I dismounted and went over and read it there and then. Not unnaturally it said the same thing. The last trains both in and out will run on Saturday week.'

'Then, Garrity,' I said, 'please take out your diary immediately.' I fished out mine as I spoke. 'A country excursion. I shall take one anyway, now I know the line's closing, but I'd like your company if I can get it.'

We agreed a day. As term had not yet begun, in that tranquil autumn of 1951, we were not necessarily tied down to a Saturday. We settled on a mid-week day, avoiding Saturday when the station might be crowded, or perhaps just sorrowfully haunted, by passengers weighed down by the sadness of finality.

Garrity and I were sitting in the Common Room at Episcopus after one of our regular dinners, enjoying a cup of coffee and a little discursive talk before going our separate ways for the rest of the evening. It was more or less by chance that he had alluded to the fact, hitherto unknown to me, that one of the two railway stations in Oxford was to close. This was the 'L.M.S. station', that wooden building, painted white and with slender iron pillars, which stood some couple of hundred yards away from the larger Great Western station at the junction of Hythe Bridge Street and Rewley Road. It was a building of some elegance, designed in a style that, in America, would have been described as 'colonial'. It had an air of dignity, almost of repose. It was a terminus, where your journey either began or ended. Once a train came in at Rewley Road, the only way to go was back out again. It also had a certain academic dignity derived from the fact that it was from here that one took the direct service to Cambridge. Once settled into your corner seat at that white-painted station, you needn't budge till the towers of Cambridge came into view across the flat, windswept grain-fields of Eastern England.

'Where shall we go for our elegiac trip?' I asked Garrity.

'Islip,' he replied without hesitation. 'Have you a bicycle?'

'Not in working order, I'm afraid.' When last seen, my bicycle had been a heap of components on the garage floor at Chinnor, Michael and his friends having dismantled it for the purposes of cannibalization into other bicycles.

'Very well, we'll walk. It's been a habit of mine for years to take my bicycle out to Islip on that line, then ride to wherever I wanted to go on Otmoor and then home. But this time we'll be coming back on the train too, so that we arrive at the station as well as depart from it. Must give the place a good send-off on its voyage into the land of memory – eh? eh?'

It was Garrity's habit, when he made a remark with a slightly oratorical flavour, to finish the sentence with a sound that cannot really be described, let alone represented in writing. It wasn't a laugh; it wasn't a bleat; but it had the explosive quality of a laugh and the vibrato of a bleat. As he uttered this sound he made brief spasmodic movements with his fingers. He did so now, then quickly put his pipe back into his mouth and drew out dense, choking clouds of smoke. All these were signs that the subject, to a greater or lesser degree, moved him emotionally.

When I got to my room I thought about Otmoor and its strange dark history. If Garrity and I were going to get off the train and walk, we would inevitably be walking over the scene of some grim, even desperate, episodes. At Islip itself, Royalist and Parliamentary armies had fought one of their bitterest battles, for possession of the bridge that carried the road over the River Ray, the thrusting little stream too deep to be forded so that the bridge was essential for the carrying of supplies to the King's headquarters at Oxford. Many a brave man had given his life in the struggle for that bridge. After that war Otmoor had sunk into lethargy, seven poverty-stricken villages dotted across an inhospitable saucer of land which, because of the low ring of hills that bounded it, had soaked up rain water for so many centuries that it had evolved into a peat bog, tolerant only of subsistence farming, and with soft spots here and there into which cattle sometimes wandered and disappeared. An ill-wished place, the local people said. Only in the Billy Morris epoch, after Oxford became congested and noisy and choked with fumes, had this dour, shelterless area in the empty space out to the north-east begun to seem attractive because it offered silence and solitude, two qualities that the motor car was making scarcer week by week. That bleak, treeless plain, its silence broken sometimes by the bubbling cry of a curlew, had finally become sought after. No wonder Otmoor was one of the refuges of Garrity. When he selected a poem for translation, always a German lyric poem loaded with suggestion and *nuance*, he would go into a trance for a day at a time while he meditated a single line, and the meagre hedgerows and silent lanes he found here were the place for such meditation.

I thought of the sleeting Otmoor winters, when even Garrity must have kept away, and of the comfortless lives of the smallholders who had scratched for a living in those dank fens, pressed between the two millstones of a harsh physical environment and an unjust social system. When was it, some time in the 1830s or 1840s, that their sullen stoicism had erupted into a version of Luddite rebellion? I must look it up and refresh my memory: that time when a small landowner, having acquired a slab of Otmoor inconsiderable enough but large compared with the pocket-handkerchief plots worked by the peasants, had dug out a drainage system which improved his land but flooded theirs. In their desperation half a dozen of them, working silently in the dark of the night, had breached his dykes with picks and shovels and left the system in ruins. They were arrested, of course, and sentenced; but on their way to Oxford Castle – at that time in use as the town's prison – they had been escorted by a file of soldiers along St Giles's Street on one of the days when the annual fair was in progress, and the crowd, moved to pity by the sight, had surged about and released them.

I pictured that crowd. They would not have been much like the urban crowd that I knew from my own experience of St Giles's Fair, as it blared and glared just outside the walls of Episcopus, an idle, casual crowd drawn by strident mechanical amusements and sideshows; those early Victorians would have been mainly from the rural working class, for it was a hiring fair then and the cowmen, shepherds, hedgers and ditchers and milkmaids who had assembled to look for work would have been easily moved to the same resentment and the same uneasy fears as the Otmoor men.

Were any of my ancestors in that crowd? Did they wrestle with the soldiers who were in charge of the file of prisoners, tear their weapons out of their hands, press them helpless back against the walls, the thick impassive walls of Episcopus College, as the convicts made their escape? They were never recaptured. I must look up the documents, I thought, and see what the Otmoor landowner did about his dykes.

I got as far as taking out a pad of paper and beginning to make some notes about where to start my investigation, when I was interrupted by the ringing of the telephone. I felt a twinge of irritation at being disturbed so late, but after all it was only about ten o'clock.

As soon as I picked up the receiver I was swept into a different area of my life and a different mood – welcoming, receptive. The voice was familiar to me, deeply familiar, familiar through many years, but not heard recently. Harry Goodenough! Holding out the prospect of a meeting! Telling me, in fact, that he and Geraldine would be in Oxford the next day and asking if a meeting would be possible. I realized with a sudden warm rush of affection how much I had missed the pair of them. I must have been subconsciously longing to see them, during all these months when the current of my life had moved me away from them. Months? It was years, four solid years with only the occasional postcard as life rushed us all along. In all that time I had not set eyes on big, clumsy, tousle-haired Harry and bird-like, bright-eyed Geraldine, he with his head permanently in a Shakespearean cloud, she hopping through life with her keen eyes and sharp bill ready to spear anything that moved, so long as it was something that could minister to the bundle of eager, impulsive, generous impulses that collectively made up her character. Neither of them cared about money; I imagined them living on sheer energy, black coffee and scratch meals. They always did me good; I felt uplifted and in a way purified by their company. I was immensely fond of them. Quickly I reached for my diary, made sure I had a space the next afternoon, and invited them to seek me out in Episcopus. 'And what's your news, Harry?' I couldn't help asking before letting him go.

'Oh, just ordinary life. Got a pasting from the crickets over my *Pericles*; you may have seen that.'

Harry Goodenough always referred to critics as 'crickets'. It was his way of reducing them to what he considered their proper stature. Since they consistently either carped at his productions or neglected to mention them at all, I felt he had a right to put a few defensive planks round his self-esteem. Ever since we had formed our friendship as undergraduates I had known that he would be a great man of the theatre. In those days he had never stopped talking about Shakespeare; now he did sometimes stop for a moment or two, usually to make some remark about Lope de Vega, Calderon, Molière, Euripedes, Pirandello or Dürenmatt. I wondered, as I rang off, whether he and Geraldine were still as passionate lovers as they had been, and my confident guess was that they were.

Harry and Geraldine! How had I got so out of touch with them? Why, for instance, had I not written or telephoned them months ago, years ago even, to invite them to visit me? It was another of those self-answering questions. I had got out of the habit of inviting people into my life because, at present, I had no life. What I had – and Harry's voice had jolted me into an awareness of it – was something that was waiting to become a life.

– 140 –

Going over the next morning for a cup of coffee in Common Room, I was greeted on entering by a burst of boisterous laughter from the end of the room, over by the window. The laughter had nothing to do with me; it came from half a dozen of the Fellows who stood, coffee-cups in hand, in a semi-circle round Manciple. He was delightedly retailing something that evidently gave him unusual pleasure, and I knew without needing to be told that he must have got hold of some morsel of gossip with a particularly spicy flavour.

'Have you ever seen one of these things?' someone was asking him as I poured out my coffee, my back turned for the moment to the group.

'Not exactly *seen* one.' Manciple spoke as if he had seen diagrams, photographs and scale models of this artefact, whatever it was, and discussed its *rationale* with its designer and builder, but was prevented by his scrupulous regard for truth from claiming that he had actually seen the object itself.

'How big is it?' the same man asked.

'Well, it has to be big enough for an adult human being to be completely enclosed inside it. If you lay it down it's something like a coffin, if you stand it up it's something like a sentry-box.'

Another questioner put in, 'What's it made of, Luke?'

'Well, there's steel wool in it for one thing. In between the layers.'

'But what are they layers *of*?'

'As far as I can gather, something fairly commonplace. Could be hardboard or even chipboard. Anyway, there are several layers and there's this steel wool in between them.'

'Any scientific reason for that?'

'There must be, but I don't know what it is. But then I readily admit to not knowing most of what there is to know. There's an awful lot you have to take on trust. But then,' Manciple added, his cunning little eyes sparkling with enjoyment, 'we shall probably soon be in a position to gather some empirical knowledge.'

'You mean,' someone said drily, 'we shall be able to observe the results?'

'Well,' Manciple said, puffs of laughter escaping round his words, 'there's no law against assessing the probabilities. I mean, if we observe the ordinarily observable facts and put two and two together we shall at any rate establish the probabilities.' Unable to contain his happy mirth any longer, he gave a loud, braying laugh in which several of the group joined. One or two of the others, their momentary curiosity fading, moved away in search of newspapers.

'What's Manciple got hold of now?' I asked one of them, a dark, taciturn New Zealander.

'Something about an orgone box,' was his terse reply.

'A what box?'

'That Wilhelm Reich stuff. You can't have missed all that business Manciple's been going on about.'

'I usually dodge him if I can.'

I could see the man was looking round for escape, not wanting to spend his few minutes of leisure on tedious explanations to me. 'Oh,' he said, 'it's all to do with that chap Hunt who was up here in about your time, if I'm not mistaken. One of Watson's friends.'

'Oh, yes.' Hunt, I remembered, had been talking about going to interview this Reich. I had meant to find out something about the man, but it had had very low priority and I had come nowhere near getting round to it. Leaving the New Zealander in peace, I went over and tackled Manciple directly, his *entourage* having now dispersed.

'Wilhelm Reich,' I said.

'What about him?' said Manciple, looking at me with that familiar mixture of defensiveness and curiosity. Familiar in him, that is. 'You another prospective customer? I wouldn't have expected it, in your case.'

There seemed to be an insolence lurking behind his words, but then there generally was an insolence lurking behind anything said, done or thought by Manciple. I ignored it and went straight for the simple information.

'Did Hunt write something about him in his paper last summer?'

'I don't believe so. I think he researched it and then there was a change of editorial policy. They decided not to run it. It seemed a strange decision at the time, considering that sex is usually their chief preoccupation and Reich has written a book on the orgasm. But when Hunt handed in his piece it turned out to have too many words of more than two syllables.'

'That's strange for Hunt. He's usually perfect at judging the kind of sludge that's expected of him.'

'Yes, but apparently Reich was an associate of Freud and at one time taken very seriously by that crowd in Vienna. He had serious claims to be a psycho-analytical theorist, and even if you're Hunt you can't altogether avoid talking about that side of his life. Not if you want it to be recognizable that you're writing about Reich at all.'

'But surely Hunt could get round that. It isn't only psycho-analysts, or people undergoing analysis, who have orgasms. He could have gone round interviewing film stars or fashion models and be damned to this Reich.'

'Well, he was prepared to do all that, of course, but they can all get that kind of material any Sunday without having to carry any ballast about psychology and such. And it seems Reich's theories take a bit of puzzling out, he's a typical German mystifier, more than half dotty, so they say.'

'But there must be plenty of ordinary scandal Hunt could rake up. It's what he's trained for, after all. For instance, I remember his mentioning that Reich had come out of prison. What did he go in for?'

'Oh, that was a technical offence, really. He had a run-in with the Food and Drug Administration, or whatever that branch of the American government's called. They told him to withdraw his orgone boxes from sale because he couldn't substantiate the claims he was making for them.'

'What claims was he making?'

'He said they gathered and stored orgones.'

'What the hell are orgones?'

'No one's ever seen them and no reputable scientist believes in their existence, but Reich says they're particles of something or other and they radiate cosmic energy and they fall from outer space. If you sit in an orgone box you can saturate your system with them and then – wow!'

'What do you mean, wow?'

Manciple giggled. 'We shall have to find out, shan't we? He's just sold one to somebody who'll put it to good use; she'll spread the message all right.'

I firmly stopped myself from asking who this person might be. I dislike gossip. But in any case there would be no need to ask. Manciple knew something – or had heard something, which to him was the same thing since the fact that a story was going about was a fact in itself; and to expect him to abstain from passing it on would be like expecting an old whisky-soak to sit cradling a glass of the finest malt for half an hour and then put it back in the bottle untouched. I waited, and I didn't have to wait long.

'You know Hunt went to America,' he said, 'to see Reich.'

I nodded.

'Reich gave him all the background on this orgone box business. Apparently the Food and Drugs people had ordered him to stop selling them. He'd ignored the order and carried on as if they didn't exist. Finally they had to prosecute. What he ultimately went to prison for was contempt of court, whatever name they give to that in America. It wasn't because his ideas were immoral or subversive or anything, as one used to hear rumoured. It was just a technical offence which he refused to stop committing.'

I nodded again.

'When Hunt met him he was out after serving his sentence. He hadn't given any guarantee about mending his ways or anything. So, I suppose, he just carried on as before.'

'You suppose? You don't know for certain?'

Manciple closed one eye and nodded slowly several times, facial sign language for 'We weren't born yesterday, were we?'

'Hunt got hold of a stock of them,' he said. 'And who supplied them if Reich didn't?'

'A stock?'

'Well, half a dozen at any rate. I'm not sure how it was done. There were regulations to be got round, and then the whole business of carriage across the Atlantic. They aren't the kind of thing you can fold flat and put under your arm. I understand the paper made it possible. He had a pretty elastic expense account, as these journalists always do or there wouldn't be any newspapers.'

No, I thought, and there wouldn't be any Hunts either. What a good thing that would be.

'And are you telling me Hunt's making a sideline out of retailing these contraptions?' I asked.

'Well . . .' Manciple winked again. It was the one thing he could do to make his coarsely repulsive face, with its low hairline, even more horrible than usual. He held the wink for about four seconds and then said, 'He certainly supplied one, whether as a sale or a gift I wouldn't know, to a certain good friend of his.'

I remained carefully expressionless.

'A friend,' Manciple pursued, 'well known to all of us here.'

This was my cue to say, 'Of course you mean Molly Whitworth.' Certainly she was the only friend of Hunt's, apart of course from Watson, who was well known in Episcopus. But I didn't give Manciple the satisfaction of actually naming her. I just nodded, and kept my face expressionless, and poured out another cup of coffee.

I now sat back in my chair, drinking this coffee and looking about me to see who was in evidence during this late stage of the Long Vacation, when the family men at least had had to come back to Oxford because the school holidays were over. Episcopus, like every college, always became more populous in September, and dons who lived within its walls felt themselves less marooned and isolated. Just as I had that thought Bax walked past me, an isolated man if ever there was one. He was on his way to the door.

'I'm off for a day or two in London,' he took the time to inform me. 'A Gibson jaunt.'

I nodded. 'I hope it's fruitful. I'll be glad to hear about it when you get back.'

'You shall,' he said and moved on.

Bax was interested in an eighteenth-century Bishop of London, by name Edmund Gibson. At a time when the division of political opinion was hardening throughout the country into the Whig-versus-Tory pattern it was to retain for so long, there was a struggle going on for the soul of the Church of England. Whig clerics followed the directives of the Court, Tories either retained traces of Jacobite loyalty to the exiled house of Stuart or, at best, settled into that general 'country' attitude of hostility to central government and suspicion of the Hanoverian establishment that became, for most people, 'Toryism' at that time. Oxford had more than its share of these and Edmund Gibson, as the most influential Whig churchman of his day, worried about Oxford and intervened continually in its affairs. Bax had long been gathering information about Gibson, whose correspondence he planned one day to edit, and whenever he got wind of a *cache* of material that could throw light on the man, he took himself off, equipped with the necessary permissions and introductions, to comb through it, describing his errand as 'a Gibson jaunt'. Doubtless a mass of documents awaited his attention – in the Record Office, in the British Museum, at Lambeth Palace. At least the quest would keep him from brooding and introspection.

Getting to my feet to go back to my room and get on with some of my own work, I was struck, not for the first time, by the strange warp and woof of Oxford society; of donnish society, that is, not the perpetually hurrying river of young people, living their lives, hitting peaks and troughs, faithfully reflecting the fashions of their day whether their day was 1650 or 1750 or 1850 or 1950; they were interesting, certainly, but in the way that young people anywhere and everywhere are interesting, because of their youth, their vitality, their idealism and their silliness. 'Oxford' itself, the Oxford where I had my being, was certainly not homogenous. At one extreme it contained solid, responsible scholars like Bax, accepting the responsibility they had undertaken to acquire as much depth of understanding of their chosen subject as they possibly could, and hand on that understanding to those with ears to hear. At the other extreme it contained people like Molly Whitworth, living in a competitive world of bright ideas and gimmicks like the orgone box, and encouraging in the role of *cicisbeo* a Fleet Street rat-face like Hunt. Bax was far more interesting, useful and generally sympathetic than Molly Whitworth. Yet she was the one who attracted the attention. There were dozens of people who knew her – at any rate by sight, and were familiar with her voice, talking whatever shallow nonsense – for any one who knew anything about Bax.

Well, I thought as I walked back to Pearce's Building, why be surprised at that? Hasn't it always been the way things are?

★

When Harry and Geraldine irrupted into the room the next afternoon, the first thing we did was embrace rapturously, Harry giving me a bear-hug and Geraldine a loving kiss on the cheek. 'It's been such *ages!*' she exclaimed, and immediately stood back to take an attentive look at me and at my surroundings.

'So here you are, Peter, a real live don.'

'Well, strictly speaking I was that when we last met. I mean, I was a Fellow of Episc—'

'Yes, strictly speaking, but now you've got all the outward trappings and you're sitting here in state in a big beautiful room and you *look* like a don.'

'All it really means is that after Heather and I split up I came back into College.'

'Yes, you told us about you and Heather. We were sorry.'

I had indeed sent a scrappy letter, just conveying the bare news. 'Well,' I said, 'these things always are a pity, but they happen.' To change the subject, I went on, 'Anyway, it's not a big room. It's a poky little room compared with what most dons have.'

'You could say it isn't as big as some, but it's very pleasant, with a view out on this bit of garden. You've looked after yourself, Peter.'

'What's actually happened is that Episcopus have looked after me. That's why I'm so pathetically grateful to them. There are times when my work-load is really more than I reasonably ought to do, because it's like a river that goes from flood to trickle and back again, but even at the worst times I don't really grudge it. I'm too conscious of what I owe to good old Episcopus.'

'Yes,' Geraldine said crisply, 'institutions that have the resources usually have a lot of experience in deploying them where they'll buy class loyalty.'

'Class loy— Geraldine, are we going to have all *that* again?'

'I mention these things for your own good, Peter. If you're going to fit smoothly into the Establishment, you might as well know that's what you're doing.'

'Yes, but Geraldine dear, you might well be describing just the ordinary human being of any shade of opinion. If I feel gratitude to my employers, who happen in my case to be my University and within that my College, doesn't the working man feel loyalty to his Union and his mates? And why shouldn't he? And don't you yourself, my love, feel a fierce loyalty to the ideal of being uncompromisingly *against* the Establishment, against the governing class, against most of the people with authority in our society?'

'Yes, because of the rotten deal they've given to the underdog majority.'

'All right, as long as you don't start telling me that the underdog majority would do any better under the Communist Party, who are always wooing them with phony hot-air slogans about a Workers' State and Power to the People, when in the countries that are actually ruled by Communism the worker hasn't even the right to strike or to make his voice heard.'

'I'm not a member of the Communist Party,' she said almost casually.

'Oh?' I was genuinely surprised. 'I distinctly remember you joining at the time of the first demonstrations over the business of the Cutteslowe Wall, and trying to get me to join as well.'

'Yes, but you also remember me leaving the Party at the time of the Russo–German Pact.'

'I thought the general attitude was that the war had washed all that out. I thought there'd been a drift back.'

'There has, but I haven't been in it. When the Communist Party teamed up with the Nazis, they lost my membership, not that I suppose it keeps them awake at night. I'm just generally Left now – pretty hard Left, I admit, but not part of the Kremlin flock.'

'Well, congratulations on that at least.'

'Thank you, and now tell me what social issue I can congratulate *you* on. Is the Cutteslowe Wall still standing?'

'Yes, I'm afraid so.'

'So all the nasty rough people who live in the housing estate still have to walk a long way round to get to the bus stop and the shops because there's a wall to keep them from polluting that stretch of road that has posh houses on it?'

'They're ordinary houses. Not posh. They're just not built by the Council, and they don't have subsidized rents.'

'What does that prove?'

'Well, I mean that the people who live in them aren't top-hatted millionaires grinding the faces of the poor, they're just people.'

'But they still don't want to breathe the same air as the working class?'

I sighed. I had never won an argument with Geraldine and it was too late to start now.

'Are the slums in central Oxford just as bad?' she pursued. 'The ones I took you to see in St Ebbe's that morning?'

That was the morning, I reflected, when she had told me about her break with Bax. I thrust that subject back out of sight and answered the one about the slums.

'The St Ebbe's slums are still standing, but there are plans on the drawing-board to demolish them.'

'That's good at least.'

'That in itself is good, but there may be an outrage of another kind in store. The City Council haven't published the plans yet, but from what's been leaked I gather that the buildings that are going up instead are of a mindless ugliness you'd never believe.'

'Oh, come. This is Oxford. There'd be a solid opposition to anything too Philistine, if only because of the tourist trade.'

'Geraldine, this city is ruled by cloth-cap types who don't care about tourists any more than they care about art connoisseurs. What they care about is factories and motor roads.'

'Well,' she said forgivingly, 'that's where the livelihood comes from, for a majority of Oxford citizens.'

'That's true, since Billy Morris. But it doesn't make me think any more kindly of Billy Morris. The damage he's done will go spiralling on for ever.'

'Is that because you'd rather have picturesque streets than people in work?'

'Look, fifty years ago there were picturesque streets in central Oxford *and* no unemployment to speak of. When the car industry hits hard times – and it's running into them already – the workers who'll be unemployed will be workers that Billy Morris *brought* here. He's created the problem, and if he succeeds in staving it off for a few years that doesn't make him a knight in shining armour, as his worshippers are always trying to tell us he is.'

'Well, don't take it out on me, Peter. I'm no admirer of Morris. I'd like to have factories like his as state-run enterprises. I don't like millionaire private capitalists.'

'Talking about state-run enterprises,' Harry said from his corner, 'I see the landlady from the Palace managed to get the stone dropped into place.'

'The landlady from the Palace?'

'Buckingham Palace,' he explained.

A moment's reflection put me on the right lines. He was referring to Her Majesty Queen Elizabeth, who, deputizing for her husband King George VI, had laid the foundation stone of the long-projected National Theatre on the South Bank of the Thames.

'You mean you read about it in the paper, Harry?' I asked. 'I'd have expected you to be there.'

'I was busy. And since by some oversight they hadn't sent me an official invitation and offered me a glass of champagne, I thought I wouldn't disrupt my programme.'

'But you wished it well from a distance, I suppose?'

'I didn't wish it ill. I just wish I could believe in it a bit more. It's a couple of years since Parliament voted it through and said, "Yes, we will spend public money on building a theatre that won't have to depend on making money at the box office", and in two years they've got no further than putting down a stone in some wet clay. How long will it take them to get four walls and a roof put up?'

'They'll get round to it, Harry.'

'In my opinion,' he said, 'it won't matter much if they don't. The Old Vic's the National Theatre in all but name, that's where Londoners go to see Shakespeare, and they're not usually disappointed by the acting or the production. I mean, you've only got to think of . . .'

Harry then talked for some fifteen minutes of the Old Vic as a repository of the Shakespearean tradition of the English theatre. Famous names flickered in and out of his discourses – Lilian Baylis, Ben Greet, Sybil Thorndike, Lewis Casson, Ninette de Valois. It was impossible to interrupt him. One felt like applauding as he fell silent.

'But the future, Harry?' I said timidly, after a pause.

'Oh, the future. That's in the hands of chaps like me. Committees don't produce art.'

'But . . . but can't committees find the money for other people sometimes to produce art?'

'As a matter of abstract possibility they may be able to, but I must say I get the wrong vibrations from this lot. They've had too many false starts already. You realize, I suppose, that the stone Herself laid down the other day was the third? Actually the *third* in a row, each one with that accompaniment of high hopes and brave words and speeches full of platitudes?'

'Oh,' I said humbly. 'No, I hadn't realized that.'

'There was the one in Gower Street some time about 1914, then there was one in South Kensington, and now this. A pretty shaky start, and on top of that they have to choose Friday the 13th as the day to do it. Probably the only day the Queen was free. Everybody else had noticed the unlucky date in time and cancelled the functions they would have wanted her for.'

'Oh, surely, Harry, that's a bit over the top.'

'Theatre people are superstitious, aren't they, my love?' Geraldine said soothingly.

'Everybody who depends on luck is that,' he said and relapsed into silence, not sulky but preoccupied as he thought of Lilian Baylis and behind her Edmund Kean and William Barrymore.

Once we were sure Harry had nothing more to say for the time being, Geraldine and I resumed talking politics. Or rather, as usual, arguing. As her first ranging shot she sent over, 'I see the Americans are up to their usual games in Korea.'

'Geraldine, I don't know whether I ought to be drawn by that kind of remark, but I have the distinct impression that you're going to be at your most predictable.'

'Perhaps we both are. I wouldn't mind betting, for one thing, that you're going to come out with the line that the Americans are only treading the righteous path laid down by the United Nations.'

'Certainly it's U.N. policy to discourage aggression where possible, and the invasion of South Korea by North Korea is a clear case of aggression if ever I saw one.'

She whistled softly. 'Phew!'

'What do you mean, phew?'

'All those years of studying political history and you can still be so *naïve* about *Realpolitik*?'

'I'm no more *naïve* about *Realpolitik* than you are, indeed I rather suspect I'm less so, since you've been through the experience of being brain-washed by a totalitarian power and that never happened to me.'

'Really? Are you sure it isn't happening now?'

I stared at her. 'Geraldine, are you just trying to be annoying?'

'I'm perfectly serious. Wouldn't you call America a totalitarian power and isn't America brain-washing the entire Western world, particularly over this issue of Korea?'

'No, I wouldn't and they're not.'

'Peter, I'm sorry for you and I'd like to help you.'

'My dear lovely friend, I appreciate that, but if your idea of helping me is to change my fundamental beliefs I must warn you that it isn't going to be easy. For what it's worth, I'll tell you how I see the situation. America is a pluralistic society that offers people choices in a multi-party democratic system. It sees many of the other countries of the world, particularly the Western European countries that were so battered and impoverished by Germany and the Asiatic countries that were so ravaged by Japan, weakened and impoverished by years of suffering, behaving like rabbits in front of a snake under the great staring red eyes of the Soviet Union that has declared war on their way of life if not actually on *them*. America's trying to put a bit of heart into them with financial help and with military leadership in defending themselves where the Communist forces have actually invaded them. As usual they can't make up their minds on any common course of action, and as usual they're frightened to disobey the Kremlin because of the blood-curdling threats as to what the Kremlin's going to do to them if they don't fall into line. And on top of that, they're war-weary. Our young men are back from fighting and we don't want them to go out again, but G.I.s are fighting and dying against Chinese troops armed and equipped by Peking and behind them, Stalin. I see the hand of Joe Stalin behind the whole nasty little plot, sending North Korea in to savage South Korea. It's the kind of thing he thrives on. The truth may not come out for a long time, but it'll turn out that Joe's in there somehow, mark my words.'

'So the conclusion is, Hurrah for the Pentagon?'

'Certainly. Hurrah for the Pentagon and Hurrah for the British Army who, in spite of all the losses up to 1945, are doing more than anyone else to back them up and make it not just an American effort.

When that young soldier, Bill Speakman, won the V.C. I really cheered. I cheered out loud.'

Geraldine looked at me coolly. 'Funny. I never thought you'd turn into that type.'

'Well, my love, I have turned into that type. On selected occasions. And if you look hard you'll see Joe's hand in that too.'

'Why can't you see it for what it is, just part of the American global effort to "contain" Communism, to put the genie back in the bottle? You can't really think they're being idealistic.'

'I know enough about the Americans,' I said, 'to know that it's impossible to understand them, even at their most annoying, without taking account of the fact that there *is* a crumb of idealism in the American character, a hard, irreducible crumb. If you think there isn't, set them beside the total, unhesitating selfishness of the French or the deviousness of the Russians. In both those cases I don't mean the judgement to apply to every individual in the country, just to the policy-makers. In America, and I think to a very slight, vestigial extent, it's true even of the policy-makers that they're not one hundred per cent cynical.'

'I can't believe what I'm hearing.'

'I'm sure you can't, darling. You've been well inoculated against it. That's why it doesn't matter to the Kremlin that you don't actually vote Communist and carry a Party card. The fellow-traveller never contradicts the official Communist line.'

'I did,' she said. 'I contradicted it once.'

'I remember that and I honour you for it. The Nazi-Soviet Pact changed the capital "C" of your politics to a small "c", and I shall always respect that. You're a non-mechanized Communist. You want to live in a communal society that has all things in common, but you don't want the Kremlin and the secret police.'

'And what about you, Peter? Are you satisfied with what we have?'

'Not particularly, but I don't want to overthrow it by revolution. I'd rather work through the ballot-box. Patiently vote things into a better shape.'

'That's all very well, but what if the voting system doesn't give us the choices? You say you're glad I don't vote Communist, but if I wanted to I couldn't. There are scarcely ever any Communist candidates at Parliamentary Elections.'

'That's not because they're not allowed to stand. It's because when they do stand nobody votes for them, so they lose their deposit.'

While we rattled out the familiar arguments, both content for the moment to restate predictable positions, I was functioning on two levels. Under the more or less mechanical repartee I was studying Geraldine.

In the twenty years since I had first met her – twenty-one or twenty-two, more likely – she seemed to have changed so little in appearance. Just as slender, just as quick in her movements both mental and physical, no white hairs yet (I couldn't see her patiently tinting them out); even her neck seemed the same age. Could this really be? Or was it simply an illustration of the principle that one's contemporaries never seem to be changed in the way that younger or older people do; it is as if one's whole age-group moves along in a solid band, and the faces one is surrounded by are like one's own face – the changes in them steal in unnoticed. No, I decided, Geraldine's case really was unusual. Was there, hanging somewhere in a locked room, a painting of her that aged instead? Compared with Harry, whom I had known just as long, she did seem almost magically unaltered. He, at forty, was manifestly the same person that he had been at twenty, but equally manifestly not the same; he was heavier, his mop of hair was receding a little, and some trenches had appeared along his forehead.

'Well, anyway, you'll never convince me about Korea,' Geraldine said finally, in a dismissive tone that indicated a willingness to have done with the tedious subject. 'I can't accept that it's harmless U.N. police action. I think it's part of the global attempt the Americans are making to contain Communism.'

'I agree that part of its motivation is to contain Communism, but what's wrong with that? Communism is aggressive and expansionist, it comes to power on the guns and bayonets of soldiers and not through the ballot box, and once it gets power it hangs on to it like grim death and won't ever consider giving it up even if the people obviously don't want it. I don't see what you can do with a political philosophy like that *except* contain it, if you want to live in peace.'

'Peace! You surely can't mean that the Americans want peace!'

'Yes, they do. At any rate they want it more than the Chinese do. They're the ones who are doing the fighting in Korea. It's the Chinese army that's actually in the field; the Koreans on their own wouldn't last five minutes without them.'

'Well, you'll never get any progressive person to believe that. And by the way,' her face took on a more interested look, 'talking of progressives, have you seen your friend Carshalton lately?'

'My *what* Carshalton? You mean that dreadful creature who was at Episcopus in my time? The one who was such a social climber?'

'The one who went to America and got himself a rich wife.'

'Yes, he did all the correct things. He was the complete opportunist. Never took his eye off the main chance for a second. I haven't seen him lately and I don't expect to. In fact I very much hope I never see him again.'

'Obviously you don't take any interest in the man, so it won't matter to you that he's become very Left lately.'

'Well, I did hear something like that.' I dug into memory; I felt I must be wrinkling my brow. 'As far as I can recall, I met his wife just after the war. They were house-hunting. Now that money was going to be no obstacle to him, Carshalton had decided he wanted to have a Cotswold manor house and her dollars were going to buy him one. She's quite a nice woman as a matter of fact. A sculptress, I gather.'

'What does she think about his politics, if she's American and rich?'

'Oh, I think she's just glad of anything that keeps him out of mischief, gives him something to play about with.'

'Well,' Geraldine said, 'he'll have to play a bit more effectively if he wants to cut any ice in Left-wing politics. I've seen him trying to join in, and he just doesn't know any of the rules.'

'Being him, he'll soon learn them.'

'There's a lot for him to learn if he's going to get anywhere. The other evening I was at a meeting and he was on the platform and tried to make a speech. He went over like a lead balloon. I never saw such a total flop. He just wasn't on the wave-length of the people there.'

'What kind of wave-length was that?'

'Well, it was a "Hands Off Korea" meeting. Americans out – stop using the U.N. as a cover for capitalist imperialism. Quite a simple message, and pretty much what the audience had come to hear, so it couldn't have been an easier wicket, but he made a mess of it. And what a mess! They heckled him, they laughed at him, and finally they shouted to him to sit down. He tried to flounder on, but one person after another took it up till the whole place was yelling, "Sit down!" at him from all over the hall. In the end he just sat down and did nothing for the rest of the evening except open and close his mouth like a goldfish trying to breathe after being taken out of its bowl. It was pathetic.'

'What didn't they like about him?'

'It'd be easier to start at the other end and try to find one thing they did like, only there just wasn't anything. His way of speaking is funny, isn't it? No flavour to it. It's like something mechanical.'

Our talk passed to the trivia of our lives, bringing up to date the mundane chronicle of our existences. I went out to the little pantry along the landing and brewed tea, and we settled down with cups of it steaming merrily in the summer air, and I began to rack my brains for anything I might have to report that could possibly interest *them*, with their lives so much more filled with colour and movement.

'A don's life is very uneventful,' I said apologetically. 'The only events in it are thoughts and emotions.' As I spoke I remembered, with a jarring shock, that I was talking to a woman who years ago had been very much part of one particular don's life. It was not for me to tell Geraldine what that life might or might not contain.

Thank goodness, I thought with another shiver, that Bax happened just now to be away on one of his Gibson jaunts. With appalling carelessness, I had taken no steps to block off the possibility that he and Geraldine might suddenly come face to face during her visit to the College. Geraldine, for her part, must be so secure in her new life, so confident of being able to face the world and have control over her emotions, that she could face the theoretical possibility of a meeting with Bax and decide just to take it in her stride if it came. It was the blow to Bax that would have been crippling. He had never recovered from the loss of her. And here I was, thoughtlessly incurring the risk of having him run smack into her! Inwardly I made a vow to think more carefully before making any decision in the future, even the most innocent social decision.

With a sudden effort I dragged my mind on to new lines – any lines, as long as they led away from that neuralgic subject. 'We've – we've elected a new President here at Episcopus,' I said. 'Salterton retired.'

'I should think he did,' Harry said. 'He was about ninety-five, wasn't he?'

'Something like that. But he was a good old boy; he wasn't senile or anything.'

'Who've you got now, another old gaffer?'

'No, we decided to take the other path this time, and elect somebody from right outside the little enclosed world of Episcopus. That type can often be very effective, though of course there can be snags – you don't, by definition, know them as well as you know a man who's given his life to the College. A new broom might turn out to be difficult in ways that couldn't have been foreseen. The one we've got now seems all right, though, I must say.'

'When you say "all right",' said Geraldine, 'd'you mean he'll keep the College on an even keel, do things the way they've always been done, and not let too many nasty disturbing changes happen?'

'No, I don't. He's a man who's had to adapt to a good many changes in his working life and be generally alert all round.'

'What's he done?'

'Diplomat. He's been British Ambassador in one or two places and he's put in a lot of service all over the world.'

'Service! Is that what you call it? Most people would see the Foreign Office as an organization devoted to nostalgia and fantasy. Trying to keep alive the dream of an imperial past.'

'Geraldine, do you actually *know* anyone in the Foreign Office?'

'I know their record.'

'Well, if you know their record you know that the chief thing they've been doing about the Empire in the last five years, since the war ended, has been to handle the practical business of dismantling it.'

'What's this man's name?' Harry asked, obviously not out of interest but merely to separate us before we started some boring wrangle.

'Mowbray. Sir Jocelyn Mowbray. Likes people to call him Jock.'

Geraldine was still dissatisfied. I could see what was troubling her. She thought I was settling too easily into a don's ideas and attitudes, accepting the conventions of a way of life that she regarded with suspicion, largely because she still associated it with the granite faces of the St Hilda's dons who had tried to stop her wearing trousers when she was a student. They wanted her to behave like a young lady. She had maintained that young ladies who behaved like such were part of the sickness of England in the early 1930s: a biased opinion, but not a totally false one.

'I don't see what a college is doing with a President or a Principal or whatever you call the head man,' she said. 'What need is there of a leader-principle? Decisions ought to be taken in common.'

'Oh, they're that all right,' I said, thinking of all those interminable College meetings. 'It's just a convenience to have someone to represent the place, that's all. A figure-head.'

'Well,' she said, lapsing into indifference, 'I don't suppose I'll ever meet this figure-head, so it doesn't matter to me.'

'I wouldn't bet on that. Life can turn up some pretty surprising things as it lengthens out, which ours are beginning to do.'

'What kind of things are you thinking about?'

'Well, let's suppose for a moment that now Jock Mowbray's in Oxford he becomes Vice-Chancellor one of these days. It's a job that's passed around among heads of colleges. And let's further suppose that his term of office as V.C., five years, coincides with Harry getting an honorary degree.'

'Me? Are you joking?' Harry was startled. 'I'll get no honorary degree. I haven't got that kind of standing in Oxford, and I wouldn't want it. My life is given to the theatre.'

'A lot of people get honorary degrees, and all of them could say their lives were given to something or other that was nothing to do with the University,' I said. 'As for your standing, these things can change very quickly. My prediction is that they'll rush to give you a doctorate as soon as they hear you've been knighted.'

'Look here,' said Harry, jumping up from his chair and looking seriously alarmed, 'have you gone raving mad? Give me a doctorate? Peter, try and get a grip on yourself.'

'Everybody who's prominent in the theatre gets a knighthood sooner or later,' I said. 'And if Jock Mowbray is Vice-Chancellor when you get your doctorate he'll give a lunch-party and Geraldine will be at it and that's when she'll meet him. So I'm right. Q.E.D.'

I had taken a bottle of white wine out of the cupboard, and I now drew the cork triumphantly. 'Let's have a drink,' I said to my friends. 'To Sir Harry Goodenough, D. Litt., or will it be a D.C.L. they'll give you? And,' I said, filling a glass for her, 'to Lady Goodenough.'

'Ugh,' she said, conveying deep and sincere distaste. 'How I'll *hate* that. But I'll bear it for your sake, darling,' she said to Harry.

'No need,' he said gruffly, beginning to be embarrassed. 'Peter's talking through his hat. Nobody's going to give me degrees and handles to my name.'

'Oh, but they are, Harry,' she said tenderly. 'You're too important to go hanging around the world of theatre without a knighthood. At a certain level it's like a union card. You don't work without it.'

'I'm not a celebrity,' he said testily. 'I'm just a chopping-board for crickets.'

'Oh, that's only a necessary stage. Every genius goes through a time of being reviled and ridiculed. Then he suddenly emerges into the sunshine.'

'You'll see,' I said to Harry, nodding.

'Oh, bollocks!'

'You can use bad language as much as you like,' Geraldine cooed, 'but they'll make you a knight and I'll have to put up with being Lady Goodenough and, oh dear, I'll hate that. It's taken me long enough to get used to being Mrs.'

'Get used to . . .' I stopped short. I didn't know Harry and Geraldine had got married, but I wanted to let the information sink in before I said anything more. It wouldn't do to say the wrong thing. Obviously it was good news – they wouldn't have got married if they hadn't wanted to – but what kind of good did it represent?

'Go on, say it, you didn't know we'd got married,' Harry said, grinning.

'Well . . . uh . . . Does it sound silly to say, "Congratulations"?'

'No, it sounds fine,' said Geraldine, taking charge. 'We never had anything against getting married; it was just that, well, we knew we weren't going to try to do without each other, we'd have missed each other too much and in any case we functioned much better as a pair. And then there never seemed to be time. And another thing was that my mother would have so liked me to, it became an obsession with her and that made her go on and on at me, and if you've got the kind of temperament that I have you don't like anybody going on at you, it makes you do the opposite.'

'I can quite see that.'

'But all that seemed to become irrelevant, it just blew away like chaff on the wind, as soon as we knew Deborah was on the way.'

'Knew *who* was on the way?'

'Deborah. Our daughter.'

'Your *what*? Why wasn't I told about this?'

'Well, we didn't keep it a secret,' Harry said half-apologetically. 'All our London friends knew.'

'Yes, but I'm not one of your London friends. I sit here in Oxford and I never see anyone from London. When did this happen? No, first of all tell me something else. How old is she?'

'Three. Well, three and a half, nearly.'

'Three and a . . . where is she now? Why haven't you brought her?'

'She's with my parents at Surbiton,' Geraldine said. 'We're having a few hours' holiday from parenthood.'

'Hard work, is it?'

'It takes your attention, but it's very pleasant as a rule.'

'To confess something,' Harry put in, 'I'm missing her already.'

'Well, you can bath her and put her to bed.'

'You needn't say that as if it were a penance; there's nothing I'd rather do.'

'Yes, I know how you dote on her.'

'Of course I do. It's the love affair of my life.'

'Completely overshadowing,' she said acidly, 'the one you used to have with me.'

'No,' Harry said, taking hold of her and kissing her, 'fitting neatly around the contours of the one I'm in the middle of having with you.'

'Oh, Harry, I'm too skimpy to have any contours.'

'I'll be the judge of that,' he said, kissing her again.

'Ahem,' I said.

'What do you mean, ahem?' Harry demanded.

'I mean ahem,' I said. 'I'm here too. And it's time to have another drink.'

Shortly afterwards they left, with a definite arrangement to meet again soon, leaving me meditatively finishing the last inch of wine and pondering on the way life was unfolding. Geraldine and Harry, parents! Well, they would be wonderful in the role. So overflowing, so spontaneous, so naturally able to share the richness of their lives with any eager, enquiring child. Deborah . . . a most attractive name, though it didn't go well with Goodenough, two dactyls, like Malachi Mulligan. I smiled to myself in the empty room, looking at the two wine-glasses and thinking how much I liked my friends and how glad I was that they had increased themselves to three. I looked forward to getting to know Deborah. Now that Michael had grown up, my life didn't contain enough children.

★

Following on from those thoughts about children and family matters generally, I sat by the gas fire after dinner, the evening being a chilly one for September, and investigated the state of my thoughts on relationships, domesticity, sex, parenthood, and Lares and Penates in general. I knew that soon, as the mills of the law turned, my divorce from Heather would become a completed event and I would be freed from my vow to put no pressure on Mairead.

Obviously I could not know what would happen after that, but I should know before long; the legal processes couldn't drag on for ever, and then the way that led to a life with Mairead would be decisively open or finally blocked. All I could do at present was take stock of how things were with me at this actual moment.

The impact of Harry and Geraldine with their mutual love and certainty, and the news of their parenthood, had of course turned my mind to thoughts of love, of family, of the possibility or impossibility of there being, one day, a Leonard home with a Leonard family in it, like the one where I had grown up.

That made me think of Michael, which indeed I never went for long without doing. His seventeenth birthday had fallen in February 1951. The release of pent-up energy it brought to him was impressive. Quite clearly, in his own mind he had emerged from a chrysalis state to take on his fully developed form; he had arrived among the human race. His generation had the same attitude towards the coming of seventeen as the young males of the Victorian and Edwardian epochs had to the arrival of twenty-one, with its insignia of adulthood, the vote and the latchkey.

> Pa says I can do as I like
> So shout hip, hip, hooray!

Seventeen, in the twentieth century, made a lad free of the glorious, shining world of the motor-car. That world contained everything an adolescent boy wanted – dash, glamour, escape from home, social and sexual adventure. Since I spent so much of my imaginative life in the eighteenth century, it amused me to meditate on the vast difference that this one change, never mind all the other changes, made between 1751 and 1951. In the former year, when everybody who could possibly afford to do so went about on horseback, this magic

–158–

wand was not there to be waved. When even the children were encouraged to have ponies as soon as they could get astride them, if only in the interests of family mobility, a strapping lad of sixteen, well able to handle a sixteen-hands horse, experienced no sea-change on becoming seventeen. The development of the car, and then of the driving test, must have made the whole landscape of adolescence look entirely different. And what problems it involved for parents! In our day, the approach of seventeen was a liberation but it was also the knell of innocence and harmlessness. Except among the rich, whose wealth put them beyond the reach of mundane troubles of any kind, it meant that the parents no longer had the undisputed right to the family car – or cars, even, if the children were plural in number. It meant a daily battle; it meant worry, expense, fretful waiting in late absences, all of them hostile to family peace. It meant careless, inexperienced driving; it meant repair bills, fines, heavy premiums. To go no further and name no worse. The motor-car, which at the beginning had been so warmly welcomed by the middle classes because of the freedom it promised, had begun, by about this date, to reveal its true nature as one of those ambiguous gifts, bestowed on the helpless infant in the cradle by the cruelly smiling witch who begins by identifying herself as the fairy godmother and ends as the Destroyer.

That kind of talk, naturally, would have meant nothing to Michael. His point of view was refreshingly simple, which was part of what made his company so delightful, as all young people's is when it is not actually irritating. (It is always, by a simple law of Nature, the one or the other.) He wanted a car and he wanted it straight away. By exerting the utmost force of my authority, an authority that resided mainly in my cheque-book, I had managed to prevent his acquiring a motor-cycle, which by law he could have done at sixteen. ('The law is an ass.') Luckily, in this struggle I had, for once, had the unwavering support of Heather, who was as horrified at the thought of a motor-cycle as I was. Our revulsion was born in the same moment, as a result of the same incident. One day, five years ago, we had been driving along together when a motor-cyclist in front of us swerved and crashed at about forty-five miles an hour, coming down Cumnor Hill. I stopped and hurried over to pick him up, but even before I began to lift him I saw that he was lying very still and blood was coming out of his ears. He had been killed instantly by a severe fracture of the skull. Since that day, crash helmets have become compulsory, but they were not so in 1951, and in any case motor-cyclists have many other ways of killing themselves without resorting to fractures of the skull. Heather and I, driving the rest of the way home and arriving shaken and troubled, had decided then and there that never, never, *never* should Michael ride around on a motor-cycle.

This lesson, mercifully, had remained with her. She had ceased to be my wife, but she had not ceased to be Michael's mother. She would do many things, and go to extraordinary lengths, to flout and frustrate me, but not when it came to a motor-bike for Michael.

Now, however, Mike had climbed by slow and painful stages to the shining peak of Year Seventeen (completion of), and our defences were blown away like chaff. It must be a car, and it must be now. On the evening before his birthday I had telephoned Chinnor, hoping to speak to him and invite him out for the evening to talk over the whole matter (in other words, stall for time), but as usual I got Heather.

'All right, I'll tell him when he comes in, but what d'you want him for?'

'I want to talk to him.'

'Well, I didn't suppose you wanted to sit there in silence and wave your antennae at him in silence like a stag beetle, but what d'you want to talk to him about, if I'm allowed to know?'

'He's bound to start demanding a car of his own now that he's legal to drive, and I just wanted to prepare the ground for whatever he's going to spring on us.'

'He's not quite legal yet, you know. He's going to get his provisional licence tomorrow, and he's already fixed up with a local driving school to have three lessons – to get him ready for the test.'

'Why only three?'

'He's so confident he's bound to get through that he thinks they could only fail him on technicalities to do with the test itself. Not giving the answers to their questions in the form they expect. Not going through all the motions in exactly the orthodox way. He's perfectly sure he's a better driver than the instructor's likely to be, when it comes to just driving.'

'He's probably not far wrong. Brian's taught him a lot.'

'Yes, I know all about that. I didn't think they'd take him on for just three lessons, they must prefer people to take the full course, but it seems the chap who runs the school is a friend of his.'

'Wouldn't you know?'

'Yes, wouldn't you? Anything to do with cars. When d'you think he'll grow out of it?'

'Well, not at seventeen. That's why I think I ought to see him.'

Heather now moved on to the attack. I'd been wondering when she would. 'Before you get together and start forming schemes and not telling me about them till they're all set up, let me suggest the obvious common-sense thing to do.'

'Oh, yes, I'd welcome that.' I hoped she would not take my remark as sarcasm though the spirit in which I uttered it was sarcastic. My hope was that she would think it only right and natural for me to agree with any idea, however crackpot, that seemed to her 'obvious' and 'common-sense'. This hope, based as it was on a sound know-ledge of Heather's character, proved entirely justified.

'You know I need a new car. I can't go on running around in this antique for ever and ever. It's ages old and it's dropping to bits.'

This was true enough. Our car, a just pre-war Wolseley saloon, was obviously preparing for the severing of soul from body.

'So the obvious thing to do is to buy me a new one and Mike can have the old one.'

'I don't follow,' I said. 'Why is that the obvious thing?'

'Because I need the car for serious business. He can get by with an old one for messing about in. And he enjoys tinkering; he'll fix it up.'

'Got it all worked out, haven't you?'

'Course I have. I've got to get things worked out. I have to look after myself, there's no one to do it for me.' Dig, dig.

'Heather, our divorce is grinding towards the law courts and when the lawyers have finished with me, you'll get a settlement out of which you'll be able to afford a showroom full of new cars and thirty years' supply of petrol. That's how much looking after yourself you'll have to do.'

'Right, that's settled, then. I'll tell Michael.'

'You'll tell him what?'

'That he can have the old car as soon as I take delivery of the new one you're going to contribute.'

'Tell him what you like, only add at the same time that I want him to ring me and fix a time when he can get over and see me and I'll tell him what's *really* going to happen.'

'What is really going to happen?' she demanded.

'I'll discuss it with Michael,' I said, 'and let you know.' After that, I hung up and left the telephone off the hook. I just couldn't face her squawking at me down the line. If I was going to be thought of as a bastard, I would behave like a bastard, which at least would simplify my life. My advice to anyone who owned Heather's present car would be to get rid of it before the day came when the supply of cars finally caught up with demand and the seller's market vanished. Since I was technically the owner of it, I intended to take my own advice and peddle it as soon as possible. That, in turn, would involve me in buying two cars, one for Heather and one for Michael. All right, I would buy two cars. But not new ones.

Further, since the whole underlying object was to spend more time with Michael, to get to know him better, to share objectives with him, I would bring him in on the whole business of acquiring both cars. We would go round to second-hand car depots, look at job lots, at rows of rusting heaps. We would answer small ads., explore scrapyards. What was more, I decided, I would remain the nominal owner of the car I bought for him. It would be a car for him, but if it were my actual property I could occasionally commandeer it and keep it at Episcopus for a while. If I played my cards right I could have quite a presence in my son's life. Gone would be the days when I would pathetically suggest that he should come over to Episcopus and visit me, for the sake of keeping up our relationship. Our relationship, immensely important to me, was to him not altogether without importance, but it had to take its place well down a long queue. By having such a powerful card as a motor-car, and playing it skilfully, I could arrange to jump a good few places in that queue; though I didn't, of course, try to deceive myself into thinking that I was going to finish up ahead of the lovely Sophy.

All this I passed in review as I sat by my gas fire that night, after Harry and Geraldine had gone on their way. The Michael-and-car programme was under way and, so far, proceeding reasonably well. The Heather part of it was already accomplished, in the months since that telephone conversation we had found Milady a meat-and-potatoes saloon car, considerably younger than the one she was giving up, and after the statutory routine grumbling she had accepted it. Michael's needs were proving more difficult to meet. Our procedure was that he explored a wide area of countryside by bicycle, taking in towns like Thame and Wallingford and Witney, frequently patrolling Cowley and East Oxford, and when he found promising material, first preparing the price by haggling with the vendor and then, if the purchase still seemed to him worth making, telephoning to set up an excursion with me. Long, dragging bus journeys followed; or, in the case of the occasional car that Michael regarded as a snip, madly impulsive and extravagant dashes by taxi.

We hadn't bought a car yet, but we had spent a good many hours together, sharing the excitement of the chase, united in hope, anticipation, sometimes leaden disappointment, but, always, shared experience. The motor-car, which had already revealed itself as the great changing and displacing force of the twentieth century, had already shown its power in my life before that century had reached its mid-point; and now, as the second half of the century began, it seemed (if I could trust what the signs appeared, on the surface, to be saying) to be giving me back the son I had been so afraid of losing.

*

This had been the pattern of life, then, for me and for Michael. Because this sensation of a shared quest had been attractive to me, I had let it drag on. I felt ashamed, now, when I thought how long. The next opportunity, I decided, must be grasped. Michael must have a car. We would get one *soon*; it was urgent now.

And that, I thought as I turned off the gas and got ready to go to bed, was pretty much as it should be. Most father-and-son relationships turn out to be failures; partial failures, at best, total failures at worst. Perhaps this one would be a success.

★

On the morning of our farewell excursion from Rewley Road, which dawned clear and tranquil, I was down at the L.M.S station a few minutes ahead of Garrity, so I bought two return tickets to Islip and passed the time looking at the engine, which stood quietly hissing and snorting to itself while its three coaches filled up. It was a saddle-tank engine. I looked at it with uninformed interest, wishing, as I so frequently found myself doing, that I knew more about what I was looking at. At that date, steam engines were still common on all British Rail routes, but the death sentence had been pronounced on them from on high. The great beasts volleyed and thundered along gallantly, but it was impossible not to feel the emanations of a certain dignified pathos coming from them, like elephants on their way to a secret graveyard. It was the perfect example of the way the perceiving eye modifies the object. It sent me back to the day in . . . when was it? 1936? When Nussbaum had asked me whether I would still find the Oxford college buildings beautiful if the day came when the Nazi Party was running the University.

From my position on the platform I saw Garrity enter the booking hall, look round for me, go towards the ticket window and begin getting out his money. I hurried to intercept him, told him I already had his ticket, and overbore his protests at being paid for.

'If you object to my standing you a cheap railway ticket,' I said, 'you can buy me a pint of beer when we get to a pub and settle it that way.'

Settling into our seats, we soon felt the train smoothly begin to pull away from the platform and out across the space beside the canal that we knew was already earmarked as a car-park. Looking out pensively, we said our farewells silently, not unduly dramatizing the small event, though we both felt the passing of something from our lives. It wasn't an historical moment big enough to need words; we were commemorating it already, by being here, by making this journey together. We spoke, when at all, of indifferent topics. Even of them there wasn't time to say much, for the journey to Islip took hardly ten minutes. And yet, looking back, I realize that I must have been preoccupied, perhaps thinking deeply at a level just below consciousness, because I scarcely looked attentively at Garrity until we had left the train, watched it pull away, and were standing by ourselves on the platform at Islip station.

I now, however, took him in, savouring his Garritism. In honour of our excursion, he was at his most Wordsworthian. I had often fancied that his manner and bearing had something in common with those of the great visionary of rock and cloud, mountain and lake. But today he could almost have been on his way to a fancy-dress party at which he was to represent the poet in his habit as he lived. Evidently determined not to be surprised by any sudden rainstorm, he was wearing one of those water-resistant hats that project fore and aft, with a hinge in the middle allowing them to be folded in two and thrust into a pocket when not needed on the head. In place of the faded khaki shorts he generally wore for walking, he had donned a pair of breeches that gave him something of an early nineteenth-century look, perfectly in keeping with the historical period of Wordsworth's greatest flowering, and in his hand was a stout ash stick, handy for scrambling over stone walls or beating off aggressive rams, though what use he intended to put it to in the tranquil, not to say somnolent, landscape of Otmoor was not apparent. The usual stout brogues protected his feet. Clearly we were in for not just a sentimental train ride but a serious walk.

'We've got three hours before the train comes back,' he explained as we walked into Islip village, 'and I thought the best use of that time would be to make a gentle circuit. Just along to Noke, then by field path to Water Eaton, on to Wood Eaton, and back here either by retracing our steps for the last bit from Noke or going along the main road at the top of the ridge, if the traffic isn't so heavy as to make it disagreeable. That's a very short distance, but it gives us time to linger over anything interesting or just to sit and admire the view.' He tapped his capacious side pockets and added, 'I have a little refreshment with me – as usual.' I remembered the small dark brown hock bottles, containing his invariable College Ale, which he had been carrying at our first meeting.

I raised no objection; Garrity with his intimate knowledge of every lane, every field path, every grassy knoll in Oxfordshire, was a man to trust on a walk. I had confidence in all his decisions, beginning with his advice that, in case the flatness of Otmoor should prove oppressive before we had finished, we ought to begin by walking straight up the hill out of Islip and standing on the brow where we could enjoy a wide sweep of landscape. So that was where we began, and a wonderful sweep it was, with Brill on its Buckinghamshire hill straight ahead of us across the level moorland, the spectacular church tower of Charlton-on-Otmoor over to our left and the village of

Beckley to the right. The sunlight was soft and clear, only the far distances melting into haze, the colours gentle and as perfectly harmonious as if they had been blended and placed by some great artist – as indeed they had; her name was Nature. I stood beside Garrity, perfectly happy in the present moment, happy in the beauty of a rural England that I had grown up with and come to love more and more as I grew. Not being gifted with prophetic foresight, I had not known, back in the early fifties, what was soon to be the fate of that landscape when the planners and developers and road-builders had destroyed about half of it and intensive agri-business got at the rest. I just accepted it, and marvelled, and gave thanks without knowing that I was giving thanks.

Down the hill we came, along the hillside to Noke, a mere cluster of stone-built thatched cottages with a delightful medieval church; nothing would do but that Garrity must go into this church to see the Jacobean pulpit with the hour-glass stand meaningfully placed beside it. 'I always think the University should long ago have adopted something similar,' he remarked. 'With the decline of Church authority in our time, we're in no danger from vicars who go on attempting to safeguard the souls of their parishioners for more than sixty minutes at a time. Twenty minutes would be reckoned a long sermon nowadays. But within Academe, loquacity has far more permission to cause misery. Many's the time I've turned up for what I expected would be a sixty-minute lecture and found when I was firmly wedged into my seat in the middle of the row, beyond all hope of rescue, that the lecturer was one of your ninety-minuters. They can't get away with it in ordinary Faculty lectures, of course, because there's always another lecturer, and another audience, waiting to use the space. But once you're into the piratical waters of the special lecture that begins at five and is supposed to end at six . . .' He sank into a mournful silence, fumbling in his pocket for his pipe. Understanding that he felt a need to light it, I led the way out into the open air. Immediately Garrity produced his quaint antique lighter, which by rights ought to have found a place in a museum of wartime memorabilia, whacked it into sending skywards a tall flame, sucked the flame violently into the charred bowl of his pipe, and was free to become articulate again. He told me, between gusts of laughter, an anecdote of one of his colleagues in the English Faculty.

'He hated lecturing, disapproved of it, thought it a medieval survival, a waste of time now that printing had been invented and people could get their information from books. It's a point of view, though not one I agree with. He chafed at being compelled to give a statutory number of lectures per year. So –'suck, suck, his head disappearing into that blue cloud, myself standing back so as not to be asphyxiated – 'he planned his strategy carefully, building it round the regulation that says lecturers are allowed to cancel the lecture if the audience does not rise above two. He decided he could easily shake his audience down to nought, and then all he had to do was to turn up every week, push the door open and look round, confirm that all the seats were empty, and then march off with some free time at his disposal and a small victory over the system to his credit.'

Garrity paused as we stood there in Noke churchyard, his fuming crater of a pipe in his hand, the September sun dramatizing his craggy Wordsworthian features, now suffused by incipient laughter.

'But –' puff, puff, wheeze – 'he had reckoned without the malevolence of certain of his colleagues. Whether they were devotees of the lecture *per se*, loyal to the idea that academic teachers have to give lectures, as in some respects I am myself,' puff, giant puff, 'or,' from cloud centre, 'whether they were activated solely by irritation at his taking the law into his own hands, I don't feel myself in a position to say. But for whatever reason,' he lowered the pipe and pointed the stem at me, as if taking aim, 'they hit on an effective strategy.'

'Tell me what it was, for God's sake, or I'll break a blood vessel.'

'They bribed two undergraduates,' he said, 'with a modest sum that varies from one account to another in a way familiar to folk-lorists but not in the least threatening to the probability of the story; they bribed them, I say,' immense puff, puff, puff, 'to attend the whole series of lectures, every week for the entire term. Week by week he pushed open the door, and week by week these two students were there, the irreducible minimum, the minority that enforced a lecture, earning their bribe. He had, you must understand, proceeded in the most careful fashion. He had announced the most uninteresting subject he could think of, he had given his first couple of lectures in a dry, perfunctory manner that must have been excruciatingly boring to sit through, and it had not worked. Everyone else gave up, but those two students were there week after week. The luckless man gave his full complement of lectures that term.'

True to his somewhat disconcerting habit, as soon as he had finished his anecdote Garrity resumed our purposeful walk with none of those preliminary well-we-must-be-off signs that are usual. Barely had he uttered the last sentence and the last bark of laughter, which as always he did with hands straight down by his sides and fingers moving in an almost convulsive to-and-fro jerk, than he was off, straight into his long loping stride, expecting me to be at his side and keeping pace with him. This was so obviously a habit born of long years of solitary walks that one never felt any trace in him of discourtesy. The habit of allowing for the presence of someone else had simply not developed in Garrity. He was a solitary, and a solitary cannot change his habits overnight, glad though he always was of company and full of interest in the friend whose company he had. He listened carefully to everything I said and gave me considered answers; he brought up matters I had raised in previous conversations, proving that he had remembered and pondered them. Only in his small, unexpected mannerisms did he behave as if solitude had made him impervious to other personalities.

His lean, muscular legs, forging on at an unhesitating pace and poled forward over any patches of soft or uneven ground by that stout ash staff, covered the distance in a surprisingly short time when measured against my usual walking habits. Following a tracery of paths beside hedgerows and skirting deep irrigation ditches, paths whose existence I had never suspected, he got us very soon to Wood Eaton with its large, quiet stone houses, its ancient cross on the green, its farm buildings and patches of woodland. Here I requested a stop. I never went past that little Early English church on the edge of the village without going inside, even briefly. It pulled me too strongly; it had too much character, too much history, to walk past unheedingly as if it were a grain store. Garrity assented willingly, and followed behind as I entered the church porch and pushed open the door.

We stood for a moment letting our eyes grow used to the dimmer light. I already knew from many visits what to look for in particular – the unusual architecture of the spire, standing on stone piers in the interior of the building, the sturdy barn-like beams of the roof, the pure eighteenth-century flavour of the handsome pulpit and the squire's pew closed off for privacy within its high wooden ramparts, the musicians' gallery at the opposite end, and in particular the wall-painting that faced the door. As my eyes adapted, I stood confronting this painting: large, flamboyant, reassuring; St Christopher bearing the infant Christ across the flooded field. Immensely protective, the saint stood directly opposite the entrance, challenging your view as soon as you stepped inside, and out of his mouth came a large scroll bearing his (literally) unreal but (physically) strengthening message, an encouragement to travellers who might face unknown dangers in their way. He had stood there with that message for a thousand years. *Ki cest image verra le jur de male mort ne murra*, it said in what I took to be Norman French. 'He who shall look upon this image shall not today die an evil death.'

I turned to make some remark to Garrity, who had put on his glasses and was staring attentively now at the painting, now at the building in general, but as I did so I saw that we were not alone in the church. Someone else was sitting in one of the rear pews, right back underneath the gallery: a grey-haired, straight-backed figure; face, aquiline and of severe cut; familiar, identifiable: yes! It was Otto Nussbaum. Here? In Wood Eaton Church?

I drew in breath to utter his name as I moved towards him, but Garrity's voice sounded before mine. 'Nussbaum!' he breathed. 'Distinguished company indeed!'

Any surprise I felt at the recognition soon died away. Of course Garrity would know Nussbaum. The first-rate seek out the first-rate; the profound gravitate to the profound. Besides, there were adventitious reasons. Garrity had spent periods of time in Oxford during the darkest years of the war, when the huddled minority of German expatriates, hungry for their own language, their own art, their own culture and history, had clung together and welcomed such friendship as they were offered. Garrity had come among them like the evangel of a scarcely imaginable rebirth – an Englishman with a passion for German lyric poetry and a love of the land of Germany, her mountains and forests and lakes, who could almost have found his way blindfold about some of her beautiful medieval towns. In that setting he had become a friend of Nussbaum's, indeed of the quasi-mythical Katzannussbaum, now existing only in the realm of memory.

We came out of the church and, in a silence broken only by trivial remarks, moved a few yards up the road and on to the village green where stood an ancient stone cross. Here, Nussbaum halted and, seeming to have made a decision to explain himself, turned and addressed us. Garrity and I halted in our leisurely pace. We could see from the concentration and seriousness of Nussbaum's face that an utterance was coming.

'Perhaps you wondered what I was doing,' Nussbaum said, 'loitering alone in that church contemplating the image of a Christian saint.'

He seemed to expect some kind of answer so I said, to drown the silence, 'You or any man has a right to sit and think in an English country church, or any church for that matter – and the image was put there to be contemplated.'

'I used often to go into that church in the nineteen-forties,' Nussbaum said quietly. His face, with the mellow sunlight full on it, suddenly seemed to me old, ravaged and unalterably gentle. In the same instant I also saw for the first time a resemblance between Nussbaum's face and Albert Einstein's. 'The *early* forties.' Garrity nodded. I had no need to nod; we both understood what he meant.

'There was no news out of Germany,' Nussbaum said. 'At least, such information as reached England would be gathered by Intelligence and obviously was not available to the public at large. In any case it would not concern private individuals. One's friends, one's family – there were no means of sending or receiving messages, of having any contact with them, of knowing whether they were alive or dead. Since all my family, and many of my friends, were Jews, it was obviously rational to hope that they were dead, safe for ever from the attentions of the killers and torturers. But humanity is profoundly irrational. It would not have been human for me not to hope, in some corner of my being, that the people I loved were still living somewhere, somehow, and that one day I would see them again.'

Garrity was standing as immobile as a figure on a tapestry, stiff in brocade, his eyes trained immovably on Nussbaum's face. I knew that he was taking in every syllable of Nussbaum's discourse, missing nothing. The sheer depth of his sympathy caused him to concentrate fiercely; there had been moments when he had been close to the horror of that *régime*. He stood on the grass beside the weather-beaten cross, his living body as motionless as the stone.

Nussbaum's eyes were distant as he went on. 'I awoke each morning with my mind heavy with grief and fear. In my sleep I always saw their faces so clearly – the faces of people who had for so long been close to me, family for the most part. I saw them all, aged women, my grandmother and one or two equally old great-aunts, and I saw some of my father's brothers – he was dead, thank God! – and . . . and,' his voice, normally deep and resonant, became almost inaudible, 'I saw children. My favourite niece, my sister's daughter, had a pleasant young husband and two enchanting little girls, but I knew they would not enchant the butchers who were sent to look for them.'

We stood in silence, a group of three human figures on a village green, lit by sunshine, united in sadness.

'Usually, I got up and went to work,' Nussbaum said. 'I walked along Walton Street and turned in at that imposing classical archway and went up to my small room at the Press. Small, cluttered, cramped, but to me beautiful. It was safe; it was in an unconquered country. My room was reached by many stairs, but I knew that I would never hear the feet of storm-troopers stamping up those stairs.'

No, I thought. You would have used your revolver by then. Your Smith and Wesson.

'But sometimes it would happen that my agony was too sharp, too urgent, to allow of my settling down to any of my routine tasks. And then, I had a contingency plan. I did not take to it readily, I tried always to avoid giving way to a mere mood that would pass after an hour or two. But there were days when I knew that the grief, the need, the anguish, would not pass, the days that followed those particularly cruel nights of shallow sleep and dreams so vivid that even after coming fully awake I still took them for reality. In those dreams, the faces I saw seemed always to be trying to speak to me. I could never hear their actual words, but always I could hear the tone of their voices, and it was always a tone that pierced the very soul within me. They were crying for help, or, if they had ceased to believe in the possibility of help, they were saying goodbye to me, sending me their farewells in voices in which love and sadness were inextricably blended. And on those days, I did not go to work.'

He paused for so long that I finally assumed he had finished what he was going to say. To wrap it up for him, to permit the day to continue, I said quietly, 'On those days you came out here.'

My words seemed to jog Nussbaum into renewed speech. He resumed almost like a malfunctioning radio which has received a sharp tap in the strategic place.

'On those days I came out into the countryside. I had a need for quiet, and solitude, and moving my limbs helped to quell, or at least to disguise, the restlessness inside me. And I needed to see things growing, according to their season, to make me feel that the life of Nature was still going on, whatever might be happening to my human generation. At first I went to a variety of places. I would go down to Gloucester Green and take a bus just anywhere – the first bus going out of the city. But it was wartime, and the buses were few and irregular, and sometimes in winter I would be wandering the country lanes after nightfall. A man with a German accent, looming up out of the darkness, was not always welcome in those years. So I came to rely on the ordinary town service to take me as far as Marston, where it ended. The bus turned round and went back into Oxford and I walked out into the country. As you see –' he gestured around – 'here we are in a place totally simple and rural, yet very near the edge of the town. So this became my usual rescuing walk. I used it to rescue myself from despair and unendurable agony.'

Garrity asked, really wanting to know, 'And did it work?'

'At first, well enough. But never quite completely. There was always a hint of something missing. Without knowing it precisely, I dimly suspected that what I needed was a symbol, something tangible that would act as a node for my thoughts whether of fear or desperate hope or just simply of resilience, the ability to go on in spite of everything. Then one day I entered this village from the direction of the Marston road. The little medieval church attracted my attention, though I do not much frequent the shrines of Christianity, which has shown so little mercy to my people and was at that time largely standing aside and leaving them to their fate. But I had no such thoughts at that moment. The modest building standing amid its fringe of trees seemed to invite me. I pushed open the door, and there facing me stood St Christopher, with his old French message: 'Whoever beholds this image shall not today meet with a bad end.' It seemed to speak to me across the silent space of that interior. I was engulfed by a passionate longing that those words might somehow be true, and that they might radiate somehow through me and out to all the unknown places where my loved ones were on that morning. Were any of them, I wondered, still in the place where I had last seen them, in what had been their accustomed home? I knew that was unlikely. Even the old women would have been taken away, for that was not a system that spared anyone on the grounds of age or gender. The children, too, would inevitably be gone. But I stood there and contemplated the message. 'Whoso looks on me will not die violently today.' I suppose the plain fact is that I was going insane. My mind was losing grip. Nevertheless, for whatever reason, the message lettered on that wall by some long-dead Christian artist suddenly came to me not as a fact only but as a message – of what? Affirmation? Hope? The offer of some kind of help, of human comradeship in that black night of hatred? I stood for a long time, looking at it. Of course what I was doing was praying, not consciously, not with volition. I felt that some strength pulsed through me from those painted words in this quiet place and that somewhere, in some dimension, it might pulse out to the people I loved but could not reach.'

He ended. His words left my mind full of questions, but I knew I would never utter them. Most of all I would have liked to ask, had the saint's magic worked for any of Nussbaum's family or friends? Or had it been healing and saving just for him, enabling him to keep some hold on his sanity? I knew that popular imagination had accepted, five hundred years ago, that to look at a picture of St Christopher kept one safe for the rest of the day and that that was the reason why paintings of him in churches tended to be, as this one was, immediately visible from the door so that travellers, whose patron saint he naturally became, could see his image without taking time to search. Had any of Nussbaum's people survived until the moment when Adolf Hitler shot himself in his bunker and lifted the curse of Nazism from the world? If it could be shown that they had, the legend of St Christopher might root itself in a corner of my imagination; not in my belief, not in my intellectual assent, but after all to imagine something is to believe it a little.

I never did know the answer to that very natural question. It was for Nussbaum to tell me if he chose to, and if he did not choose then the veil of an inviolable grief must always remain in place. Garrity, obviously, felt the same. Our thoughts and our talk turned to other matters. Garrity explained why we were out in the country on that particular day. Nussbaum had not heard of the closure of the Rewley Road station and said that instead of walking back into Marston and waiting for a bus he would come back with us, since he too had been fond of the old station and would like to use it once more. He could get a ticket at Islip.

So it came about that I was in a railway carriage with Garrity and Nussbaum on that gentle September late afternoon and that all our minds, just below the surface, were occupied with thoughts of tragedy, of exile, of persecution, however our talk on the surface seemed to distance these things. For this reason, or perhaps some other reason, it did not surprise me when, as the train slid in through the last mile or so of our journey, Garrity suddenly introduced the subject of the Nuremberg trials, which were much referred to at that time, having recently reached their conclusions after long-drawn-out, agonizing investigation of the appalling data. He asked Nussbaum whether the trials, with their inevitably clumsy but perhaps justifiable effort to bring to the bar of international justice the perpetrators of unspeakable cruelties, had made any difference to him personally.

Nussbaum was silent for a moment and then said, 'As things are, no.'

'As things are . . . ?'

'If the Nürnberg trials, and the sentences imposed, had really left the world a cleaner place by purging it of a significant number of bullies and fiends and inhuman robots, I think it would have rejoiced my heart to some extent even though it could not restore to life those that I loved most. It would have seemed to me that justice had been done, and that can never be a bad thing.'

'But you don't feel,' I said, 'that justice has been done?'

The train was slowing now. My last run into the old L.M.S. station was nearly over.

'Justice?' Nussbaum said. 'To the east of the River Elbe there exists a reign of terror as hideous as anything carried on by the Nazis, and extending over a far greater territory, from the Black Sea to the Arctic, from Central Europe to the Pacific. Not only is that reign still in place, it is enormously strengthened by events since 1940. In its soundproof cells and its remote punishment camps, cruelties are enacted that need fear no comparison with the most sophisticated methods of the Nazis. And in total security, guarded by vast armed forces and justified by a world-wide propaganda machine. Its commanders, its torturers and executioners, are all of the same black dye as those of Nazi Germany. Their propaganda is as stuffed with lies and cynicism. Their aims are just as ruthless and expansionist. Their appeasers and lackeys are just as fawning and cowardly. But there will never be a Nürnberg for the men in the Kremlin. The concentration camps in the Arctic ice-fields will never have their gates burst open by an invading army. This time the enemy of the human race is too strong and too well entrenched. And what remains of the free world is too weakened and too lacking in confidence to carry through an effort like the one it has just completed. On the contrary, country after country is vanishing into that tangled thicket of misery.'

'The free world still exists, you know,' I said, trying to sound confident but aware of not feeling it much. 'And it's beginning to see the wisdom of arming itself and being watchful. NATO . . .' My voice trailed off under Nussbaum's gaze.

'NATO is a useful defensive step,' Nussbaum said. 'But NATO by itself will never produce a Nürnburg. It will never even have the power to silence the Fifth Column these monsters have established in our midst, the creatures who send up an obedient round of applause every time some new country disappears into the Communist game-bag.'

'You see them as a Fifth Column?' Garrity asked. 'You don't accept it simply as a difference of opinion?'

'I see it as a Fifth Column,' Nussbaum said. 'These people, unless they are mentally diseased, cannot actually wish to live under a regime that would deny them any glimmer of freedom and dignity, where they would openly be treated as faceless serfs, fit only to breed, work and fight. That is not civilization. That is not humanity. I concede that many of them belong to a type that is quite content to see other people treated in that way, as long as they emerge with a safe position and privileges for themselves. Most Fifth Columns are made up of that type. They hope for an enemy victory because they hope to profit by it. That is not a difference of political opinion. It is betrayal, *simpliciter*.'

'So it's your opinion,' I said, 'that the world will never see another Nürnberg?'

Nussbaum shook his head. In the changing light that came in through the windows as we moved across the quiet fields, I suddenly saw that his face resembled that of a tragic sculpture by Jacob Epstein.

'Nürnberg was a brave attempt to demonstrate that international standards of humanity and justice do exist and can be enforced. It was good to see it, I grant you. But there will be no successors. Nürnberg was the end of that line.'

A few minutes went by, during which none of us spoke, and then our little tank engine pulled up at the platform of Rewley Road station, and once more stood peacefully hissing to itself. We descended, and took our leave first of the graceful white-painted wooden building, then, thoughtfully, of one another.

*

It had become something of a habit, on a Sunday morning, for Cynthia and myself to drive out into the country. She had a little

–173–

buzzing Continental car, and I would take my place beside her as she drove out into the alluring perspectives of Oxfordshire and Berkshire, making for some delectable pub like the Bull and Butcher at Finstock or the Sparrow at Letcombe Regis, where we would drink beer and eat whatever was going, after which I would accompany her back to her flat for some more of whatever was going. They were easy, carefree days, especially once I had accustomed myself to the fact that, during such part of the voyage of life as we were destined to make together, Cynthia was on the bridge and I was, at best, First Officer; or more accurately, perhaps, Chief Engineer, working mainly below decks. I used to steal admiring glances at her as she sat Minerva-like behind the wheel, bolt upright and imperious, her helmet of orange hair gleaming in the morning sun as her impatient glances willed other drivers to swerve into the roadside ditches.

On the Sunday that followed the Otmoor excursion, Cynthia and I had a date to spend the day in our usual fashion. Mostly she drove over to Episcopus and picked me up, and then we set out for an excursion. Today, however, she had told me that she wanted to finish some work left over from the week and wouldn't be ready to set out till eleven; so, as I had nothing to do for once and the weather was soft and fine, I decided to walk to Headington and join her there.

It was pleasant enough; I simply left Episcopus at the far end of the garden, crossed over Parks Road, went down to enter the Parks at the point where the Cherwell divides into two channels and walked along the causeway between them known for a century or so as Mesopotamia (in that Victorian university slang that never tried to break free of the Classics). From there I left the Parks at the bottom of Headington Hill and climbed up past the site of Joe Pullen's Oak. Cynthia lived in a large house that had been divided into flats, somewhere near the crossroads where you turned left off the main road to go to Old Headington. It amused me, as I drew nearer, to realize that I was passing very close to that horrible Holyoake Hall where I had, in my first year (or was it even in my first term? – so impetuously had my burning needs hurried me along) taken Vinnie to an evening's dancing. Phew! Overall, seen in its entirety, the evening had been simply one more in that succession of humiliations and frustrations known as my adolescence – had remained in that category, at any rate, until Vinnie's surprising gesture of encouragement and incitement when, in the taxi going home, within a minute of our journey's end and leave-taking, she had suddenly brushed her hand over my fly – a fleeting, seemingly casual movement, but in fact, as she and I both knew, calculated with fiendish intent to rouse the murderous energies that slumbered so lightly within that frail enclosure. Immediately I became totally insane with desire, but – and this well illustrated her cat-like cruelty – within thirty seconds, as she well knew, the taxi began to slow and the driver to bark questions over his shoulder about where exactly to stop. I became involved in giving directions, counting out money, paying the man off and wondering how much would be a correct tip – which, young as I was and coming from the background I came from, I was doing for probably the first time in my life.

Approaching Cynthia's building I thought briefly but intensely of Vinnie, whom I had not seen for years apart from that one glimpse behind the counter of a tea-stall on Port Meadow the day before the war broke out. I thought of her soft, shining brown hair that she wore with a neat fringe at her forehead. It was straight and had reddish lights in it. Perhaps it had been her best single feature. But then her whole being, the entire impression she gave, was in itself a good feature: her slender agile body, pale intent face which became more intent as her erotic pleasure increased, till at the moment of final spasm it relaxed into blankness and became completely expressionless.

Vinnie in those days, Cynthia in these – the two women with whom I had sought a relationship that was sexual and nothing else, and had been met with an exactly matching need on their part. Had they, I wondered, anything in common, beneath their obvious differences? And the answer came at once: yes, much. Particularly I remembered, halting for a moment on the pavement and looking over towards Holyoake Hall, the expression of utterly dedicated, selfish pleasure that used to take possession of Vinnie's face when she threw away all restraint and really let her sexual impulse power her. That pleasure involved another person and the awareness of another person, but it was selfish, essentially, totally, relentlessly. Years were to go by before I met that expression again, until, with a curious blend of surprise, shock and relief, I recognized it on the face of Cynthia.

Temporarily banishing such thoughts, I greeted her on this Sunday morning with cheerful matter-of-factness. 'Have you,' I asked her, 'ever been to the Maharajah's Well in South Stoke?'

'No, is it a pub?'

'You bet it is, the most traditional one you could imagine. There's no bar. You just go into a room with a flag floor, like a farmhouse kitchen, and the landlord goes down into the cellar and fetches up your pint of beer straight from the barrel.'

'Does that make the beer taste better?'

'Well, I always think it does. Come on, get in and we'll go for a run in my dream country, where the beer comes straight out of barrels.'

We had hardly reached our destination, though, and gone into the attractive old inn, before I became aware that something in Cynthia was not responding to the occasion as I had hoped. You couldn't exactly say of her at the best of times that her heart was on her sleeve, but what I felt now was a reserve that seemed steadily to be growing cooler and more impenetrable. To make conversation, I began discussing a film we had seen during the week and had not had an opportunity to look back on since. In it, an actress had movingly conveyed the heartbreak of a girl callously abandoned by her lover. I found much to praise in her interpretation of the role; Cynthia firmly, and laconically, disagreed.

'I get sick of all these films and plays about women being left by men and making such an emotional meal of it,' she said dismissively. 'Why go into these things if you're not going to be able to handle them?'

'Well . . . One doesn't always foresee—'

'A woman who takes a man on as a way of enjoying herself, ought to realize that there's also its own kind of enjoyment to be got out of kicking him off.'

'Oh.' What was she telling me? Or rather . . . Wasn't it pretty obvious what she was telling me?

'I know at points in my life when I've decided to get rid of a man, I've always approached it in a positive spirit. I've held my head high.'

'I've never seen you hold your head any other way than high.'

'No, and I hope you never will. I don't think one ought to whinge. Having fun with men is a matter of sometimes getting hurt, but you don't show it and you forget it as soon as you can. The girl in the film didn't do that.'

'No. She was representing a character who wouldn't have found that a natural thing to do – a character who would have found it not only natural but right, in a way, to express grief at being betrayed by the man.'

'That's what I call whingeing. If she doesn't like the heat she ought to get out of the kitchen.'

We didn't stay long at the Maharajah's Well. As I drove Cynthia back to Headington I didn't feel confident of being invited in when we got to her flat. But I had one more surprise to come. She not only invited me in, she swept me into bed and put on the performance of a lifetime. Not since my youthful ecstasies with Vinnie had I hit such high jagged peaks. And yet . . . 'performance', after all, is the right word for what she was doing. There seemed to be, at the core of all her forthcomingness, something held aloof, something objectively apart and observing, calculating the effect on me rather than participating. It fitted my idea of how prostitutes must serve their clients. It so happens that in all my life I have never used the services of a prostitute, less from fine moral scruples than from a conviction that they must all, sooner or later, become carriers of disease. But when I have idly imagined how they must proceed (and I mean high-class ones, not assembly-line scrubbers), I have thought of them much as I found Cynthia that Sunday afternoon.

Be all that as it may, she found me plenty of work and I was glad to measure up to my responsibilities like a man. And when I got back to Episcopus – in time to have a long, restful bath in which I twice fell asleep, awaking only when I began to draw in water through my mouth and nose, before listlessly climbing into the obligatory Sunday night dinner-jacket and going in to dinner – I was entirely certain that the episode of Cynthia was closed.

A couple of days later I received from her an unceremonious but not unfriendly note, telling me that she was accepting a research post that would take her for a couple of years to Vancouver or some-where, and saying she didn't think it would be worth our while to try to keep up. I wrote back agreeing with her, and sending my best wishes for her research. I might have added, while I was about it, my congratulations on the thoroughness of the research job she had done on me. I certainly had found it an eye-opener.

However, as things turned out I didn't have much time to think about it. My life, which for some years had been very lacking in events, was about to gather momentum and move forward at a surprising pace.

PART THREE

My divorce lawyer, he of the light grey suit and horn-rimmed glasses, had warned me some time in the summer of 1951 that it would soon be time for the last ragged knot to be untied and that I would have to attend court. Divorces took an incredible time in those days. It was part of the generally punitive attitude of society towards them.

I protested at the bit about having to go to court, pointing out that I was not defending my corner at all and was willing to pay anything they ordered me to pay and in every respect to be completely spineless, which was presumably what they wanted of me. (I had just got round to reading *1984*, and when I read the chilling words with which it closes, 'He loved Big Brother', I immediately recognized aspects of my own situation.) But the sallow face behind the horn-rims looked at me across the desk with that same mechanical patience. It wasn't allowed for, the man explained. Appearing in court was something I *had* to do. We both understood, though neither of us said, that the fact of my finding it searingly unpleasant was exactly the reason for its being insisted on. People who broke their marriage vows had to have their noses rubbed in their misbehaviour; the law was going to treat me like a criminal, and on the whole I accepted this. Perhaps my leaving Heather *was* a criminal act. I reflected that many of the things we do without hesitation are criminal if you look at them scrupulously. Certainly many of the things we would *like* to do are criminal.

So I went through with it like a sheep going into the slaughter-house. And my frozen carcase duly came out at the back door, packed up ready for transport. Heather's counsel had looked at me with practised distaste. The judge had looked at me with judicial distaste. Heather had looked at me with icy distaste. In the decision she had been awarded the house, the car, everything we jointly owned, plus alimony of a third of my salary for life or until her death or remarriage, whichever came first. She also got a private health-insurance policy and maintenance for Michael till he was eighteen. After that she got the cost of his higher education till he was twenty-five or graduated. There was a mortgage on the house which I had to pay until it was finished with, another fifteen years. In exchange I had the right to see Michael once a week. If I wanted anything else, I had the impression that they would look round for an old clothes-line I could hang myself with, if I asked them nicely.

I left the courtroom with a wonderfully lightened heart. Money, after all, is only money, and I still had two-thirds of my salary left, which I could manage on even after deducting the mortgage, so long as I lived in College. God bless the college system! I thought. And, as a matter of history, it's worth noticing *en passant* that the college system, at about this time, began to bless the divorce courts. Before 1870, an Oxford don had to be unmarried or he couldn't be a don at all, end of argument. Between 1870 and about 1945, the rules formally permitted matrimony, but it was widely understood that a young man who wanted a career at Oxford would derail that career at the outset if he got married before he was in his later twenties. Colleges had a statutory number of bachelors who were required to live in the actual building, and a married man was out: that was why I had had to keep Heather's existence a secret from everyone at Episcopus for three years – to the detriment, I felt, looking back, of our marriage during the stage when it should have been forming its bones. Increasingly, as the late 1940s moved into the 1950s, young academics would not tolerate that kind of interference in their lives; with the expansion of higher education, and the tremendous upsurge in wealth and prestige of the American universities, a career at Oxbridge no longer seemed so essential to them; and the colleges became more and more stuck for bachelor dons to live within their walls. The system was visibly cracking when, just in time, the institution of marriage began to crack in its turn. I was one of the first, but very soon I was followed by others – first a trickle, then a flood – who found themselves landed with expensive settlements to keep up households of which they could not be a part. Thankfully, they came trooping back into college. The problem disappeared, and stayed disappeared until the floodgates of the 1960s and 1970s opened and all rules and regulations simply danced away like bits of matchwood on the flood-tide. Who cared, once everything had become 'permissive', who lived where and with whom? When a don was the same as anyone else, who cared whether he was in college or out of it?

In the days when my divorce happened, of course, people still did care, and this was not the easiest period of my life. People who didn't like me (Watson *et al*) took full advantage of the many opportunities that came their way to inflict little cutting touches of the lash in places where my skin might be supposed still tender. The trick was not to wince and I became a great non-wincer. I had to be ready for the next flick to come from any direction, at any angle. Watson would, for instance, mention some acquaintance who had formerly owned a house in the country and now no longer did. Then with his eyes resting very lightly on me, 'like certain among us'. One evening when a guest was speaking of the fine open country beyond Watlington, where the bare Chiltern Hills come close to Oxford, one of Watson's allies put in, 'Pretty familiar to you at one time, I believe, Leonard.' It was like one of those testing ceremonies you read about among Red Indian braves, to see if they can get one of their number to show any sign of pain.

At last, about three or four weeks along from the court case, I received news that my marriage to Heather was finally a thing of the past. And the trailing bits of business were completed in their turn. One fine day in early September the morning came when, after reading rapidly through the two or three letters I scooped up from my pigeon-hole in the lodge, I knew it was all over and the way was clear. I went into my bedroom, sat down on the bed and looked at myself in the mirror on the dressing-table. Peter Leonard, free man. Candidate for matrimony. 38 years old. Health, reasonably good. Appearance, not far deteriorated from when younger; face not noticeably thinner or more lined; forehead more creased, lines running from corner of nose to ends of mouth more deeply incised, but not to a disfiguring extent. Own teeth, fairly intact. Hair not thinned, not showing grey; people originally fair-haired soon darken, but don't go grey as soon as the really dark-haired. Expression: watchful; not hostile, but on the other hand not trustful. The face of a *good* person? I pondered that one. Exactly what kind of face is a good person supposed to have?

It was time to act. I was . . . well, not at peak – I wouldn't pick out any period in my life when I could have been called 'at peak' – but at a point from which the only changes would, on the whole, be deteriorations. No more delaying. This was the moment of the decisive swoop upwards. Or, just possibly, of the final nose-dive. On my two earlier, impulsive calls to Mairead, all I had asked of her – all I had had any conceivable right to ask of her – had been patience. The tolerance to put up with my voice on the telephone for a few minutes. She didn't need to come to a final decision, let alone acquaint me with it, because the chips weren't down yet. Now, the chips were down. If there was any reason why she couldn't face joining her life with mine, the only thing she could do now was to tell me of it and send me packing. (But I would have nothing to pack.)

My fingers trembled slightly as I dialled her number. Apart from that I gave a pretty good imitation of someone being calm. I tried to imagine that I was an actor and that the plot of whatever he was appearing in called at this point for him to make a routine telephone call: say, ringing up to order a delivery of tonic water and cheese straws in readiness for a party. He had the drinks all ready, but had forgotten any tonic water for people to have with their gin if they wanted it, and a few cheese straws are always useful at a party. I imagined the audience relaxing after some particularly tense scene that had just happened; this was a breathing-space in the action. Audiences, after all, expend nervous energy as actors do. The drama is dramatic for both of them. I sat and looked unconcerned, keeping still.

The telephone rang on. My performance was so realistic and convincing that I actually felt a wave of quite genuine irritation that the shop was so slow to answer. What kind of way is this, I thought, to run a business? Then I remembered it was not a business. It was Mairead, it was my whole life, and it was her whole life as well if she wanted to have it with me. Did she want to have it with me? Why the hell doesn't she answer? Wrong number perhaps? I rang off and dialled again, obsessionally this time. Then I waited while it rang ten thousand times. *Nishte*. For the first time in five and a half years I had something important to communicate to Mairead, something posit-ive – at least, it was positive if she took the same overall view of our situation as I took (but was that a big 'if'? Was it too big an 'if' to be assumed without further discussion?) – God, would this torment never cease?

Well, one thing was clear: it would never cease until I had a chance of a straight, uninterrupted talk with Mairead. That meant getting her to the telephone. If the explanation was simply that she was not at home, I would have to keep ringing.

She might have been away overnight and gone straight to work from wherever she had spent the night. NO! NOT DOWN THAT PATH! MADNESS IS WAITING THERE! She might have gone to work early. It was a delicate balance; I hadn't wanted to ring too early, in case it irritated her, but then there was the opposite risk of ringing too late and finding her gone. She might have chosen this time to have a holiday. She might be away for some days, for a week. She might be away for a month. The telephone-answering machine had not, in those days, been invented. The only way to get in touch with people who were away was to write to them. But I had no address. That frail telephonic link was all I had.

I kept calm. I stood up from the desk where I had been telephoning and stared out of the window into the little strip of garden. The bird world came to my rescue. The seventeenth-century wall I could see stretching away on my left was covered with a handsome, long-established climbing shrub. After a moment, a pair of tree-creepers, small brown birds no different from hedge-sparrows at a distance, emerged from cover at the bottom of the walk and started their characteristic exploring, searching, fossicking movement, turning over every scrap of cover with their rapid bills in their quest for nourishment. As I watched, they moved upward, searching the tree from branch to branch as is their wont. It was only by their movements that I identified their species. I felt cheered and buoyed up by this sudden totally frank demonstration of the Life Force.

I would keep calm. I would not go to pieces. To go to pieces would be the worst thing of all, the most useless, the most humiliating. It was still vacation, the undergraduates were not yet back, but quite a lot of my colleagues were. Dons who have children at school in the Oxford area tend to be back in Oxford, and usually spending a lot of time in college, any time after the first week in September, from whatever adventurous or sybaritic thing they have been doing since July. If I had to be led away from Pearce's Building by men in white coats, they would all see me, ashen-faced and stumbling, or gibbering and mopping and mowing. Watson would see me. Manciple would see me. The gravely sympathetic ones, the satirical ones, the hard analytical ones, would all see me. I would remain collected. My outward appearance would give away nothing. I would think of the great tradition of the eighteenth-century thinkers who preached, and practised, a bleak but heartening realism. All may yet be well. The tension I was feeling at being unable to speak to Mairead might be that and nothing more – tension caused by waiting and uncertainty. When she returned – and perhaps she wasn't even away, just out – everything might be the best and I might be overwhelmingly happy. But whatever was coming to me, be it joy or agony, I must hang on to my dignity and self-respect. I must remember the example of the great men of the eighteenth century, that period where I liked best to be and whose heroes were my heroes. And I repeated to myself, aloud, the noble words of Bishop Butler in his great work of 1736, *The Analogy of Religion*: 'Things and actions are what they are, and the consequences of them will be what they will be; why then should we desire to be deceived?'

Holding myself together, summoning these heroes to my side, I sat down in my study, looking at the desk and the telephone. It was still early in the day, and a fine unclouded late-summer day it was. Lots of people were still having breakfast and slitting open their letters; they had the whole day in front of them. But I knew that the day I had in front of me was going to be useless for anything that involved concentration. I could pay attention to nothing except the need to talk to Mairead, tell her my news, get her reaction. The fact that the way to her was now at last unblocked, that it had resolved itself into a matter of choice on her part, had suddenly brought her devastatingly close: even physically. It wasn't just that I wanted to fuck her, in fact I hadn't yet dared to wind up to the point of imagining that. If I had thought back even for a second to what it had felt like to get between her legs I would have fainted dead away. Even the degree of physical contact involved in a telephone conversation with her had unsettled me completely. She had spoken, her voice had sent out sound waves, and those sound waves, electrically transmitted, had impacted on my eardrum. That in itself had brought her beauty, her gazelle-like poise in sitting and standing, her weightless grace and precision as she moved about, straight to my nervous system. It had even made me remember the smoothness of her skin, even the fleshy sensual feel of her ear-lobes . . . I knew I would go insane if I sat there imagining Mairead, all day today, and not only that but all day tomorrow till seven-fifteen in the evening. No, no. It was not to be thought of. I stood up. I had no engagements that day, and even if I had had any I would have paused no longer than it took to cancel them hurriedly. I went out of the room like a charging bull.

Fortunately the weather showed no sign of turning wet, because if the sky had been full of rain-heavy clouds I would not have had the presence of mind to pause and collect a raincoat. I simply galumphed out. I strode recklessly across St Giles's Street, along Walton Street and down to the Thames. Turning upstream, I walked along the towpath, with the wooded hill of Wytham rearing up on my left hand. At Eynsham I left the towpath and took to the road, passing through Stanton Harcourt. I would have rested there to drink beer and contemplate the tower in which the exquisite sensibility of Alexander Pope, trapped in his ugly stunted body, had stared out across the quiet fields and composed couplets that turned the fierce vertical light of Homer into the dappled sunshine of Oxfordshire. But I didn't because it took my thoughts back to the savage lyricism of my first love with my first wife, and that made me think of pain and disillusion. In a ramshackle hut on the river's margin near here, I had devoured forbidden fruit by the truckload, and now my teeth and hers were set on edge. I walked on. Northmoor Lock, Appleton, Bessels Leigh. I was coming close now to exhaustion. I had had nothing to eat or drink, and the day was sultry. Pubs were closed now, and there were no teashops. I gulped water from a tap in a farmyard, and strode on. A sign said 'Sunningwell'. I had not meant to walk this far. Never mind, I wasn't going back now, and as my fatigue mounted it was more and more successful in taking my mind off Mairead. Mairead, Mairead! I cried out inwardly. God, send her to me! Don't give me what I deserve or I shall get nothing. Give me Mairead! What's this, I said to myself, calling on God? You know you don't believe in God. Bollocks, mate, I replied, we all believe when we get into this kind of state. From somewhere down by the river bed I heard a long, hollow laugh. I knew it to be Tertullian enjoying his victory. *Credo quia impossibile est*, he said with a soft, mocking chuckle. I made no reply. Abingdon was the next town I reached. I would have paused there, but it was where Heather and I passed our honeymoon of precisely one night. And it was where the M.G. factory still stood, where Billy Morris had cheated Brian out of an ideal. Abingdon was no place for me. There was quite a frequent bus service to Oxford, and I caught one. There was also a railway station. But for Brian's sake I didn't take the train; it would have seemed like betraying him.

★

Michael's eyes smouldered as he looked towards her, lingering on every detail of her shapely body. I could see he was deeply in love.

'There's one thing, Dad,' he said. 'Nobody, nobody *on earth*, could tell you you hadn't got a bargain. I wonder,' he dropped his voice conspiratorially, 'if this bloke realizes that he's just about giving her away, at that price.'

We were standing in a couple of inches of mud in a combined scrapyard and used-car outlet situated down a side turning off the Witney Road. Clearly the place had once been a small farm; the cottage which now served as the mildly disorganized 'office' had been the modest farmhouse and the area where we were standing had been the farmyard. For generations, it had been trodden by slow patient cows – brought in twice a day to be relieved of their cargo of milk distilled from the soft lowland grass – and pecked about by chucking, drawling chickens; over to one side there would have been a row of pig-styes, and, over the wooden fence near to the house, a haystack. Now, all those things existed only as a hovering memory. One side of the space contained a large dump of what were quite clearly pieces of cars, the boneyard of an industry just as the factories away over the skyline were its maternity wards. The other side contained a row of disconsolate vehicles all nearing the end of any possible life-span, offered for sale to the indigent, to those handy with blow-torch and spanner, and (as in Michael's case) those who saw them with the eyes of love.

Most of these waifs were well-used, indeed over-used, vans or family cars, products of Lord Nuffield's faith in no-nonsense motoring for the ordinary man. But Michael's eye had spotted one among them, still jaunty under its layers of grime, that testified to the opposing opinion, the counter-movement that for about five years had been kept alive at the very heart of Nuffieldom: the determination of Cecil Kimber and his dedicated band of outlaws to build fast, stylish cars to go racing in. This small *enclave* had been, among other things, the life-area of Brian Leonard; and now, exactly like an animal whose habitat is commandeered

–187–

by the relentless outward thrust of the human race seeking profit or power, he was left wandering in territory so denuded that he was compelled to leave it behind. Thank God he had an alternative habitat, behind the beer-pumps at the Bargeman's Arms!

Thinking these thoughts, I gazed at the dented little racer that stood before us in the converted farmyard on that cool, showery October afternoon, with its tyres in the mud, looking as if it would never start again.

Exactly as if he could read my thoughts, Michael said, 'I don't suppose there's anything wrong with her that Brian and I couldn't put right. No charge to you, of course.'

He strode over to the car and, expertly undoing the catches, opened the bonnet. The two metal shards flapped upwards like a beetle's wing-case. Only the octagonal 'M.G.' on the radiator still stared bravely at me.

The proprietor, a ruddy man in overalls, came over to us. I thought what a traditional bucolic type he was. Take off his overalls and put him in moleskins and leggings, and he would have been a groom, ostler, horse-dealer *circa* 1850. He almost gave off the smell of oats. But now it was cars, cars, cars; petrol and tyres, petrol and tyres. The new overlay was so shallow upon him, it could have been peeled off in an instant. With his sons it would be different. Billy Morris would have their souls as well as their bodies.

While Michael plunged into an animated discussion of the merits of M.G. sports cars in general and this one in particular, I looked at the car and tried to imagine myself owning it. Dark green in colour under its layer of dirt, light-weight wheels with multiple spokes, knock-off hub-caps, it certainly looked purposeful. The bonnet was long in proportion to the overall length, taking up at least half of the total, with everything else crammed in behind the steering wheel. This lengthy bonnet terminated at the cockpit end in a raised section which I believe was called the 'scuttle', rising from the horizontal and emphasized towards its upper edge by two sleek bulges like the upper half of a well-filled bikini. The windscreen was folded flat and lay forward on the bonnet; behind it projected two semi-circles of glass, designed presumably to 'shelter' the occupants slumped in their bucket seats. To preserve the narrowness of the skimpy body, which ended abruptly at the back in a rump as short as a duck's, the wheels were thrust out into the open air, though in contrast to the sports cars of the 1920s this car had at least managed to ingest its exhaust pipe.

I stared down at it. It stared up at me, balefully.

'Nought to fifty in twenty seconds,' I heard the proprietor's voice behind me. Then Michael's. 'Twenty point seven. I remember the figures.'

'Remember them?' the man chuckled. 'You can't have been born, young sir.'

'On the contrary,' Michael said crisply, 'I was born in the exact year when this model came out: 1934. It was the first with the 847 engine and the three-bearing crank.'

'What does all that mean, Mike?' I asked him.

'It means that it's one of the famous ones. It's the PA.'

'Yes,' the proprietor said challengingly. 'It's the A, and that's why she's going cheap. If she'd been a B she'd cost a lot more.'

'The PB had some improvements over the PA, certainly,' Michael conceded. 'Less bumpy. That's why it did better in racing. More controllable, specially on a rough circuit like Brooklands.'

'Ah, well, I can see you knows your M.G.s. No point in giving you any sales information. I'll get the key for you. Got 'em all hanging up in the office, I have. Then you can have a little test drive.'

He looked with a touch of hesitation from Michael's face to mine, as if not certain which of us should have the initial drive; then, evidently deciding that the first thing to do was to fetch the key, he stumped off to the old farm kitchen. In the few moments it took him to fetch the key, Michael made one of those small gestures – small, that is, to the external view – that actually reveal the true nature of a human being, separating the fine from the commonplace, the chivalrous from the selfish.

'All ready, Dad?' he said in a deliberately casual tone. (I knew him well enough to know that the casualness was deliberate.) 'In the mood for a good fast drive?'

'I don't know about fast,' I said. 'If I manage to make it move along at all I shall be quite satisfied with myself. I've never driven anything like this before.'

'Don't let him know that,' he said, indicating the returning figure of the proprietor. 'Let him think you're an old hand. Then he'll know he can't put anything over on us.'

'On you, you mean,' I had just time to say before accepting the ignition key from the man's meaty hand. Inwardly my heart was over-flowing with gratitude at having a son whose character showed such delicacy. I knew how strong was his craving to get behind the wheel of this fierce little car and urge it forward; I knew how easily he could have rationalized and justified to himself a decision to be the first to drive, the first to exercise mastery over this fascinating prize. It was a kind of *droit de seigneurie*, and he was assigning it to me so graciously, without a hint of struggle, as if it were the obvious thing to do. And why, forsooth? For no better reason than the dry, formalistic, sapless fact that I was going to be the actual purchaser, the formal owner. The PA, if it proved to be in a mechanical state that would warrant our buying it at all, was going to be 'my' car, 'belonging to' me. In reality, as we both knew, she belonged to Michael, she was Michael's car. His aching need of her had impelled us here. It was not the routine sale of a clapped-out used car I was about to witness: it was a wedding, and he was allowing me over the bridal threshold ahead of him, though my claim was nothing in comparison. He was doing it to allow me to keep up a good front, not to lose face, not to be there as that mere appendage in so many episodes of youth, 'the old man'. I blessed his goodness, his considera-tion. And, as if taking my priority for granted, I lowered myself into the driving seat.

'All right, sir?' the proprietor asked, bending down to me. I supposed he meant, was I inside the car and more or less ready for whatever was to come next, so I nodded. I wasn't all right in any other way. 'The young man and me'll get her started and then you can take her for a little run round.'

'A little run round? Where to?'

'Oh, just down the lane to the Witney Road, and run her till she gets warm. You'll soon see she's a good goer. That is, if you're seriously considering . . .' He gave me a judging look.

Getting her to run along proved a lengthy business. Michael and the proprietor managed it only by a determined effort lasting at least a quarter of an hour. I did not scruple to inform them that I hadn't this kind of time available whenever I wanted to go anywhere in the car. They patiently assured me that I wouldn't need this much time. 'Once we get her warmed up,' the proprietor told me soothingly, 'and she gets used to the idea like, she'll be as sweet as a bird.'

When she finally did start she wasn't anything like any bird I had ever seen, but then I don't know much about fighting cocks. The rasping and crackling noises that followed the initial coughing fit settled down ultimately into a drumming vibration that caused the vehicle to shudder feverishly from stem to stern. Michael's face was flushed with excitement and adoration. Already, I could see, she was *his* darling. Glancing across at him as he bent over the cockpit and stared at the instrument panel, I thought of Sophy. I couldn't picture her because I had never seen her, but I thought of a pretty, long-legged adolescent girl. If someone took Sophy away from him, would it hurt as much as taking this infinitely desired object? I doubted it. Sophy, in all probability, was repeatable; whereas only a limited number of M.G. PAs had been built.

'Well,' I said, raising my voice above the noise of the engine (three bearings! 847 c.c.!) and trying to maintain some outward semblance of calm, 'let's put her through her paces.'

Michael smiled kindly. 'Hardly, Dad,' he said. 'You'd need a racing circuit for that.'

'Well, let's say trundle along the road in her, then,' I said sullenly, and tried to open the door on the driver's side.

It wouldn't open, and Michael explained tolerantly that though it had originally been built to open, it must have long since rusted into the shut position. Apparently the owners of M.G. PAs didn't open doors to get into their vengeful little cars; they climbed into the cockpit with the loose-limbed agility of youth, as into a light aeroplane.

I could just about muster the agility, if not the loose limbs, at the age of thirty-nine, and I was soon behind the wheel and Michael beside me.

I could drive reasonably well in an ordinary car, but this one was determined to be different. It was a struggle to get into gear and move off, it was a struggle to get used to the turning circle, it was a struggle, with the hard springing, to pound over the deep ruts in the lane.

'Not very good for the suspension,' I shouted.

'You don't have to worry,' my son shouted back. 'The frame's made of ash wood. Light and flexible. Nothing to touch it in metal.'

Setting my teeth, I trod on the accelerator and we slammed down into a particularly hostile rut and up again. I had the vague feeling that if I could break something on the car I would have made my point and won a small victory.

'You're getting the hang of it,' Michael shouted approvingly. Apparently what I had done was the right thing.

By this time we had reached the Witney Road and I had to ease out into the traffic stream. This was a dangerous road even in those days, with a volume of traffic that would nowadays seem pastoral. It was designed in the lethal three-lane pattern that came in during the 1930s, with two lanes howling in opposite directions and between them an overtaking lane which was a standing invitation to get yourself killed in a head-on collision. We had spent so much time at the scrapyard that the evening rush-hour was already beginning, the road was busy and the drivers in a hurry to get home. I tried to get the blunt little snout out into the stream of nondescript tin-kettle cars as gradually as possible, but the impatient snorter wasn't designed to do anything gradually, and with a bad-tempered snarl we bounded forward into a space nothing like adequate. That my life did not end at that point, and Michael's with it, I owe to the fact that the driver of the next car along was possessed of a respectable level of skill and quick reactions. Joseph Conrad once remarked that not to believe in luck is a mark of inexperience. From that moment on I was experienced.

We were facing towards Witney. I thought I would run as far as the turn-off to Eynsham, which would give us a chance to get off the main drag, turn round circumspectly, and rejoin the road going back the other way with a proper system of white lines and laid-down procedures. I couldn't afford to take any chances; I was only just in control as it was. The traffic stream was moving at about fifty miles an hour, and I soon found that it was extremely difficult to drive the little racer at that speed. In the lower gears she would grind along at about thirty-five, nothing like fast enough, but if you changed up there seemed to be no speed short of about seventy at which the engine was comfortable – and when it wasn't comfortable it snorted and protested and went along in a series of abrupt kangaroo-leaps. More than once I came within a millimetre of slamming into the rear end of the car in front, and then again I would slow right down and have the driver behind breathing angrily down my neck.

Ah, here was the turn to Eynsham. I saw it approaching with more relief than I had ever seen the nearing of a road junction before. It signalled my release, and the end of Michael's frustration. I slowed, pulled on to the grass verge, stopped. The engine was still running and the car trembled like a washing-machine, but at least we were standing still. I had triumphed. Honour was saved and now Michael could take over and enter into his new kingdom. All I stipulated was that before going back to that roaring main road, we should go on into Eynsham village and drive around in a few lanes and *culs-de-sac*. Michael made no objection. For the next quarter of an hour we drove round Eynsham at speeds varying from a saunter to a brisk bicycling pace. We stopped abruptly, we stopped slowly, we turned in a tight circle, we turned in a wide circle, we reversed, we stopped to let old ladies quaver over the road, we stopped for children, we accelerated, we did everything. Then Michael expressed himself ready to drive us back to the scrapyard.

'To buy?' I asked in a casual tone that deceived no one. 'Or not to buy?'

'To buy, for certain. Unless you've suddenly turned against the whole idea of getting a car, Dad.'

'No,' I said, still keeping up that phony lightness of touch, 'I haven't done that.'

We drove back to the Kidlington scrapyard in a way that felt totally different from the same trip we had just made on the same road. If I had shut my eyes I could have imagined that the car had grown wings and was flying over a mountain range through bumpy air, which caused us to jolt up and down, but not with the kind of bumpiness you get from a road surface. It was as if the little dragon had taken the decision, right from the beginning, to obey the new young master. We pulled up outside the dilapidated farmhouse like an eagle alighting on its nest. Michael turned off the ignition and the engine shuddered to a halt. The silence was delicious. The proprietor was waiting for us.

'Did you see a play?'

'A play?'

'Yes, you must have had a good long stop at Stratford-on-Avon.'

I gathered he was being sarcastic about the length of time our little test-drive had taken. 'You've made a sale, anyway,' I said stiffly. 'We'll have the car.'

Beside me Michael let out a great exhalation.

'You're spot on, Dad,' he said to me in an emotional undertone. 'Right on beam.' I gathered these were terms of the highest praise.

In his happiness, he jumped out of the car like a Jack-in-the-box. I followed more slowly. My buttocks felt bruised after a drive of only about five miles.

'Gives you a hard ride, doesn't she?' I murmured to Michael.

'Well, naturally the springing's hard. She's sprung for racing. The springs don't actually come into play till you hit seventy-five or eighty. Obviously it'd be hopeless if they came on sooner. She'd roll. She's built for racing, that's all.'

I agreed that that was all and stood for a moment stiffly massaging my nates. Some procedural discussion now followed. Apparently there were formalities about insurance that could not be completed on the spot. (Insurance? *Insurance*?) It struck me, also, that the proprietor wanted to satisfy himself that my cheque for £180 would not bounce. Michael, who obviously would know no rest until the car was safely and certainly the property of the Leonard family, offered to act as go-between in any way he could, during such hours as they let him out of school: to be anywhere, to go on any errand, to whirl about Oxfordshire on his bicycle, that humbling symbol of juvenility so soon to be discarded. We set it all up. I was to wait quietly in Episcopus College until the car was ready to be collected. Then I was to collect her and take her immediately to Brian who, with Michael's help, would see what could be done by way of rejuvenation. Only when everything was ready could I enter into full ownership.

Michael and I walked over to the Witney Road and got ourselves to a bus stop. They were about every fifteen minutes in those days and our wait was short. The early evening was a bright one and the sun shone levelly on the trees, fields and farm buildings we passed. Michael was very happy.

We took the bus to Gloucester Green and went to the Welsh Pony for a drink before I went back to College and Michael continued on his way to Chinnor. As we drank our modest half-pints of beer, he told me again that it would be money well spent. I said I had never doubted it. Sharing our new status as M.G. owners, we drank a toast to the memory of Cecil Kimber before separating with a promise to be in touch and meet soon.

The next time I talked to Brian he told me I had been swindled, that the car was a wreck and it was monstrous to charge any three-figure price for it. I made no defence of my action, but remembering how the brightness in Michael's face had rivalled that of the clear evening sky, I reaffirmed, in the silence of my mind, that it had been money well spent. At the same time, I wondered how he had represented the transaction to Heather, and whether my promptness in handing over £180 would give her the idea that I had plenty of money to spare. If it did, I could expect a few tradesmen's bills, passed on to me without comment, in the next few weeks.

★

All this time I kept on telephoning Mairead, and she kept on not being there. I got up each morning, washed, shaved, put my clothes on, had breakfast, went through the day, did what was expected of me. Particularly I was glad of any diversion strong enough to take my mind off the situation. One of these, about the fifth or sixth evening of this numb period, was the appearance of Norbert at College dinner. I had always liked and admired the man. In a corrupt world he had seemed to me an example of the fact that people existed, here and there, who gravitated towards power and authority not from self-importance, not from sweaty reaching out for the material fruits of important positions, but because by nature and by certain habits of thought implanted by their upbringing they naturally assumed control when things became difficult. They recognized, as clearly as the rest of us, the truth of Lord Acton's remark, 'All power tends to corrupt; absolute power corrupts absolutely,' but instead of drawing from it the usual moral that the pure in heart should simply shun and renounce power, choosing rather to be incorruptibly insignificant and have no influence whatever on events, thought it might be better to try to influence these events from a position of responsibility while keeping an eye on oneself for the beginnings of the familiar infections – self-importance, lust for power, jealousy, disdain for the insignificant. Norbert, I knew, did keep such an eye. It was obvious that he did so – obvious from his expression, his bearing, the tones of his voice, the kind of remarks he came out with. I had felt this about him since we were both undergraduates, he third year, I first. I felt it still now that, entering middle-age, he was evidently moving closer to the centre of decision-making in his work at the Foreign Office, and it did me good to notice that Jocelyn Mowbray obviously had a high opinion of him, inviting him frequently to the College, sitting next to him at dinner, listening attentively to what he had to say, retiring with him to the Lodgings later in the evening, doubtless to pursue

–194–

Foreign Office shop over a whisky and soda and perhaps exchange thoughts and speculations that were not altogether appropriate for unscreened audiences.

Personally I was quite content with the material that was not classified, the things that could be said before a general audience. If you had the sense to know what you were listening to, you could always distil the truth out of them. As an historian I had already been well trained – by Bax, largely – in the essential skill of recognizing what my source material was likely to be able to tell me. On this particular evening, fresh of mind and alert for stimulating talk and for diversion from Mairead-emotions, I positioned myself as near as possible to the long settle where Norbert and Mowbray sat together drinking coffee.

As usual they had a half-circle of listeners about them. It was always interesting to hear these two professionals talk about their world. Some-one, it seemed, had prompted a discussion by bringing up the name of Senator Joseph McCarthy, at that time cutting a wide swath in American political and social life, with repercussions throughout all Western coun-tries, by his probings and questionings, his accusations of 'un-American Activities', his 'Loyalty Oaths' and witch-hunting generally.

'I suppose the interesting thing that emerges from the whole McCarthy boil-up,' Mowbray was saying reflectively, 'is that he's far from being altogether wrong, he has a case, but he's managed to make that case seem so repulsive that no one with any sensitiveness wants to be seen standing beside him.'

Norbert nodded, his broad, capable hand cradling his coffee-cup thoughtfully. 'He has this ghastly knack of going at things the wrong way, hasn't he? What he's succeeded in doing is to convince the ordinary decent voter that it's a cad's trick to accuse anyone of being a Communist, even people like the Rosenbergs who undeniably *were* Communists. The backlash even went as far as to make people want to defend Alger Hiss. McCarthy's made himself into the kiss of death for any anti-Stalinist, which can't have been what he intended.'

The venerable *savant* Weatherby was listening now and he said wistfully, 'But is it essential to be anti-Stalin?'

'I'm afraid so, if you want to be a human being,' Jock Mowbray replied evenly.

'I do hate the situation,' Weatherby said, 'of having to be pro or anti. It's like finding out that a field you'd always taken to be a pleasant space, where you could take a walk and collect your thoughts, was in fact a football pitch with a game going on – so you couldn't set foot on it without wearing the jersey of one side or the other.'

'But don't you think, Sir Thomas,' Norbert addressed him with careful politeness, 'that the old liberal green-space attitude towards Stalin died the death at Yalta?'

'It died the death in 1936, with Stalin's murder of Kirov, if we'd only known it then,' said Mowbray aside. But he spoke so quietly that I believe I alone heard him.

'I had hopes of Yalta,' Weatherby said, disconsolate.

'So did we all,' said Norbert. 'But they weren't fulfilled, were they? Stalin's game came out into the open immediately after the military defeat of the Germans. What price Czechoslovakia? That was where the Communist technique of taking over a country really showed itself as the well-oiled machine it is. First infiltrate – get your Party members into just about every key position in industry and politics and administration, whether they publicly admit to being Party members or not. Then, at a given signal, the *coup*. The country wakes up to find itself part of the Communist empire. And if there's a democratically elected President to whom the people might rally once they realize what's going on – that's easy. Push him out of a fifth-floor window. He won't give much trouble after that.'

Mowbray put down his coffee-cup and took a cigar from a silver box on the table. 'Yes,' he said meditatively, 'Czechoslovakia. That was a smooth job. I saw it at close quarters.'

'Very depressing,' Norbert agreed. 'It showed what we were up against.'

I thought, suddenly, of Carshalton. His decision to become a convert to the Stalinist faith and an admirer of Stalinist methods, if I remembered rightly, had been taken very early on; he had already been in the fold when the Czechoslovakian state was blackjacked and President Masaryk hurled from a window. How good the news must have made him feel! How smug about having chosen the right side to be on!

'The only cheerful feature,' Mowbray was saying, 'was that it was such a success for Soviet gangsterism that some people, at least, were simply jolted into seeing what was going on. The Left couldn't see it, of course, because they were deep in a love affair with Stalin that hasn't ended yet, and probably won't end until they're gobbled up like the male spider whose task is done, but ordinary sensible people did begin to ask themselves, if a sequence of events like that could happen in a civilized country like Czechoslovakia where they had one of the showpiece democracies, was there any country where it couldn't happen?'

'From that point of view,' I said, 'it's a pity Britain and France let the Czechs down so heavily at the time of Munich. That must have left them with an ingrained suspicion of the West that made it easier for Stalin to pull them east.'

'That's true as far as it goes.' Mowbray had got his cigar going by now and spoke through a fragrant mist. 'If there was any general prejudice in the mind of the populace, the Party machine would naturally exploit that prejudice as it would exploit anything else. But if you'll take the word of someone who was pretty close to the action from beginning to end, I can tell you that the whole thing would have unfolded in exactly the way it did even if there had been a strong prejudice to shy away from involvement with the Kremlin. After years of being dominated by the Gestapo, I don't think they were in any mood to be dominated by the K.G.B. using much the same methods. They just weren't given the choice. They wanted freedom, yes – but in the event it didn't matter what they wanted. And I agree with Norbert that the only positive fruit of the episode was the suspicion it aroused all over the world.'

'Certainly,' Norbert said. 'Just look at the order of events. First, the Czech take-over. Then the Marshall Plan, then the setting-up of NATO. We'd never have got the other two if we hadn't had the shock of the first. They both meant the spending of a lot of American money and you can depend on it that Congress wouldn't have agreed to either, let alone both, if the Czech business hadn't shaken the American people out of their isolationism.'

'And you can see McCarthyism as a by-product of that anxiety?' The interception was young Manciple's. 'Rather than what some of us take it for, the expression of a Ku Klux Klan type of xenophobia?'

Norbert shot him a look that seemed to me to combine interest with wariness. 'I have no tenderness for the Ku Klux Klan and very little indeed for McCarthy,' he said, 'but if you can think of a way of bridging the differences between them so that they actually look similar, I'd be interested to hear it.'

Manciple drew a happy anticipatory breath, glancing from face to face, deeply grateful to the luck that had given him this first-class audience. 'Well, I don't know the area personally,' he said, 'but surely the economic and political objectives of the agrarian South would lend themselves very easily to the manipulation of a McCarthy. I mean, the common targets of suspicion . . .'

As unobtrusively as possible, I slid along the bench seat till I had quite a gap between myself and the central knot of the others; then I stood up and moved away. Common Room etiquette dictated that one avoided directly showing boredom, but I could see there was a monumental slab of it about to fall on us and I quailed at the prospect; besides, I knew that Manciple wasn't aiming to impress *me*. Looking back from the doorway, I saw Mowbray's face was perfectly expres-sionless, while Norbert was actually leaning forward in an attitude that seemed to indicate that he was paying profound attention. He was even watching Manciple's face as if spellbound by his burble of words. Not for the first time I thought: *the man is an observer of the decencies.*

Back in my solitary room, I reflected that the conversation had done me good by drawing my attention away from the turmoil of emotions inside me and making me think of wider, impersonal issues. It had reminded me, as Common Room conversation so often did remind me, that I was part of a community of intelligent beings, trying individually and collectively to play our part in the essential work of the world and discriminate among its issues and concerns. To that extent the familiar magic had worked, and if it had been jarred and interrupted by the self-centred crassness of young Manciple, well, I could live with that. A Common Room has to contain all types, and there were some at Episcopus who considered Manciple able and interesting, though I personally found him pushy and insensitive. Both parties, obviously, were right in their own way; they simply looked at the same qualities in the man and interpreted them differently. If I had had the patience it might have been instructive to stay and see how Norbert handled Manciple, whether he would end up by trying to broaden and liberalize his outlook or politely give him up as a bad job. But that evening I had less than my usual amount of patience, which truth to tell has never been much at the best of times. The sudden plunge into excitement and uncertainty had totally unsettled my mind. Mairead! She had come back into my world. Or at least the idea of her had. Or at least her voice had. I couldn't go on folding her away like a washed and ironed garment that might be worn some day, lying in a drawer to await some occasion big enough to justify an outing.

Switching on the lights, I sat in my armchair. Surely, I thought, if Mairead had decided, during these years, to break away from me, she would have simply said so on the morning when I rang her for the first time and broke the silence. She would have done it in so few words, so quickly. 'Oh, it's you, Peter. Well, you might as well know that there's no need to bother getting in touch with me. It's all rather faded away, hasn't it? I mean, presumably you feel much the same yourself, don't you? No? Well, I'm sorry about that, but obviously it would be much better for you to get used to the idea now, and less painful for you in the long run. I'm sorry, but I really can't discuss it, I have to go to work, but in any case there's nothing to discuss — that's just the way my mind has gone. Be brave now, and go and find someone to be happy with; I'm sure you will, and now I really must go. I'm late already.' Once my imagination had formed the words they seemed so natural and probable, I could hear her voice so clearly saying them, that with the greatest effort I could hardly make myself believe that I hadn't actually heard them. I got out of the armchair and moved over to the sofa. But the thoughts that came to me there were just as bleak and nightmare-ish.

There was only one thing to do: go out. Walk about under the dark sky and call down some calm from the heavens. I let myself out at the far end of the garden and walked north. It was a calm, thoughtful autumn night, still early, not yet ten o'clock; though mild, it was not quite outdoor weather; people who were not at home tended to be still inside the places they had chosen to go to – pubs, theatres, restaurants, at meetings, in the homes of friends. There were very few about in the streets, and not much traffic. An unusual peace brooded over the whole northern part of the city and, I could imagine, the countryside beyond. Even within that peace I chose the quietest residential streets and back lanes. I paced meditatively along Parks Road, into Norham Gardens, thence into Crick Road, over Norham Road, and found myself walking along the quiet pathway behind Park Town.

I reflected as I walked how much I had always liked Park Town. There was something defiantly urban, even Londonish, in its atmosphere, with the two graceful curved wings that formed its main section, the central space filled up by an area of trees and shrubs that had had plenty of time to mature and develop its own character. The archway at the top end, connecting the two halves of the straight terrace, added a touch of diminutive but not absurd grandeur. The place had an air and, with its fresh stucco and well-tended shrubs, had not been allowed to grow seedy. Most of all I liked the sharp nostalgia it aroused in me for an Oxford that had disappeared long before I was born. In the 1850s, when it was built, Park Town must have been surrounded by open country. There can have been very little building, at that time, to be seen north of Wadham. Even the stately, leafy suburb of classic North Oxford, Victorian don-land, was still twenty years in the future. How pleasant, I had often thought, to have walked and wandered in those peaceful fields and lanes, and to find in the midst of them that trim, self-possessed little enclave of houses! Where the richer dons kept their mistresses, tradition said. I wouldn't blame them if so. But it can't have been, then or later, anything like a discreet academic Storeyville. Most of the houses – tall, neat, prim, without bathrooms but with plenty of basement kitchen space for servants – must have been occupied by families, no doubt the families of respectable tradesmen with old-established Oxford town names. One fragment of information flashed into my memory as I walked past those back-garden fences: Mr Cavell, one of the two partners who founded Elliston and Cavell's, for so long Oxford's largest department store, lived in Park Town. No doubt he was just the type.

I was pondering these tranquil considerations, allowing peace to steal into my churned-up mind, when I was abruptly startled by a loud crash, such as would be made by a grandfather clock falling on to a plank floor. I stopped, transfixed. The noise came from over to my left; that is, from one of the houses in the crescent of Park Town.

The back gardens of those houses terminate in a brick wall, uniform with the walls that separate the gardens from one another, and doubtless put up by the original builders as part of the general architecture of the area. Past this wall I was now walking, keeping it on my left-hand side, for I was moving northward. In more recent times, the ever-rapacious demands of the motor-car have caused some sections of this wall to be demolished and replaced by garages made of cheaper and uglier materials, so that the rear view of Park Town has lost some of its elegance, just as the constant passage of motor vehicles has made the lane itself more rutted, muddy, and at times dangerous, to walk along – a history of modern Oxford in miniature. But back in the early 1950s none of this had happened.

When that sudden crash halted my thoughtful walk I naturally turned and looked over the tidily closed garden gate, more accurately described as a latched wooden door, set in the boundary wall. All seemed much as it ought to be. There was the garden, about thirty yards long, mostly lawn with a strip of flower-bed down each side. Had I imagined that loud crash? It seemed impossible. But if it had really happened it must have been caused by some mischance: and there seemed no sign of . . . No! Wait! Directly leading into the garden, and therefore facing me as I looked down the garden's length, was a pair of French windows. I had been in a number of these Park Town houses and knew that this was the downstairs sitting-room. One of these windows was now hastily thrust open and the figure of a man emerged, his quickly striding form draped in what at first sight looked like a white hearth-rug.

The light from the room was not bright; it evidently came from a smallish table-lamp that had been on, routinely, when the room was unoccupied. Still, since the garden was dark and such light as came from the room was behind the man, it was hard at first to be certain of details. But then he turned so that his profile was towards me, and I saw that it was Hunt. Another figure, female, was moving about in an undefined way just behind him, not emerging from the room. As I watched, enough light fell on her to reveal her identity too: Molly Fishman, alias Whitworth.

Yes, I was seeing this. I was watching Hunt, wearing some strange accoutrement which he was making fretful attempts to wrap securely round what I now saw was his naked frame, leaving the ground-floor back entrance of the Fishman residence in Park Town (I remembered now someone telling me that the couple had bought a house there), clad in a hearth-rug, or perhaps a table-cloth. No, I saw now, it was a towelling dressing-gown, white or off-white in colour, and considerably too small for him. In short, and unmistakeably, it was Molly's towelling dressing-gown or bath-robe.

Ergo, Hunt had been in the bathroom at this Park Town house and he had had his clothes off. Perhaps he had been having a bath. And why not? He was a friend of the couple, especially of one of the couple, and doubtless a familiar guest at their home. But why, in that case, should he rush out into the October night immediately after emerging from the bath, wearing only a too-small dressing-gown not his own? Was it perhaps part of some austere health regimen? Something like cooking oneself in a sauna and then emerging to hurl oneself into a snowdrift, as in Finland? I would willingly have thought so, but there seemed to be difficulties in the way of this explanation. I stood patiently in the lane and waited for elucidation.

It came immediately. 'I need my fucking clothes, damn you!' I heard Hunt's voice hiss in furious anger. 'I can't stand out here like—'

'Be quiet and take what you're given!' came Molly's voice on an equally deadly note of hostility. 'I'll throw your clothes down if he's still in the bathroom. If he's come out, you'll have to wait till I—'

'*Wait*? How the bloody hell can I wait? You throw those clothes out or I'm coming in. It's no good locking the door, I'll smash the glass!'

I was glad I hadn't missed this. What glorious luck that I had been going past just at the right second! On the other hand, I reflected, for all I knew it wasn't the one-in-a-million coincidence it seemed to be. Perhaps the tempestuous lovers put on some kind of show like this several times in the average week. Perhaps the neighbours were accustomed to overhearing their *al fresco* altercations; that could even be why no windows had flown up, no exterior lights snapped on, during the moment of eerie silence that had set me wondering whether that frightful crash had happened in my head. The neighbouring houses stayed wrapped in their decorous slumber: Park Town remained Park Town, discreetly incurious. All the same, by any standards this show was a good one. It involved the philosopher-husband, Fishman, which must surely be unusual.

Molly had closed the French window in the time it took me to formulate these thoughts. I heard the key turn in the lock. Then the oblong of light vanished as she rapidly drew the curtains.

Hunt was about twenty-five yards from me. The night was not totally dark, and I could make him out dimly, swathed in Molly's robe. His bare calves looked cold as he moved restlessly to and fro, and I heard his voice, subdued but intense, through clenched teeth. 'The fucking thing . . . Curse the bastard thing . . . *Curse it.*' I imagined his numb, bare feet. I could tell he was clenching his teeth to stop them from chattering; the noise would probably have been loud enough to give away his presence.

I was just beginning to feel sorry for him, which considering that Hunt was Hunt and I was I, was a fairly extraordinary state of affairs. I don't suppose more than two or three minutes had gone by since Molly had whipped the glass doors shut on him, but that must have seemed enough to be going on with, and he had besides the tension of not knowing when she would get round to letting him have his clothes. What did it depend on, I wondered? The 'he' who, to suit their plans, was required to be 'still in the bathroom' must be her husband, who presumably had arrived home early and surprised Molly and her *cavaliere servente* (if the phrase is not too dignified, and too much associated with an elegant and stylish way of life, to be used of a dipstick like Hunt), in the midst of, or preparing for, or relaxing after, their raptures. This would account for his exit, hasty and unclothed. I still wondered how she could have appeared downstairs, in short order, apparently dressed; but perhaps it would be easier for a woman, especially one who was in her own home, to drag on a dress and thrust her feet into slippers. Anyway, she had managed it, clever lady.

A window opened on the first floor and a bundle of clothes was flung out. At least, it started as a bundle but during its descent the individual garments began already to flap loose from the collective mass. Hunt pounced on them. The window was still open, and before it rapped shut a pair of shoes followed the clothes. One landed on his back as he bent over the scattered items on the ground, snatching them up and shaking them out. He had them now – shirt, trousers, a pullover, a jacket. I never saw anyone get dressed so quickly. The shoes went on, I noticed, over bare feet. Hunt was thrusting the socks, and some other raglike objects that were probably his underwear, into his side pockets as he turned and started along the garden path. Straight towards me! My head, protruding over the gate, was fully visible from where he came striding on. But perhaps his preoccupation and confusion, plus the fact that he would not be expecting to see anything of the kind, would safeguard me. With a rapidity that matched his own, I bent down to bring my head out of sight and darted away along the lane with the crouching gait of one of the larger primates, my knees bent and my head tucked well down between my shoulders. Hunt, with feverish haste, dragged open the garden gate, which was evidently sticking a little, and as I heard the sound behind me I swerved to the side of the pathway where I was partly screened by foliage spilling over from the other side of the wall, turned my back to the gardens, and stood still as if lost in contemplation of the night. If Hunt came up to me, I was ready for him. In fact he never noticed me. Turning in the opposite direction, towards Norham Road and the Parks, he set off with great lunging strides. I could almost feel the anger boiling in his veins at the things that had happened to him.

Slowly, I moved back to my position just outside the Fishmans' garden gate. Everything was very quiet, and my senses were fully alert. Across the space that separated me from the house I heard the rush of water from a pipe. It was the unmistakeable sound of someone's bath water draining out. Fishman's, no doubt. If he had travelled back unexpectedly from wherever it was in Scotland that he was a Professor – too absent-minded, perhaps, to telephone ahead, or perhaps under the impression that he had done so – it would have been natural, after so long a train journey, for his wife to propel him in the direction of taking a comforting bath.

Since this bath had immobilized him while Hunt made good his escape, it had quite clearly been comforting to her as well as to him. In the long term, it might even prove to have been comforting to Hunt. When the immediate sensations of shock and alarm, followed by cold, rounded off by discomfort as he charged off through the North Oxford night with his underwear and socks in his pockets, had died down, they might seem to him preferable to being at the centre of an unpleasant and much-publicized row.

In any case, I reflected as I strolled back to Episcopus, I had no means of knowing. And no motive for caring. If I had a shred of sympathy with any one of these three, it was the relatively harmless Fishman. And he had been a bloody fool to marry Molly Whitworth in the first place; I could have told him that.

Only one question still nibbled away at my mind: what was that loud crash? I was certain now that I hadn't imagined it and that it had come from that house. But what could it have been? Something to do with the orgone box, perhaps? But if so, what?

*

One shouldn't, I know, make too much of small matters, but on the morning when I found in my mail a postcard from Brian saying that the M.G. PA was 'as ready as she'll ever be' and I was to go down to the Bargeman's, preferably that lunch-time, and pick her up, I felt a distinct sense of having to nerve myself.

I had a substantial meal, not hurrying, and then took a taxi down to the Bargeman's to avoid standing in the bus queue in Cornmarket, already becoming an ugly street with the removal of graceful landmarks like the old Clarendon Hotel and the arrival of the first wave of cut-price superstores with their headquarters in London. I sat back, trying to feel paternal, authoritative and calm, as the taxi buzzed me the mile or so down to my old home, but it was an unconvincing pretence. The driver chose to turn into East Street at the top end, upstream from the Bargeman's, and as I looked down the length of the short street over his shoulder I saw 'the little demon' waiting by the kerb outside the Saloon Bar. Two schoolboys, hands in pockets, were examining her keenly. We stopped, and as I paid off the driver I saw that he was looking at her too.

'Somebody goin' racin',' he commented, nodding towards the car.

'Looks like it,' I said and went into the pub, careful not to cast a glance in the direction of the PA so that nobody, least of all the two boys, should associate me with her and start asking questions.

My father was behind the bar, my mother in the kitchen; the universe was in place and its parts functioning normally. Brian had delivered the PA that morning, and left her outside with the message that with Michael's help he had done what was necessary 'to make her run along the road'.

'Not quite the car I'd have expected you to get, Peter,' my father commented carefully.

'Join me in half a pint, Dad,' I said. 'I wouldn't have expected myself to get any kind of car. I'm really buying it so that Michael can borrow it sometimes.'

'That'll be fun for him,' he remarked, still in his careful none-of-my-business tone.

'That's the idea. To see to it that he gets some of the fun that he'd be getting in a normal family life, with Dad around.'

I knew very well, as I spoke, that most boys of seventeen get precious little fun out of having their Dad around. Most fathers, as seen by their growing-up sons, are either hostile and obstructive, or so mild that they might as well not be there, or fairly sympathetic but just overwhelmed by drudgery, responsibilities and the dragging weight of unfulfilled dreams.

Whereas I, of course, would have been different, simply by virtue of being myself. Well, we all have to have some illusions.

After a few more minutes' routine conversation with Dad, and the same with my mother, I went outside and got into the PA. The two boys had cleared off now, thank goodness – the wholesome discipline of the schoolroom, no doubt – and I had no witnesses. The sun had come out in a clear sky, for it was that kind of autumn afternoon, and it struck me that in colour, light and air temperature this was a repeat of another journey by car from the Bargeman's Arms, Oseney Town, to Episcopus College: the afternoon, twenty-one years ago, when my father had driven me and the trunk containing most of my possessions over to Episcopus to begin my new life as a real live undergraduate, a member of Oxford University after all those years of wanting and striving to be. How rich the colours had seemed, how strongly the current of life had flowed, like a river irresistible in force though its fast-sliding surface was flecked with misgiving and self-distrust. And how beautiful Oxford had looked, the infinitely desirable at last attained, the greatest place in the world! I wondered if it seemed like that to Michael. But no, of course, it couldn't, it was too familiar, too worn into a shabbiness, with Episcopus College the normal background of his father's life that he, the son, found uncongenial.

These thoughts laid hold on me so strongly that I almost failed to notice the racket as I started the PA's engine, the vibration, the suddenness of the acceleration, the way people turned their heads to watch as I piloted the busy crackler along the street. Somehow I reached Episcopus without mishap: should I keep going, drive around for a while, get used to the car? No, said a voice in my head, stop while you're winning, live to fight another day.

Arriving at the heavy wooden boom which was always kept locked, I got out of the car and left her growling and quivering at the entrance to the drive while I unlocked. Some undergraduates who were passing stopped and stared. Among them I recognized one who was among my current crop of pupils, in fact I had a tutorial with him at five o'clock that very afternoon. This sudden intrusion of a new element in my life would cause immediate comment; since I knew that I was generally considered anonymous, quiet, rather characterless, in any case inconspicuous, I must be ready to be looked at with new eyes, though what kind of eyes I could not foresee. Puzzled? Satirical? Admiring? Disdainful? If a combination, how could those qualities be combined?

As I drew up the PA next to the Senior Dean's stately Armstrong-Siddeley, I asked myself these questions, but with no hope of answering them.

It took the news of my sea-change, incidentally, a very short time to reach Frank Penney. As a matter of routine I telephoned him in the lodge and told him that I had added one to the number of cars habitually using that parking space. He asked me for the registration number and I gave it, but said nothing else about the car. When I ran into him he was ready with the quizzical grin that was one of his two or three standard expressions.

'Just been taking a look at your car, sir. Gave me quite a surprise.'

'A surprise?'

'Yes, when I first saw it a distance off I thought there must be some mistake and I went and looked all over for the green light. When I couldn't find one I came back to the lodge and checked the registration number.'

'And you found it was correct?'

'It was correct all right, sir.'

In those days junior members of the University had to get permission from the Proctors to keep a motor-car in Oxford. And if it was granted, they had to display a green light on their car to make it immediately recognizable that they were students.

'Mind your own business in future, Frank,' I said to him. But not in words. I looked at him silently and said it with my expression. Nobody had told Frank Penney to mind his own business in all the years he had been at Episcopus, and he was retiring in a few months.

★

The Library at Episcopus College took the form of a capital L. The somewhat longer line of the L ran along the upper floor of the Garden Front, its windows overlooking the lawn, trees and flower-beds. The slightly shorter side formed the southern wall of the inner quadrangle. In those days the entrance to the Library was the end of this wing; it was about fifty years older than the Garden Front, and was in consequence known as the Old Library. It was built in about 1590, and indeed was a fine specimen of Tudor construction, with a timbered ceiling that irresistibly suggested the long gallery of some great Elizabethan house. With its alcoves and wooden desks for reading and writing that folded down when they were needed and hinged up to make more space when they were not, it looked the kind of library in which Francis Bacon might have sat in lofty contemplation, mapping out in his head a new direction for the intellectual flow of the Western world, leading it away from scholasticism and towards empirical scientific enquiry; or a profound theologian like Richard Hooker prescribing for the religious life of a nation; one could, even, imagine William Shakespeare coming quietly in and sitting unnoticed among the alcoves, leafing through volumes of Boccaccio or Cinthio or Ser Giovanni Fiorentino for stories that would spark off another play set in Renaissance Italy. No matter how many times I pushed open the tall wooden doors at this entrance and went inside, as I had done on that evening when I spoke for the last time with Salterton, I always felt a touch of the same *frisson* at being in such a place. It encouraged me in the thought that I was carrying a torch that had shed a long, steady light for humanity and was capable of going on shedding it.

This entrance to the Library was reached by climbing a short flight of stairs which curved gracefully to the left as it ascended, and as it happened the modest eighteenth-century building where I made my home was reached by going past the foot of this staircase. One evening I was late in coming back to College, having spent some hours in professional shop-talk with a fellow historian elsewhere. I had only just finished reading a book he recommended to me, Holland Rose's *William Pitt and the National Revival*, which throws a good deal of light on the sugar lobby in Parliament in the eighteenth century, and it had caused me to see the opposition to Pitt's Irish Resolutions of 1786 as part of an attempt to safeguard the prosperity of the West Indian sugar planters by keeping up the demand for British sugar – the same motivation, at bottom, as for the Molasses Act of 1733, very little changed in the half-century that had gone by. We had opened a good bottle of claret after dinner, sat by his fireside and talked out our ideas: a very pleasant evening, but it did mean that we forgot to watch the clock at all closely, and by the time I walked home it was late and the streets dark and silent; I heard my own footfall.

I let myself into Episcopus, for the gate had shut at midnight, went across the first quad, into the second, turned left along a passage, and had just reached the foot of the short Library staircase when something made me glance up towards the next floor, which I might easily not have done. The doors of the Library were correctly closed; the only light left burning was the single bulb on the staircase which would be on till morning; huddled on the stairs about half-way up lay a brown-coloured huddle, as shapeless as a heap of sacking carelessly thrown down, with the cold light of the electric bulb staring indifferently down on it. I stopped; I stared; then I hurried up the stairs and bent over the unstructured mass.

It was the brown colour of the material that first suggested an identity, even as I climbed hastily towards it. Bax possessed a suit of that colour. It was Bax's suit, Bax was inside it. He was unconscious. I moved him on to his back; he was breathing. I felt his limbs; nothing seemed to be broken. He had not fallen far, and must have bumped the side of his head as he hit the floor, because his glasses had been pushed over to one side and the frame was slightly twisted. I took them off. His eyes did not open and when I let go his head, it fell back. He was out to the wide world and he smelt like a distillery. I felt his pulse; it was normal, though a trifle rapid.

Bax was not a big man but he was a dead weight. I could not lift him, so I went and got the porter. Together we hoisted Bax up and took him to his rooms. His door was not locked, as it would have been if he had intended to leave College, and the reading-lamp on his desk was on. Books and papers were on his desk, obviously in process of being used. There was also a decanter, with not much left in it.

There were no prizes for reconstructing what had happened. Bax had been driving along the lonely night hours by working, and helping himself to whisky to keep his spirits up. At some point or other he had realized that he needed a book that was in the Library, and had let himself in and got it. But he must have been more drunk than he realized. Coming out of the Library, he had duly locked the door, but on turning to continue downstairs he had lost his balance and fallen. Had he stunned himself? It didn't seem likely. I felt his head for anything like a large bump, but found nothing. He had simply blacked out.

The porter and I stretched him out on his bed, flat on his back.

'Shall we call a doctor, sir?' the porter asked me. His name was Bob Clack and he had only recently joined the College. I supposed it was the first time he had ever had to deal with a situation of this kind.

'No,' I said. 'We'll just leave him. His pulse is normal and I don't suppose there's anything wrong with him that a good long sleep won't cure. Who's his scout?'

'Len Wright, sir.'

'Well, Bob, you get hold of Len Wright when he comes on duty in the morning and get him to bring Mr Bax a good pot of strong tea at about eight o'clock. If he won't drink that, it'll be time to call a doctor. But my guess is that he will.'

We parted and he went back to the lodge. I turned Bax's reading-lamp off and by the faint beams that came in through the window made my way to the door, which I closed gently. I stood for a moment outside it, thinking compassionately of my old tutor, re-membering how often I had knocked on that door and waited for his summons to go in and read my essay to him.

Before going back to my room, I went across to the spot where I had first seen the bundle of rags. If my theory was correct, Bax would have been carrying a book when he came out of the Library. I hadn't noticed any book, but then I had not at that stage been looking for one. Now that I was, I found it soon enough. It had fallen between the banisters and was lying in the shadow at the foot of the stairs. I picked it up, went up into the Library and put it back on the correct shelf. Then I looked in the box for 'Completed Slips' to see if Bax had gone through the formality of signing for it.

He had; or, at least, he had tried to. The book was one of the volumes of the Chatham Papers from the Public Record Office, of which Episcopus Library possessed a full set. He had filled out a slip, getting as far as putting the volume number. After that the writing became illegible. Then he had tried to sign 'R.S.C. Bax' and the result had just been a squiggle. There are some people who make a squiggle every time they sign, as if the simple act of spelling out their name were too much for them. Bax was not one of these. I had never seen his signature when it was not crystal-clear. Until now. Obvious-ly his drunkenness had suddenly hit him like a wave, and made him incapable of holding a pen.

I took the slip, crumpled it into a ball and put it in my pocket. Then I went and listened outside Bax's door, to see if I could hear any moaning or bumping about. But all was quiet, so I went to my own bed. But it was a long time before I slept.

*

The long, shadow-haunted frustration of regularly dialling Mairead's number and never, never, *never* finding her at home had now settled down into a solid, immovable part of my life. To hear her telephone ringing was no longer an experience that caused my heart first to leap skywards in a delirium of mingled fear and rapture, and then come thudding down helplessly on to the earth's crust like a shot bird. It was just something I did sullenly, inescapably, with neither dread nor hope. I did it because I had once started to do it. The monotonous repetition of that rite, morning and evening, gave me an insight into how religions gather about them their cults and observances: to dial that number, to sit for a certain number of minutes listening to the telephone calling, forlorn and ignored, into the empty air, and then to replace the receiver – it was something I went on doing because it was part of my nature. I could foresee a time when I would have forgotten why that procession of letters and numerals (for London telephone numbers in those days began with three letters, indicating the exchange, and went on to four numbers, as in WHITehall 1212) was the ritually correct combination to make. My worn-down brain, broken by disappointment and loneliness, would know only that the combination had once stood for something, or someone, of immense importance. I would never stop dialling that number, morning and evening, as monks never cease their praying and chanting. Unless, of course, the ringing should one day result in my speaking to Mairead. But that, after about the ninth day, began to seem to me like the kind of thing that might be expected to happen on another planet, not on ours.

Then, one morning at about half-past eight, she answered. It was so unexpected that I didn't even have time to feel any surprise. My voice just went ahead automatically and I began talking to her as if the event were not earth-shaking at all, just ordinary.

'Hello,' she said, just in that ordinary way.

'Hello, it's Peter,' I said. I said it flatly and unemphatically. Take it or leave it, this is Peter.

'Hello, Peter.'

'Mairead,' I said, feeling excitement mounting in me but fighting hard to hold it down. 'Mairead.'

'You must be ringing to say something more than just my name.'

'Don't bank on it. Just saying your name, especially saying it to you, is a tremendous pleasure to me. Mairead, Mairead, Mairead,' I added by way of illustration.

'Peter, I have to go to work.'

'I'm not ringing to waste your time. I'd hate to do that. Mairead, Mairead . . .'

'I'm going to ring off. I'm all ready to go to work and it's time to leave now. I can't stand here and listen to you babbling.'

'I won't babble. I've got news.'

'Tell me later.'

'I can say it in a second. I'm divorced. Legally dismarried.'

She said nothing. I was listening carefully, and I distinctly heard her say nothing.

'Mairead? Are you there?'

'Yes, I'm here but I have to go to work.'

'I've been trying and trying to get you on the phone.'

'I've been away.'

She was silent again. I said, 'When can we talk for longer?'

'You want to talk for longer, do you?'

'Well, for Christ's sake, of course I do. Obviously I do. For Christ's—'

'I'll be in tonight.'

'What time?'

'Any time. I'll be in all evening.'

'Well, I'll ring tonight, of course. I mean for Christ's sake. I want to get your reaction.'

'Do I have to have a reaction?'

I swallowed. 'You mean . . . I've been waiting for four and a half years to be able to tell you I'm legally free and now it's happened you've no reaction?'

'I don't know. I'm frightened. It's very sudden and I had my mind on other things and all at once you drop this on me. I feel cold. All my body's gone cold. And I have to go to work.'

'I'm sorry,' I said. I really meant it, I could see how ham-handed I'd been. 'I'm terribly sorry, darling. Do go to work and don't worry and just have an ordinary day and feel useful and wanted, which you are. And I'll ring you this evening and I'll try not to give you any surprises.'

'All right.'

'All I ever want to do is to love you and care for you.'

'All right. I feel cold. I'm going to walk fast. It'll warm me up. I oughtn't to need warming up because it's a lovely mild day. It must be the suddenness, the shock.'

'It's just the unexpectedness, darling. It came as a surprise. But don't think of it as a shock.'

'I don't know what to think of it, Peter. I'm going to work. That's the only thing I feel certain about.'

I started to say something, rehearsing the stuff about ringing her that evening, but obviously she didn't want to hear all that again, and I heard her put down the receiver and then she was gone.

I got through that day somehow; fortunately I had plenty of routine things to do. I tried not to be too thrown by Mairead's hesitant and dubious attitude. After all, it was quite likely to be due to surprise as to anything else. It was a pretty hard ball to throw at her, suddenly, and expect her to catch it and look glad at the same time. I must go gently, I thought. Give her a bit of time to draw her breath.

And for that matter I would try to set everything up as normally as possible at my end. I would not, for instance, take my name off the list for dinner, as had been my first impulse. About seven o'clock would be the earliest feasible time to ring Mairead, but if I actually did ring her then it would mean doing without an evening meal, and while I would gladly have gone without food for a week if it had served any realistic purpose, it seemed to me just now that I might as well have a meal inside me to help carry me through whatever ups and downs this evening was destined to bring.

Dinner was at 7.15. It took just over half an hour to eat the customary three courses and be ready to leave the Hall. Those taking dessert would then peel off to the Common Room where it was served; the rest were free to go about their business. My business was to get back to Pearce's Building and telephone Mairead. After the long period of waiting, during which it had begun to seem an impossible ambition that I should speak to her again ever in my life, there was something almost surreal in the way it had now decided to go with laughable ease and smoothness. *Nihil obstat!* Just as I had done in the morning, I dialled the number and immediately found myself talking to Mairead. It was not yet eight o'clock; the evening lay calmly ahead.

'I must have seemed a bit thrown this morning, Peter,' she said. What was this, an apology? 'It all came a bit out of the blue and I didn't know how to react at first.'

'I don't know what kind of reaction I expected from you,' I said. 'After all, everything in the situation was unpredictable except the one bedrock fact that the whole situation is built on. I mean the fact that as soon as I knew I was no longer someone else's husband, I was going to tell you so. That you'd known all along. Everything else was an unknown quantity – when it would be, what each one of us would be doing and thinking at the moment when it suddenly surfaced, all the circumstances.'

'Yes, and add to that the fact that you'd already rung me a couple of times when you hadn't actually anything to communicate.'

'Those two calls didn't do anything to make the situation worse, did they?'

'Well,' she said, and seemed to be thinking carefully, 'there were already enough bad things about the situation that it could hardly have been any worse. But it did mean that when I first heard your voice this morning I just gathered that you were ringing me and I had no idea what to expect.'

'Whereas now,' I said, 'you've had a day to let it sink in.'

'Yes.'

'So you know I've come round to the same point I was at in 1947, only now I've sweated it out and earned my right to approach you.'

There was a little pause and then she said, 'Is that what you're doing, Peter? Approaching me?'

'Yes, Mairead. I love you and I want to be close to you.'

'What does it mean, be close to me?'

'It means anything you want it to mean. If I'm really lucky it could mean that you'd be my wife. But if that's too much to ask for all at once, couldn't we just begin by getting to know each other over again? Seeing each other and talking and just sharing the same space and breathing the same air and hearing each other's voices?'

'Ye-e-es,' she said as if forcing herself, for the sake of fairness, to agree to something she wasn't keen about. 'But how would we begin? How would we set up the first time?'

'Anyhow you like. Why make it complicated? Let's just fix on somewhere to meet and meet there and get started.'

'Peter,' she said, 'it isn't me and it isn't you who are making it complicated. It *is* complicated. It's just complicated by its nature.'

'But look here, why should it be? Mairead, for years I haven't known your address. All I've had is that one little magic number to keep me alive. Why don't you just tell me where you live and I'll come to you there?'

'No,' she said.

'Why no?'

'I can't quite explain. I'd feel . . . uncomfortable somehow, suddenly bringing you into this space that I've had to surround myself with . . . I can't explain.'

'Well, come to me.'

'Come to you? In Oxford, you mean?'

'Where else? It's where I live.'

'I suppose you're ringing now from wherever you live. What kind of place is it?'

'It's a college.'

'Oh,' she said. 'I wouldn't like that.'

'My love, you've absolutely no means of visualizing where I live.

−212−

It's a modest and very elegant eighteenth-century building overlooking a secluded strip of garden.'

'Oh, I don't think I'd want us to have an important moment in our lives . . . well, if that's what it's going to be . . .'

'That's what it's going to be,' I said firmly.

'. . . in an Oxford college. It sounds so *institutional*.'

'Oh, I promise you it's nothing of the kind. It's just where I live. It's my *home*.'

But she went on just as if I had said nothing. 'If you had a house you'd rented and I came to see you in it, I'd just be a normal visitor.'

'Mairead, you'll never be just a normal visitor.'

'You know what I mean. But if I come and see you in your grand college rooms, I'll be an appendage.'

'Oh, come on.'

'It wouldn't be just you I'd be coming to see, it'd be Oxford. The whole top-heavy system with porters' lodges and servants' halls and leather armchairs in the Common Rooms and priceless works of art on the walls and rare editions in the library. And I'd just be one small person.'

'I never expected to hear this line of talk from you.'

'You don't know what to expect from me. It's been a long time since we met.'

'Yes, but it doesn't seem like you to . . . that line of talk is so *external*. An Oxford college isn't just the stuff you see in the first ten minutes. There's a cosy side to it all . . . domesticated . . . . You don't know it, that's all.'

'No, I don't know Oxford, but I've visited plenty of people at T.C.D. in my time and that's modelled in the same way. It's like Oxford or Cambridge except that everything's a bit more frayed and worn and the silver's tarnished. Our first meeting should be somewhere ordinary, and human, and impartial.'

'Oh, God – not another hotel bar.'

She laughed. 'No, I wouldn't want that either. I won't come to Oxford, not to begin with. But fortunately I've got a counter-suggestion.'

'Oh? Where *you* live, perhaps? I'll come anywhere,' I said quickly.

'Well, it's only to Barnes.'

Barnes? Oh yes, on the river. Over Hammersmith Bridge and turn left, or right, or something. 'I can find that,' I said. 'Where and when?'

'I have a friend who lives there, and she's going to be away in Rome for a month. It's Siobhán, as a matter of fact, the one you met long ago in Dublin. She has a small flat and she's asked me as a favour to go there now and again and see that everything's all right, and that it hasn't been broken into or anything. I thought of going there for a day or two one weekend anyway. I know she'd be glad, especially if I rang her up from there. So I've more or less decided to go.'

'And I could come there and see you?'

'Yes, Peter.' Her voice had a gentleness that stirred my heart. Oh, how lyrically it stirred my heart.

'What day? Friday evening? Saturday?'

'Saturday. In the afternoon, about four.'

'This Saturday?' I pressed.

'No, a week on Saturday.'

I knew it was no use showing impatience. At the moment I had to be grateful for whatever I got. 'Well,' I said, 'it'll come, if I wait hard enough.'

'If you mean because you're eager to see me,' she said, 'you've just waited four and a half years.'

'Yes,' I said. 'But as I've just explained, it's all different now I've heard you.'

'Has that brought it nearer?'

'It's working with two hands. With one hand it's brought our actual meeting much nearer, and with the other it's pushed it away to an immeasurable distance.'

'Sounds a very complicated state of mind,' she said, gravely but with an undertone of amusement. And, somewhere within the *nuances* of her manner, there was sympathy, too, and warmth. I heard them, I swear.

'May I have the address of Siobhán's place in Barnes?' I asked.

She gave it to me, and after a few sentences more we rang off. Before doing so I got in one more 'I love you' and this time she said, 'I'm glad to hear that.'

★

I'm not very good at timing journeys in London. I find it difficult to predict how long each leg of the journey will take. Never having lived in London except for that spell in wartime, when everything was so different, I'm more or less permanently reconciled to being too early or too late when I turn up anywhere. If it's anything of importance, the only thing is to get there ridiculously early, establish exactly where the place is, and then while away the time somehow until the moment comes to show up.

So this is what I did on the Saturday when I was bidden to meet Mairead at her friend Siobhán's flat in Barnes. Catching a train from Oxford that arrived at Paddington just after three, I took a taxi to

Barnes and let the driver have the job of finding the actual building. When he dropped me, which because of the traffic stream he did on the opposite side of the road, I had forty minutes to wait. That suited me. I crossed over to the building – 1930s, featureless, a block of flats similar to countless others – and checked the names against the bells.

Mairead had given me Siobhán's address and the number presumably indicated what number her flat was. Nervous as I was, I would have liked to know Siobhán's surname, as a double check, but she hadn't given it to me. In any case, was the name outside necessarily Siobhán's surname? Was it a temporary address or permanent? Questions of this kind flooded into my mind, testifying to my anxiety. You would have thought I was a dispatch rider trying to get through an area under heavy bombardment rather than a sedate 39-year-old citizen who had been given a perfectly normal address in a perfectly normal part of London. And yet I wasn't wrong either. Nothing in my situation was perfectly normal when you stopped to think about it. And I had stopped to think about it.

I stood there in the hallway of this lifeless and rather spotty block of flats, peering at the names. The one beside the number I had been given was 'O'hUid.' No initial. None of them had initials. They all looked as if they had been tapped out on the same slightly battered typewriter. Well, if a surname in isolation can say anything, this one certainly said 'Irish'. And Irish in spades too. *Echt*-Irish. Witness the wacky spelling. It must be one of those names that have been decolonized, re-Hibernicized. So far, it all seemed solid.

Not long now till four o'clock. Did anything remain to be done? Oh, yes. Shaving-cream. I had with me a small knapsack in which I had packed the things I would need for the journey. Not only the journey there and the journey back, but an overnight stay. Two overnight stays, if need be.

It had taken me a great deal of thought and puzzlement and speculation to pack that knapsack. I had emptied it out and filled it again at least four times. It contained a couple of books I might want to read on the train, and beyond that nothing except the basic requirements for a night away from one's home. Toothbrush, sponge-bag, that kind of thing, plus a pair of lightweight slippers and a change of underwear. It was the overnight stuff that had caused me the thinking and puzzling. I had so little basis for speculation. When Mairead had said that I could meet her at Siobhán's flat in Barnes at four o'clock on a Saturday afternoon, how long had she anticipated our staying there? Would it be a full-scale weekend together, or would it be a cup of tea with a slice of lemon in it, an earnest conversation in quiet voices, and then off, leaving the place tidy and being careful to take the door-key away in Mairead's handbag, parting on the pavement to go to our respective destinations, perhaps with an arrangement to meet again? Either alternative seemed artificial and unlikely when one looked at it closely. If Mairead and I still meant to each other all the things we had meant, then obviously we would not be meeting in a flat that we were to have to ourselves for any other purpose than to spend the weekend together. Ah, but did we still mean to each other what we had meant? Or some of it? Or parts of it? And if so, what parts? And in what proportions, as between her and me? I wanted the whole bag, that was easy enough. But what did Mairead want? Was it likely that she even knew, at this stage? Was she going to make up her mind, on the strength of what it was like seeing me again, after (wait for it) FOUR YEARS AND SEVEN MONTHS? If she was going to make up her mind, how would she react if she happened to find out that I had brought my overnight kit with me instead of just assuming humbly that I would be back in Oxford after a few hours? Come to that, wouldn't it have been better not to bring anything, and just let my stubble grow, and clean my teeth with my fingers dipped in salt? Who needed overnight bags? Had Romeo taken an overnight bag, when he swarmed nimbly up on to Juliet's balcony on that myth-creating night in Verona? To hear Shakespeare tell it, he seems to have knocked her off pretty satisfactorily without benefit of toiletries.

Of course there was no need to let Mairead know what my knapsack contained. I could easily manoeuvre it out of sight. But quite apart from Mairead's knowing what I had in there, what about the immortal gods, the never-sleeping ones up there? The Fates, the Parcae, whoever it was who kept a jealous eye on people who got pieces of good fortune and took them for granted or enjoyed them too conspicuously? Human beings have always believed that the gods are jealous, that if they think you are getting away with anything they will punish you for it. If I succeeded in pulling it off with Mairead I would indeed deserve punishment if good luck is punishable; it would be such a huge, resplendent, over-the-top, walloping, king-size slab of good luck and happiness. Even to be conscious of it, let alone to brag about it even in the silence of one's own mind, would come perilously close to *hubris*.

Standing here, knapsack on my shoulders, staring at the word O'hUid, I abruptly made a decision. When I was finally re-stowing my overnight kit in the bag that morning, having packed and unpacked and then packed and unpacked again, I had noticed that my tube of shaving-cream had terminally squeezed flat when I had shaved. I had no shaving-cream. I had made a note to get some, and I had not done so. It would be four o'clock in a few minutes. If there was a shop anywhere near where I could get a new tube, I would buy one. In view of the fact that

I had to have one anyway, that I would be shaving the next morning whether I was here in Barnes or back in Oxford, I decided that to purchase one wouldn't look conspicuously like a show of *hubris*. Glad to have the decision made, I hurried out of the building.

Barnes didn't seem to have a main shopping street, or if it did I wasn't successful in finding it in that hasty exploration, but I ran across a street with a parade of shops and one of them was a pharmacy. It even had my usual brand of shaving-cream. I bought one and stowed it carefully in the knapsack. The chips were down now; it was Mairead or bust.

I settled the knapsack on again and walked back to the flats. As I drew near, I became aware that someone was walking behind me. I was moving fairly fast, in my tension and eagerness, but this person, with a light feminine step, was moving faster. I didn't look round; in a city environment it often happens that someone else is treading close behind you for a few moments, till your paths diverge. But when I turned in at the entrance to the hallway, this lightly-stepping person turned in also. I knew that she, for it must be a she, was now no more than a couple of yards behind me. I wasn't afraid of being attacked from behind – our urban society had not yet reached that phase – but I felt curious. I stopped and immediately turned round. The person who had been behind me, and was now in front of me, was Mairead. She was carrying a shopping basket.

She smiled at me and said, 'I think we're going to the same place.'

She went up a flight of stone steps and I followed her dumbly. Coming to rest before a door, she unlocked it and opened it, then went inside and with her free hand held the door open for me. I entered still dumbly. She let the door shut behind us and turned to look at me. I was still mute as I stood and looked back at her. Would I be speechless for ever, I wondered. Had my vocal cords vaporized or snapped or something? It didn't matter, I didn't need words, all I needed were my eyes to look at her. Her beauty was totally unchanged. No, not unchanged. It had become more dramatic, more assured, more exquisitely true and right in every detail. I just wanted to look and look and look and look.

Then she kissed me. She took her time about it. During that time I ceased to want nothing more than to look. I ceased to be of the opinion that I could respond to her adequately using my eyes only. I took her in my arms. We stayed like that for a long time. We had still come no more than two steps into the interior of the flat. But it was enough.

When we finally let go of one another, I had the impression that it wouldn't be for long. I let the knapsack slip from my shoulders and slung it over a chair. I knew it didn't matter, now, what was in it or not in it. Mairead and I were together. We had come an immeasurable distance, and we had arrived together. My voice returned, but it was not much needed. The events of the next hour or two, by themselves and with no verbal garnish, were enough to establish once and for all that Mairead's opening remark to me had been true. We had, indeed, been going to the same place.

After we had finished making love . . .

No, that doesn't get it. I could come a little nearer by saying, 'After our fierce sexual need for each other had used us for its purposes till our limp and sated bodies were no longer usable and it had cast us aside to be renewed in sleep . . .' And even that would still be only one way of putting it; anyway, when that stage had come and gone, and when we had slept, Mairead rolled on to her back and turned her dark head on the pillow and looked at me and said, 'I will marry you if you like.'

I was awake in an instant: up and running, you might say. 'What d'you mean, if I like? Isn't it the one thing I've been asking you to do ever since I found you again?'

She laughed gently. 'You're getting quite an Irish inflexion. "Shure, and isn't it the one thing I'm after asking ye to do ever since I found ye again?" ' She uttered the question in a stage-Irish brogue and laughed again, softly, moving towards me in the warmth of the bed.

'Well, sure and it is, and why wouldn't it be? That's settled then,' I said. 'We'll get married as soon as ever the arrangements can be made. Gretna Green if necessary!'

That was fine, as far as it went. That is, it was all right as a verbal gesture at a moment that called for verbal gestures. Unfortunately, it was also true that, profoundly in love as I was, I also possessed a memory. I had a pretty good recollection of the conversation we had had in the bar of the Great Western Hotel, Paddington Station, on that bleak evening in 1947. I could even hear my voice, quiet and desperately in earnest, entreating Mairead to let me share her life on any terms, any terms at all. I remembered her saying, 'What about my career?' and the exact words of my answer: 'You needn't interrupt it if you don't want to.' She: 'How on earth could I combine going on with it with coming to Oxford and living with you?' I: 'Who said anything about coming to Oxford?'

And then I had given her all that bullshit about buying a house in Ealing because that was as far west as the London Underground got out to, and the pair of us getting up early every morning and she going to London and I to Oxford. I couldn't remember, now, what had actually been going on in my head when I uttered those words. Had I really found them credible? Obviously they were forced out of me by desperate need, the need to keep her talking and stop her from breaking away and ending the interview, but had I been doing any more than improvising, just flapping my mouth and sending words out into the air?

And even if, in my desperation, grabbing at the flimsy story as a drowning man grabs at a straw, even if there had been a momentary crumb of belief behind it that some such arrangement *could* be worked out, how could that possibly apply to the sheer raving I had gone on to utter a few moments later? That stuff about how if Mairead got posted abroad I'd come with her and try to pick up any kind of odd job – lift attendant in the Embassy building, for instance, or security guard. What rubbish! I wondered, now, how even in the fever of that moment I could have brought myself to utter such drivel. She had shown unusual patience – or was it indifference? – in listening to it at all. What kind of security guard would I have made? Come to that, what chance would I have had of even being considered for the job of security guard? And by an *Irish* government agency, yet?

Never mind, it could all wait. I lay back and held Mairead close to me. She showed no reluctance; I hadn't expected her to. After what had happened in the – by objective standards – brief time since we had entered the flat, I knew that reluctance on Mairead's part was simply not part of the programme. My energies had not yet recovered to the point where I felt the need to do more than just hold her close and revel in the nearness of our bodies. As we lay there, squashed up together, I could feel the aforesaid energies beginning to seep back along my veins, like a superbly fit combat force reporting for duty in twos and threes. The next explosion was not far away. But it was not here yet.

Outside, it was a bright October afternoon. The long windows of Siobhán's bedroom faced west; her sitting-room, and the kitchen where she obviously had her breakfast, were on the other side of a central corridor and they faced east, doubtless to get the morning sun. So much I made out by a mixture of peering around and using my common sense. I had not, so far, set foot in any of Siobhán's rooms except this one, which was now bright with sunlight. I thought, kindly, of Siobhán. I thought of her large eyes that spoke both of intelligence and emotion. I thought of her physical, and doubtless psychological, femininity. I thought of the softly rounded shape of her jawbone. It was a firm jaw but it did not thrust forward aggres-sively. She was a gentle person. I was glad that Mairead had her for a friend.

She had me for a friend too, of course, and as I lay there looking up at the ceiling without paying any attention to it, I knew clearly that the immediate next task was to convince her of the reality of this friendship and to cement it immovably in (a) her consciousness and (b) the structure of her habits and expectations. Some of this convinc-ing would have to be done by words, and very prosaic words at that, because my objective was dailyness and domesticity and all the calmly unsurprising but joyous things that go along with them. But there would be a time for that. I wanted to be Mairead's husband, but I knew that the best way to be a woman's husband is to be her lover first. If the suitor is successful in that, then the move from the first role to the second is not like the move from one position on a chart to another position. Rather, it is like the way a tree grows by adding new rings. The rings simply accumulate with time, and they change size and shape to fit in with the tree's developing needs.

Was it time, yet, for the tree-rings to begin changing? I didn't think so, not yet. On the other hand, new growth was always a good thing.

About three hours later we woke up ravenously hungry, went into the kitchen and devoured some of the food supplies that Mairead had in her basket. When we were no longer hungry for food, but still hungry for each other, we came back and dived into bed and I pursued the policy some more. Finally we both fell asleep till morning.

When I became aware that Mairead had woken up, I said softly into her ear, 'Good morning, darling. This is the first day of the rest of our lives.'

'No, darling Peter,' she said. 'Yesterday was that.'

I wasn't going to argue. I knew it was one or the other. Or both.

★

Sunday morning was fine and blowy. Mairead and I agreed that we would spend the day together till early evening. We had no plans, it was enough just to be together, but naturally we went out for a walk. We walked on Barnes Common, and sometimes we sat down on the grass. The fine autumn weather went with us everywhere. For a couple of hours in the middle of the day it was as warm as August, but without the sultriness. We were happy; we laughed a lot and we kissed often.

Sometimes, though, a serious mood came to us. Happy as we were, we had no wish to spend the time just skipping and gambolling like lambs. We weren't lambs, whose only responsibility is to be happy until the day comes for the butcher's knife. We were people, who intended to live a life together.

'Of course,' I said, meditatively chewing a grass stalk, 'it's going to involve a completely new start.'

'Marriage always does. But I agree that ours will be more than usually thorough-going.'

'Yes. Everything points to that. Not only that we've had years of not seeing each other and having no contact, but even before that, during our previous life, as it were. We knew each other so well, in some ways we knew everything there was to know about each other, and yet if you look at it another way we were almost strangers.'

-220-

She leaned over and kissed me and said, 'Strangers who met on a train.'

'There were such huge areas of silence. Things it just wouldn't have done to talk about.'

She nodded. 'I knew nothing about your home, your background. I had to treat you like somebody who just didn't have a background. Somebody who materialized at my door and then just de-materialized when it was time to go. Very artificial. Still, we lived with it.'

'I wonder,' I said, 'whether it'll seem easier now that there won't be any silences, now that people and places and situations will come flooding in to those vast areas of vacuum, or whether . . .'

'Whether it'll become harder, you were going to say?'

'Well . . . Not harder, just like that, but more complex. More to take account of.'

'No,' Mairead said decidedly. 'Silence is the most difficult thing. Whole areas that you can't mention, and don't even allow yourself to think about, are the ones that have to be taken account of most of all. They never lie down to sleep.'

Wordlessly, I had to acknowledge the total justice of this.

'But now,' I said with a bound of relief, 'we can open the doors and windows on all of it. Our relationship is now in the broad daylight, except for those bits of it that are sacredly our own business, just for the two of us. There's nothing we need keep secret from anybody. It's free, and open, and between us there needn't be any silences. Let's talk, talk, talk. Look at the amount we've got to talk about! You've never met my parents or Michael.'

'I've never met Heather, either.'

'That'll have to be a matter of choice. Your choice and hers.'

'Still, at least I don't have to confront her as the new element in the situation: the sudden interloper, the marriage-wrecker. Even if at bottom that's what I am,' she added so quietly that I hardly caught the words.

'Mairead, meeting you wouldn't have done any harm to my marriage if the marriage itself had had any strength to it. I know every husband in my position says that, but there have to be cases where it's true and ours is one of them. If you want to go on brooding along those lines—'

'I *don't* want to,' she cried out with sudden loudness.

'—then do, if you must, but at least you won't have to brood in silence. Or loneliness. You can tell me anything it's a help to tell me, and that'll make a difference, you'll see.'

'So go on,' she said, sitting very composedly, her hands laced round her knees. 'I've never seen your home, your birthplace or where you live now, I've never met your parents or your son or your brother Brian – that'll do to be starting with.'

'Does it all matter very much?'

'In one way, very much, because getting to know them is part of getting to know you. And in another way it doesn't matter a jot, because whatever they turn out to be like won't make any difference to how I feel about you because I love you.'

The grass, the wind, the blue sky, the bushes, the straying white clouds, seemed to hear her words and to believe them and to add their blessing. That's what grammarians who write about poetry call the Pathetic Fallacy. Used to good effect by a poet like Wordsworth, for instance, in such lines as:

> There's not a breathing of the common wind
> That shall forget thee.

I could have done with a few poets of that stature around me at that moment. I had a subject ready for them. But they were not there. It was the only thing in the universe, at that moment, that I could have found to grumble about.

'Your parents,' I said to Mairead as we walked on. 'Will they like me? Are they very Irish? Is there anything I can do to present myself in a good light to them?'

'They're very Irish in some ways. They're Catholic, so I'm a disappointment to them because although I've never formally re-nounced my Catholic upbringing, it doesn't play an active part in my life. I've never mentioned it to you, for instance.'

'No. I suppose it was one of the areas of silence.'

'Yes, though not one of the most urgent of them because it was an issue already settled. I just found belief, of that kind and along those particular lines, an impossibility.'

'So do I. I particularly detest Tertullian.'

'My parents see me pretty much as a lapsed Catholic, which is about like being a fallen woman. They can just about cope with that, because they've got a category ready for it: they can get it into a box and give it a name, *lapsed*. Of course my father, being a professional scientist, has a slightly more elastic mind than my mother. But it's not all that elastic. Years of poring over forms of mutation in marine plant cells don't do all that much to broaden your outlook, though they may do something to keep you in a state of readiness for the unexpected.'

'They must love you very much.'

'Why must they?'

'Because anyone would. And because the people who brought you into the world would naturally be very proud of you. Any brothers and sisters? From the fact that in all the time we saw so much of each other you never mentioned them would lead me to think you hadn't, and yet you don't seem like an only child to me.'

'What does an only child seem like?'

'Oh, I don't know . . . Someone who's used to getting all the attention, I suppose.'

Mairead looked away into the distance. 'I have a brother.'

'No! How strange that you never spoke of him. Is he, at a guess, much younger than you?'

'As a matter of fact he's a couple of years older.'

I've picked another younger sister, I thought. Ah, well, this one will be different. At least I know her brother hasn't crowded her into a corner of her own life.

'Why,' Mairead asked, 'did you think he might have been younger than me?'

'The fact of the war. If he's your kind of age-group, he'd probably have been drawn into some sort of proximity with it. He'd have wanted to help us or help the Germans. Or perhaps he'd be a fanatic for Irish neutrality. In any case it would be strange if he'd been completely absent from your thoughts during the war years, as an Irish member of the diplomatic staff working in a combatant country.'

'Well reasoned. I can see you're going to grow into a good historian.' Then the gently teasing smile faded and she said gravely, even sadly, 'Dermot was very confused about the war.'

'That's his name, is it? Dermot?'

'Yes. Dermot Hoey. And that's his real name. He's not one of those Irish people who started out in life with names they grew to feel uncomfortable with because they were too English. That was the generation of Sean O'Casey, people who started out with run-of-the-mill English names and re-named themselves to show their solidarity with the Irish national movement. Come to think of it, I suppose my parents are just about of O'Casey's generation so they made the re-alignment with their children's names rather than their own. If I'd been twenty years older I expect I'd have been christened Mary.'

'I'm glad you're not twenty years older,' I said. 'I'd have felt just the same about you, because in twenty years' time you'll still be you and just as magical, but I don't suppose I'd have had a chance. You'd have been snapped up.'

'I don't know whether I would or not. I wasn't one of those marriage-at-all-costs girls. I had a career and I always thought that would make a life for me, if it turned out that I didn't have any other.'

That brought me slap up against the problem that was obviously going to be the most difficult: Mairead's career. Could she still pursue it while being the wife of an Oxford don? Come to that, would being the wife of an Oxford don, me or anyone else, suit her? Or would the major adaptation have to come from said Oxford don? It was all very well, I thought, to tell myself that I could float her on a tide of sexual bliss that would somehow lift her over these barriers, but it obviously wasn't going to work for ever, or even for long.

These thoughts began to make me feel very hemmed in. To push them away for as long as I could, I switched the conversation back to where it had been a few moments earlier. 'Why was Dermot confused about the war?' I asked.

'Well, obviously. He wanted the Germans to win and yet he was afraid of what they might do if they did win.'

'What they might do to the Irish, I suppose.'

'Of course. He wouldn't care what they or anybody would do to the English. If the English were made to suffer as horribly as the Poles, for instance, or the Jews for that matter, he'd only say they had it coming and they weren't going through anything they hadn't put other people through in their time.'

'Is that your opinion too?'

She hesitated for about a second. 'I'd say that my own opinion was along more or less the same lines as Dermot's, but I don't push it all the way as he does.'

'Well,' I said, 'thank goodness he had the intelligence at least to be frightened of what the Nazis would have done if they'd occupied Ireland, as they certainly would if only on the pretext of rooting out scattered guerrilla activity. Naturally there'd be pockets of English who'd managed to get across the Irish Sea and they'd fight. The Germans would have taken over and then Dermot would have found himself living under Nazi occupation like the English and the Dutch and the French and the Norwegians and the Greeks and the Poles and the Czechs and the Channel Islanders and, and . . . have I forgotten anybody?'

'He wouldn't have liked that,' Mairead said, 'and I expect that's why he didn't let himself actually be recruited by the German espionage system and give them active help. But I have a mood when I believe his chief objection to a German victory would have been that it meant sharing a common fate with England. He wouldn't want to share *anything* with England.'

'What's he going to think about his sister marrying an Englishman?'

'He won't like it. But he won't do anything concrete about it. He won't attack you or anything. He'll just keep away.'

'Well, that'll be something,' I said. 'What does he spend his time doing, anyway?'

'I haven't the slightest idea. No one in the family has.'

I began to hope that I might join the rest of the family in that untroubled category. It would have been foolish to deny that Dermot had ample justification for his grudge against the English, in view of what they had done to his countrymen and women since the smaller island was first invaded by the larger in 1169, during the reign of the king who had had Thomas à Becket cut down in front of the altar in his own cathedral. I admitted that I participated in the collective guilt of the English for what they had done to the Irish, but I had enough of the ordinary selfishness of *l'homme moyen sensuel* to hope that I personally would not have to pay for my particular share of it.

'So,' I said cautiously, 'we don't actually have to *do* anything about Dermot?'

'Nothing in the world.'

'If he meets me, will he feel obliged to insult me?'

'He might perfectly well insult either of us, but that won't be the end of the world. The English have had such a long period of being top dogs that they don't know how to put up with being insulted. There are plenty of nations who are insulted so routinely that they hardly notice it. They retire into their own inner landscape and let the insults bounce off them. And perhaps they compensate by being nice to one another, which the English quite noticeably aren't.'

'What it all means,' I said, 'is that I must be willing to learn. I must even learn from Dermot.'

'Not so free with that "even",' Mairead said. 'Dermot is an awkward, unsociable being but he is my brother, which must mean that there's a bit of him in me somewhere and a bit of me in him.'

'I'm sorry, I truly am,' I said. 'I hope you'll forgive me for being clumsy and stupid.' I really meant it.

'I'll forgive you, sweetheart, unto seventy times seven or whatever it says in the good book. And what I'm forgiving you for isn't anything to do with being stupid because it's all so new to you. I never met an English person yet who had any idea what it really feels like to be Irish.'

'I'll only say in my own defence that I don't share the usual complacent English view that everybody loves us because we're such nice people. I know that's just because we're very good at sweeping our bad qualities under the carpet and looking at the past through sentimental eyes.'

'Certainly, not everybody loves you but not everybody has the same motive for hating you. The Welsh and the Scots have been kept poor by the English, but neither of them have been as poor as the Irish. Even the Hebridean crofters didn't have to go through anything like the Potato Famine of the 1840s, when a million Irish starved. It would have been so much more noticeable – they were too close to Glasgow, not stuck away in a forgotten area of bogland over in the west of Ireland where no English person ever went.'

As usual in conversations of this kind, the John Bull in me began to feel a need to hit back. 'You mean,' I said mutinously, 'that I, and every other English person, have to go on paying for the Potato Famine?'

She turned and gave me a level look with those blue eyes that always pierced right into the centre of my being.

'Yes, I do mean that.'

'Oh.'

'Look, Peter, try to understand one thing. When an outrage as colossal as the Irish famine of the 1840s, or the murder of the European Jews in the 1940s, is perpetrated, somebody always pays for it. The human race can't just cross it off and turn over a new page in the ledger. It's paid for, either by the people who did it or the people who suffered it. And in some ways probably by both.'

I nodded silently. Of course the Irish Potato Famine of the 1840s had been inflicted on them by the English. It didn't result from any negligence or laziness on the part of the Irish work-force; it was purely the chance introduction of a virus that attacked one plant, the potato. In other areas Irish agriculture was producing an abundance of food, but the terms and conditions of trade had decreed inexorably that that food was destined for England. The Irish, who actually produced the food, were forbidden to consume it. They had to exist on potatoes, and when the potato crop failed a million starved.

Incredible? You couldn't possibly keep a starving people from eating food they had produced? Stalin did exactly that to the Ukrainians in the early 1930s. Nine million died that time. I knew Mairead had not imagined what she was telling me about her country. I had known it already, as a matter of objective information, but knew it with my whole body and mind now that I heard it in her words.

How did it all affect me, personally? I, Peter Leonard, native of the English Midlands, child of (at best) blue-collar stock, intellectual by profession, loved and desired this young Irishwoman who sat beside me on the grass of Barnes Common. In outward manner and appearance she was a typical young woman of the mid-century, articulate, agile, unshackled from the heavy Victorian past. Wearing a crisp outdoor shirt and casual trousers, she looked full of possibility, full of health and enjoyment, ready to cope with whatever life brought to her. I, deeply in love, wanted to be part – to be a central part – of what it brought. Was there still a barrier? Were a million corpses, their limbs and faces dreadful with emaciation, rising now from their mass graves to forbid my love, to drive me away with deep ancestral curses?

'Enough!' a voice cried in my head. 'These are not real thoughts, these are the fantasies of a sick child. If you want a man's life, live like a man!'

I got up on to my feet and looked down at her as she sat there, her legs carelessly stretched out, her body tilted slightly backwards, the weight of her upper half supported by the flat of her hands on the grass behind her.

'Mairead,' I said, 'I love you and I want to marry you no matter what my people did to your people a century ago. I want to take care of you and cherish you without any thought of nationality or of race, Anglo-Saxon or Celt; I just want it to be because I am I and you are you and because love and permanence are the right things for us.'

I fell silent. I had said everything I had to say. She looked up at me with that warm, tender smile and said, 'I can name another thing you want.'

I looked at her enquiringly and she continued, 'You want what an Englishman always wants about mid-day on a Sunday. A pint of beer in a pub.'

'Doesn't an Irishman insist on that too, after Mass?' I asked.

'No,' she said and smiled again. 'An Irishman has a pint of porter.'

She stretched out her hand for me to help her up and when I gave her the initial pull she sprang lightly to her feet. 'Let's go towards the river,' she said. 'I want to drink in a riverside pub.'

We walked briskly towards the Thames. Mairead's tread was springy as if she were dancing. She seemed happy. And surely it was not just seeming – surely she really was happy? What reason would she have for counterfeiting it? Timorous and pessimistic as I had become, suspicious of any promise of happiness that might reveal itself as a let-down, I believed it and started to feel happy myself, more and more so with every jubilant step we took. We went over Hammersmith Bridge and down on to the little paved promenade known as Lower Mall. From there we could keep company with the river, walking upstream on the left-hand bank. In this immediate neighbourhood there were two pubs we could choose from, the Blue Anchor and the Doves. We chose the Doves, which was a few minutes' walk further on but had a yard with seats where one could sit by the Thames.

So Mairead had her wish. And I, being next to her, had my wish. And she had a bottled light ale and I had a pint of draught, pulled so skilfully and with such a perfectly judged head that my father himself couldn't have done it better. And when I say that, I say everything.

By coincidence, or at least I assume it was pure coincidence unless Someone Up There had been watching for exactly the right moment, the clouds just then cleared away from the sun and it flooded the scene with a warmth and light that seemed to startle not only the two of us but everybody in the vicinity. People leaned back in their seats, or paused in their steady walk. They unbuttoned jackets, loosened collars, half-closed their eyes happily against dazzle from the water. One could almost hear them saying to one another that it was like having summer back again. It was not that they were astonished; every October has such moments. But it took them unawares and gave them a temporary lift of the spirits. For Mairead and myself, who were in high spirits, it provided a boost into the stratosphere.

We both experienced – and we compared our impressions afterwards – that feeling one very rarely has after the age of about eighteen, the feeling that you are very happy and that the entire world understands this and is happy with you. The earth, the stones, the sky, the plants, the animals, the fish, the birds, even the people, have simply no choice but to be happy in the face of this enormous example.

We finally bestirred ourselves to get some sandwiches, just before they ran out, and eating restored our sense of normality enough to make us look at watches and calculate what to do with the rest of our time that day. Mairead had to go to work the next morning, I had to go to work the next morning. Sixty miles separated the places where these obligations would have to be discharged. Train times had to be thought about. Our original intention had been to go our separate ways, for the time being, at about nine o'clock. We now recognized that this plan had been unrealistic. Obviously I was going to be on hand right up to the departure of the last train to Oxford. We were going to return to Siobhán's flat to collect our belongings and leave the place tidy, then go on to Mairead's own dwelling, and finally I would go on to Paddington. I extracted a promise that she would not think of coming to the station and seeing me off or anything of that kind. I wanted to think of her safe at home, and preferably tucked up in bed.

Before we left Siobhán's flat I stood in the doorway and took a last look at it. I knew I was extremely unlikely ever to see it again, and yet this one visit had made it worthy to be remembered for ever. I would revisit it in memories, in dreams, in sudden flashes of imagery, in long streaks of stilled memory like the water of canals seen under bridges. I would never enter this place again, yet it was also true that I would never leave it. I stood there and photographed every detail on my memory. The doorway I stood in was not that of the main entrance, from which in fact you couldn't see much, since it was at the end of a corridor with rooms opening from it. I chose the doorway of the main living-room with the kitchen beyond. The pictures on the walls, the light fixtures, the standard lamps, the gas fire, the shape and disposition of the windows; in the kitchen, the shelves and the things on the shelves; I missed nothing.

And before finally leaving I halted again on the mat just inside the front door, where we had stood immediately on first entering. You couldn't, as I said, see much from there, but it was where Mairead had, in that sudden kiss, given me the first love-sign of this new and deeper stage of our life together: given it so impulsively, so decidedly, so unexpectedly: where everything had burst into a new life in a single transforming instant.

And now we were leaving it behind, and leaving a part of ourselves in it for ever. Mairead had gone out ahead of me and was standing outside on the landing, waiting to shut the door behind us. She made no sign of impatience, she knew what I was doing.

We took a taxi to Mairead's habitation. I had been wrong to visualize it as a flat; it was in fact a tiny house, one of a little secret terrace hidden away down a back alley near the Notting Hill end of Kensington Church Street.

Originally, I had had some notion of going along to Paddington towards midnight and taking the next train. But I was in Mairead's bed at midnight, not just in her bed but entwined in her limbs, and all the trains in the world could have left for all the destinations in the world without me as a passenger for all I cared. We just lay there in that nurturing darkness and I lost all sense of the passage of time. All I was aware of was our incredible closeness. I felt that our two bodies had almost succeeded in merging into one. There was my heart, then my rib-cage, then Mairead's rib-cage, then her heart. It was almost a state of symbiosis; and of course from time to time we essayed each other means of knitting ourselves together physically and emotionally.

At last – how many hours had gone by, and where we were in the journey of the night I had no idea – Mairead asked me, 'Do you hear anything?'

'What kind of anything?' I asked.

'A sound. A continuous sound.'

I listened. London is never completely silent. Even if you manage to get into a quiet corner of it, out beyond that quiet there is always the unstoppable rumble of traffic: sometimes close and urgent, sometimes distant and even soothing, but never quite absent, as pervasive as the sound of the sea in a coastal village. Beyond that, and the sudden sharp cry of a cat among the nearby chimney-pots, I heard nothing.

She laid her head on my arm and said, 'It's like a kind of humming.'

'A humming? Like the sound a generator makes, you mean?'

'Well . . . not quite a generator in that sense.'

'I'm completely lost. Is it something we ought to attend to?'

'Yes,' Mairead said. 'I'm going to attend to it. I'm going to reposition my whole life so as to attend to it.'

'I'm willing to believe that I'm delirious,' I said, 'but you're not making sense to me.'

'I won't be mysterious. What I'm hearing is obviously in my own mind, but it's none the less real. It's the house saying yes.'

'Yes? The house saying yes? Is it actually uttering the word yes?'

'No, it's making an affirmative sound, partly like a cat purring and partly like a very musical chorus of human voices uttering the various words that human languages use for the word 'Yes'. Some are saying yes and some are saying *si* and *oui* and *ja*. But it's one collective voice, and it's speaking to me and it's saying yes.'

'Darling, I think I'm understanding you, but fill it out a little.'

'All right. This is my home where I've lived for the last three years and more. I'm like most women in that the place where I live is very important to me. I daresay it is to a lot of men, but on the whole it's more a woman's thing. That's why we're always fussing about, comparing curtains and buying little things to hang up here and put on tables there. Our home is our personality. This cottage is full of things I've gathered round me because they speak to me, and together they make a statement about me and I make statements back to them. And since you came in, my house has had to get to know you. And because I love you, the house didn't show any sign of resistance when you came through the door. I welcomed you, so it welcomed you.'

'And that's why it was saying Hum?'

'It was saying yes. And I'm not being cosy and quaint and what men call feminine, meaning irritating. I could put it into quite clinical terms and say that the decisions of my mind have to be ratified by the decisions I make unconsciously, in the depths of my being, and they don't always emerge at once. I'll admit in the most rational way that it isn't the house that's humming and saying yes, it's me.'

I considered for a moment. 'Ought I to feel worried because I didn't hear it?'

'Not at all. I was humming and vibrating, but not necessarily to you. To you I can use words. I can address your conscious mind with my conscious mind.'

'That sounds awful. Like a pair of robots.'

For answer she took hold of my phallus, which immediately began to swell. I pictured it lying in her soft little hand like a glossy aubergine. After a while she released it, allowing me to pay attention to her discourse.

'Never mind all that talk of robots,' she said. 'But listen now, because this is important. My house has said yes and that's all I was waiting for. I wasn't conscious of waiting for it, but I must have been, because when I heard it – and I'm still hearing it now – the last traces of hesitation died out in me.'

'Hesitation? Well, I suppose you naturally would have some, considering the amount of—'

'Let me do the talking, darling, and I'll save us a lot of time. The problem's actually quite simple and so's the solution. Starting point: we want to get married.'

'Of course we do. I don't want to settle for a jot less. I want the whole outfit – marriage, children if we're lucky enough to have them, every kind of involvement all the way down the line, and I hope you do.'

'Naturally I do. Right, that part of it's behind us. Next point. You have a job and professional connections and a setting that's both your life and your work. I have a job too, and mine isn't without its professional connections and its meaningful setting in my life. In theory I've got as good a right as you have to stick to what I'm doing and where I'm living and the place where I'm living. In practice, I'm not going to.'

I squeezed her, but said, 'Don't make a hasty decision, my darling.'

'It's not hasty. I've been thinking it over very carefully ever since you first telephoned me and got back in touch. Straight away, that very second, the whole situation was staring me in the face, with all the decisions it involved. I suppose the truth is I'd been carrying it all around with me for four and a half years. I must have kept gnawing at it, and always with a kind of subconscious governer on it that stopped it from coming to the surface. I was very busy with our relationship, but that cut-out always came into action before it appeared to view. To make it real, and to get me to deal with it, I needed your physical presence, plus the proof that you'd really be able to carry out your promise and get free. And after that, it was left to the unconscious areas in me. I just had to wait for those. Your love-making had done most of what was needed, but through it all there was an area that stayed just out of reach. And when the house waited for us to be lying here together and then said yes, I heard it and I understood. And now,' she finished, 'you've heard me.'

'Yes,' I said, and I remember that my voice sank to a whisper. 'I've heard you and understood you, and it's left me with nothing to say that I haven't said before, that I love you and need you, totally and for ever.'

'Don't feel inhibited about repeating yourself,' Mairead whispered. 'Just say the old things to me again. Say them and keep saying them.'

So I did.

★

I awoke the next morning, just at first light, calmly accepting the fact that I had to be in Oxford by about nine o'clock. The last grains of the summer vacation were running out; full term would begin in another week, and the habit of regarding the last week of the Long Vacation as effectively a preliminary week of term was already fully established, though it had not yet been given its unpleasing modern name, 'Noughth Week'. I had, that morning, to attend a meeting of the committee that ran the History Faculty Library. Lying calmly beside Mairead, I decided that it would be best to take a very early train and walk into the Hall at Episcopus College before breakfast was cleared away. I felt no sense of haste or harassment. I accepted, with tranquillity, that duties had to be performed and appointments kept. I was in control, my life was now resting firmly on its true centre. Nothing could ruffle me or give me the sense that my life was going out of control. It was not going to go out of control. All that was over.

I left for Paddington before seven o'clock, not fully waking Mairead, quitting her with no ceremony beyond a cup of tea cooling on her bedside table and a kiss on her warm, sleepy mouth. I didn't trouble about a taxi. I felt no trace of bodily fatigue, and as for my mind, it seemed to be in a dream, yet alert and expectant as one so often is in dreams. I preferred, while in that visionary state, to stand at the kerb beside a bus-stop, looking at the street, the houses, the sky, the early-morning Londoners, until the tall red bus, displaying the friendly '27' that meant Paddington, glided to a majestic halt and welcomed me on board. At first I was strap-hanging, but in Bayswater I got a seat, and stared with a tranquil joy at the world, the urban, unconcerned London world that didn't know what I knew. And then the train journey, with the level morning sunlight still giving every scene a touch of magic, and a wholesome hunger for breakfast, a breakfast I knew to be many miles away, beginning to stir in me.

Breakfast-time at Episcopus, very distant when I left Mairead's little house, grew nearer as the train journeyed on. Once we had left Didcot, with only the last ten country miles to go, I could almost smell the coffee and see the rashers lying on my plate. The thought completed my sense of what a wonderful morning it was. Wittenham Clumps, over to my right, stood up challengingly on the sky-line, those two clusters of trees each crowning its own round hilltop, as mysterious and powerful as they are in Paul Nash's paintings: perpetually affirming something, but exactly what? What they said to me this morning was, 'Be happy.'

Oxford came into view. As the train slowed to enter the station I picked up the little knapsack from the seat beside me, and almost laughed out loud at the thought of the agonies and indecisions with which I had packed it, only three days ago. Three days! Not quite so much, even! From Friday noon to Monday morning! And nothing, nothing at all, was the same. But that was in another country.

★

What the next three or four months showed me was how fast two people can get on with building a life if they work as a team and have a clear idea of what they are doing. Mairead had to serve out notice at her job; I had to arrange to leave College and find a house. We each had to alert our families and those about us generally to the change in our situation. And it had to be done one-two-three. Mairead's next period did not come punctually and it was soon confirmed by her doctor that there would, for the usual length of time, be no more where that came from. We were going to procreate our kind! – had, indeed, already begun to do so! I felt upbuoyed, elated; and so, less demonstratively, did she.

Apart from sharpening up the urgency of the whole matter, the news had some repercussions on my state of mind that were, I suppose, foreseeable. For one thing, it made me convinced that I must, without delay, put Michael in the picture. I was still of an age when the news of my intention to try my luck again, after parting from his mother, would be unsurprising. But the fact that I and his new stepmother were going to present him with a new little half-brother or half-sister, and in short order, was something he had to begin getting used to at once. Every day that went by without his knowing it was a day lost. Mairead's pregnancy had put us all on board a train that had already begun to move, and was gathering speed. There was no time to pussy-foot around the matter, picking and choosing the time and the venue. As soon as Mairead could get down, which would be a week-end, and wherever we could arrange to meet Michael, would have to do. On the other hand I shrank from arranging to see him at the Bargeman's, which was so much the easiest place to get him to; he went there as a matter of course, usually in company with Brian. That would be fine once he had already met Mairead and knew that the family was about to be augmented. But not everything at once. Mike first, then a general family encounter. That would be enough, at present, for Mairead to be subjected to.

Anxious to get in touch with Mike and arrange to see him, I had to cut through the customary manoeuvring and do it by telephoning Chinnor. This meant, of course, that I got Heather. I asked her to give Mike a message to ring me but, with the casualness of youth, he didn't. I telephoned again, choosing a time when I was reasonably certain he would be at home, and got Heather again. She said he was out.

'You gave him the message, didn't you?'

'Course I did, what's the almighty hurry? You quite often see him down at the pub, don't you?'

'Just get him to ring me, all right? Tell him I need to speak to him and it won't wait.'

'Pretty damned mysterious, aren't you?'

'Oh, it's just a bit of business,' I said, feeling evasive and a cad but determined, on the other hand, that I wasn't going to tell Heather *first*. I didn't look forward to telling her at all, come to that, but at least she wasn't going to be the first to know. That would put her in the position of passing on the news to Michael, and I felt obscurely that if she did so she might put some kind of curse on it.

'How are you?' I asked Heather.

'Don't tell me you care.'

'Of course I do, but in any case I know that if anything was conspicuously wrong I'd have heard about it from Mike.'

'Yes,' she said in a flat voice. 'The things that are wrong in my life are just that: they're inconspicuous.'

She made her troubles sound like cancers not yet diagnosed. Perhaps that's how she thought of them. I didn't say anything. There was nothing that occurred to me that wasn't either a *cliché* ('We all have our troubles') or untrue ('I'd like to give you more help if I knew how').

Then she said, 'I've started a business. A riding school.'

'Oh,' I said. Her words caused so many thoughts to form in my mind that they jammed in the doorway, and again I said nothing.

'You don't sound very interested,' she said.

'I'm interested all right.'

'That's good, because I need some money. The initial expenses are shattering.'

I couldn't think of anything to say except, 'Well, I didn't think they gave horses away for nothing, and I suppose you need a few.'

'To make even a modest beginning I need at least three horses, with stabling and equipment.'

'Well, how much will that cost?'

'I could get started – very modestly, mind – with two thousand pounds.'

'Two thousand – where are you going to lay your hands on that much?'

'From you,' Heather said calmly.

'*From me?*' This was in the days when people earned ten pounds a week. 'I haven't got two thousand pounds.'

'I'm sure you can get it. You could scrape it up.'

'*Nyet*,' I said. 'I simply haven't got that much to spare. You know what our divorce settlement cost me. You'll have to borrow it from the bank like anyone else.'

'I am borrowing it from the bank. They want two thousand pounds collateral.'

'I'm not believing this. You think I've got two thousand pounds to hand over to some *Gauleiter* of a bank manager just so that you can . . . you can . . .'

'So that I can set up in business and earn a bit of money – yes, I do, and I bloody well think it's the least you owe me.'

'Nothing of the kind. The amount I agreed to hand over in court was what I owed you, and the full extent of it according to the

−234−

judgement of society as expressed in the law. And a pretty harsh judgement it was, in most people's opinion.'

'What do most people know about it? Most people haven't tried to live my life.'

'No, people don't go about trying to live one another's lives, they just look at what they see happening and form their own common-sense judgements. And most of the people who've mentioned it to me are of the opinion that the court caned me up pretty hard.'

'Well, I'm going to cane you some more, or I'll know the reason why. Two thousand pounds, please, a cheque in the post as soon as you can manage it.'

I could almost smell the gin on her breath now. I began to wonder whether there was any objective truth in the story at all. A riding school? It sounded credible: places like Chinnor were well provided with families whose daughters wanted desperately to get to horseback and be the kind of girl of whom men in red coats said, 'By Jove, sir, she has a good seat and a good hand.' Heather had a good seat and a good hand. I remembered how impressed I had been when I first saw her. As against that, I thought, to demand two thousand pounds from me, just like that, seemed evidence of a weakening hold on reality. If only I could ring up and find her sober for once!

'I might as well tell you, Heather,' I said, holding my spine very straight and deciding to face whatever came back along the wire, 'it's out of the question for me to put two thousand pounds into your riding school because, for one thing, I'm going to marry Mairead and I need the money to set up a home.'

'A home for what?' she said in a thin, venomous voice. 'Lost dogs?'

'No, lost people,' I said. 'I'll be the first. And I might as well add that Mairead is very probably pregnant. A household for three is what I'm talking about. Now do you understand what I mean about the riding school?'

'So,' Heather said. 'It won't be a riding school that your money goes into; it'll be a home for lost bitches.'

'Stop it, Heather,' I said. 'Stop it now.'

She didn't stop, so I rang off and left the telephone off the hook. And that was the manner in which I acquainted my first wife, Heather, with the approach of my marriage to my second wife, Mairead, and the birth of our first child, Keira. I could wish it to have happened differently. But then, when I look back over my life, I could wish that many of its most important episodes had happened differently. Am I alone in that?

Meanwhile, I had to face the fact that I had blown it as far as Michael was concerned. He wasn't going to be the first to hear about the marriage and the baby. He was going to get the news *via* Heather, which did mean inevitably that it would be filtered through a layer of hostility. I spent all one evening trying to come up with a solution to this problem, and in the end decided that there wasn't one. I would just have to forget about it and soldier on.

It didn't, after all, make any perceptible difference. Once I had decided to go with the current of life and stop trying to stage-manage everything, life looked after itself pretty well. We found a house that suited us, small but not too small, in Kingston Road just beyond Jericho. Since it was one of those on the left as you move away from the town centre, that meant that the back garden ran down to the canal, which suited me. I had always been fond of the canal; I liked to see the trees reflected in the water and the swans gliding by, and the families of ducks living their humbler lives with each mother in charge of a cluster of ducklings like little hyperactive balls of fluff; and I didn't object to the muddy, reedy smell that standing water always tends to have. I was used to it. One week-end when Mairead was in Oxford, we went on a shopping expedition to buy things for the house and ran into Michael unexpectedly, on the pavement. It was all so sudden that introductions had to be performed at once, lightly and casually. Mike came back with us to take a look at the house, climbed up and down the uncarpeted stairs and looked into the empty rooms, and said he liked it and was looking forward to coming to see us there. Mairead said he must certainly come, often, and I heard real welcome in her voice. The two of them seemed all ready to be good friends. I had been worrying for nothing. Perhaps I'm not unusual in that either.

★

'You're sure you picked the right place?' Mairead asked me as we sank down on the sofa and looked about us.

'No, I'm not sure. I've never stayed here myself. But I took good advice and I came and looked at the place, and I liked the neighbourhood and it seems to have the right atmosphere, and for God's sake it's only for one night.'

'I know I must seem very fussy.'

'You don't at all.'

'I'm sure I must do. Fussy and obsessional. But I do want them to enjoy staying here, and be at ease and look back on it as a happy experience.'

'My darling, if it makes you feel any better I'll give you a signed statement that I don't see anything fussy in your wanting your parents to look back on our wedding day as a happy experience.'

'There are times, Peter,' she said, looking straight into my eyes, 'when I honestly don't believe that you're as completely lacking in imagination as the rest of the male sex. You're an exception. Don't slip back. Keep working at it.'

'I promise,' I said and we kissed.

In the middle of that kiss a woman's voice said, just behind my head, 'Hello. We're here. Very sorry to keep you waiting.'

I let go of Mairead preparatory to turning round. As I did so a man's voice said, 'It doesn't look as if they've minded very much being kept waiting. They've found a way of filling the time.'

I looked over my shoulder. A middle-aged couple stood behind me. They wore the sort of clothes one wears for a journey: comfortable, well-worn, nothing that minds becoming a little creased and baggy. But good materials, well cut. Over by the door, obviously just put down by the man, was one of those zip-up canvas suitcases that stand up to air travel. The woman wore a mackintosh hat, the man's hat was tweed. They looked like country-dwellers: that is, not like peasants but like professional people who lived in the country from choice. I let Mairead fall back against the sofa cushions and struggled to my feet.

'Stephen Hoey,' the man said, extending his hand. 'This is my wife Kathleen.'

I blurted out something. Mairead had now risen and embraced her parents. I stood for a moment taking in my first sight of my new parents-in-law. Mairead and I were to get married the next day, at the Register Office in her district of London, and her parents were to make their first acquaintance with me tonight, in this modest but comfortable hotel in Highgate selected for them by me. Mairead knew more about London than I did, but I had taken on this part of the administration, especially since I was settling their bill.

During that initial handshake, as they must naturally have been taking stock of me, I tried to gather my wits sufficiently to take stock of them. Mairead had obviously inherited her father's appearance, which is as much as to say that he was a fine-looking man. His hair was iron-grey now, thick and strong in texture, but doubtless it had once been black, and he had blue eyes, so that was where her striking colour combination came from. His build, like hers, was neat; he looked light on his feet for a man in his later fifties. The mother had obviously been a beauty, indeed she was still beautiful but her beauty was not of the same kind as Mairead's; she had red-gold hair, whitening now, and the outlines of her face and body were soft, flowing, quintessentially feminine. I put that clumsily, making it sound as if she was running to fat, but not a bit of it, she was trim and looked well exercised; you associated her colouring with country walks in soft Irish rain, and the gentle lines of her mouth with innocence. I at once formed the impression that she would be beautiful now, this afternoon, if it were not for . . . if it were not for what, exactly? I couldn't put my finger on it. Something was dimming her, weighing on her spirits. There was a sadness that had taken possession of her. Was it permanent, a lifelong sadness that had touched and possessed her at birth? – Something that had clouded her mind in her earliest years? – Or was it now, in the present phase of her life, that the trouble had fallen on her, so that she looked out at the world with saddened eyes? I had no way of knowing, but naturally the thought came to me: have I anything to do with this? Is it her daughter's marriage to me – an Englishman, a foreigner, someone who cannot but threaten to take her away from the familial network of Irish life – that is touching her with foreboding?

She shook hands with me and said the correct things, and gave an uncertain smile; but perhaps her smile was always uncertain. I glanced across at Mairead for reassurance, but she was saying something to her father and at present neither I nor her mother had her attention.

Oh, well, I thought, time will come to my aid because I shall make Mairead so happy that to see her would do any mother's heart good. Time will prove me right, time will help me. And beneath it all I knew, as an historian, that time is always very slow and very reluctant to do any such thing for human beings either in the mass or individually. I passed the buck to time because I didn't know what else to do with it.

Then I was talking to her father and my mind was held to attention by the intelligent alertness of his eyes and the brisk authority in his voice.

'I'm very glad to make your acquaintance, Peter. All this has been – well, very sudden and very unexpected for us, but then Mairead is the kind of girl who springs surprises. We never thought we'd be getting an Oxford don in our family.'

Is that what I actually am, an Oxford don? Did your family ever think your family would contain the son of the licensee of a side-street public house in Oseney Town?

I mumbled something. I didn't, I discovered now, know how to proceed. This conversation might have all kinds of hidden reefs and snags in it. Did he, or his wife, know anything about the long underground history of Mairead's and my relationship during the war years? Had they been told, or learnt from some random source, or intuited, or in any way become aware that their daughter, in whom they had laboured to instil good principles, good *Catholic* principles, had been immersed in a passionate love affair with a married man?

I had never asked Mairead what she had told and to whom. The avoiding of all such questions was part of that thick black-out curtain we had drawn around our love, the pretence that nothing existed outside the four walls of our own little cube of space. Now, faced with the parental couple I had so long been careful not to think about, I was lost for words because I was lost for thoughts.

'Peter,' Mairead said in a tone of half-comical expostulation. 'Don't let me down. You're supposed to make brilliant conversation, or, if you can't manage that, just conversation.'

'I can't,' I said. 'I'm tongue-tied. I can't hit a natural tone. The occasion's such an important one for me that I've dried up.'

'I can assure you,' Mairead said to her parents, 'I've never seen him like this before. It's rather touching. He's like a boy of eighteen.'

'That's what I feel like,' I said.

Stephen Hoey laughed, threw back his head and looked at me in a way that almost convinced me that he knew all my thoughts, whether or not I ever got round to uttering them. 'I think we can deal with this on a practical level,' he said. 'First, we all go into the bar and have a drink. That'll probably loosen our tongues, and if it doesn't we'll have another.'

'Seconded,' I said.

'After that, Kathleen and I will take our bags up to whatever room they've given us—'

'That won't be necessary, surely,' I said. 'The hotel people will do that.'

'No need. We're travelling very light. I always carry my own luggage – I'm trying to stay in trim and stave off old age. Where was I? Yes, we'll go up to our room, settle in briefly, and then we'll all go out and have dinner. Our treat. You come as our guests – no argument. And while we're upstairs, you think of a good restaurant, somewhere where we can eat well and relax in quiet surroundings and get to know each other. Will that suit you, wife and daughter?'

They signified that it would. Son-in-law likewise signified that it would.

'Well,' he said, rising from his chair, 'we'll do that.'

So we did that.

★

The ice-breaking, then, had gone off reasonably well. The wedding itself followed on the next morning. Our getting married in a Register Office was a circumstance that, in the 1950s, must have caused its quota of raised eyebrows among the quota of orthodox Catholics from country districts who made up a large part of Mairead's family, but it couldn't be helped. In fact, only a light sprinkling

−239−

of these good people were present. They were mostly of the kind who needed anything up to a month's notice before being able to leave their premises for two or three days, the minimum it would have needed for people who shrank from air travel. They mostly kept animals of one sort or another, alongside the cultivation of some sliver of the earth's surface. They were not in the habit of travelling; it was an upheaval for them. To get as far as London was formidable and expensive. From the start, immediately after the despatch of the wedding invitations, the regretful refusals began to come in. A series of long telephone conversations followed, between London and Newtownmountkennedy, in which Mairead discussed with her mother what seemed at first the advisability, then the necessity, of holding a house-warming party in Kingston Road that would be a larger-scale affair than the wedding itself.

That decided, we drew breath. The wedding itself attracted a few friends and relatives on either side and, numbering a good deal more than a third of the total, Mairead's friends and colleagues from the Irish Foreign Service. Nothing much of moment happened, except what was supposed to happen, which was of moment enough. We got married! I was Mairead's husband! This lovely young woman was declaring herself to be mine: not only in our intimate close-knit life as lovers, but right out where everyone could see it, manifestly, even legally – she was actually going to change her name, as if marrying me would have the power to confer on her a different identity!

I am aware, of course, that in the time that has since gone by, most of those assumptions have been challenged and rejected by a new generation of women, who no longer change their names, no longer think of themselves as becoming attached to their husbands in any way that entitles him to say, 'You are mine', no longer allow anywhere near their consciousness the notion that marriage might change or even slightly modify their identity. So be it. In those days we (whether 'we' were male or female) went along with these things, inwardly making our own bargain with them, inwardly deciding how far they were to be obeyed in any literal sense. We accepted them because they were the pattern of our society. Forty years ago people accepted many things without bristling because they were the pattern of society, and did so without being appreciably harmed. Their attitude was easy-going. Yes, that's the expression I've been searching for. They were not weaker or more brainwashed or more docile than contemporary young people. They were more easy-going, a state of mind that has now passed from the world but was no great burden in its day.

In any case, there it was. Mairead and I were married, she was Mrs Leonard, and here we were entertaining a total of twenty-seven people (I counted them) in a room we had hired in an ordinary run-of-the-mill hotel, people whose one feature in common was that they had some connection with one or other of us. The net was spread wide enough to have caught Harry and Geraldine at one end and, at the other, two maiden aunts of Mairead's who shared a house in Tralee and took paying guests in the summer-time. It was a strange, lumpy mixture but it stirred together well enough as the afternoon went on. I made no real attempt to influence or direct anything or anyone; I just let it wash round me. Our catering was of the simplest — two large cakes and a trainload of champagne, all supplied by the hotel. We were trying to get by with as little permanent scarring as possible, and on the whole we were succeeding.

There were of course on Mairead's side a few people I was particularly interested in meeting for the first time, characters, so to speak, whose names I knew from the *dramatis personae* and whose arrival on stage I had been awaiting with interest. One of these was Mairead's friend Siobhán, in whom she had confided for so long. It was in fact the second time I had met Siobhán, the first time being in Dublin in 1947, before either of us knew who the other was; she had also been present in spirit when we had met again and re-launched our lives in her flat in Barnes. I liked Siobhán. There was an openness and warmth about her; one felt that she was not afraid of life, that she trusted it, not to let her down lightly (when did life ever do that, to anyone?) but to meet her as a fair opponent, not to throw anything at her that she couldn't handle. I remember her very clearly from those few minutes of talk in that impersonal lobby of a public building, five years earlier; when she spoke, the tones of her voice came back very distinctly; I felt I knew her, though I had yet to hear her speak a hundred words. I gathered she had very recently got married. I hoped she had a husband who appreciated her.

My own family was represented by my parents. Brian, unable to leave the pub, had sent a friendly message and a bouquet for Mairead whose magnificence slightly embarrassed her — though, as with a slight ruefulness she admitted, in making a gift of flowers the only possible policy was to overdo it: to send a meagre bouquet is a way of saying nothing, and to say nothing at a wedding is to say something negative. All this she understood and acknowledged, but somehow still did not know what to do with the huge, demonstrative mass of flowery, leafy, frondy goodwill from Oseney Town.

My father meanwhile, stiff in a new brown suit, was squinting knowledgeably at his glass of champagne as if trying to guess its vintage; I knew, as a matter of fact, that he had very little experience of champagne and did not much care for it. Every now and again he produced from his top pocket a swizzle-stick in the shape of a hockey-stick, relic of some long-forgotten revel, and stirred it vigorously to activate the bubbles. As they foamed on the surface, more briefly with each repetition, he would offer the swizzle-stick to my mother, who always shook her head with a kindly smile, as if indulging a child. She too had on what I judged to be a new outfit, one of the Easter fashions from Elliston and Cavell. I was glad that our nuptials had, among other things, been good for my parents' wardrobe. I could imagine the elaborate consultations, the calculating of monthly budgets, the hang-it-all resolution to press on. Their costumes spelt out plainly: 'This is a special occasion. We are *dressed up*!' At intervals throughout the proceedings, I gazed at them fondly. An invisible banner, suspended above their heads, was emblazoned BARGEMAN'S FOR EVER.

I now began to sniff the air for traces of the scent of release. The wedding ceremony had been at two o'clock. By a quarter to three everybody was assembled for the reception, for which we had hired a first-floor room. The room, like the hotel itself, was characterless but adequate to the purpose. I had the sense, looking about me, that the people I saw had been drawn together by the pull of a magnet and, once assembled, had been quickly bonded together by a not very strong glue. Now, at four o'clock, the magnet had been removed and the glue was rapidly losing its adhesive quality. I fancied I could almost see it melting, beginning to drop on to the carpet in the form of simple water, leaving no deposit and causing no damage.

My parents, as if picking up the same message, now approached the spot where Mairead and I stood side by side. 'We'll have to be off now, Peter,' my father said. 'We told Brian we'd help out for the first hour or two this evening. Have to be there by six, you know.'

He used my name but he was looking as much at Mairead, glancing from her face to mine and back. I could tell he was avoiding using her name because he found it strange and exotic, and was uncertain how to pronounce it. On one of her scrambling week-end visits Mairead had met my parents, but they had not had time to get used to her or anything about her.

My mother, for her part, wore a shy expression as she walked over to us, but something seemed to move in her as she drew near. Perhaps it was the sight of this young couple, as we must have seemed in her eyes, standing together, ready to launch themselves into the old dangerous, endlessly necessary process, one of them her own son launching for a second time. With a sudden glowing smile in which I read the beginning of a strong, rooted devotion, she drew Mairead's arm through hers and kissed her cheek. Then, still with that linked arm, she said something into her ear which I did not hear and perhaps was not meant to. Mairead smiled too and they stood close together for a moment, not moving.

'Well,' Dad said, 'drop round and see us when you get a bit of time, Peter. Michael not here, then? We're driving back – we thought we might give him a lift.'

'We didn't think it was worth taking him out of school for a day,' I said, keeping my voice flat and matter-of-fact. I had in truth wrestled long and hard with this decision. *Question*: What is the correct thing to do about your adolescent son, who is making his home with his mother, your ex-wife, when you celebrate a second marriage – invite him or not? *Answer*: There is no correct thing. Either course you follow will be wrong, probably in an unguessable number of ways.

I don't know whether my father read any of that in my expression-less voice. I knew he was at least normally sensitive, pretty accurately tuned in to other people, though like Brian he chose to hold back from showing it. It was my mother who showed her feelings. In the social *milieu* they had always inhabited, it was the women who had the feelings, or at any rate were allowed to reveal them. Within reason, of course. Emotions were womanly, but not turbulence.

'Well now, Katie, we must be off,' my father said. He held out his hand, a trifle awkwardly, to Mairead, and I believe would have launched into a little speech welcoming her into the family; but she ignored his hand and instead moved swiftly towards him and kissed his cheek.

'I'm going to enjoy being your daughter-in-law,' she said to him softly.

His square, strong-jawed face, engraved as it was with deep lines of effort and watchfulness, relaxed and his smile matched hers. 'Just enjoy being Peter's wife, my duck,' he said, 'and everything else'll follow.'

I relished the way he unexpectedly came out with that Oxfordshire 'my duck'. It recalled his roots, his family, his oldest associations and habits. It must have sprung to his lips quite automatically, propelled by the depth of his acceptance of her. In sound, of course, it was very close to 'moy duck' rather than 'my'; but as everyone knows, in the complex and ungraspable matter of trying to represent the sound people make when they speak, spelling is the bluntest of blunt instruments.

Some formalities followed: my parents went over to Mairead's parents, my father repeated the business about having to get back to Oxford, friendly handshakes were distributed all round. That side of things was evidently buttoned up to everyone's satisfaction. Then my father began to steer my mother towards the door; he did so with an arm round her shoulders, as if fearful that she might suddenly pitch forward in a dead faint or, alternatively, make a break for freedom. I, however, knew the real reason. He always held her close to him at times when he was emotionally moved. It was because he felt the existence in her of an unquenchable spring of life, some instinctive sustaining force that arose in her and not, or only intermittently, in him; and at any important point in time he wanted to stay close to it.

I went with my parents to the door, intending to see them out and then return to the fag-end of the occasion, which I expected to extend to the consumption of any left-overs of champagne. Everyone was melting away now and as we reached the door and paused for a moment in valediction, we were overtaken by a knot of people also on their way out, so that for a brief moment there were about six or seven of us bunched in a doorway that would admit, at most, three abreast. The usual shuffling, hesitation and good humoured 'After-you' gestures ensued, in the course of which I became aware that the slowness of movement was partly caused by the fact that the people trying to go out had become slightly snarled up with one person who was coming in, and who showed no inclination to draw back and wait for them. This new arrival, a man of average height and slender build, was wearing a mackintosh and trilby hat, appropriate enough to the season but inappropriate among the present company, who had all checked in their outdoor clothes in the cloak-room on the ground floor before coming upstairs. The newcomer cut through the loose scrum of leave-takers and, as I turned briefly to follow him with my eyes, gave me a view only of his back as he advanced towards the centre of the room.

I stayed at the doorway another few moments, receiving with what I hoped was a becoming show of appreciation and gratitude the repeated and pressing invitation of some uncle of Mairead's twice removed to come and stay at his house with the main purpose (I gathered) of eating Dublin Bay prawns with him at a little restaurant he frequented in, I think, Dalkey. I am not enormously fond of prawns, though willing for any lack of of contrary evidence to concede the claim that those to be found in Dublin Bay are unusually succulent. I got rid of this good man with a certain amount of difficulty, but he went down the stairs at last and I turned and moved back to the now whittled-down party.

At once I knew that I was in the presence of the fabled Dermot. Without actually admitting the thought of him to my conscious mind, I had been, all that day, subliminally willing him not to turn up. Without actually believing, in any literal sense, that he would put a curse on the marriage, I had an obscure but powerful conviction that his presence would bring down bad luck of one sort or another. Mairead was standing between her parents at this moment, having by sheer chance fallen into a grouping that looked rather posed, as if someone had said to her, 'Let's have you in the picture, Mairead – come and stand between them.' They were in the positions they would have been in if Dermot, who was standing to one side of them, had been just about to take their photograph. But he did not in the least resemble a photographer. Neither his expression nor his stance had in them any element of that curious manner, half greasily affable and half bullying, that photographers assume at weddings. On the contrary, judging solely by his manner he might have been about to produce a revolver and tell them to clasp their hands on their heads. As I approached, he turned to face me with the same manner.

'At a guess, you must be Dermot,' I said to him. 'Glad to see you.' It was the first remark I had ever made to my new brother-in-law, and it was a lie. 'Why don't you take your hat and coat off? Are you in a hurry?'

'I'm not staying,' Dermot said. He looked very steadily straight into my eyes, as if he had been assigned the job of interrogating me. Now that I was examining his face at close quarters, I felt overwhelmed with sheer surprise. I simply did not believe Dermot; I found him, quite literally, non-credible. How could anyone look so much like Mairead and yet so unattractive?

It was not that Dermot was ugly. His features were regular, like Mairead's. His hair, like hers, was raven-black, and his eyes vividly blue. He had all the elements of good looks – startling good looks, in fact, as she had. But he was unattractive in the sense that nothing drew one towards him. He did not invite proximity. He did not invite dialogue, or any kind of sharing, or even communication. His expression, his manner, his bearing advised you to go away if you knew what was good for you in the future. He was, in the strictly literal sense of the word, repulsive. He wanted to repel, and he did repel. Not surprisingly, I felt repelled.

As I uttered the words 'Glad to see you', the muscles of my right arm and shoulder experienced a slight tremor. Those words, spoken on meeting a man for the first time, would ordinarily be accompanied by a handshake, or a gesture that offered a handshake. But at the last second I drew back from extending my hand because Dermot was so obviously not going to extend his. He just stood there fixing me with Mairead's eyes looking out of Mairead's face; the resemblance didn't go any further, needless to say.

'Dermot, you'd better have a drink,' his father said affably. 'Presumably you won't turn down a glass of champagne. I think there's some left.'

'I could always get them to send up another bottle,' I said through the curtain of anger that was beginning to come down on my mind.

-245-

With a considerable effort I managed to speak pleasantly. If there was going to be a breakdown of courtesy, it would not be on my side.

'How are you, Dermot?' Mairead asked. 'Have you been in London?'

'And other places,' he said in a tone of voice quite sufficient on its own to close the door to any further questioning. I had no means of knowing whether to reveal nothing about his movements was particularly important to him just now, or whether it was simply that secrecy had become such a way of life for him that he could never let any information pass his lips. In either case the effect was the same, and I was mildly surprised when Mairead pressed on.

'I left messages for you with so many people, telling you we were getting married and the where and the when,' she said. 'I had to hope one of them would run into you, or know somebody who was going to run into you.' Her manner was cool and businesslike rather than affectionate, as if it were a business deal she was talking about, but her motive for wanting to give her brother a chance to be at her wedding must have had some love in it somewhere; if not love of the brother, I thought, then love of the parents, to whom it was obviously a satisfaction that both their offspring were present if only for a few minutes.

'Your plan worked, as you see,' Dermot said to Mairead. 'As a matter of fact, I got the message three separate times. You must have been very thorough.'

'Yes, I was thorough,' she said composedly. 'You have to be thorough when you're looking for a needle in a haystack.'

'Or, to put it with more suitable precision,' her father added, 'sending impulses through the haystack in the hope of making magnetic contact with the needle and attracting it out.'

I essayed a good-humoured laugh at this mild sally, but in Dermot's presence it was difficult to feel amusement at anything.

Mairead confronted him squarely, as if she had made up her mind to say something decisive that she had been wondering whether to keep to herself.

'I suppose, brother, you won't ever have an address that's common knowledge where you can be reached at any time?'

'No,' Dermot said. The single word came out unemphatically, even casually; which made it all the more lethal.

'That's something we've all grown used to, Dermot,' his father said levelly. 'But none of us have ever grown to like it.'

Dermot did not shrug, he kept his body entirely still. But I had the curious impression, watching him, that if he had made any movement at all, even the slightest, a shrug is what it would have been.

'It's the way I live,' he said.

Mairead made a slight gesture of helplessness, a gesture that said, 'All right, be like that: I give up.' Kathleen Hoey looked at her son with a sudden wave of pain and longing so evident in her face that I wondered how he could bear not to gather her up into his arms. Stephen Hoey reacted into bodily movement: he held out to Dermot a glass in which he had amassed a certain amount of champagne by up-ending two almost empty bottles. 'It's not quite flat,' he said, keeping his voice casual though I was sure he was angry. 'Here, Dermot, drink to the happy couple.'

I watched tensely, acutely aware of Mairead's arm through mine. Instinctively I wanted her close, where I could touch her, lay claim to her, protect her even. Something violent and destructive was in the air. It was obvious that Dermot had made up his mind in advance that I was the Enemy, the invader, sweeping his sister off not only to England, not only into the English middle class, but to Oxford, which in his mind would be a hated symbol, a concentrated essence of everything he thought of as *echt*-English ultra-middle-class. And here was his father, standing beside him, putting a drink into his hand and prompting him to drink it ceremonially, honouring our wedding-day.

But if I expected this to throw Dermot, I was reckoning without his years of battle-experience in such matters. He raised the glass with his eyes on his sister's face. As he actually brought it to his lips he switched his gaze to mine and uttered, clearly and with no hesitation, a phrase in Irish. Then he drank.

I had no idea what the words meant. He uttered them without smiling, but with a resonance that would go naturally with their being a toast, though I knew that they were just as likely to be a curse. I glanced at Mairead. She was standing very still; I couldn't read anything in her expression.

The mother spoke next, reaching out to Dermot with her warm, affection-proffering voice as she would have liked, but for the fear of coldness and rejection, to reach out to him with her warm, affection-proffering hands. 'Dermot, it's a pity you weren't here a little earlier – even just a quarter of an hour ago, before people started leaving. You'd have seen your cousin Rose.'

'So I missed her. I'll have to live with that.'

'You'd have had so much to talk to her about, I know.'

'You think so?'

'You always used to chatter away together like a pair of jackdaws when you were growing up. You used to be very fond of Rose.'

Without answering, Dermot tilted his head back and drained the rest of his wine. Then he set down the glass.

Kathleen Hoey soldiered on about cousin Rose. What else could she do? 'She's always full of enthusiasm for something. Takes up so many interests and always seems to make a success of them. Just now, she and Jack have taken up breeding fox-terriers.'

Dermot gave a look which said very clearly, 'I did not come here to talk about fox-terriers.' When this had reduced his mother to crushed silence, however, he made a concession to her that I couldn't imagine his making to anyone else: he uttered to her a few words which came close to being an explanation, even in its fashion an apology.

'I came a bit late because I thought if I was early I might run into one of those pestering photographers who always want to line everyone up in groups and get pictures of them they can sell to you.'

'And you wouldn't want that, would you?' Mairead asked him, still in that cool, matter-of-fact tone.

Dermot turned to look at her. 'No,' he said coldly. 'I've known photographs cause a lot of trouble.'

No one knew what to say to this, we all just stood there. The wedding reception was well and truly over now; we were the only people in the room except for a couple of hotel staff who were beginning unobtrusively to clear up.

Dermot now said, addressing his father, 'I must be going. I have to get to a meeting.'

'A meeting, eh? What kind of a meeting is it that's more important than your sister's wedding?'

'It's at Shepherd's Bush,' Dermot said as if that explained anything. To his sister he said, 'Well, take care of yourself.'

'I can relax some of my efforts on that front,' she replied good-humouredly. 'It won't be just a matter of me taking care of myself any more. I'll have help.'

Giving no sign of having heard this remark, Dermot gave me a stony nod, kissed his mother perfunctorily on the forehead and took himself off. I watched the door swing to behind him. It was fitted with one of those compressed-air devices that hotels used to provide to stop customers from slamming the doors or opening them too abruptly. Every time it closed it emitted a noise like a sigh; this time the sigh could equally have come from any of us who were left standing there. In my case it would have been an expression of pure relief at Dermot's departure; on his mother's part, pain and regret; in the case of Mairead and her father, both these emotions together, mixed according to their individual natures, with a touch of exasperation thrown in. But at least it was over. Dermot had paid his duty visit to our wedding reception (Why? To take one look at me, preparatory to avoiding me for the rest of his life? To imprint my appearance firmly on his memory in case he was ever motivated to assassinate me in a country lane?) and now he was gone.

After that I felt I needed a drink. I was standing near a table and had just put down my glass, with a little left in it; but now, looking down, I saw that there were several used glasses standing fairly close together and it was hard to identify which was mine. Better to go in search of a fresh one, I thought. Looking up, I saw Stephen Hoey standing beside me, his expression conveying seriousness and a gentle, concerned sympathy.

'Marrying into an Irish family can have its surprises, Peter,' he said, speaking clearly but not so loudly as to be overheard. 'You may be ready for them, I don't know. Obviously you're the sort of person who wasn't born yesterday, when it comes to understanding in-grained political attitudes and inherited grudges.'

'I'm acquainted with the general ground-work,' I said. 'And Mai-read's done her best to prepare me for one particular case, the one you've just seen me run into. But I don't, on reflection, think there was any way of getting ready for that one.'

My father-in-law shook his head, still regarding me with that sym-pathetic eye. 'We Irish are a people who take some getting to know. You won't need me to tell you that, and I wouldn't have brought up the subject at all if it hadn't been for Dermot's behaviour. It left me with a wish to set the record straight. To apologize to you, even.'

At that, I felt moved to protest. 'For heaven's sake banish that feeling. The notion of your needing to apologize to me is preposter-ous. It's I who ought to thank you for fathering Mairead. That's the greatest service you could have imaginably—'

'I fathered Dermot too.' There was a steely quality in his tone as he cut into my protestations, something that ran counter to the soft lilt of his speech. 'That's the duality you have to be aware of in our nation. It won't have been lost on you that we have a layer of welcoming softness on top – rather like the Austrians and their gemütlichkeit. But slice down through that just a little way . . . and there's granite. There has to be. There wouldn't be such a people as the Irish if they weren't stubborn. So much effort has gone into exterminating us, as if we were rats or locusts, that it stands to reason we must have exerted an equal effort just to be still here.'

'As you say. If you hold people down by force for seven hundred years, by the end of that time they're either stubborn or not there at all.'

Stephen Hoey inclined his head gravely. 'I should have realized that you, an informed man, an historian by profession, would know these things. Most of the English I've encountered in my lifetime aren't aware of them. The English, even those in quite responsible positions, seem extraordinarily unaware of the past, except for the parts they can glamorize like battles between Cavaliers and Round-heads, with the dashing Cavaliers always satisfactorily winning.'

'Yes,' I said. 'Which, in reality, they didn't.'

'Precisely. And in that kind of historical perspective, all the Irish can do is disappear.'

'Or have funny stories told about them,' I agreed. 'I'm afraid it's just human nature. On the whole, the English have benefited from the injustices of the last six or seven hundred years, so of course they're very ready to have harmony and forget old quarrels. It's people with scores to settle who linger over the past. I'm never surprised that there are people like Dermot in Ireland. The only thing that surprises me is that they're not all like that.'

He gave me a swift, clear look. 'We *are* all like that,' he said quietly. 'It's just that most of us have that top layer of *gemütlichkeit*. Dermot just doesn't happen to have it.'

I made no answer to this beyond a compliant nod, but inwardly I was thinking, 'It's not that he just doesn't happen to have it. He totally rejects the very notion of having it, spurns it away with all the concentrated energy of his being.'

By this time the wedding reception was just about finally over. The last knot of lingerers was dispersing; they came over to say their goodbyes and repeat their good wishes. There was a general air of benevolence which almost formed a curative dressing over the burn left by that encounter with Dermot. Almost.

Mairead's parents were catching an evening flight back to Dublin. By tonight they would be back home in Newtownmountkennedy and the wedding-day would be a memory, completed, framed in the past, marooned within its own beginning, middle and end. It would be like a photograph mounted in a family album.

But if our wedding-day was going to seem like a dream, it would be a strange one to look back on, with the sombre figure of Dermot brooding and hovering up there somewhere in one corner of the picture. Dermot hadn't exactly been with us, he had just materialized, curiously like some supernatural presence – witch, wizard, or fairy godmother – in Irish folklore. And though he had gone, he was still with us as we said our farewells and exchanged handshakes and good wishes and observed all the little rituals that human beings do observe at such times; times, that is, when life pauses for a moment, gives itself a shake and then sets off in an altered direction. Everyone feels they should signal that moment in some appropriate way, but no one knows quite what to do. So we took refuge in detail, and the scurrying activity that is needed to attend to detail.

Stephen Hoey, with his quiet efficiency, had brought down the luggage from the hotel in Highgate where they had spent the previous night, and checked it in at the hotel we were in now. Now I went and asked the girl at reception to call a taxi for us, to take my parents-in-law to the airport. Mairead came with them into the downstairs lounge to wait. Stephen and I hunted up overcoats, wraps, parcels, odds and sods generally. We trampled about, chucking things down into armchairs, gathering them up again and putting them into different armchairs. I went back to reception to make sure the taxi was on its way, though there was plenty of time. We strode to and fro, we stood up and sat down, we said the same things over and over again, and all for the same reason – that we did not know what to do about Dermot.

This was the thought in my mind as I looked at Stephen and Kathleen. Neither they nor we knew what to do about Dermot. I was marrying their daughter and they were glad of it, or at any rate not sorry. They were prepared to give it a chance. But Dermot was not glad about it, not prepared to give it a chance. Dermot did not wish well to anything that boded any kind of amity, any kind of knitting-up, between England and Ireland. Mairead was Irish. I was English. To Dermot, that settled it. That we should try to come together on the common ground of love and marriage between a man and a woman was, to Dermot, an outrage and the betrayal of a host of martyrs.

I was in no danger of liking Dermot or agreeing with his opinions, but at the same time I could not deny that I saw his point of view and understood why he held it. From the twelfth century when the Normans, then masters of England, had trampled down the resistance of Strongbow and his followers, to the 1840s when the wails of starving children had echoed thinly through the valleys and villages and a million had lain down to die, England had mortified Ireland, and who was I that I should not live with the results of that wickedness? If Mairead and I came out of our respective strongholds and tried to meet on some kind of common ground, and tried to meet in the middle, that was no use to Dermot. To him, there was too much blood soaked into the ground under our feet. The very grass that grew up, the very hawthorn blossom that made festive the hedges in May, he saw as red because their roots were in that underground lake of blood. I wanted him to be wrong: but how could I tell him he was wrong? How could I undo the past, except by building on it as I planned to do?

I don't know whether Mairead had the same thoughts. What I do know is that after the taxi came, and we helped her parents settle their luggage in it and exchanged kisses and handshakes one more time and it drove off, we were both rather silent as we made our way over to what was still, for a few more weeks, Mairead's London home in the quiet Bayswater mews. Then at last our mood lifted, when with exclamations of gladness and relief we sank on to the sofa and kicked off our shoes. The house was still saying Yes.

In the end Heather got the two thousand pounds she needed to set up the riding school: she borrowed it, interest free, from a neighbour of hers named Meg Bolsover. When she gave me this news on the telephone, coldly but with an undercurrent of triumph as if I had been actively trying to stop her from setting up in business, I asked Michael who Meg Bolsover was.

He grimaced. 'She's someone Mum knows.'

'I know I'm stupid, Mike, but I've got that far on my own. She's just lent Mum some money, so I know they're acquainted.'

'Oh, I didn't know you knew about that. About the loan, I mean.'

'But you knew it?'

'Yes, but Mum asked me not to talk about it to people.'

'I'm not people, I'm me.'

'All right, she didn't mention you by name, she just said, "Don't go talking about it," and as it doesn't interest me very much I just sort of forgot about it.'

'But you know what she's going to use it for?'

'Horses,' he said laconically. 'You don't need the car this week-end, do you, Dad?'

'I suppose not. You've had it for the last three, you know.'

'But week-ends are the only time I have off.'

'Tell me about Meg Bolsover.'

'There's nothing to tell about her.'

'Is she a great friend of Heather's?'

He appeared to consider the matter for the first time, but only for a moment. 'She seems to drop round quite a lot. I don't think she's got much to do with her time.'

'Not like some of us, eh?'

'You can say that again.'

'What kind of age is she?'

'Oh, old. I can't tell people's ages when they get as old as her. She's older than Mum, anyway.'

'Is she nice?'

'No, she's a horrible old boot. She's got a loud voice and she's very boring. She drives a big Bentley and it's so big and heavy she thinks she owns the road. She's usually either on the wrong side or smack in the middle; it's as if she *wants* to hit something. Of course in a thing like that you must feel you're in a tank. She'd knock anything off the road – anything smaller than a bus, anyway.'

From one or two other enquiries I made, I constructed a reasonable Identikit picture of Meg Bolsover. I had no wish to get to know the woman, merely to be reassured that she actually was sufficiently well-heeled to be able to throw four-figure sums of money around without being led away to a debtors' prison. It turned out to be a fairly usual pattern for a country-dwelling Lady Bountiful: her husband had been a Midland industrialist, no tycoon but certainly not poor, who had spent his working life making huge quantities of something respectable and useful like fork-lift trucks, and after years of stress and overwork had dropped dead in his early sixties. Meg, in her late fifties and brimming with energy, had moved out of Wednesbury or Wolverhampton or Walsall or wherever they had lived, bought a country house and looked round for a manor to be lady of. Unfortunately for her she had arrived in the countryside some twenty years too late, when that kind of rural life – centred on a landowning squirearchy, a resident peasantry and a flourishing tradition of hunting and fly-fishing – had ceased to survive even as a memory. In short, Meg had no role and nothing to do, and to fill her time and spend her money she made visits to London to buy expensive tweeds and woollens, plus the exactly right style of shoes and raincoats, dabbled a little in antiques, and generally did the things that women of her kind did. Heather must have seemed to her a wonderful resource, always there to be dropped in on, good enough social background to be invited to dinner-parties, and to cap it all she had her roots in precisely the kind of country life that Meg would have enjoyed buying her way into, if only it still existed. But mechanization and suburbanization had done their work, the local rivers were too polluted for the kind of fish that rose for flies, and the crack of sporting guns from neighbouring woodland only signified that some party of business men were enjoying a day out, shooting at intensively reared English game-birds at a fee of £300 per day, cash down. In this *milieu*, Meg Bolsover must have felt a joyful relief at being allowed to finance Heather's riding school. At least it was, in its own way, real.

There were other factors at work too. Quite apart from the question of what Meg Bolsover was like as a person, I was glad to know that she was on hand. The time had come when Heather would begin to face loneliness. Michael had got himself accepted at Birmingham University to read Mechanical Engineering. He seemed to be patterning himself more and more closely on Brian; certainly his main ambition, as far as I could make out, was to become a designer of racing cars. He had enough sense to know that this was not a profession one could just walk into, and obviously accepted that to work for a degree in engineering was the necessary groundwork. I raised no objection, naturally. Young people being what they are, so much at the mercy of fads and fancies, I was just glad that he wanted to work at *something*: and if he never got to be a designer of racing cars, at least a trained engineer could make a living somewhere.

But it would mean his leaving Chinnor for most of the year. Heather, somewhat to my surprise, did not seem to have a man in her life; at least, if she did it was all carried on so discreetly that no rumour ever reached me, and knowing people's readiness to spread rumours I believed I could take this as confirmation that she was wearing the white flower of a blameless life. (Unfortunately.) Having this Bolsover woman around and sharing the responsibility for the riding business would prevent her life from being lonely or aimless. So Heather had a predictable future. And Michael had a predictable future. And I had a predictable future. It was almost enough to make me believe that it was time to stop worrying and switch off the alarm system.

Luckily, though I have never considered myself a wise man, I am at any rate not quite such a fool as to do that.

*

Of course Mairead and I had a house-warming in Kingston Road. And of course a large contingent of Mairead's family came from Ireland, many of them her older relatives who had done very little travelling in their lives and found it a novel and daring experience to venture so far, not only to England – that was already foreign enough – but to Oxford, about which they entertained strange and fanciful notions. They struck me, collectively, as the kind of people one reads about in Somerville and Ross; without the quaintness, because after all people in real life are not quaint, but true to the mental and spiritual outlines described by those two ladies, particularly in their charming rural fantasies concerning the 'Irish R.M.' When we were in the planning stage I was apprehensive that Dermot would take it into his head to show up, but Mairead treated the idea as laughably preposterous.

'Dermot! You must be joking, Leonard!' (Calling me 'Leonard' was a sign that she was modulating into affectionate raillery.) 'He'll never come here if he lives a thousand years. It's a symbol of everything he hates about England.'

'Does he actually know anything about Oxford? Has he set eyes on the place?'

'Never. He'd take good care not to. He only knows the things about Oxford that everybody knows.'

'The things that everybody knows about Oxford are mostly myths and illusions, as you'll find out when you come to live here.'

'I'm expecting to find that. All the same, Leonard, you don't need me to tell you that myths and illusions are very powerful forces. People who are the victims of injustice console themselves by creating them and disseminating them. And people who inflict injustice get consolation from them in their own way. They simply view the same myths and illusions from the other side.'

'Yes, yes,' I said, heading her off; although I was in very substantial agreement with my wife's views on Ireland and its treatment by England, I didn't want her to go into the matter at that precise moment, when we were trying to draw up lists and make practical arrangements. Some of Mairead's relatives would find it no easy matter to dig into their pockets and pay for such a long journey, and if they had besides to pay for somewhere to stay for a couple of days, the burden would be heavy. Mairead spent a long time on the telephone to Newtownmountkennedy, reading over to her parents the list of people we intended to invite, checking whether we had left out anyone who wanted to be asked, and then tackling the (apparently, to judge from the telephone time needed) agonizingly delicate task of deciding an order of priority among the ones who would find the trip financially crippling unless we put them up at our house. Its modest size put a strict limit on how many we could take, but with goodwill all round and a general readiness to undergo some inconvenience and discomfort, we had decided the house could sleep five besides ourselves, so long as four of them could be grouped as two couples.

I could see it was going to be a whale of a party with five (comparatively) indigent and (absolutely) elderly people needing to go to bed at various stages between ten and midnight, but I recollected that these were Irish and not English people, therefore less shy and more gregarious. As it happened all were from the Republic of Ireland with no participation from Ulster, but even if the gathering had been equally balanced by guests from either side of the Border, I would, in that year of 1953, have had no apprehension. The time had not yet come, was not to come for fifteen years yet, for the bitter clan warfare of the two Irelands to be rekindled and fanned into flame by the shifts and counter-shifts of history, abetted by the likes of Dermot. At the moment, as I recognized, Dermot was suffering the fate of all pioneers who were ahead of their time: he was isolated. Part of the sourness that possessed his mind came, indeed, from that isolation. What I did not foresee was how soon, in historical terms, his day would come round again, and what a terrible day it would be.

But that martyrdom was in the future. Nothing concerned me at the moment except that Mairead and I were going to fill our new home with guests and that these guests would be Irish. I hoped for the best and on the whole the best happened. Mairead's contingent also included her friend Siobhán. It seemed recently she had married a man who worked at the Imperial College of Science and lived in West London, placing Siobhán not far from Paddington, which in turn meant that she and Mairead could exchange frequent visits.

I fielded a few of my own family and friends, largely just to demonstrate to my assemblage of new relatives from the Emerald Isle that I was neither an orphan nor a social outcast and did in fact have some family and friends. Since they were people I could see at any time, I felt that I was inviting them more in the capacity of character-witnesses than fellow revellers, but when the wine merchant's van drew up and the driver delivered the gargantuan cargo of lubricant that I had decided to lay in, I thought – as crate after crate came clinking into the hallway and the accusing face of my bank manager hovered in the air before me like Macbeth's air-drawn dagger – that some revelling would probably manage to get done.

It turned out to be a happy evening. I had expected it to be a duty occasion, something I just went through because there was no way of avoiding it but which was going to need all my patience. Instead, it became steadily warmer, more animated, more building of relation-ships; after about the third hour I felt that I had known these people all my life. Mairead moved about among the knots of people, smiling, listening, welcoming, performing introductions; I kept stealing glances at her and thinking each time that I had never seen her so beautiful. I swelled with pride at the knowledge that the seeds of a new life were quickening within her, and that I had been so unutter-ably privileged as to put them there. This emotion was not novel, it was not original or even unusual. It has been felt ever since the world began, by every married man who has been happy about being married, by every father who has been glad to be a father. Its very universality is precisely what makes this emotion so precious: it is the emotion with which we greet the dawn, or the return of the spring, or the sight of the moon breaking clear of a bank of cloud. The happiness I felt in looking at Mairead just now was a satisfaction I shared with my entire species, or at least those members of it who are capable of strong, uncomplicated, positive emotions. And they, even after all the corrupting and sophisticating influences have been let loose to do their work, are still in the majority. Most men, I knew, would feel as I felt when I looked across the room at my wife, and most men would be right.

Well along in the proceedings – towards midnight, indeed – I was suddenly made aware that the front door had been opened by someone standing near to it in response to a series of rings at the bell which had been going unheeded amid the general tumult, and I was glad, but at the same time rather guilty, to see Otto Nussbaum come in. I had forgotten inviting him, though his was one of the first names I had put down. In view of my affection and respect for him, and the fact that he lived so near at hand, it had never occurred to me not to invite him to come and help warm our house. He explained his lateness by saying that after his solitary evening meal he had sat down in his armchair by the fireside, and had fallen asleep. On waking at half-past eleven, he had immediately telephoned for a taxi and here he was, refreshed by his nap and ready to bring us his good wishes.

I was grateful to him. I wanted to introduce him to Mairead, and his presence in our house was an important symbol to me. Also, I knew that a certain sacrifice lay behind his casual description of the pattern of the evening. I conjectured that he very often, usually in fact, sat down by the fire after his evening meal, closed his eyes, and slept, and that in his sleep his dreams were shot through with memories, so that at times it would have been difficult to say for certain whether he was evoking his memories within a dream-landscape or dreaming with his dreams fuelled by memory. He had told me, sometimes, of his childhood spent in some little town in the foothills of the Bavarian Alps, and how in his dreams he would be transported back even now to the forests where the red deer were to be glimpsed everywhere, and wild strawberries and blueberries grew so prodigally, and where the cold streams from the mountains ran ice-green. He would wake, he said, with tears of longing streaming down his face, knowing that he could not afford to go back to Bavaria, and that if he did it would only be to find that that childhood paradise had been obliterated in one way or another.

Looking across the room at Nussbaum where he stood talking to Mairead and Siobhán, I thought how much I admired and pitied him, though I was not free of the thought that it was presumption to feel pity for a man so brave and so wise. He seemed fabulously old, yet in terms of ordinary arithmetic it was impossible that he should be. He had served in the First World War; the oldest he could possibly have been, to see trench service in that war, would be something like 25 in 1914. Anyone who was 25 in 1914 was eleven years older than the century. It was now 1953, which would make Nussbaum what? An incredible 64, and that at the maximum. Why, the man was almost a youngster. Looking over at him again I thought he seemed more like an octogenarian, and one moreover who had not worn well. The effect was to bring home to me, as words or statistics would never have done, that our century, at least from half-way through its fateful second decade, had not only been a terrible one in general but specifically cruel to a particular and valuable human type. Its vast load of chaos and evil and cruelty had lain with special force on men like

Otto Nussbaum: sensitive, thoughtful, not protected by any highly developed sense of self-preservation nor cocooned in anything like wealth, depending on the surrounding society to support and tolerate them while they pursued their difficult, idealistic labours in the realm of knowledge and imagination. For such as Albert Einstein, who proved able to wield power in a form immediately recognizable by the multitude, rescue and comfort were available from a fortunately early stage; not so for a scholar like Nussbaum, whose devoted and meticulous work must always have struck 'the blunt monster with uncounted heads' as irrelevant and incomprehensible. The European civilization he had been so willing to serve had not given him anything like his due; at best, it had flung him scraps, kept him from actually starving. Yet here he was, still alive, still straight-backed, still as brave as ever though no officer any longer mentioned him in despatches. I was glad he had come to visit our home, and to leave a little of his spirit within its walls.

PART FOUR

Harmless, innocent Ransom with his clear eyes, outdoor skin, and the stance that made one look instinctively for the cricket bat under his arm, was our College Tutor in Roman Law, an innocuous subject – or at any rate one that in his hands could be made to seem innocuous. Going into the Common Room one morning for a cup of coffee, I saw him settled in an armchair staring doggedly at a magazine. Something in the flimsy appearance of the magazine gave it a familiar air, and I looked down at it as I passed. It was one of the undergraduate weeklies of that epoch, *Cherwell* or perhaps *Isis*.

'Keeping abreast of the young?' I said to him genially.

'Faint but pursuing would be more like it,' the honest creature replied. 'Come and tell me if you can make anything of this.'

I poured myself some coffee and joined him. He handed me the magazine, open at a poem. Well, a wodge of verse. More accurately, perhaps, versicular prose. It was headed, 'POEM'. I began reading.

> Violet-haunted snowscapes of desire
> images of conquest in multiple exposure
> refracted as hesitant velleities.
>   Consider, maidens,
> what it is you do, when through apertures
> inflicted surgically on the rind of time
> your eyes regard in mute dubiety
> the stone mask swinging from its bough.

There was more, but I thought that would do for the time being. I handed the magazine back to Ransom.

'Well?' he asked.

'Well, what?'

'Can you get a meaning out of it?'

'I'm not convinced that there's meaning *in* it. What it tells me is that the author wanted to write something that looked like a slab of verse, get it published and think of himself as a poet.'

'I don't think I'd have the confidence to say that. I mean, I never really expect to make head or tail of modern poetry. It's always complex, isn't it?'

'Complex or disorganized,' I said. 'One's not always clear which.'

'Well, I suppose that's always apt to be the case with poetry,' Ransom said humbly. 'I mean, those daring metaphorical leaps . . . I mean, I remember when I used to have to read poetry as part of my general education . . . The logic always seemed to me difficult to follow. Of course I've got a legalistic mind. It doesn't do to be too much of a stickler for what someone like me would think of as precision.'

'It doesn't,' I agreed, 'and yet it must have struck you that this kind of thing is just about the easiest stuff to fake.'

'Fake? Why should anyone fake it?'

'Well, I wouldn't and you wouldn't. But it's worth a lot in certain circles to have the reputation of a poet.'

'Really?' Ransom was so guileless that I sometimes wondered whether he was laughing at me, but I always concluded that he wasn't. 'There's no money in poetry, surely?'

'There's prestige, and prestige can be cashed in for money. I gather there are all sorts of positions one can get if one can play that card along with one's others.'

'Oh, well, I suppose you know these things.' Why he should make that assumption I had no idea, but then I always found Ransom's mind impenetrable. What really was his idea of me? For that matter, what really was his idea of anything?

I looked down at 'POEM' again. It was attributed to one Christopher Pettifer.

'Why are you reading this?' I asked Ransom. 'Do you know this man?'

'He's one of my pupils. First year. You must have seen him at Collections.'

I thought. Pettifer, Pettifer . . . 'Oh, you mean the chap with the cloak?'

Ransom nodded. 'Of course I knew he wrote poetry. He told me half-way through his first week. It's his standard excuse for being late with an essay, or not having read something I told him to read. Struggling with the Muse.'

I remembered the tall, skimpily-built student, pallid of face and languid in manner, who had materialized from the realm of Infinite Possibility at Collections during the last few terms. My thought then, which I now voiced to Ransom, was that he didn't look the kind of man who would be doing a degree in law, Roman or otherwise.

'Well, he's not the usual kind,' Ransom said. 'It's just that his father offered him what I understand is a pretty hefty allowance, on top of his grant, if he read law. He's quite frank about it. Says he has expensive tastes. The father came to see me, actually, as his tutor, and we had quite a talk. He's a very successful barrister, earns enough not to notice anything he gives his son, and he's hoping the boy will give up this stuff about being a poet. Grow out of it. And meanwhile he'll have picked up some knowledge of the law, which will prevent his years at Oxford from being a complete waste of time.'

'I don't think this father sounds the kind of chap I'd like much, if I knew him.'

'I don't awfully like him myself. But he's entitled to his point of view, I suppose. He says that whether his son gets a qualification in law or not, it'll be a help to know *some* law, whatever branch of business he decides to settle down to.'

Well, I thought, it's a perfectly normal calculation, as the world goes. Just boring, boring, boring. Surely life's about something more than surviving and having plenty of cash. And then the thought followed, as it always does: how few people would agree with that? And after that came the counter-counter-thought, which also follows each time: yes, but that few always will, always and everywhere, and they are the ones to live your life among.

Meanwhile, what of Christopher Pettifer? Just about the only fact I had hoisted in about him, apart from the fact that his poetry was pseudo-rarified piffle, was that he wore a cloak. It was made of black velvet and had a pale blue lining, and he secured it round his neck with a heavy silver brooch. It made made him look like a minor, a very minor, poet of the 1890s. With one important difference, I thought. It would have been possible to feel sympathy with a young poet of the 1890s, however tiresome and untalented, who drank absinthe and struck all the fashionable poses, because he was doing so as a gesture of defiance against a society that was very prosperous, very Philistine and very powerful. To flout social and moral conventions in the 1890s was to kick against people who were very willing to kick back, and hard. But what did it mean now, in the mid-twentieth century, to flout the assumptions of such people, who had lost authority, lost conviction and now barely existed as a homogenous class? Who was really going to care that Christopher Pettifer was walking around with a sensibility that had slipped sixty years in time?

On the other hand again, it was probable that he saw some point in it or he wouldn't have done it. I trusted the social perceptions of the young – more than I trusted my own. There was a touch of the Ransom about me; I was, for all my suspiciousness, something of an innocent. The young, ever watchful of the barometer of social pressures, were always a couple of jumps ahead of me. But where precisely did that put them? I thought of asking Michael, but he was preparing to go and join the young engineers of Birmingham, who, I was sure, saw things differently.

★

For the record, I will put down here that the first member of Episcopus College to sign a contract to appear on television was Watson. What was more, he pulled off a spectacular deal, arranging to appear as commentator and anchor man in a series of ten weekly programmes about Life, no less. Life in the purely physical sense was his subject: how cells develop, why a species is not the same thing as a genus, that kind of topic; Watson, though his academic field was microbiology, could always, when called upon to popularize, broaden out into any aspect of biology. I saw one of his programmes. It succeeded in making sense of a number of biological classifications, largely with the aid of imaginative visual presentations not set up by him, though his coaxing voice could always be heard explaining the significance of everything. The series was called 'Looking for Life' or something equally cheery.

The chief reason why I watched a sample programme was curiosity, because I had never associated Watson with anything designed to attract the general public. He had always taken such care to keep up a parade of being supercilious, withdrawing into an arcane cloud of connoisseurship and viewing average humanity through a haze of (at best) tolerant irony. It was true that he very rarely said anything that revealed the sensibility of a real connoisseur, or was flavoured with genuine irony; he relied on the ability to suggest these qualities by his manner, and on the whole his manner did the job for him.

As a TV commentator, also, his manner proved able to rise to the occasion. Never having seen television before, I could only guess at how much of the effect was owing to artful studio lighting, but on the screen his predatory little eyes seemed friendly and twinkling, the unpleasing scooped-out quality given to his face by the abrupt declivity under the lower lip was cleverly illuminated away, and the self-congratulatory sarcasm of his smile came over as cheerfulness, a healthy good humour. He was a success! Watson the ringmaster of cliques, Watson the nose-in-air snob, was a success at the art of hypnotising the masses by means of the cathode ray tube. I could test and confirm the reactions of these good people because I started from the same point; never a one of them was more ignorant of the science of biology than I was. In my boyhood it was a subject very rarely offered at the ordinary secondary school, and the school I went to was very ordinary; and it was a gap I had never tried to fill in the years since. I was perfect material for Watson's TV series, and I can testify that he had a very beguiling way of standing in a Salvador Dali-like setting of charts and plastic mock-ups and saying things like, 'We shan't get very far in trying to see our way through this business unless we can get to terms with a team of very busy little fellows to whom biologists give the name "enzymes". They're the special class

-264-

of proteins who recognize *both* the glycene molecule *and* the end of the DNA molecule — that's the little character you see over to the left here — and bring about the chemical reaction that bonds them together.' Then with a sudden flashing smile (Why? What was funny about it?) he would make some clinching observation such as, 'Of course it's important to remember that though all catalysts aren't enzymes, all enzymes are catalysts.' Freshmen arriving in Oxford in the autumn of that year, 1953, looked at him with a keen but shy interest in suddenly recognizing his features among the assembled dons who were going to interview them. Here was a face they knew and they could write home about to their parents, who would also know it, for it was a Famous face. *Dear Mum and Dad, Today we had Collections in the College Hall, and guess who . . .*

The whole thing baffled me, but of course I was being green and innocent again. Christian doctrine teaches us that the human soul can be corrupted by three temptations, the World, the Flesh and the Devil. I had been open to temptations of the flesh (in spades); the Devil, if by that expression is meant the power that causes spiritual sins like pride and envy to infiltrate our nature, had by no means drawn a blank with me; but the World, on the whole, had retired defeated from my shut drawbridge. I didn't, in the last resort, care enough about rising in the World. Watson, like many academics, could not resist the World. Like them, he delighted in knowing, and dropping the name of, anyone who after a student period at Oxford had gone on to win success, more or less any kind of success, and fame, in the wider scene outside. His instinct had told him that television was to be the golden key to unlock the World, and he was the first of our little community at Episcopus to pounce and get that key in his hand.

I soon saw what could be unlocked with it, had one cared to try. 1953 was the year when television took command. It was the Coronation that brought this about; how ironical if it had transpired, when all the tale came to be told, that the last decisive intervention of the monarchy into English life had been the rapid and irreversible spread of the TV-watching habit, probably in the end fatal to the monarchy itself, as to anything hierarchical. At the beginning of that year, a minority of British homes had a television set; at the end of it, a majority. They wanted to watch the Coronation and so they went out and bought themselves the square-eyed household deity, and once they had it they sat in front of it in an obedient coma.

In retrospect, when more years had gone by and Watson had established himself firmly as a TV don, it was all clear even to me. But now, in the initiatory year of 1953, there were still things I found entirely beyond me, and I look back with gratitude to a terse explanation given to me one evening at dinner, or rather at dessert among the ritual of wine and fruit and conversation, by a brisk young man who happened to sit next to me. This man was a Junior Research Fellow, one of our birds of passage, a high-flyer who stayed with us only while he balanced himself to take off again and soar higher. I liked him, what little I saw of him; he frankly didn't need us, except as a source of a little money for a few years, but he wasn't aggressive about it. He thought we were quite harmless dinosaurs, a species with its own interest whose extermination would probably leave a gap, and should preferably be avoided if possible. Beyond that, our fate couldn't possibly concern him because he was already one of those picked out as worthy to spend their lives in the stratospheric heights of scientific achievement; ultimately, I believe, he came back to the neighbourhood to work at Culham, that high-powered Eurocentre of scientific thought which seems always to be spoken of with bated breath.

Watson was not present on this occasion, though I am sure that if he had been, the young scientist's opinions would have found just as trenchant expression, in or out of the victim's hearing. Someone had brought up the subject of Watson's new-found screen fame, and the wise youth ('a Daniel come to judgement') merely remarked tolerantly, 'Oh, yes, he was very keen to get into all that.'

'Why d'you think it mattered to him so much?' I asked. 'I mean, was it just for the pleasure of being well-known? I suppose it's nice to be a celebrity, but is it always a help in one's essential work?'

'It is in his,' the young man answered, rapidly peeling an orange, 'because his essential work is to survive. He wants to hang on to his job, naturally, but I don't know anyone in his branch of science who thinks him any better than a mediocrity who got in at a fortunate time when there was a shortage of people to teach his subject. If he can become a household name with a lot of popular appeal he'll be all right because they like that sort of thing here.'

The company then spent an enjoyable ten minutes furnishing examples of this general truth. There was the famous historian with a weekly page in a cheap Sunday paper: the scholar of English literature who presided over a mass-market Book Club: the lecturer in Politics who actually spent a third of his time in the bar of the House of Commons, a third in broadcasting studios, and only the tired-out last third on his Oxford concerns. Game sprang up in abundance, shotguns exploded, and a spirit of keen sportsmanship took over among the decanters and finger-bowls.

'Anyway, Watson was dead keen,' the youthful savant went on, when calm again descended. 'It was the joke of the lab. He never made the slightest attempt to hide it from us, though I expect he kept the mask on when he got out of the immediate scientific circle, in fact I remember he very rarely mentioned it in College here. But we saw him with the mask off because there'd have been no sense in trying to disguise it. The crowning thing was his nervousness when the prize was almost in the bag – when he'd got everything but the producer's signature on the contract. I never saw anyone so jumpy. He was doing one pilot programme, so that they could decide whether they wanted to sign him up for the series. When they were settling the details, the producer wrote and said, "The fee will be £50," and Watson wrote back by return saying he was delighted to accept and enclosing a cheque for £50.'

There was a ripple of laughter, but through it Tonson, the Arabic scholar, whose memories went back to the early thirties, leaned forward slightly in his chair and said, 'That story's a chestnut.'

'Oh?' said the young genius imperturbably.

'Yes. I'm not saying it isn't true in spirit, but considered simply as an anecdote, resting on a base of ascertainable fact, it's simply a recycled joke. I remember exactly the same story going round when academics first got invited to take part in radio programmes, which must have been about the time the B.B.C. left Savoy Hill and moved down to Broadcasting House. Oxford had its Watsons then, of course, and of most of them in turn the story was told that the producer had written and said, "The fee for your broadcast will be £x," and he'd written back in nervous haste and enclosed £x.'

'I expect,' I put in, 'that if one really looked into the matter one would find that the story was common enough when dons first began to earn big fees by writing in the Sunday papers.'

Someone wanted to know whether I meant the heavies or the tabloids, and the conversation drifted away into a general drawing of distinctions between newspapers and audiences, and whether the cheap press actually increased its audience by attracting celebrities from Academia. (Not until they became TV personalities, it was finally decided, after which anything went.)

The young man who had originally told the story showed no surprise at being told it was a chestnut. As a scientist, he would have learnt already that most of what is offered as new information turns out to be not so new when you examine it. In any case, the subject had very little interest for him; he was just coming as close as he ever did to 'making conversation', an activity he doubtless despised.

Nevertheless, I did notice one thing. *Les absents ont toujours tort*, and no one put in a word in defence of Watson; indeed, it seemed to me that the earth opened up for an instant and I had a glimpse of the soles of his dapper shoes as he was swallowed into its entrails. On one or two faces I even thought I discerned an expression of relief, as if someone who had had the power to be an irritant in their lives had suddenly lost that power. For of course Watson had managed to find several habitual butts for his lightly feathered shafts of sarcasm; I was not alone in filling that role.

★

To turn to more serious matters, our daughter Keira was born one morning in July 1953. She arrived at breakfast-time. Mairead had had her first contraction at about four a.m. and I had taken her the short distance to the maternity wing of the Radcliffe Infirmary, where Michael had been born nineteen years earlier. The sky was just beginning to be dappled with grey as we came out of the house and got into the car to drive down there. In that curious way the mind has of bringing up some absurdity at a point of crisis, I remember thinking that it was a good thing I had something more suitable to provide in the way of transport than the M.G. PA I had bought to make Michael happy. I had kept up the fiction that it was 'our' car, shared between him and me, right up to the point when Mairead had finally left her little house in Bayswater and come to live with me in Kingston Road, when I had ceded it to him and bought a dull, ordinary saloon car that would chug from A to B and do it unobtrusively. Unobtrusiveness, by that time, was what I wanted in a motor car in the same way that I wanted it in my internal organs. (It's better not to be aware that you have a liver.)

The custom of inviting – requiring, indeed – the presence of the male parent during the process of birth had not at that time taken root. Most people, in fact, had never heard of such a thing, though a few pioneers had begun to press for it. Once it did become established, many husbands claimed that the experience had been immensely positive and contributed greatly to their joy in the event and in the love they felt for their wives. I was glad to hear it, though it didn't seem to make any impact on the steadily increasing rate of divorces. (To be fair, of course, we didn't know how fast that rate might have increased if the custom of having the husband attend the birth had never taken root. As Bax had taught me at eighteen, speculation is a fruitless activity.)

In any case, in my and Mairead's day, the husband sat in the waiting-room, or paced the corridor, or went home and sat by the telephone, or whatever. All I can say is even under these conditions it was a joyous and fulfilling experience. Apart from her mother and the doctor and a couple of nurses, I was the first to set eyes on Keira and welcome her into the world. Then I kissed Mairead, knowing as I did so that I stood on sacred ground. The Christian religion is true in one respect at least: every child who is born is the offspring of God.

Then I was shooed away from the room; gently, kindly, but shooed. I walked back along Walton Street, into Kingston Road, into our house, and straight into the kitchen where I cooked myself an enormous breakfast. I ate for myself. I ate for Mairead. I ate for Keira. I ate for the earth, the forests, the rivers, the mountains, the birds and the animals. Then I sank down into an armchair and slept. When I woke two hours later I thought it would be all right to go to the hospital again.

It was all right. It was better than all right.

That second visit lasted ninety minutes, till I was chucked out again. I went to a wine merchant and bought a case of champagne – good champagne. Then I fetched the car and took the case home. There was room in the refrigerator for about three bottles to start cooling, so I laid them there. Then I went to the telephone and started to scatter invitations. I drew some blanks; Garrity wasn't there – being, like many solitaries, a man of fixed habits, he used July to explore northern parts of the British Isles, then briefly returned to Oxford before setting out in September for Continental Europe. I was glad he took such pleasure in travelling and exploring, even though I knew he was only escaping from one loneliness into another. But even a change of loneliness must be something.

In the evening, after another visit to Mairead, I went down to Oseney Town to give the news to Brian and our parents. Brian was serving behind the bar as usual, but the place was not very busy and, having a capable middle-aged woman to help him, he neglected his duties for a while to hear the news and give me his congratulations. I had drunk a fair bit of the champagne by then, and as he pressed me to have a drink on the house I asked for some wine rather than the beer I would normally have chosen; I reasoned that if I put beer down on top of the champagne it would make me feel very ill. There was no call in those days for modest side-street public houses to stock good wine; it was all cheap stuff, just about good enough to cook with, but I discovered this evening, Keira's first evening on the planet, that it was also good enough to celebrate with. By the time I had had a glass of it, plus another one for luck, then another one for the road, it seemed a pity to waste the rest of the bottle, so I had that too. I had intended to go and call on Mother and Dad in their cheerful little house in the next street, but when I got down from my stool and noticed that my walk was slightly unsteady I thought it would be best to go home and telephone them with the glad news. But when I got home I sat down in an armchair and went to sleep again, waking up at about 1.30 a.m. when there was obviously nothing to do but crawl stiffly off to bed.

So ended my first day as the father of a girl-child. I lay back in bed and noticed how the world was slowly rotating, which I knew couldn't be right; but it was a very happy world for all that.

★

Hannah Carshalton, in the fourteen years I had known her, had never lost the habit of laying her hand confidentially on the wrist or forearm of the person she was speaking to. She had indeed never lost or even dimmed any of the speech habits or body language that had characterized her when her horrible bridegroom, horrible Carshalton of Episcopus, had brought her to visit me in my College rooms that August afternoon in 1939. She herself would have attributed her speech and manner, in those days, to the influence of her background – what she engagingly referred to as 'never having been out of the liddle golden ghetto'. Certainly a whiff of moneyed Jewish Manhattan – in those days, incredibly, a flavour something of a novelty in Oxford and not common even in London – had accompanied her then and still accompanied her now, after years of California and then years of alternating between a cosmopolitan life in Europe and sending down some kind of roots in the English countryside. Her wealth had bought the Cotswold manor house that Carshalton's daydreams had figured to him as the ideal launching-pad for his schemes of social and political aggrandisement – somewhere to relax between adventures, to be photographed in, to entertain and impress in, and also somewhere convenient to dump his wife if she showed signs of sticking too closely by his side and interfering with his plans: for his ambitions, one gathered, were erotic as well as social, financial, political, and generally geo-egocentric. To this end he had fed her with a number of placatory titbits, as one might keep a fretful child occupied. He had paid her at any rate sufficient sexual attention to make her three times pregnant, and her own earth-mother fecundity had done the rest, so that the couple had a daughter, a son and another daughter in that order. He had also encouraged her to persevere with her work as a sculptor, which she took with immense seriousness and pegged away at year after year. Carshalton, not averse to adding the art world to the various spheres of influence in which he was trying his strength, took a pleasure in learning the patter, dropping the right names, fishing for introductions, throwing parties and inviting exactly the right people; it was a game of skill that he enjoyed, and he soon discovered that it didn't involve any boring waste of time actually *looking* at works of art and coming up with a response to them. The responses were all there, pre-packed; you just helped yourself on the way in.

I never could decide, nor did the question much trouble me, whether Hannah Carshalton actually *saw* her husband. What she saw when she looked towards him must have had some elements of the actual Carshalton, but on the other hand it must surely have been, in the main, a construct, as much a product of her own imagination as one of her bulky, dropsical sculptures; no one who looked at Dominic Carshalton straight and dispassionately, without distortions and without imaginative accretions, could ever have seen anything in him that was not repulsive or at least unattractive. For myself I distrusted him so completely that I did not even believe that his first name *was* Dominic, as he had given out ever since his undergraduate days. I suspected that D., his leading initial, stood for something more commonplace, more predictably in tune with the *milieu* I knew he came from: Hounslow, where his father had done something like managing a furniture shop. No disgrace in that! People need furniture shops and those shops have to be managed, in Hounslow as everywhere. But I knew that men who manage furniture shops in Hounslow, and the wives of such men, do not — or at any rate did not in the 1920s — cause their sons to be christened Dominic. Or, for that matter, Cyprian, or Graeme, or Marcus, or Tristan. In short, Carshalton was lying as usual.

Hannah Carshalton, transparently honest, too rich and too protected since birth ever to have felt the need to deceive anybody, too straightforward in character to derive any pleasure from masquerade or falsity, laid her hand on my forearm confidingly as we paused, our paths crossing, on the steps leading up to the Ashmolean Museum that May morning in 1953. Pearly discarded blossom strewed the lawns of Oxford: the cheerful, boisterous spring wind was just closing down the season of full display from almond and flowering cherry, and out in the fields and along the canal banks the hawthorn, smaller and more tenacious, was clinging like soapsuds to the thorny twigs that were already coated with young green. Bursting vitality was in the air; I felt it everywhere, not least in the presence of the burgeoning, still young matron who inclined her ample form slightly towards me, gave me that wide smile that so engagingly emphasized the small gap between her two central front teeth, and said, 'Oh, I've been hoping to meet you, Peter. You won't be offended if I give you a word-of-mouth invitation? Sending out cards through the mail is udderly time-consooming and I'm into some new groupings.'

'An invitation to what?'

'Oh, I thought you knoo. Our sculpture pardy.'

'I'll come if I'm free on the date,' I said. 'But what's a sculpture party?'

'It's just a brawl in the grounds of our house. Maybe forty or fifty people with drinks and bits of things t'eat. And dotted about, the sculptures I've done since we've been living there.'

'Date?'

'July fourteenth. Might as well pick one people can remember. Bastille Day.'

I took out my diary, looked at it, and made a note there and then. 'Are wives invited?'

'Of course. I'm a wife. But warn her that there'll be a lot of sculptures to look at. I do five or six a year.'

I looked at her strong figure, her decided face. Carshalton was a nothing, but she was a something, and I wished her well.

'Thank you for the invitation. We'll certainly come. Quite apart from the sculpture, which will interest us, there's the house. It's a treat to get the chance to visit a Cotswold manor house, particularly one that's in private ownership.'

'Well, there aren't that many, and most of the ones that are still owned by the original families have to let the public in, at so much a head, a couple of days a week. I suppose that's the kind of thought that ought to make me feel horribly guilty, with being an interloper from way outside the right circles, and being pretty dam' loaded and all. Still, it helps to have a bit of ice. It helps me and it helps Dom.'

I don't need telling it helps Dom, I rejoined silently. And it helps you if you happen to regard it as a piece of good fortune to be Dom's wife. Because you must know, whether you admit it to yourself or not, that you wouldn't see Dom for dust if your bank balance was an ordinary size.

Exactly as if I had spoken the words aloud and she were calmly responding to them, she said, 'Dom's got so many projects going and most of them need money in the early stages.'

'I'm sure he's full of ideas,' I said.

'Well,' she said, 'see you then. And no matter how many brilliant and famous people there are there, please talk to me. I'll be lonely.'

'Lonely?' I said. 'Supported by a whole crowd of your own sculptures? Never.'

She gave a quick, derisive flap of both hands – a very Jewish gesture, wafting away hyperbole, blocking *chutzpah*. 'You're just laughing at me now.'

'I swear,' I said, meaning it, 'that if I'm laughing at anything it's at the idea of your being lonely at a party at your own house. Or anyone else's house.'

'With or without sculptures?' she asked, two steps below me now, twisting round to look up at me, poised to hasten on her way.

'With or without sculptures. What's the kick-off time?'

'Noon. But it goes on till everyone collapses. It's open-ended.'

'Mairead and I will be there,' I said. 'Noon on July the fourteenth.' And what new Marquis de Sade, I wondered as I thoughtfully continued up the steps, shall we release from what new Bastille?

I went on through the glass door and into the building. My visit had a specific purpose, which was to check certain details about eighteenth-century keyboard instruments in the Bate Collection, but as I began to climb the central staircase I saw first the lower, then the upper half of a familiar figure coming down towards me. It was Garrity.

'Well met, Leonard,' he greeted me. 'I've just been refreshing my memory of the Palmers.'

I nodded appreciatively. Like anyone in Oxford with a grain of discernment, I much appreciated the wisdom of that succession of curators at the Ashmolean who, in the 1930s and the war years, had realized, a step ahead of everyone else, that Samuel Palmer was a great painter. These connoisseurs had, by wisely laying out the modest funds available to them, built up a fine collection of his work, including some of the great symbolic landscapes of the early Shoreham period and the wonderful 'Self-Portrait' of about 1825. Once Palmer had come into his own, paintings like these never came into the saleroom except to shoot straight through the ceiling into the financial stratosphere, and the fact that they were hanging in the Ashmolean for casual inspection by anyone walking in the streets of Oxford was and still is a great monument to the discrimination and shrewdness of a generation largely unsung by posterity. Garrity, at least, was encouraging the young to appreciate them; trust him!

From a commanding position on the main staircase, he surveyed the Ashmolean Museum benevolently. 'I make a policy of encouraging my men to become familiar with this place,' he said. 'I want it to be second nature to them to drop in and just look, simply look, at paintings – and, for that matter, ceramics and tapestries and art-objects generally – that were produced at the same time as the books that their syllabus requires them to read. I'm a great believer in understanding one art through another. Of course it's equally important to know the music too. The sensibility of an age expresses itself in all those ways, and you're out of step with any art if you don't begin by getting a feel for the sensibility of the age. How else can you tell whether an artist is swimming against the tide or allowing himself to be carried along with it?'

I had turned and come down, step by step, into the entrance hall, so as to keep pace with Garrity. He hadn't quite stopped dead in order to engage me in conversation, but he hadn't exactly walked on at an even pace. What he had done was walk on at about a quarter of his normal pace. I therefore had a choice of staying where I was and allowing his voice to float up to me from a greater and greater distance, or turning and going slowly down beside him. Had I chosen the former course, he would probably have raised his voice as he got further away, and he was already speaking loudly enough to cause heads to turn in his direction.

He said nothing more until we were standing in front of the sales and enquiry counter, then resumed in ringing tones. 'Samuel Palmer,' he assured the surrounding space, 'was a major visionary painter, consciously touched by the mantle of Blake. But what made him so unusually important was that his first flowering came during the time of William the Fourth – that is, of Macaulay and Bentham as well as the later Wordsworth and the earlier Tennyson – in other words, when there were many cross-currents swirling about . . . H'mm? H'mm?'

As usual, he ended by emitting the peculiar Garrity-sound he always made in conversation when the ideas inside his head began to bubble and boil. It came out through his nose, with mouth closed, and did in fact suggest the escape of steam under pressure; it was, also, invariably accompanied by one of his most characteristic physical gestures – the arms straight down by the sides, hands held rigid as if there were no wrist-joints, fingers pointing straight downward and twitching rapidly. A knot of visitors, in the act of pushing their way through the plate-glass doors into the building – either Americans, or on their way to attend some fancy-dress function at which they would be required to dress like Americans – regarded him with expressions of frank amazement.

Garrity was now ready to make his exit, but before doing so he turned to me and asked with one of his abrupt changes of subject, 'Did you know Arthur Dobson was to be in Oxford this evening?'

'Arthur Dobson?' I searched for the name. 'You mean the man who writes a lot about primitive epic and folklore?'

'That's a rough description of his field. Done a lot to carry on the work adumbrated by Albert B. Lord. *The Singer of Tales*, you remember?'

'Well, it isn't my field. . . .'

'Old friend of mine, Arthur, from years ago. And I so seldom get a chance to see him now he's working in Aberdeen. Always found his a peculiarly stimulating mind. A talk with him would leave me pondering fresh perspectives for weeks. Months, often. As well as the sheer pleasure of his company.'

'You must be very glad he's making a visit to Oxford.'

Garrity stopped short and the expression of happiness and eager interest faded from his face. Instinctively he plunged his hand into a side pocket, pulled out his pipe and then, recollecting that he was in a building where he could not smoke it, thrust it back again. During these actions an air of despondency was spreading over his features as a cloud steals over the sun.

'Rather unfortunate timing, I'm afraid. He chose today for his visit, and because it's Thursday I'm simply not available in the evening. I told him this some years ago and I've repeated it all along, but it must have slipped his memory. Of course he's a busy man, and he gets very wrapped up in his work – it's so original and speculative. But it's a pity he couldn't have kept it in mind. Never on a Thursday evening in term. Any other day of the week and any day at all in vacation. But Thursdays in term I keep for my men.'

Oh, yes, I thought, his men. It was that streak of old-fashionedness in him that made him use that quaint, almost Edwardian term for his pupils, harking back to the days when it seemed natural to a certain kind of college-bound bachelor don to refer to the undergraduate body with unceremonious geniality as 'the men'. In the etiquette of those days, it was *de rigueur* that you set aside certain regular intervals of leisure for your 'men'. Garrity understood this tradition, was loyal to it, and had remained loyal to it while the world changed around him. What did the 'men' themselves, who in any case were by now increasingly apt to be girls, think of it? Their attendance at Garrity's evenings was, as I knew from other sources, patchy and fitful at best. They had grown up in a world in which the old college solidarity did not exist; there was not much chance that they would make common cause with someone like Garrity, so different from themselves, so uncomprehending of their ways, unless they happened to share his love of the arts and particularly of poetry. They would have different motives for showing up at his *soirées*; some because they were at a loose end that evening and Garrity always laid in unlimited bottled beer; some because they saw it as a source of unofficial extra tuition – as Garrity rhapsodized over this or that poet, he might let fall *aperçus* which could be stored in a canny memory and later used to freshen up a jaded and perfunctory examination answer. One or two came because they liked Garrity; others because they found him comical and wanted to perfect the mimicry of his mannerisms that would win applause and laughter in the Junior Common Room. It was, at best, a loosely-tied habit, one that would come untied for any one of a wide range of reasons. An undergraduate might vaguely intend to spend an evening at Garrity's and then be deflected at the last minute by an essay crisis, or being needed for a darts match, or seeing a chance to go out with a girl or in search of a girl. Or just inertia. Garrity set so much store by these evenings; no one else, it seemed to me, set any at all.

'Oh, cancel it for once,' I urged him. 'This is a chance you get very rarely. Leave a note pinned to your door, apologizing to your men.'

I felt myself using the phrase in quotation marks. 'They'll live, if you're not there for once.'

'That's just what Arthur Dobson said, when I spoke to him on the telephone. I explained that this was the evening I always kept for my men, and he said exactly that.'

'So would anybody. Think of yourself for once, Garrity.'

He shook his head. 'I'm afraid it's quite out of the question. I think it's very important for the men to find me at home when I've said I'll be. If they're disappointed once, it sows doubt in their minds on subsequent occasions. If they're not sure whether I'll be there or not, they could start staying away.'

'I imagine they stay away pretty often as things are, don't they?' I said brutally.

'Some do,' he said with dignity. 'Of course there's no obligation on their side; it's just recreation. But I think it's a good thing to set them an example. I shall just have to see Dobson another time.'

I perceived that important issues of principle were involved for him and I had to admit defeat. He longed to see his old friend and to allay his deep loneliness with an evening of delightful talk. But even more than that, he wanted to keep faith with his men. I hoped the little featherheads were worth it.

★

The agreeable Noel Arcady, who had for some year held the teaching Fellowship in English at Episcopus, was leaving us. He had accepted a position as literary editor of a prestigious weekly paper. The weekly press, with its inevitable awareness of fashion and gossip and the charting of ephemeral reputations, was a more appropriate habitat for one of his tastes and preferences. The academic life, as glimpsed fleetingly on a casual visit, can easily seem to consist largely of sitting in graceful panelled rooms, strolling in idyllic gardens and consuming an endless succession of good meals with excellent wines. But strip away that surface and what lies beneath it is a great deal of hard work, often boringly repetitive, undertaken in the knowledge that one's best efforts will usually go unappreciated and almost certainly unthanked. It was not Arcady country, decent man though he was. He needed a gentler climate, and was off to find it.

His decision was a blow to Watson and to the Episcopus *claque* over which Watson presided. Watson, as our grandfathers would have put it, 'loved a lord', and though Arcady was not actually a lord he was some kind of minor scion, an Honourable or something of the kind, and to Watson this was quite enough to be going on with. Quite innocently, because it was the only world he knew, Arcady tended to sow into his conversation many fascinating seeds in the form of well-known names in the higher worlds of literary and theatrical fashion – fascinating to Watson, that is.

In particular, Arcady's social circle evidently included a number of people who had grown rich by the writing of detective stories. He seemed to have devoured the output of all the celebrated practitioners of this curious sub-branch of fiction, and was always starting conversations about them at meal-times or in Common Room. The fact that I never joined in the conversations inevitably acted as an irritant to Watson; he claimed that my lack of interest in this harmless form of recreation confirmed his view of me as a long-nosed, over-earnest killjoy.

'I don't take any notice of phrenology, either,' I said to him. 'I don't collect old sweet wrappers and file them away. I don't haunt salerooms buying up cuckoo-clocks. Why don't you attack me for not being interested in those things?'

'You read books. You read novels, I expect, from time to time. You just have a superior attitude to detective novels.'

'Exactly. You've put your finger on it. I do have a superior attitude to them; they're below my angle of vision.'

'So,' he said, inviting me to step into the purple limelight as the pantomime demon. 'You regard people who enjoy them as likewise beneath your notice.'

'Some of them are,' I said, giving him a long look as if I had never noticed before what a rat-bag he was.

And there, for the moment, we left it. Most conversations with Watson ended inconclusively. I think he believed there was something *bourgeois* and mundane about going for conclusions. He thought everything should be glancing, deft, light-fingered. The most casual conversation, no more than a sentence or two, was enough for him as long as he could extract from it something he could store away and use as ammunition when the right time came. And he never, *never* forgot anything.

★

If Bax ever knew that he had been gathered up and carried away to bed on the night when he fell over on the Library stairs, he never made any reference to the fact. It was always possible, of course, that he simply woke up next morning with a headache, which must have been a frequent occurrence with him, and never knew that anything unusual had happened. Certainly he made no allusion to the incident when, not long after the beginning of the autumn term, he knocked on my door one morning and came in to discuss what he called 'a small point of tutorial allocation'.

It turned out that of the batch of second-year undergraduates whom he had agreed to teach, there was one he wanted to get rid of. Since all the Episcopus men had to be taught either by him or by me, that meant of course that we had to do a little horse-trading, one of mine for one of his, and as we had devoted some thought at the end of last term to sorting them into pairs who seemed reasonably consonant with one another – able to profit by each other's contribution to three-cornered discussion and with no obvious personal hostilities – unpicking the pattern now was not to be done without taking trouble and giving up quite a lot of time to the job. He apologized for this while keeping up his dry, somewhat distant manner, his eyes as usual masked by their thick lenses. I had long since ceased to confuse this manner with any kind of superiority, as I had naturally done when I was a raw eighteen-year-old from Oseney Town; I knew it was the natural defence of a shy man, and I knew besides that, in a society constituted as English society was at the time constituted, Bax had every reason to be extremely wary of revealing the systole and diastole of his emotional life. It turned out, now, that the problem centred on a student by the name of Robertson.

'In a word,' Bax said, 'I would prefer not to tutor Robertson.'

I passed the names and faces in review. Robertson? Tallish, fairish, no particular characteristics that I could remember, just an undifferentiated slab of male humanity, waiting to be structured into a thinking being. Weary work, weary work, and largely unappreciated at the end of the day. Yes, I recalled Robertson, as far as there was anything to be recalled. But then I went back to my old method of switching genders, and thought how often a girl who could perfectly well be described as an undifferentiated lump of young female humanity had sent some middle-aged man wandering distractedly into the surreal landscape of unfulfilled desire, 'mopping and mowing through the sleepless day', as the poet sings. And I understood, and was humbled.

I plotted; I considered; I wrote on scratch-pads; I conferred with Bax; in the end I took on Robertson, relinquishing in exchange a pustular leprechaun from East Lothian who fiercely disputed every word that issued from my mouth. He had no more than a modest allowance of grey matter, but someone had told him at a formative stage that disputation was the essence of the intellectual life, and he took this as a perpetual summons to argument, the more stubborn the better. In his presence I never advanced a proposition, however uncontentious and well-worn, without having it furiously contested, with the result that our discussions never made any progress at all and his unfortunate tutorial-mate was rapidly sinking into apathy and despair. Bax bore away this gladiator and fought with him from then on until he took some kind of degree and left us in peace, and I inherited the amenable and, to my eye, entirely featureless Robertson.

Bax's eye, needless to say, had discerned qualities in Robertson that had unsettled him emotionally. Since his disastrous experiment with Geraldine, his sexual needs had been (I conjectured) unassuaged, and though he must have been hoping that the mere passage of time would begin to dowse them, his present age, the early to middle fifties, is well known to be highly inflammable. He never discussed the reasons why he found the proximity of this or that youth impossible to take calmly, while looking with indifference on the bulk of them; he merely pursued the policy of refusing to join battle with an adversary whose success record has always, through the centuries, been close to a hundred per cent. A wise retreat is more honourable than being slaughtered on the battlefield. We were beginning, at that time, to get more and more requests to tutor girls from the expanding women's colleges, and if I had been sent one who particularly engaged my sexual emotions I would have got rid of her faster than you could say 'Emily Pankhurst'. (She would not have had to look far for a tutor to replace me; Oxford has always been well supplied with dons who have pursued a policy diametrically the opposite of mine.) Bax, of course, was in a much more difficult position. He was in the position I would have been in if I had (a) not been married to a woman I was in love with and (b) actually employed full-time at a women's college.

*

'I wish I thought more of it. I think the trouble basically is that I don't find much sensitiveness to the ambiguity of perspective. Surely that's the awareness a sculptor needs most of all.'

The words were part of the buzz of conversation around me, to which I was idly listening. I, and the rest of the throng, were standing in a graceful room at the end of a gallery on the third floor of the west wing of the Carshaltons' manor house in the Cotswolds. Nearby, their backs turned to me, were Mairead and Hannah Carshalton. Mairead was inclining slightly towards her hostess to indicate that she was giving full attention to the latter's discourse, which concerned her art.

This was forgivable because the company, of which we were a part, was assembled to pay attention to the art and the artist. This was Hannah's big moment. The graceful mansion in its dream-like setting had been given over for this one summer day to the display and discussion of Hannah Carshalton's *oeuvre*.

The man who felt dissatisfaction with Hannah's philosophy of perspective uttered his opinion from beside my left elbow. Turning further, I saw that he was addressing a man of about his own age, fifty or so, with a nut-cracker face and rimless glasses, who now replied, 'Personally I'm in two minds about her compositional use of the voids between the spaced-out elements. Whether they're meant as counterpointing or corresponding, I mean.'

The other, whose curved bill and round unblinking eyes gave him somewhat the look of a parrot, stirred restlessly and said, 'Does it really matter?'

'From the point of view of praxis, yes,' said the nut-cracker man firmly. 'Theoretically you could always get round it, I suppose.'

The parrot-man shrugged, a gesture conveying part resignation, part indifference. 'There's not much else to talk about, is there? I mean, she's sticking very doggedly to the old "truth-to-the-materials" movement. She may have to break away from that if she wants to be taken seriously.'

'I agree, it's old hat. But she'll have to be careful just *where* she goes, won't she? I can't see any evidence that she's really in touch with the newer currents.'

I had a quick vision of Hannah Carshalton helping herself absent-mindedly to currants from a paper bag marked in large letters 'OLD'. It takes boredom to invite into one's mind foolish fantasies of that kind, and I was certainly bored. I had come into this room in order to get a drink and to find my wife, who was loyally keeping our hostess company and calming her nervousness. Said hostess's husband was nowhere to be seen. Obviously he was not going to bother with his wife; he would be too busy feathering his own nest in any one of a dozen possible ways.

'Of course,' the nut-cracker man said tolerantly, 'there may be the hint of a quest for fresh theoretical impetus in the tendency one notices in the more recent work, to juxtapose completed geometric forms with fragments of broken mass. Rather gives the impression of someone struggling to escape by breaking down solid barriers, wouldn't you agree?'

Feeling that I needed to escape and, if I did not, would be driven likewise to breaking things, I interrupted the conversation between Mairead and Hannah to say that I was going out into the grounds, where the sculptures were dotted about on view. I added an invitation to come with me, though I knew it would involve hearing Hannah talk non-stop about her work. She was too nervous to stop talking. I understood; I liked her for not being entirely at her ease, for feeling that the whole grand occasion was beginning to run away with her. She was a decent woman who simply wanted to produce some interesting forms by carving and modelling. She wouldn't want to be swamped with art-talk by the likes of the two critics standing beside me. Yet she had wanted critics to turn up and look at her work. It was the old problem of the artist. Even Harry Goodenough had to endure having his productions pronounced on, however uncomprehendingly, by 'crickets', who as a rule either stay away from imaginative work or affect to despise it; but he acknowledged that they have their necessary part to play in the world, if only as a news service. I didn't think this was going to be a happy day for Hannah, but it might be a day that, looking back, she would consider usefully spent. Now would be a good time for her to receive some support from her cold rice-pudding of a husband, but was she going to get any? Was she, hell.

Why was Carshalton such a cold rice-pudding? And one made with curdled milk and low-quality rice, at that? But then, why do some people become concentration camp guards? These questions are unanswerable. It must be something in their childhood; or further back, in their genes. And then people say there is no Original Sin!

I wandered off into the grounds. They at least were beautiful. These, demonstrably, were solid achievements of England, a country that had not always been the rat-infested rubbish tip it was now beginning to turn into. Behind the cheap cracked plastic of the modern scene one could still discern the outlines of the epoch when England, the England of Shakespeare and Byrd and Hilliard and Raleigh and Bacon, had seemed a spacious enough home to five million people, who seem to us who look back to have been so marvellously endowed with genius and energy.

Hannah Carshalton wanted very much to have genius and energy too, and the sad thing was that while the second quality was evident enough in her work, the first was achingly absent. I had already spent an hour looking at them with Mairead, and we had jointly come to this conclusion, but because I liked the woman I was willing to stroll about some more and see if I could form a more positive judgement – to get them up, so to speak, from $\gamma+$ to $\beta-$. It seemed worth doing. I gave the figures my attention once more, in the most benevolent spirit I could summon.

Obviously with the most careful eye to effect, she had caused them to be strategically placed at various points in the gardens and grounds, so that one saw them at the end of long avenues, or was abruptly confronted with them on rounding a corner of an outhouse, or walked among a cluster of them on a terrace. They were vaguely humanoid in form and executed in bronze or, occasionally, metal and glass. I found personally that I was not baffled by them, since they followed well-established modern tendencies and spelt out a conventional series of messages; I was simply rather damped. I found them uninspired and uninspiring. As she had explained to Mairead and myself as soon as we arrived, she had got 'Dom' to take her to the Venice Biennale in 1948, when the British Pavilion had been dominated by the work of Henry Moore. This had been the turning-point in Hannah Carshalton's life, and while I couldn't quarrel with her taste I couldn't see that she had done anything but admire and imitate. 1952 had seen her back at the Biennale, and this time Moore had been accompanied by a British contingent that included some of the most energetic and original of the younger sculptors. Hannah had looked; she had admired and absorbed; but when she put out what she had taken in, she added nothing to it. From the evidence of her work, the single piece that had made the greatest impression on her was Kenneth Armitage's 'People in a Wind'; the same tugged, pressed, elongated or squashed-in quality was aimed at, and sometimes achieved, in her careful figures. It was interesting enough. Or perhaps, to be candid, it was interesting, but not quite enough.

The time slipped away. The shadows slanted. Servants appeared with immense pots of tea and platters holding mounds of tiny sandwiches, which they dispensed from tables here and there. I ate and drank. I looked round for Mairead. I wondered where she was. I vaguely began worrying about her. Finally, towards six o'clock, I set off determinedly to find her.

Almost at once I found her. There was a large area of shrubbery, mostly rhododendrons, and as I was about to plunge into its shadowy mass Mairead suddenly emerged.

'Ah, you're here,' I said, not saying anything about my anxiety because it might have sounded like a reproach, and after all a grown woman has a right to stroll about in a garden. 'At least the pieces are improved by being in the open air, aren't they? But then I think nearly all sculpture needs to be under a changing sky to bring out its . . .'

I stopped. Moving towards me, she had swiftly come close enough for me to get her face in full view. Normally I loved to contemplate Mairead's face; but this time, I did not like what I saw. Her expression was tense and angry and she was walking rapidly, evidently making for the house. I was sorry I had started blathering about sculpture and changing shadows and all the rest of it. Obviously my wife was distressed.

'What's the matter?' I demanded.

'We're going, Peter,' she said through set teeth.

'I can see that,' I said. 'I don't know what's happened, but it's something that's made you very unwilling to stay here.'

'Yes. Come on. Let's get in the car. I want to leave here now, this minute.'

'I'll get your stuff from the house,' I·said. It didn't sound to me as if we would be coming back, and I didn't want to leave anything here. Who had upset Mairead? Carshalton himself? Or had one of those art critics been supercilious? Was it a brush with some insolent journalist? But no, she wouldn't mind that. Ordinary rudeness she could handle. This must be something unusual.

Almost running into the house, I retrieved a light raincoat I had brought along, largely to give myself a few extra pockets, and a light cap I wore for driving, plus a cardigan of Mairead's, and dashed out with them over my arm. We were ready to leave.

'There really isn't time to find Hannah and say goodbye to her?' I asked tentatively as we went towards the car park.

'No. I'll ring her later. What I want now is off. You'll understand when I tell you about it.'

We got into the car and I started the engine. In a moment we had swung round in a tight circle and were moving through the gates of the Carshalton estate, out into the lane and away. Only then did Mairead's face begin to resume its familiar gentle outlines and her eyes begin to look rather than glare.

I drove steadily. The evening was coming down now; it was just about time to switch on the car's lights. I waited for Mairead to speak. She sat with her head bowed forward a little, as if she were staring into the darkness below the dashboard. When she began, it was a narrative without preamble.

'I thought I'd take a little wander round the grounds, after I felt I'd done all I could for the poor bloody wife.'

She stopped again, so I prompted. 'Is that what she seems to you? Poor and bloody?'

'Married to him, yes. Wait till you hear.' I waited, driving on through the shadowy landscape. 'I don't know whether you explored all over, but that area of thick shrubbery suddenly opens out into a little open space, left clear so that it has a look of wild nature. Well, Milady had put a couple of figures in that space, just about life-size, doing what I don't know. One seemed to be trying to get away from the other – perhaps it was Pan pursuing Syrinx or something, or possibly an emblem of her husband's pursuit of the British voter. Anyway, talking of *pursuit* . . .' She stopped again.

'Is this going to be about something Carshalton tried on with you?' I demanded. 'Shall I turn round now and go back and punch his head?' My foot moved towards the brake pedal.

'No. But stop anyway. I want to talk quietly.'

I pulled off the road into a grassy space, and let the engine die. As usual when a car engine stops, the world seemed unnaturally quiet for a few moments. Into the quiet, Mairead's voice resumed.

'I was standing there looking at these misshapen objects and seeing if I could find any form or drama in them. Then suddenly he appeared from the opposite direction, from behind them.'

'He?'

'Nicky, or whatever the stupid swine calls himself now. As soon as he saw me he came straight towards me. Almost as if he'd been looking for me.'

'Perhaps he had. Let's hear more, though I don't think I'm going to like it.'

'He was smoking a big fat cigar, but as soon as he saw me he threw it away and he looked at me and leered. I know it sounds like a *cliché*, a certain kind of man in a certain state of mind is always supposed to *leer*, but he actually did it, he leered.'

'I shall punch his head just for that. Very hard, very accurately, and probably more than once, though once may turn out to be enough.'

'Then he said, "All alone, sweetheart?" and I started to say, coldly, to choke him off, "I'm looking at your wife's sculptures," but I hadn't got any further than "looking" when he said, still giving me that awful leer, "And I'm looking at you, darling. I like looking at you. I've always fancied you, sweetheart," and a lot of stuff like that.'

'The *bastard*! I'll—'

'Then he grabbed me. There was just one tree in this little clearing, and he got my back against it and pinned me with his weight. He's quite heavy. And I wouldn't call him strong but he's not exactly weak, when he's going for something he really wants. I was trying like mad to push him off, and after a moment or two I managed it, but not before he'd managed to run his hands pretty well all over me.'

'Run his hands . . . Christ! What was he doing?'

'Well, you won't want me to spell it out. Just kind of . . . rummaging.'

'I'll crush his balls,' I said. 'He'll never get away with this. I'll drive you home and then I'll turn straight round and drive back to his place and march straight in and get hold of him and I'll—'

'Be quiet, Peter. You'll do nothing of the kind. When we get home you're going to take me to bed and be very warm and very close to me because I need you.'

'But, damn it,' I said mutinously, 'if I don't chastize him he might do it again one day. I couldn't bear the thought of—'

'It's pretty unlikely. You know how canny he is. You've described him to me as someone who's always kept a very tight control of himself, always very aware of the impression he's making. Only now and then he gives way to his impulses and the result's disaster. I think this is one of those times. He's had a long day and he's kept himself going by taking a good swig at a bottle now and then. I got him at the end of the process, when the journalists had gone home and he was relaxing. He was pretty drunk. Anyway, let me finish the story and then you'll *really* be angry with him.'

'Really? What d'you think I am now, pretending?'

'No, darling, no. I know you're very riled at the thought of him pawing at me and going on in that disgusting way. But what he did is only part of it. I'm just as annoyed at what he *said*.'

'Well, it must have been pretty bad if it comes anywhere near what he—'

'It was targeted at you, and that's what chokes me with disgust. That a phony and liar like him should say such arrogant things about an honest man like you – I'd be enraged even if you didn't happen to be my man and I didn't happen to love you.'

'Well, let's have it,' I said. 'I'm getting chilly sitting here, and a rush of blood to the head'll make me feel warmer. I don't see how it could possibly be any worse than what I've heard already. What does it matter what a slimy rat like Carshalton *says*? Or what he does, either, if it wasn't a matter of his daring to lay hands on—'

'After I shoved him away and got clear of him he gave me that leer again and then he said, "Playing the faithful-wife game, are you? Why don't you grow up and take a look at your opportunities – what life could *really* bring you?" I didn't want to hear any more, I wanted him to shut up, but he was barring my path back towards the house, and I thought if I went away from him I might get into some tangle of shrubbery where he'd have the advantage of me through knowing the terrain. I thought of calling for help. But as I was just about to shout, he went on talking and I had to listen because I was so astonished. I forgot to be frightened of him and just stood there trying to believe my ears.'

'All right, what did the fiend say?'

'The main burden of it was that I was throwing myself away. I'd landed myself with you and you'd chosen the losing side. There was no future with you because you had no future yourself. He was absolutely certain that the world's going to give one last big heave and settle down in a new shape, that if I wasn't brainwashed by you I'd see it happening all round me already, and if I had any sense of self-preservation I'd cross over the bridge now, while there still is a bridge and it's still open.'

'All this covered over with a pretence of caring what happens to you. A dusting of benevolence like glitter powder.'

'Oh, yes, it must be a standard technique of his for getting girls. Join the future and start by joining him. Believe it or not, he actually offered me a job.'

'A *job*?'

'He said he needed a campaign co-ordinator. That he's planning a publicity tour round the West Country to give himself a higher political profile. Plymouth, Bristol, all the coastal centres and then as far over as Cheltenham and Swindon. I'd be signing on for three months, personally responsible to him. A good salary and everything I wanted. All I had to do was get rid of you, and there wasn't much time left.'

I was boiling like a kettle.

' "Think of yourself, sweetheart," he kept saying. Kept calling me that, "sweetheart". I wanted to dash his brains out. "There's no future in being the wife of a reactionary like Leonard. He's just a fly caught in the machinery of history. He'll be crushed and nobody'll even notice. Leonard! What d'you imagine is likely to become of him, when the shift comes? He'll either be shot out of hand – just knocked on the head to avoid wasting a bullet, more likely – or he'll disappear into a labour camp for dissidents and we'll see how long he lasts there. In any event you'll never see him or hear of him again. So where will it have got you, all this high-souled faithfulness?" Then he grabbed for me again. I dodged and he missed me. "Don't be a fool, sweetheart," he kept saying. "Don't be a fool. There's a new world coming in, and there's a cosy place for you in it, right beside me. I'll see to that for you. If you're with us, the sky's the limit, but if you're against us . . ." He waved his hand, made a gesture like throwing something away. As he did that I managed to dart past him and get clear. I heard him panting after me, but he was too drunk to keep up a run. Then I heard him cry out – I think he'd caught his foot in a tree-root or something and gone over. I didn't stop to look round.'

I drew her close to me and sat holding her while the darkness gathered around us. A car went by; three or four young people in it were singing a song. They sounded happy. They didn't know that the country they lived in was targeted for a take-over by the iron-faced Communist world, and if that happened they would only be able to sing Party songs, and then only when they were massed together in a well-supervised crowd. No more driving around the countryside singing whatever you wanted to sing, just because you were happy and liked being together.

I switched on the engine. 'Let's go home,' I said to Mairead.

'Yes, let's.'

I moved the car forward, accelerating. We were on our way to Oxford, to Kingston Road, to our house, to our bed.

When we got there Mairead said, 'I ought to have a bath. But I can't be bothered. What I want is warmth and closeness with you and to be bundled up together with you, and I'll have a bath in the morning.'

'It's what I want too,' I said.

'Besides, I didn't actually have any contact with his skin, you know. All right, he grabbed for me, and for a moment he actually got hold of me, but it was just my clothes he touched. And I can always send them to the cleaners.'

'It would be better to burn them,' I said, unbuttoning my shirt.

'That won't be necessary. I'll either wash, or have cleaned, *every-thing* I was wearing,' Mairead said. 'Even my shoes I'll give a good brush to.'

'Let me do that part of it,' I said. 'I'd like to do my share in the scrubbing-away of Carshalton.'

Mairead smiled; it was the first smile I had seen on her face since her ordeal. Then we went to bed.

But when I woke in the morning, and lay on my back looking up at the ceiling and gathering my thoughts, I didn't remember that I had joined her in that smile. Mairead was the one who had suffered the distressing experience, but I didn't exactly feel unscathed myself. The episode had left a deposit of thoughts in my mind, sombre thoughts for the most part. Carshalton was a swine, but was he a fool? Hardly. As a man whose life was given unswervingly to the pursuit of his own advantage, he had so far made very few mistakes. In the world struggle for power, he had his money on a victory for the Communist side. He trusted in their ruthlessness, their deeply in-grained habits of lying and deception, and their monolithic central-ism which ironed out local variants and made all Party decisions instantly applicable everywhere. If he was right, and they came to inherit the earth, Carshalton would be at the top and I would be at the bottom, and I knew what to expect then. Would the time come one day when I would regret being myself and not he?

Then Mairead awoke and rolled over and smiled sleepily at me, and I knew I would rather be I.

*

Doubtless with my habitual *naïveté*, I had imagined that by lifting from Bax's shoulders the burden of temptation and inner turmoil caused by having to give tuition to young Robertson, I had conferred a benefit on him and that the results might be visible by outward signs. Getting rid of Robertson was, as far as it went, a positive step, but it was too trivial to effect anything on its own. Bax's inexorable decline continued. Month by month he looked paler, more haggard; there were times when I felt positively shocked to see him. Unhappiness of that intensity can actually break a person up, even someone as strong as Bax; indeed, his strength was part of the overall problem because it contributed to that air of independence and self-sufficiency with which he confronted the world. Even at his worst times, even when it seemed plain that he was hastening towards final disintegration, there was about the man a suggestion of inviolability, some citadel of his inner personality that one knew would remain unconquered until death. To try, for whatever good motive, to force an entrance into this citadel was unthinkable. I used to think that if I saw Bax walking determinedly to the edge of a cliff, obviously to throw himself over it, I would just stand there and watch him although the prospect of his death would fill me with terror and grief. He was a man who made his decisions, and lived his life, in some inaccessible area of his being. There were times when I longed to urge him to go and see a doctor, or apply for sick leave to give himself some essential rest, but I could never nerve myself to do it. When I confided this to Mairead, she suggested that my attitude was a hangover from the time when Bax had been my tutor, so that for me to give him advice or suggest trains of thought to him would be too much of a reversal of roles. I thought not. I had been Bax's colleague, by now, for much longer than I had been his pupil. The reasons for his unapproachability lay not in me but in his own personality.

Then, one evening, I was surprised and heartened by the signs of an extraordinary change. Mairead and I were married by now and settled in Kingston Road, which meant in turn that I dined much less frequently in College. Married dons, if they have anything like a normal fondness for home and family, tend to return to them in the evening – a fact which on its own is enough to explain the long and stubborn defence of the requirement that Fellows of colleges must be unmarried, a defence mounted in the 1870s and not finally abandoned till about the 1950s. I went home early most evenings, though I still dined half a dozen times a term to avoid seeming to drop out of the College community, and because I genuinely enjoyed the more leisured evening atmosphere with its ampler talk; over lunch one tended to discuss the day's business.

Going into Hall that evening in the early spring of 1953, some eighteen months after the night of Bax's collapse on the stairs, I stood chatting to him for a moment before we took our places at the table, and was at once struck by the change in him. Since the last time I had seen him at close enough quarters to note his appearance, he seemed more responsive, more energetic – in a word, happier. His face had not yet had time to lose its deathly pallor, but the lines of strain had begun to loosen and be smoothed out. He stood taller. What had done this?

We had both put down for dessert, but I did not get a chance to sit next to him there, though I could see him talking animatedly at the other end of the table, and his eyes were bright; they seemed to be looking outward rather than hiding behind his lenses. After we broke up and went into the Common Room for coffee he came over and asked me if I had a little time to spare before going home.

I did have some time, and he took me over to his rooms with a laconic, 'I want to show you something.' When he led the way in, switched on the lights and stood aside to give me an uninterrupted view, I stood still, taken aback. Every surface I could see was covered with stout box-files. On his desk they were piled three or four deep; on the table the wall of files was not so high, but on the other hand there were large areas covered with bundles of papers, some clipped together, some held down by paperweights, a few bundled up and tied with tape.

'This must be Gibson,' I said at last.

'Edmund Gibson it is,' he replied.

I moved forward. 'May I look?'

'Open anything. It's all gathered for your inspection.'

'*My* inspection?'

'No one else's, I assure you.'

I moved about, opening box-files here and there. Some were filled with carbon copies, others with typescript. The ones I opened, and doubtless the rest for the most part, were all letters, or annotations on letters, or copies of material calculated to illuminate annotations of letters. I read stray sentences of the Bishop's correspondence; cajoling, arguing, confiding, instructing, directing, commanding. I was looking at a man's life.

Bax was bending down, lighting his gas fire. As I looked over towards him he straightened up and stood looking at me in its bright glow. He smiled. It was a very long time since I had seen him smile.

Naturally I wanted to know why he had put on this show, parading the intensive work of years in this spectacular way. It was impressive, but impressing *me* surely wasn't a major objective. There must be a reason. What was it? The question rose to my lips, but I waited. Let him tell me in his own words, I thought.

'This is as far as I've brought it,' he said lightly, almost conversationally.

'There's an enormous amount,' I said. 'Can there be much more?'

'Oh, yes. I think I've got the bulk of his letters here, but I've hardly done more than make a start on gathering in the other side of the correspondence, the letters *to* him. And then there are the usual knotty problems. You know, the bits of research that you put aside thinking you'll clear them up when you have a week to spare, and six months later you've just about started to unpick them because they turn out to be knots as hard as roots of teak.'

I nodded. I knew.

'There's plenty more work to be done,' Bax said. 'In my more optimistic moments I tell myself that the job might be something like half-way completed. I've been at it for eight years, ever since peace broke out and we had a chance to get back to historical work. So possibly it might take another eight – say ten with the inevitable hold-ups. Then another couple of years to see it through the press.'

I looked at him. I happened to know that he was exactly ten years older than me, born in 1902. When I had first come up to College at the age of eighteen and become his pupil, I had naturally seen him with the eyes of adolescence as a middle-aged man; actually he had been a lad of twenty-eight! No wonder he had fallen in love with the under-graduate Geraldine. Everyone at twenty-eight is in love one way or another with one person or another. It had taken that love six more years to flounder its way into the *impasse* that had broken his heart. From that time on, pity for his sufferings had always blended in my mind with the admiration I felt for his intelligence and his courage.

'So,' I said, turning my attention again to the formidable array of box-files, 'you think in about another ten years, perhaps twelve, you'll be done with it.'

'No,' Bax said. 'I'm done with it now.'

He spoke quietly, but not too quietly for me to hear him with perfect distinctness. He was giving me a steady look, making sure I was taking in what he said, just as he sometimes used to do in our tutorials of long ago.

'You've . . . done with it *now*?'

'Yes. I've taken it as far as I can. I want to hand it on to someone who's qualified to finish it properly.'

'But . . .' I struggled for something to say, for something to think. 'You don't mean you're . . . tired of it or anything like that? Perhaps if you just put it aside for a year or so, you might find . . .'

'I'm not in the least tired of it,' Bax said. 'I'm as involved with it as ever I was. Edmund was an interesting man and he lived at an interesting time. No, I'm giving up this project because I'm giving up historical work altogether.'

By now I was thoroughly alarmed. The only thought that occurred to me was that Bax's miseries had been too much for him and his mind had given way. Yet even in that instant I was impressed by the calm and the strength that radiated from him. Was it perhaps a good thing to have one's mind give way? It did not seem to have been bad for Bax.

'Could you, perhaps, expand a little on that statement?' I asked him, polite and interested, one historian addressing another. I had to keep the conversation on that calm objective level: it was either that or telephoning immediately for an ambulance.

Bax went to a cupboard and took out a decanter and two glasses. 'Will you join me in a whisky?' he invited.

'It may be unwise, after so much wine, but I will. I have the feeling that I'm going to need something.'

'A straight malt never hurt anyone,' he said genially. He poured me some and added, 'There's Malvern water if you'd like it.'

We got our drinks the way we wanted them, settled into comfortable chairs, and Bax began to talk seriously.

'I won't make a long recital of this, Leonard. It's bound to be a surprise to you and I'll give you plenty of time to get used to it – there's no particular need to come up with a reaction now, or make any decisions. But you're the first person I'm telling this news, and I want you to know now, tonight.'

I felt vaguely flattered: but still apprehensive, still anxious. Giving up historical work? Bax? The ancient Greek proverb floated into my mind: *Whom the gods wish to destroy, they first make mad.*

'I don't know what your personal philosophy is, Leonard,' Bax said, 'but I know you well enough to be confident that it's about the same as mine. It's not a philosophy of hedonism. Neither you nor I are likely to follow the example of Maurice Bowra, who stridently proclaims the value of pleasure because he's always lived a life of austere discipline and incredibly hard work, and the flamboyant pursuit of pleasure during his few leisure hours is the only outlet he's left himself. In such a man, a *voulu*, schematic hedonism is pardonable, even lovable. To people like ourselves, whose aim in life is the satisfaction of knowing themselves useful rather than the moment of gratification, the ideal is rather one of self-fulfilment. Am I right?'

'You are right, Bax.'

'What is called happiness is one element in that fulfilment. Perhaps not even a major element. But it must be present, and it must make its presence felt. An altogether unhappy man is a disabled man. Presumably the same is true of women: possibly even more true. I don't understand women.'

'I don't think I understand them myself. I just need them.'

'There, in a nutshell, is the essential difference between us. The essential difference between myself and the majority of men. You understand me, Leonard?'

'Perfectly.'

'It's a situation I have had enough of. I have tried to control it, to assimilate it into my life, to live comfortably with it, and I have failed.'

'How can you say you've failed? You've survived, you've functioned, you've met all your obligations, and you've built up a colossal work like this.' I indicated the stacks of files and papers.

'I've survived in the sense that I haven't actually died. I've survived at the price of incessant strain, incessant effort, incessant misery. I've had enough of it and I've finished.'

'Finished? What do you mean, Bax?'

He drank up his glass of malt whisky, poured himself some more and put the bottle where I could reach it. Then he spoke, gently, thoughtfully.

'Leonard, I've always had a lot of trust in you. I spotted you as a champion colt when you first came here, and a shaggy, leggy colt you were too. I backed you for a teaching Fellowship and you've amply justified my choice. Now I'm backing you again. I hope you'll take over Edmund. At least give me some of your time to show you where the joins are, the points where the work will have to be taken up by whoever does it. But one thing I do know. I'm leaving University teaching. I've spent my life in it up to now, and as a result I've reached a point where my personal problems simply aren't soluble. I need a bold, tmesic new beginning. I need the psychic release of starting my life completely afresh.'

'You could have a research post. You could give up tutorial work altogether. A man of your eminence, you've earned the right to work on your own terms.'

'That's like saying to an engine-driver who wants to retire that he can get a job as a fireman and still stay on the footplate. I want to leave altogether. I want to be a new man in a new incarnation. I'm still young enough – just.'

'Of course you are. You're at the height of your powers.'

He smiled again. 'That's kind of you. Oddly enough the very same thing was said to me by the only other person I've told of my decision.'

'Other person . . . ?'

'I'm sorry. There was one mis-statement in what I said to you just now, when I told you you were the first person I've talked to about this. I meant the first one in our academic community. Actually I have told just one person already. The Director of Oxfam.'

'Oxfam!' My exclamation began in astonishment, but even before both the syllables were well uttered I had begun to understand. 'So that's the kind of work you want to do.'

'When you get down to a certain level of unhappiness,' Bax said, 'you begin to realize that you've joined a world-wide fellowship of people whose lives, usually through absolutely no fault of their own, have become altogether unliveable. If your unhappiness has made it impossible for you to go on, so has their hunger, their disease, their destitution, their agony at having to watch their children starve. They can't go on with their lives any more than you can go on with your life. The difference is in your external circumstances compared with theirs. You may be just as desperate as they are, but you can tap material resources, you can set up networks and supply lines, you can write letters and make telephone calls, you can get in there and work and with any luck you can distribute food and stop people starving and halt epidemics and bring some hope. Then they become less desperate, and perhaps some of that rubs off on you and you become less desperate. But that isn't the motive. It can't be the motive. It may be a benefit that you receive, but if so it's a by-product and you get it by a fortunate accident.'

'You make me feel,' I said, 'that I ought to resign my Fellowship too and come along with you.'

Bax was pacing about the room, not in anything like agitation but calmly, reflectively, his slowly moving figure lit by the warm glow from the gas fire. But when I said that he stopped, stood still and looked across at me. His eyes, behind those rounded lenses that made them look rather like an owl's, had always had the power, in my student days, to make me feel nervous; they had not quite lost it now.

'I'm sorry to hear you say that, Leonard,' he remarked, conversationally rather than heavily.

'Sorry?'

'Yes, because it gives me two disagreeable alternatives. If you said it without meaning it, that amounts to a degree of insincerity I've never noticed in you before. And if you did mean it, I just don't understand how you could be such an ass.'

I swallowed. Bax had so much authority that any kind of adverse judgement from him was enough to make me feel seriously inadequate.

I took a swig at my whisky and said, 'If I have to admit to one of those two charges, and I can't think of a defence that would rebut them both simultaneously, I suppose I'd rather you thought me stupid than insincere.'

Bax chuckled tolerantly. That was another rare sound. 'Being an ass, which is the word I actually used, isn't the same thing as being stupid. It's more just a matter of making a misjudgement, which we might all do in a very unexpected situation.'

'Which this is, to say the least,' I said feelingly.

'Which this is. But it can't be very difficult to see, at first glance, that the reason why I want to leave University teaching is nothing at all to do with any feeling of disillusionment with it. I'm just as convinced as I ever was that it's important work, and I'd cheerfully carry on with it if it didn't present...' his voice flickered for a moment into hesitation, then out of it again, 'special problems in my case.'

'Oh,' I said. 'Well, I'm glad to know that. I mean I'm glad there's nothing more.'

'There's no need of anything more.' Bax's voice was flat and drained of expression. 'The degree of emotional suppression in my life was quite enough to be going on with, I assure you.'

At that moment I felt close to him. I knew that he had drawn aside the curtain as far as he ever would, at least to me. I felt a pity for him, and an admiration for his bravery in suffering for so long. I had witnessed his suffering over the loss of Geraldine, witnessed it not at close quarters but close enough to recognize it for what it was. And having, as it were, seen the negative side, I could imagine the positive side, the strength of the emotional tie he would form with anyone whom he loved and who loved him.

'You're right, Bax,' I said. 'I *was* an ass. Obviously it was stupid and irrelevant for someone like me to talk about being tempted to throw up the work here and come with you. That's a step that could only be justified by special motivation, which in my case is lacking.'

Bax did not look towards me, but into the steadily burning gas fire as he replied, 'Don't say that too lightly. You should thank God it's lacking.'

'I do thank God,' I said. 'It's one of the chief things I have to thank him for.'

He sat down now in the armchair facing me. 'So,' he said in a brisker tone, 'you know why I'm going and you know what it'll involve you in. Whether or not you carry Edmund along, you'll obviously succeed to my position here. You'll be the Senior Fellow in History, and someone else will come in as the new Junior.'

'Oh, I'm not ready to think about that yet.'

'I wouldn't want you to. But it's bound to come unless the Fellows decide collectively that Episcopus is going to cut down on historical studies, accept fewer students wanting to pursue them, spend less on that department of the Library, and so on. And I see no reason why they should. Episcopus history is thriving. It's well regarded in Oxford generally because we get good Schools results and undergraduates want to come here to read it. And of course you know why: you and I have made it a success.'

'You mean you have, Bax. First you and good old Gadsby, and then you on your own with some help from me.'

'No false modesty or I really shall call you hypocritical. Why should you take the trouble to flatter me? You know how much hard work you've put into it.'

'Anybody can work hard,' I said. 'Having a real flair for teaching a subject is something else again.'

'All right, believe what you like. Only you'll be the senior historian in this College, young as you are, because they just won't have the nerve to insult you by putting someone in over your head.'

'If there's one thing I've learnt about Oxford dons,' I said, 'it's that they don't mind who they insult.'

'That's true. But it's also true that they're very canny by nature and they know what's going to work in their best interest. You're a good work-horse. And it isn't that I've slave-driven you into being one. We've simply tackled the work-load together, as colleagues.'

'What you've done from first to last, Bax,' I said, 'has been to set me an example of serious interest in history. You believe in it so passionately, I couldn't help absorbing that belief.'

'Of course I believe in historical study. All civilized societies value it – it's one of the things that distinguish them from barbarous societies. They need to think back over the past, to rake in as much accurate information about it as one can, and then to consider the issues that were raised and whether the decisions that were taken were the best ones. And the individuals who at the time appeared to be the prime movers – were they really the prime movers or just the instruments of blind impersonal forces? Is there a moral pattern in history? If one studies the way human beings have behaved, one keeps being brought up against values – questions of right and wrong. Are they simply hampering to an historian? Ought he just to brush them aside? Some people certainly think so – but shouldn't their opinions be looked at critically in their turn? What right have they, what right has anybody, to assume the mantle of impartiality, let alone infallibility?'

Bax stopped short. He had caught my eye and seen a gleam of amusement in it.

'All this piling up of clichés, Leonard – no doubt after all these years as an historian you find it risible.'

'No, just endearing. You're such an historian, Bax – it's your life, it's your body and breath, it runs all the way through your being. I only had to say something about your interest in the subject being a crucial example to me, and it was like putting a coin into a slot-machine. The whole thing started whirring.'

'I'm sorry, it sounds depressingly predictable.'

'On the contrary. The thing I like most about scholars is their devotion to their subject. They all have it in common, it's the only thing they *do* have in common, and in many of them it's the one good quality they have. Some scholars are nice people, good friends, generous, kindly, unselfish, ready to see beyond themselves to the common good of humanity. Others are the opposite – narrow, selfish, excluding, calculating, five-star shits in every way. Every way but one, that is. They put all that aside when they enter the contemplation of their subject in exactly the same way that a Muslim takes off his shoes before going into the mosque. So as not to put the dirt of the common world on to the sacred floor.'

'And you think,' Bax said carefully, 'that I am putting my shoes back on in the porch, in readiness to go back into the common world and tread among all the dirt of ordinary suffering?'

I stood up. 'Bax, if this wasn't a time of fundamental decision-making for you, that might have disturbed your ordinary compass-readings, I might find myself resenting that remark.'

'I'm sorry.'

'How could you possibly imagine I meant any such thing? Whether or not we accept the claims made for the divinity of Jesus Christ, we accept him as a moral example, the bearer of an exceptional message of unselfishness and service, and your impulse to give your life to alleviating the suffering of the world's poorest people must surely be seen as Christ-like.'

'No,' Bax said calmly. 'It's purely self-protective. Divine impulses don't come into it one way or another, unless you accept the sexual instinct as divinely implanted in the human race.'

'And if I do?'

'If you do,' Bax said, 'the whole matter takes on a more timeless aspect. You presumably accept that the reason for the persecution of homosexuals is traceable to the biological wish of the majority to keep blemished individuals out of the genetic pool. Most species will maltreat and drive away any individual showing abnormal characteristics. That's the action of the selfish gene. Chickens, for instance, will peck a maimed or malformed specimen of their race. So will most socially organized creatures. The object is to kill or drive away the deviant.'

'How is that relevant to your decision to take up relief work?'

'Relief work offers me a socially approved alternative to my present profession. As things stand I am, and must be, targeted by the flock of normal chickens who see me as a candidate for pecking to death.'

I thought for a moment, but nothing came. Finally I said, lamely, 'That's rather an extreme way of putting it – pecking to death.'

'How else would you put it? What was the imprisonment of Oscar Wilde? He never got over it.'

I was silent.

'So I'm going,' Bax said. 'I'm going where this kind of issue doesn't bother anyone because people are so immersed in struggling against enormous, urgent, intractable problems that they simply haven't time for them. Where I shan't be in a position of moral responsibility towards the young, supposed to set them an example of how to live and what to do. As if morals entered into a matter of this kind that's concerned solely with the orientation you're born with.'

'Anyway, all that moral-example stuff is obsolete now,' I said. 'What the University offers in the mid-twentieth century is a professional training, not moral instruction.'

'If only that were true,' said Bax, shaking his head gently. 'The problem is that it's only half obsolete. The heart of it has crumbled to dust, but the outward casing is proving itself durable enough, and that casing is concerned with social adjustment. An Oxford graduate is supposed to have the *savoir faire* to fit smoothly into the pattern of society and not jam the intricate machinery. If I were to get involved in a scandal – the only kind of scandal that would be likely to arise in my particular life – that would definitely not fit into a smooth pattern of adjustment. For one thing it would be an offence against the law as it stands in England. It could land me in a prison cell, which is more than any amount of girl-chasing or drunkenness would do – or even financial dishonesty, unless it was on a colossal scale. If it could be proved that I'd swindled somebody out of twenty thousand pounds, I'd be asked to resign my Fellowship and the money would have to be paid back. I expect that rather than have a scandal about one of its Fellows being a crook, Episcopus would pay the money and get it out of me in instalments. The matter would be swept under the carpet somehow. But a full-scale scandal of the kind I would bring down on them' – I saw that he could not quite bring himself to say 'homosexual' – 'couldn't, in the present state of opinion and the present state of the law, be softened.'

'That, I'm sure, will change. The opinion will change and so will the law. Capital punishment will go first and this business will follow it.'

'That may be,' Bax said, 'but I'll be gone before that. Oxfam are ready for me and I'm going.'

'In the first instance, going where exactly?'

'Oh,' Bax said, 'I've got an estate agent sending me details of small, easily maintained flats that come on the market in North Oxford. I've lived pretty economically all these years and saved a fair amount of money, so I've got a fair choice of whether to rent or buy and I probably shan't need a mortgage. There's that at least to show for my selfish, solitary life. I just want a place where I can store my belongings and come and go as my life dictates. I don't suppose it'll be long before I've got something.'

'You'll need a pretty big place to have room for your books,' I said, surveying the tall, crowded bookcases.

'I shall pick a couple of hundred that I can't do without for one reason and another,' he said, 'and the rest I'll give to the College. In that way I'll always have them where I can get at them if I want to. It's only fair – they gave me the money that I spent on them in the first place. I'd like you to look through them, by the way, and take anything you fancy.'

'That's good of you. I might take two or three, just as a keepsake. But like you, I'd rather have them in the Library and give the College the fag of looking after them. My bookcases are bursting anyway, though my books are a pretty ratty lot compared with yours. I've hardly ever bought a new book in my life.'

'Of course,' Bax said, 'the Edmund stuff will have to be kept as an intact collection.'

'Now it's my turn to call you an ass,' I said, 'to think you needed to say that to me.'

'I'm sorry,' he said, smiling again. 'It must have been the whisky.'

Not long after this I said I must be going and stood up to leave. I was sorry to have to do this. In my single, in-college days, Bax and I would obviously have settled down to a long conversation in which we would have explored the situation very fully and doubtless broken new ground. But I was in a position that plainly made this impossible. I was not only married, but married in spades, as it were. I was a newlywed with a wife who was five months pregnant – a situation not so frequently encountered in the earlier 1950s as it subsequently became. We had only just moved into the house in Kingston Road and the furnishing was still sketchy. Under these circumstances I didn't relish leaving Mairead alone in the evening at all, let alone staying on in College till quite late, and I wouldn't have done it for anyone but Bax.

It wasn't all that late, though – barely ten o'clock – when I let myself in and, finding Mairead sitting comfortably in the one decent armchair we possessed at that time, sat down on a chair beside her and started to pour out my story. At first she had some hesitation in taking in the details. She did not really know Bax. She had met him a total of twice, once with only the three of us present and once at an Episcopus social function. The meeting à trois had been when, not long after her arrival in Oxford, he had invited us round for the inevitable glass of sherry, hardly more than a formal introduction at which they could set eyes on each other. And of course he was not a man to be really knowable on such slight acquaintance. Naturally, then, when I said, 'I've been talking to Bax,' she wrinkled her brow for a moment and searched her memory.

'Oh, yes, your colleague.'

'Well . . . yes . . .'

'You sound a bit hesitant. Ought I to have called him something else? Your guru?'

'No, well, he's my colleague, only – he soon won't be any more. He's leaving.'

'Oh? Got a better job, has he?'

'It's not a better job he's after, in quite those terms. It's a complete change.' I ran through the whole story, while she settled back and listened.

'So for Bax,' I finished, 'it's Oxfam and a new start.'

'H'mm. I hardly know what to say. But then I wouldn't, would I? I don't really know him, and now I never shall.'

'Perhaps one shouldn't be too sure about that. He's leaving academic work, but he's keeping a *pied à terre* in Oxford, he's bound to be here sometimes, and I'll make sure he keeps in touch. Besides, I didn't tell you, but he's got a huge editorial job he's set himself to do, editing the letters to and from an eighteenth-century bishop, and he wants me to carry it on.'

'Why you?'

'Well, I'm the logical person to inherit his material, and I'm an eighteenth-century man like himself, so it made sense to ask me at least.'

'Are you going to do it?'

'I didn't say anything one way or another when he put it to me, and that was barely an hour ago. But suddenly now, when you put the question to me directly like that, I know I'm going to say yes.'

'Will it be an awful lot of work?'

'Yes, but I'll have an awful lot of time to do it in. Obviously the whole thing hinges on my living at least seventy years.'

'You must. I won't settle for less. Besides, we have to think of the one in here.' She patted her belly. 'He, or she, will need two parents.'

'Well, everyone needs a mother, but some fathers are not much more than a nuisance.'

'I daresay, but you're not going to be that kind.'

'No,' I said, 'I'm going to be the kind you like having around.' I moved to be close to her and we went into a long kiss.

'Just think,' Mairead sighed, 'poor old Bax is all on his own. He never has anything like this.'

'What's even worse,' I said, 'the only thing anything like this that he'd care to have is something that, if the pair of them were caught doing, they'd have to go to prison.'

'Ugh,' she said. 'How horrible. How meaninglessly inhuman. You can tell from examples like that that the laws were all framed by men. No woman would be so punitive about any kind of search for human affection.'

'Well, at least the fact that men make the decisions gives the women an inbuilt moral advantage. They've always got someone to look down on.'

'That's a silly way of putting it.'

'I don't think so. My mother thinks that if women ran the world there wouldn't be any wars. I never contradict her, but I don't really believe it. Women are just as fond of getting their own way as men, and there are plenty of them who'd resort to force if that seemed the best way to get it. Look at Maud Gonne.'

'No, I won't look at Maud Gonne. Maud Gonne was the daughter of an English officer. It was the Anglo-Saxon blood in her that made her act like a bully.'

'English or not, she gave her life to the cause of the Irish people.'

'That's like saying she lived for others. It's a certain way of spreading misery.'

I laughed, thinking how much I loved her.

'Darling,' I said, 'one day, just once – when I have a birthday, perhaps, or at Christmas – will you let me win an argument with you?'

Her eyes were soft as she looked at me. 'I might. Specially if you're good. Come to bed now.'

It was very early; much earlier than we usually went to bed. But I didn't argue.

★

I heard my wife put down the telephone and then she came into the sitting-room and said, 'They're coming on the twenty-seventh.'

'You've decided that's the best bet?' I asked.

'That's as near as we can get. Apart from the fact that it's what the ante-natal people told me, I've been going on the assumption that it's better to have them here for a few days doing nothing than have you messing about here by yourself while they make all their arrangements and come over.'

'I'll be all right here by myself.'

'I daresay you will, Leonard, with all that good food at Episcopus, but I'm thinking of Keira. It's all a bit of an upheaval for her as it is.'

'I'll take good care of Keira. I love her the most of anybody in the world, next to you.'

We were discussing a plan for Stephen and Kathleen Hoey to come over and stay at our house for the time during and immediately after the birth of our second child, an event that was now visibly imminent. My mother would gladly have come and stayed for a few nights, but we had decided on Mairead's parents for a cluster of reasons. They were enthusiastic about being grandparents, which meant that they would in any case have been making the trip over to see the infant as soon as possible, whereas my mother was ten minutes away. They doted on Keira: not that my mother did not, but she saw Keira more often; in any case my parents were some years older than Mairead's and ought not to be landed with the hard work of looking after a young child if there were others ready and eager to do it. Lastly, but with its own importance, I found the Hoeys easy to get on with in a domestic setting, as easy as my own parents. We had spent a week with them at their home in Newtownmountkennedy, where they had originally moved because the laboratory where Stephen studied marine plant cells was there, and he was the kind of man who liked to walk to work in the mornings; he said his best ideas came to him then.

For all these reasons, therefore, they were coming to us on the 27th of that soft, tranquil month of September 1954. Our second experience of reproducing our species was obviously going to be very different from the first, for me at any rate, though for Mairead the basic similarities would doubtless overshadow the differences. When Keira arrived on the planet, I had nothing to do but hang about and wait until the birth was accomplished and afterwards, apart from that one joyous phone call, equally nothing to do but go down to the Bargeman's and get as drunk as a skunk in the company of Brian.

But that was pre-Keira. That one imperious little manifestation of the Life Force, now just crossing the great frontier between scuttling on the floor and tottering upright, had altered everything. And, amazingly, when I thought back over the things I had relinquished in order to adapt to these changes, I found that I had relinquished them without protest.

In the event, the baby was born while the back-up force was on the way to join us. Instead of making her bow on the 27th, our second daughter Moira arrived on the previous day, when they were making the journey, at about lunch-time. I was able to leave Keira with a kindly neighbour while I made my first visit to the Radcliffe Infirmary to wait for the birth, which was rapid as these things go – it took till five o'clock – and by the time I was allowed back for a longer visit, at about 7.30, the Hoeys had come and I had thrust Keira into her grandmother's arms.

In one respect the second birth was very much like the first, and I imagine that if Mairead and I had ten children it would have been the same each time round. I refer to the first time I emerged, rather dazed and weightless, from the rear entrance to the Radcliffe Infirmary into Walton Street. It was just coming up to six in the evening, and I decided that I wanted a quiet drink. I could, of course, have hastened along to Kingston Road and had a triumphal drink with my parents-in-law. But I decided to do that a little later. It was also open to me to walk rapidly down to the Bargeman's Arms, arriving there at just about the moment that Brian opened the doors for the evening. But that, too, could be done later. I don't know whether it is a consequence of having grown up in a public house, and from early memories associating peace and quiet, and calm reflection, with the opportunities it sometimes gave me of sitting alone in a comfortable corner of the deserted bar, but to sit in a quiet tap-room, freshly swept and polished and ready for trade but with the trade not yet arrived, has always been for me an emblem of civilized well-being.

I had decided, by now, where to go: the Baker's Arms, a little way down Great Clarendon Street and then to the right. It was, in those days, an unpretentious, quiet little place, serving mainly the local residents. Towards this valuable place I bent my steps, slowly and thoughtfully because it would be a mistake to arrive before six o'clock. In those days the permitted opening hours for licensed premises had the advantage of also being compulsory hours. If the pub was compelled to shut at 10.30 in the evening, to the accompaniment of grumbling and scolding from people who reject any kind of social regulation on the grounds that it robs them of their civil liberties, it was also compelled to open its doors at six, whether or not there were customers waiting to come in. Pubs, at six p.m., were clean, bright and empty; not profitable to their owners, but a priceless resource to me and people like me, of whom there were a fair number in a population of fifty million.

The evening of Moira's birth, though, was some twenty years ahead of the time when the reformers got to work on the English tavern and liberated it from its old-fashioned restrictions into the carefree paradise of unregulated chaos: since when I don't suppose pubs like the Baker's Arms have ever opened at six o'clock, or ever been peaceful and unoccupied.

At all events, at that magic hour on that tranquil autumn evening as the daylight began to dim towards dusk, I was moving along the Jericho pavement towards the Baker's Arms, full of a sense of fulfilment and gratitude. Mairead and I had another child, which was wonderful. Mairead had sustained no harm from the experience, which made it more wonderful. The child was perfectly formed and evidently normal and healthy in every way, so far as first impressions could reveal. (They were subsequently confirmed by later impressions.) That made it just about perfect. These things being in place, the only other unknown quantity, gender, had not mattered a straw to either of us. Both of us were ready to love and welcome either a son or a daughter. So the baby was a daughter, fine! If it had been a son, fine!

I was almost at the Baker's Arms when a figure crossed my field of vision, walking northwards in the general direction of the Woodstock Road, with its back towards the canal and the St Barnabas area. This figure was moving at a loping pace that covered the ground prodigiously. On its head was a mackintosh hat with a peak fore and aft, deer-stalker fashion. In its hand was a stout ash stick, and on its feet were mighty brogues.

This figure was that of the only being in the world whose company, at that moment, I would have preferred even to golden solitude. I could imagine only one person with whom I could hold converse as joyously, just then, as with my own thoughts. His eyes fixed determinedly ahead, he was marching at right angles to my own trajectory, at a distance of some thirty yards. 'Garrity!' I called. 'Garrity, can you spare a few minutes?'

Garrity halted, recognized me, and smiled. 'Ah, Leonard. No, I'm not pressed for time. I've been for a walk. Nothing elaborate, just over the top of Wytham Wood, dropped down into Eynsham and on to the river bank, then back along the towpath to Godstow and Binsey, and so to Jericho and home. Good to see you.'

'I'm just going into this pub for a drink,' I said, indicating it. 'I'd be glad if you'd join me. It's a moment of celebration.'

Garrity held up his hand, palm foremost, like a policeman stopping traffic. 'Don't tell me till we're sitting down,' he said. 'I want to savour it. I get a particular satisfaction from the good fortune of my friends.'

We went into the Baker's Arms and I told him the news. Against all my protests he insisted on paying for our drinks. He was wreathed in smiles, he shook my hand, he repeated several times the message of congratulation I was to give to Mairead. He was openly, sincerely, transparently glad that my family had increased by one, both because he knew it was something I myself wished and because it was a benefit in general. I knew I had been right to obey my impulse of a few moments ago and call out to this good and selfless man.

Only once, for a brief moment, did I become conscious of the thought, lurking somewhere in the far recesses of my mind, that I might be giving him cause for pain: that tonight or tomorrow night, or in a hundred nights from now, he might find himself waking in the chill darkness and feeling the pain of his isolation – of the impossibility for him now of ever being at the centre of a natural cluster of people who belonged to him and to whom he belonged – lying alongside his heart like a cold steel blade.

At one point, feeling the threat that this thought might surface, I shoved the conversation along by bringing up something he had mentioned the last time we had talked.

'That friend of yours who came to speak in Oxford,' I said, 'the one who's such an authority on orally transmitted epic poetry. Did his talk go well?'

I had a vague feeling as I spoke that I had said the wrong thing, but just recently I had had too much to think about to be able to recall the details of our conversation. Garrity's face became rather set as he replied, 'I believe Arthur Dobson's talk went well.'

'Oh, yes, I remember,' I said, feeling, as my memory came back, like a three-coil dog-turd on the pavement, something you could only step round. 'You weren't there. You stayed in as usual for . . . your men.'

'Yes,' Garrity said, a gentleness in his voice that made me feel even more ashamed. 'I stayed in, and nobody came.'

I was silent for a moment and then said, 'I think that's disgusting.'

'Why is it? There's no need for them to come and see me if they don't want to.'

'Don't *want* to? If they were the type who had any right to be up here they'd want to. If you can give up your time . . . They don't realize what they owe you.'

Garrity picked up his tankard, examined it carefully, and abruptly drank off the three inches of sediment-flecked brown liquid that remained in it. 'My time isn't anything,' he said and set down the empty glass.

★

One morning in early September the post arrived while I was shaving, and when I came down to breakfast Mairead said, 'Who d'you know in Yorkshire?'

'Where in Yorkshire?' I asked, putting a match to the grill. We each made our own toast.

She peered at the envelope. 'Heck-something – I can't read the postmark. Not a big place, anyway, that I've ever heard of. Somewhere in the country.'

I opened it. Though neither of us had, or intended ever to have, any correspondence we wanted to keep to ourselves, we always opened our own letters. Living together involves certain small ritual courtesies that lift it above the mere shoving of pigs in a sty.

'Oh,' I exclaimed, pleased. 'It's from Lamont!'

'He must be someone you like,' she said, watching me and smiling.

'He certainly is. He's one of the people I like and admire most.'

'What's he doing in Yorkshire?'

'I've no idea.'

'You can't know him very well, then.'

I was silent, racing through the letter.

Dear Leonard,

How are you? Well, I hope. We have not met for some time, but I propose to put that right during a visit to Oxford I'm planning for October – if, that is, you're not too immersed in your work and in domesticity (I heard of your re-marriage: congratulations!) to spare an hour for sociability.

The main purpose of my visit, apart from the natural wish of any ghost to revisit the glimpses of the moon, is to have an orgy of reading. The rural North is a fine place to live in, but now and then I reach a stage when I've read every book that is of any interest to me within thirty miles of my cottage, and my notebook is crammed with the titles of books I feel the need to read or at least consult. Then the call of the Bodleian begins to drown everything else in my head. At the moment I'm happily planning what I shall be reading and where. Some of the reading and consulting I'd like to do in Episcopus Library, to get a change from Bodley and, frankly, to indulge myself by just being there for a few hours, looking out at the garden whenever I lift my eyes from the page. Did we appreciate, when we were young, how beautiful the place is? I think we did, in our fashion, but the young are so absorbed in what is going on in their own minds and bodies, I don't think they see beauty as they learn to see it later, though it probably affects them subliminally, as people say now.

Lamont went on to ask me another favour: to book him in at some modest bed and breakfast place ('not too far out in the suburbs and not totally squalid, otherwise anything goes'). He concluded with thanks and good wishes, adding that he hoped to see Garrity and would like to stand the two of us a dinner.

During my reading of this letter I had noticed with the fringe of my mind that Mairead had left the room, gone upstairs, and returned with Moira, whom she had placed in a high chair at the table and supplied with a plastic dish containing nutrient of some kind which the little pixie, following her usual custom, had begun to distribute with scrupulous equality one-third into her mouth, one-third on to her clothing and one-third on to the floor. The menu this morning was stewed apple with a Weetabix crushed into it. To me it looked innocuous but unappetizing, like the dung of some vegetarian animal.

'I don't think I've told you about Lamont,' I said, waving the letter at Mairead. 'I've never had a letter from him before, though I've known him since we were undergraduates at Episcopus, being taught by Bax. He's a poet. He was the first poet I ever met, and I was lucky in that. I expect a lot of the people going about calling themselves poets are making pretty large claims for themselves, but Lamont's the real thing. His vision of life and of the world is – well, penetrating and imaginative, the way a poet's ought to be.'

'Have you got any of his stuff? I'd like to get to know it.'

'I'm not sure. I'll ask him to bring me up to date with that when I reply to his letter, which I'm going to do straight away. For years, ever since I first met him, he was working away at a huge poem about Euhemerus.'

'You who?'

'Euhemerus, the mythographer.'

Mairead wrinkled her brow. 'Wasn't he the fellow who said it was all history really and you just had to straighten it out?'

'Flying colours. Most people just look at me as if I am raving when I tell them I know a poet who's organizing a long poem round the figure of Euhemerus.'

'Ah, but you forget I went to High School. I've heard of the Second Law of Thermodynamics as well.'

'You must tell me what that is some time.'

'I think it's something like, What goes up must come down.'

'Anyway, Lamont publishes chunks of this Euhemerus poem every now and then but I don't know whether he's ever published a slab of it in volume form. If he ever got to the point of doing that he'd probably pull back at the last minute and say it hadn't yet reached the point of being a final statement.'

'Well, have you got a chunk?'

'Sometimes if I'm looking through magazines on a bookstall and there are any literary ones, I see his name on the cover. Not very often, I admit, but it has happened. I always buy the magazine and turn to that page and it's always a slab of the Euhemerus poem. They're pretty varied in character. That must be the fascination of the thing. He seems to have meditated on this man, about whom we don't actually know very much, to the point of making him a symbol for the enquiring human mind.'

'Was he a good symbol for that? Euhemerus the asker?'

'Well, he was a Greek of the early second century B.C., which was a very exciting time because the conquests of Alexander had opened up a lot of the world to the Hellenistic consciousness and started a lot of new trains of thought. He seems to have been an islander, perhaps from Chios, so of course a central idea in his mind was the idea of making a voyage and discovering something really eye-opening.'

'That's what he did, is it? Moira, in your *mouth*, darling.'

'Evidently. His principal work's lost, so we only know about it from references by other writers. But it was a prose work, a novel, and it seems to have been called *Sacred Scriptures*. Apparently the hero, who's a stand-in for Euhemerus himself, is imagined as setting out on a voyage into the Indian Ocean, which at that time hadn't been charted by Europeans, and finding an island. He goes ashore to explore it and there he finds a massive gold column with inscriptions that say of certain of the gods that they were great kings in their time, great human kings, who did such wonderful things that their subjects worshipped them as gods. There's a lot more to it, but of course we get it in fragments seen from different angles as later writers made use of it for their own purposes. Greek writers did that and in due course so did Latin. I expect Lamont just sees himself as continuing that tradition after a lapse of a couple of thousand years. The time-lag wouldn't have worried him any more than that sort of historical leap worried Yeats. He liked to hark back to ancient prophecies and that sort of thing, didn't he?'

'So,' she said, 'I'm going to meet a Yeatsian poet.'

'Not on the surface,' I said, 'but just as dedicated.'

'Well,' Mairead said, 'you're a deep one. I never know what you'll throw at me next.'

'It isn't me that's the deep one, it's Oxford,' I said. 'It's like a watering-hole in a desert. Most people stop here now and again. The thing is to be here and to be ready for them. It saves a lot of rushing about.'

On the words 'rushing about', as if on cue, Keira – who had been in the garden – entered with an earthworm which she put down in the middle of the floor.

'Would this be good to eat?' she asked, stooping down to examine the creature minutely.

'No,' said Mairead.

'Well, birds think it would. I saw one pulling at this one. I wreck-sued it.'

'Birds think a lot of things would be nice to eat that you wouldn't like,' I told her.

'What kind of things?'

'Slugs.'

She considered. 'Slugs might be nice. They're black, like licorice.'

'They're not nice. They're very bitter.'

'How d'you know they're bitter, Daddy? You've tried eating them, I know. You must have. My Daddy eats slugs! My Daddy eats slugs!' she chanted, pirouetting.

The earthworm, making good time, was headed for some inaccessible corner under the sink from which it would be difficult to extricate. I rose, darted across the room and captured it. 'Goodbye, worm!' I shouted, opening the door and flinging it out. 'Have a happy day!' It described a high arc and landed at the far end of the lawn.

'What would Lamont have done with that worm?' Mairead asked me.

'He'd have done exactly as I did.'

'Wouldn't he have communed with it?'

'Of course he would. So did I. I wished it a happy day.'

The conversation moved back to Lamont.

'When's he coming, exactly?'

'At an excellent time, as it happens. Term starts formally on October twelfth, that's the Sunday. He wants to come on the Monday before, and stay till Thursday. Since Thursday's the day the undergraduates start homing in, and that night'll be the first full night in Hall, it's essentially the end of the Long Vac. It'll fit his visit neatly into the last week when I'm free – not to be with him all the time, of course, but to make choices. I wonder if he planned it that way or whether it's just a lucky chance. Anyway, I'll write to him and tell him he must stay in a guest room in College while he's in Oxford. I'm not having a man like that staying in a shabby hotel. And then I'm going to bring him round here and you can meet him and he can meet you.'

'Suits me,' she said. 'I haven't met a poet since Oliver Gogarty backed me into a corner at a party in Dublin when I was seventeen.'

'I don't want to hear about that,' I said.

'Why not?' Mairead said demurely. 'It's a better topic than earthworms.'

★

During the day I had a dusty search through cupboards, both at home and at Episcopus; and not only cupboards but the kind of bookcases into whose less accessible shelves (badly lit and awkwardly low down, or chair-standingly-high) one has in desperation rammed single issues, or very short runs of a few issues, of magazines that one doesn't quite feel able to throw away. Finally I found a poetry magazine, published with a certain aplomb in about 1950 – large page size and good typography; predictably, it had survived only for two or three numbers – which featured under Lamont's name an excerpt from *Euhemerus: a sequence*. It began thus:

> Grate of the boat's keel on the shingle
> the smoothed stones easily shifting
> to make room for the hull, but not much room:

adapting, parting, slipping aside,
but not far aside, coming together
in a new shape that remembers the old shape:
adaptation of the impermanent diagram.

The stones are smooth because of the waters'
continual fingering from year to year
a ritual disturbed only by passionate storms
for water and stone are married from the beginning,
and will stay married till time swallows all endings.

Some of the stones are flung and fractured by waves
that hammer in mountains of fury over the beach,
and afterwards pour crazily back to base,
in contrast with the harmony of the stones
that lie about them, glad to forget the storm,
till time when they are sucked back from beach to sea,
and the water touches and touches them, calmly,
until their sudden edges are touched away
and they go back to the long patience of nature.

And next in the shadowless light, a smaller sound:
a man's sandal stepping from the boat
disarranges the patient stones again
with a small, unparticular rattle of interrogation,
like an enquiring knock at a plank door,
a simple door, not locked, just casually closed.

Euhemerus the Greek steps on to the shingle.
A Greek, therefore a voyager: a Greek,
therefore an enquirer: a man native to islands,
to rocky uplands and the dividing sea.

His eye is accustomed to reckoning distances,
his ear to the many voices of the waves:
the voices of the multilingual sea.

They bring him news of human and divine.

I read this through several times, bore it home, and said nothing
about having found it till later that evening, when our two little
tsarinas were in bed and Mairead and I had finished our simple meal.
Then, with a sigh of contentment (we both loved the quiet of the
evening, when we were permitted to enjoy it together in peace) we
sank back into comfortable chairs and I produced Lamont's lines.
  Mairead read them, and looked up at me.
  'What d'you think of him as a poet?' I asked.

'Oh, Lord, I don't know. I have to find out what I think of him as a man first. I want to check if the impression he makes on me in his work matches up with the one he makes on me personally, as a living being.'

'That seems a funny way of going at it, to me.'

'That's because you're an intellectual.'

'Is that a bad thing?'

'Yes, probably. But you can't help it. Now it's my turn to ask *you* a question. Am I going to like this Lamont?'

'Can't you tell from the poem?'

'Could you tell from "Ode to a Nightingale" whether you were going to like Keats or not?'

'Um,' I said, thinking.

'Try having a guess. Shall I like Lamont when I meet him? What do you think?'

'Well,' I said, 'I can't think of anyone who knows him and *doesn't* like him. No, to put it a bit more exactly . . . I can imagine people knowing him and not reacting much to him one way or another, but I can't imagine anyone actually *disliking* him. If they weren't on his wavelength they wouldn't think about him at all. He's very un-pushy.'

'Usually,' Mairead said, 'people who don't inspire dislike in any-body are nonentities.'

'I agree, and I also think that some of the people who are the most famous for being good and lovable must have been intensely disliked by at least some of their actual acquaintances. I'm sure St Francis of Assisi must have been perceived by some of his neighbours as a terrible bore and a bit of a show-off too, the way he made such a thing of calling the birds and animals brother and sister. They must have crossed the street when they saw him coming, some of them.'

'Is that how I'm to imagine Lamont – like Francis of Assisi?'

'On the surface, not at all; that would be a side-track. I was just thinking about the question, what kind of people are liked by what kind of people. I *would* expect you to like Lamont, though these things aren't ever totally predictable. At the very least I'd expect you to recognize in him somebody who has a very strong inner life, which you also have, so it should be deep calling to deep. I know some people who strike me as having hardly any inner life at all – they're entirely directed outwards. Lamont isn't indifferent to other people – he's very understanding and responsive to them, in fact – but one has the very definite sense that his real life goes on deep inside.'

'Is he married?'

'Will you believe me when I say that although I've known him for a quarter of a century I don't actually know anything about his personal life, even whether there's a Mrs Lamont or not?'

'Of course I would. You're very vague about things like that.'

'It may be that I'm vague, or it may be just that that's how Lamont affects people. He seems to have such a single eye. All his thoughts are so concentrated on the central issues of life, death, immortality, joy and sadness that he gives you the curious impression while you're with him that irrelevancies don't exist.'

'Irrelevancies like wives, you mean?'

'Darling,' I said, laughing, 'that's just point-scoring. Not worthy of you.'

'Well,' she said, training her deep blue eyes on me till I felt my bones begin to melt, 'it's nice to score points sometimes. When people will let you.'

So I let her score this one. It took some time, and then we went to sleep for the rest of the night.

*

'Daddy, I can dance,' Keira announced, coming into our bedroom on a Saturday morning in late September. 'Look, I'll show you.' She raised her skirt, which was not long enough to require much raising, and began executing a series of curious bounding movements in which I saw the beginnings of a repetitive pattern.

'I think that's very good,' I said from the bed. It was my turn to lie there an extra few minutes while Mairead went down to the kitchen and made the tea.

'Guess who showed me how to do this,' Keira said, continuing her *pas seul.*

'Mummy, I suppose.' I marvelled at the elasticity of her little lungs. She could leap about like a dervish and still talk with no more breathlessness than if she had been sitting in a chair.

'No, not Mummy. Siobhán. And tonight I shall be able to dance better than I can now.'

'Why tonight?'

'Because Siobhán's coming to see us today and she's going to teach me some more steps. That's what it is with dancing. You can walk by just walking, but dancing, that's something somebody has to show you how to do.'

'Yes. Like riding a bicycle.'

'I don't think Siobhán's got a bicycle.'

'No, perhaps she hasn't.'

'How could she teach me to ride a bicycle if she hasn't got one?'

'I didn't say Siobhán had a bicycle.'

'You did, Daddy. You said Siobhán could teach me how to dance and how to ride a bicycle.'

'I didn't. I was distinguishing between categories. Walking's something you do without thinking about it, but dancing's something you have to be shown how to do. And so is riding a bicycle.'

'We'll ask Siobhán when she gets here if she's got a bicycle, but I've never seen her with one and if she hasn't got one how's she going to teach me?'

'I didn't say she was going to teach you, for Christ's sake.'

'You did, Daddy. You did. You're a story-teller.' Keira executed a particularly vehement leap to underscore the accusation.

'Stop shaking the house, you up there! The plaster's coming down!' Mairead shouted from downstairs.

'Daddy,' said Keira, calmly desisting and coming over to sit on the bed, 'when will Moira be old enough to sing?'

'When she can distinguish a tune,' I said. 'The physical part of her training's completed already. Her lungs are powerful enough to give her the volume she needs to fill La Scala. She just needs to cultivate absolute pitch.'

'That's what one of the boys at school said.' Keira had just begun nursery school. 'Miss Hammond brought us a jug of lemonade and we all had some and this boy said it was absolute piss. Why does Moira have to cuttley-vate it?'

'Pitch,' I said. 'It's the sound you make when you sing. Moira's tops for volume and breath control, but she's amateurish in pitch.'

'Well, I want her to start singing as soon as she can.'

'Any special reason?'

'Yes, then we can do an entertainment.'

'How d'you know that word?'

'Miss Hammond has us doing them. An entertainment is when you do something you're good at and everybody watches and listens. Moira and I could do one. I could dance and she could sing.'

'Both at the same time?'

'*Together*, not just at the same time. You're a bit stupid, aren't you, Daddy?'

'Outstandingly,' I said.

'You're outstabbingly. But I still like you. I could dance and she could sing in time to my dancing.'

'Not the other way round?'

'She's too little to dance, stupid.'

'No, I mean wouldn't it be a case of her singing and you dancing in time to what she sang?'

'No, she'd have to watch me and sing to what I danced.'

'That sounds a bit difficult.'

'Well,' Keira said, 'I speck she'd pick it up. People do pick things up, don't they?'

'Yes,' I said.

'Tell me some things you picked up when you were young.'

'Whistling,' I said, 'and pessimism.'

'If you'd known me then you could have whistled to my dancing.'

'It wouldn't have been possible for me to know you when I was doing my whistling,' I said. 'By definition. You couldn't come into existence till I grew up and met Mummy and got fond of her.'

'Then she let you put me into her tummy, didn't she?'

'Yes, that was nice of her, wasn't it?'

Keira gave me a considering look. 'Did you say thank you?'

'You might say I did, in my own way.'

Mairead came in with the tea-tray and we all began discussing Siobhán's forthcoming visit. She was coming from London, for the day. Her scientist husband was infected with a mania for fishing, and he had passed on this disorder to their young son. The two of them would often spend a Saturday or Sunday, sometimes both, sitting side by side on a river bank, drowning maggots. They planned to squander today in this fashion, leaving Siobhán free to be with Mairead. She was going to drive down from London, on the way dropping off her husband and son at somewhere like Cookham, picking them up on her return in the evening. The two women delighted in each other's company, and the presence of the children did not seem any bar to desultory talk, shared memories, confidences, jokes, all that nourishing thick stirabout that makes a friendship, feminine or masculine. Obviously there was a happy day in the offing, partly indoors, partly out under this fresh piebald sky. That left me with no particular role to play. They wouldn't have driven me away, but they had no actual need of me, and since term was approaching and I had to get a course of lectures ready, besides putting Gibson's ramifying correspondence into mothballs for another eight-week period — ten weeks, in the autumn, because of admissions papers and interviews at the end of term — I had more than enough to get on with in my study in Pearce's Building. I waited long enough to greet Siobhán and enjoy a few minutes of her pleasant cheerfulness, then went over to College.

As I walked there I reflected that I knew where all the members of my family were going to be that day. My wife and daughters would be with Siobhán, in and around our home. Heather — if I was still entitled to think of Heather as one of my family; certainly she was one of my dependants — would be teaching people, young girls mostly, to ride horses over the chalk hills that came down as far as Chinnor. She would be spending the day in the fresh autumnal breeze, or in and out of the stables, handling leather, drawing in the smell of horse-sweat and straw and oats. Michael, for his part, would be amid the smell of high-octane fuel and the note of high-revving unsilenced engines, for he was slated to accompany Brian on one of the two sacred days in the year when the K3 went racing at Silverstone; for some weeks it had been impossible to get him to talk of anything else. For two or three seasons now, the K3 had been officially listed in the programme as 'Entrant: B.Leonard. Driver: M. Leonard', and at this year's spring meeting, six months ago, he had managed third place in the chief event of the day, triumphing over more experienced drivers and faster cars. I knew the barely suppressed excitement that bubbled in the veins of my son and my brother, and the only reason I was not going with them to the event was the feeling that I, with my ignorance of the racing scene and generally vague attempts to be part of it all, cramped their style. No, let them enjoy drinking this dram together, and enjoy, just the two of them, the fiery ecstacy of gulping it down.

My destiny was humbler. Work, solid work, took up this day as it took up the huge majority of my days; it was what I had asked for in life, and what I had got. I had lunch in Common Room at a table of men largely as silent and preoccupied as I was myself, then took a turn in the garden for ten minutes before settling back to the steady reading, note-taking and systematization that awaited me. At four o'clock, another visit to Common Room for a quick, silent cup of tea. But when I got back to my room, the telephone was ringing as I opened the door.

'Lodge here, sir. There's someone asking to see you. Shall I send him over?'

'I don't think so. I'm busy just now. What kind of a someone?'

'A policeman, sir.'

I suppose everyone feels some kind of jolt when unexpectedly told of the arrival of a policeman. In the next second I even found my mind rapidly spooling back to think if I had done anything illegal in the recent past, but nothing came to mind. My conduct had not always been creditable, but it had always been legal. My sins had been sins of the mind and spirit: envy, uncharitableness, petty selfishness, a wish to score in argument even at the cost of cutting corners intellectually. A sorry record, but not the kind of thing you went to prison for, I reflected as I replaced the telephone after asking for the officer to be sent up.

I rose from my desk and went to sit down in an armchair, then, after a moment of hesitation, returned to the desk and hastily tidied it a little, sorted the books and papers into rough heaps, and sat down again in my writing chair. It seemed the best place to be when receiving a representative of the law. Sitting back, I imagined the policeman making his ponderous way over from the lodge to Pearce's

Building. What could it be about? I found it impossible to speculate; my mind seemed frozen, immobile. Something serious? It could hardly be trivial, for a constable or a sergeant or whatever he was to be spared from his other duties to come to Episcopus at six o'clock on a Saturday evening. It seemed a curiously long time before I heard his tread on the stairs and then his knock.

He turned out to be a tallish man with a heavy, serious face and dark brown hair that was beginning to recede; bare-headed; carrying his helmet in one large, capable hand; age, forty-ish. I began by acknowledging that I was who he thought I was, in other words that my name tallied with the name neatly painted above the door, and I invited him to take a seat.

'Thank you, sir, I'd rather stand.' But he laid his helmet down on a corner of the desk, as a kind of concession to the idea of sitting down.

'Well,' I said above the noise of my pulse, 'what can I do for you, officer?'

He looked at me steadily, a man determined to do his duty. 'I ought to say to begin with, sir, that I'm here at the request of your wife, Mrs Leonard of Chinnor.'

'My former wife,' I said.

'Beg pardon, sir, your former wife. She asked us to get in touch with you and inform you.'

Terror gripped my heart. 'Inform me . . . ?'

'I'm sorry to say there's been an unfortunate accident, sir.'

I just sat there at the desk and looked at him.

'Our information being that you and Mrs Leonard lived apart and that your son lived with Mrs Leonard, she having the custody.'

'Well, yes, but he's grown-up now, words like custody hardly apply any more.'

'No, sir, but we have a procedure we have to follow. Since Mrs Leonard was granted custody and the young man was making his home with her, that made her legally the next of kin.'

'Next of . . . what precisely are you trying to tell me?' But I knew. In some desolate, terrible way, I knew. My mind didn't know yet, but my body did. That was why it felt so cold.

The policeman dropped his eyes for an instant, then levelled them and held mine. 'Your son, Mr Leonard. Your son, Michael.'

'Yes, my son Michael. That's his name.'

'He was at Silverstone this afternoon. Silverstone racing circuit.'

'And there was an accident. And you went to tell Heather about it. And she sent you to tell me. *Tell me what?*'

'This is very bad news, sir. I want you to collect yourself.'

'If you want me to keep calm, stop torturing me. Michael's been hurt. He had a smash in that damned car. Is he in hospital?'

−315−

'In a sense, sir.'

I opened my mouth and drew in my breath, intending to ask him loudly and angrily, 'In *what* blasted sense?' I was going to put the question in the tone of a justifiably anxious man whose patience had snapped. But no sound came out. Something else, before I could speak, had already snapped, broken, fallen away: the thin membrane of resistance that had been preventing the knowledge I already held in my body from flooding into my mind.

'You mean . . .' I whispered and stopped.

'Yes, sir, the accident was a fatal one. Your son was taken to Northampton General Hospital, but he was . . .'

'Dead on arrival,' I finished for him.

'Yes, sir. I'm very sorry indeed to have to bring you this news.'

'You must be pretty used to it.'

'Well, it's part of our work, sir, but somehow you never do get used to this one. We'd like to offer you all our sympathy, sir, myself and colleagues.'

A note of emotion had come into the policeman's voice. It seemed, for this moment, almost as if our roles were reversed – as if I were calmer, more in command of myself, than he was. He had known the facts for some time and the sadness of them had had time to settle into his mind. Having to break the news to me had brought that sadness to the surface. Now that it was on the surface it would soon blow away. In an hour's time it would be no more than a gentle melancholy and within a week it would cease to affect him at all. He was a decent man, but Michael had not been his son.

I, on the other hand, had entered a brief calm because I was in shock. I knew that the shock would not last. It had knocked out my perceptions and emotions, but they would come back. The sudden blow had disconnected me from my feelings and the only thought I had in my mind was that I was terrified of being reconnected, of knitting up again. *Leave me alone, please*, I prayed inwardly, to Whom or What I had no idea. *Leave me spinning in space.*

I remember nothing more of my conversation with the officer. Doubtless it wasn't memorable. After his departure I continued to sit at the desk. I tried to think of anything I ought to 'do', in a practical sense. But it seemed to me that if it really was true that Michael's life had ended, that there was no longer such a person as Michael, then it didn't matter whether I did anything or not. I might just as well sit in that chair as do anything else.

Arnold Cantwell, my scout, now knocked and came in, squeaky boots and all, for what purpose I don't know. He often came in on some small business at about this time, before he went over to serve in Hall. That reminded me, from another life on another planet, that

I had put down my name to eat in Hall. I told Arnold I wouldn't be doing that and asked him to convey it with my apologies. He asked if he should bring me over anything from the kitchen. I told him not to trouble himself. He did whatever he had come to do and shrilled out.

Alone again, I went on sitting there. Time did not seem to be moving, but then why should it be, with nothing to move to? The desk was positioned in the room so as to give me the light over my shoulder as I sat working, which meant that I had my back, or at any rate my three-quarter back profile, towards the window. But I became aware now that the light in the room had become clearer and more dramatic. I turned in my chair and looked out of the window. A magnificent sunset was in progress. The sky was unbelievably beautiful: clear, serene, its pale blue conveying the sense of infinite depth. But that blue was not uniform; it was broken up here and there by small clusters of cloud, now tangled with the fire of the sinking sun. The thought came to me that Michael would not be able to see that sky. For the first time in twenty years, I could not say to myself, 'I hope Michael, wherever he is and whatever he's doing, will pause long enough to look up at that sky and its beauty.' Not that I had always had that thought when the sunset happened to be a splendid one. But now I could never have it. The possibility of having such a thought had gone from the world.

Then I wondered whether Michael, now that he could no longer see the sky as living people saw it, might be *in* it. Perhaps he was part of the sunset, giving a portion of the beauty that was coming to me from its fiery transience.

I didn't dwell on that thought. I didn't dwell on any thought. I knew that I ought to go home. Even if anything had been normal, even if the state of affairs had been exactly as it was this morning when Mairead and I made our plans for the day, this was about the time when she would begin to expect my return. And of course it wouldn't be normal. By this time, Mairead would know what had happened. She would have been told by some means, by someone. I knew that I ought to know the details. I knew that I ought to telephone her immediately. Why, then, couldn't I? Why was that single action impossible to me?

Never mind why. It just was. I crossed the room to the panel with its two light switches. Sunset was fading into a deep dusk now and I automatically put the lights on. I turned them off again. The hard, unyielding edges, the uncompromising definition of everything in the room, was too much for me. I needed to sit in a nest of shadows. Outside, the light was draining from the sky, but as long as the sky was lighter than the interior of the room I had the sense of being sheltered, of being in a refuge of sorts, however easily breached.

I sat down beside the window. In a moment I would get out of this chair and go home and be with Mairead. I would re-connect myself with life. But first I had to gather strength. I had to find, from somewhere, the solidity to stand up, to go on existing, in a world that had no Michael in it. I would never hear Mike's voice again. I would never meet his quick, intelligent eyes or speak to him. There wasn't any Michael. There was his body to dispose of, and there were his belongings to sort out, and after that there would be the silence and the emptiness where he had been.

Looking out into the dark, I thought of the silence of not-Mike. And I thought of Keira and Moira. I was not childless, I had those two little girls who had the power to make love flow out of me like a miraculous gush of water from a dry rock. I adored them. I cherished them. But they were not a consolation for losing Mike. The joy they brought me held no possibility of compensation: they were too different. I had made them with a different woman, in a different place, at a different point of my own trajectory. They were not less than he was. They were not more. They were simply different, and the same feelings did not stretch to cover both him and them. If the three of them had been part of a shared family life, their lives and my life of the single warp and woof, it might have been possible. But it wasn't possible. The grown young man and the puppy-tumbling little girls were different in kind. And now one of the kinds was extinct, and with it a great part of my own life.

Getting up suddenly from my chair, I left Episcopus, taking a route through the garden and out into the road at the back for fear of meeting anybody I might have to speak to. Once I was on the pavement I walked home to Kingston Road at a determined pace. It took me about ten minutes.

Mairead opened the door. Her eyes were big and disturbed; her face looked thinner than it had in the morning. I let the door slam behind me and we stood holding each other, silently, in the narrow hallway.

'Who told you?' I asked at last.

'Brian,' she said, laying her head against my chest and giving a little shiver.

'Did he ring up?'

'No, he came here. But he didn't stay long. He said he hoped it would be all right for him to come over some time when you are here.'

We went into the sitting-room and sat together on the sofa.

'Would you like a drink or food or anything?'

'No, just to be with you and not feel I have to say anything.'

She nodded. 'If the phone rings, do you want me to answer it?'

I tried to think. 'Is it likely to ring?'

Mairead took my hand for a moment before answering. 'I think it is, my darling. But it all depends.'

−318−

'I'm not understanding you.'

'Of course you're not, because I'm not being clear. So I'll be clear. I think the phone's likely to ring because Brian hadn't long gone before it rang, and before I had anything like a chance to get myself together Heather was screaming at me. And then she'd have a fit of sobbing and then scream some more. "You killed him!" she kept shouting. "You bitch, you killed him!" '

'I wonder how she makes that out,' I said.

'Oh, Peter, it's easy enough to see how she makes it out. Anyway she's got to blame someone, it's the only way she can get to terms with it.'

'Yes.' I thought, Shall I find myself blaming someone? Or just myself?

'And the reason I say it depends is that she sounded drunk, and what it depends on is whether by this time she's gone beyond being able to telephone.'

'My God,' I said. 'My God.'

'Is she all alone out there?'

'As far as I know there's no other member of the household.'

Mairead stood up. 'Somebody ought to be looking after her. She might set fire to the house or anything.'

'Well, she runs a riding school and she's got horses stabled out there. She must employ a groom or a stable lad or something.'

'Peter,' she said, 'will you let me take this one over? I'll give my mind to it and I'll handle it. There must be something common-sense we can do. I'll just think for a moment. The fact is I've only just begun to pick myself up. When Brian first telephoned, life was all swirling along around me. Keira was playing some game with Siobhán and the pair of them were laughing their heads off, and Moira was joining in and making happy noises very loudly. And of course while I was in the kitchen telephoning, they knew nothing about what was happening, so all the merriment was going full blast when I came back in here.'

'What happened then? Did Siobhán go?'

'She's a true friend. I told her, quickly, and she helped me to get the kids to bed and stayed with me a little longer. Then she said I knew where I could speak to her any time, and kissed me and told me she was ready to help in any way and then she went.'

'That's the sort of friend . . .' I said. I was going to finish the sentence with 'to have', but the telephone rang. I must have been subconsciously listening out for it, because the alarm it struck into my being was enough to bring me to an instant silence.

Mairead got quickly and decisively to her feet. 'I'm going to answer it, Peter.'

'I ought to,' I said bemusedly.

'You go and get yourself a drink. I'll tell you who it is, and if it's someone you want to speak to you can.'

She was going out of the door as she spoke. The telephone was in the kitchen. The drinks cupboard was in the front room, where I was. I went over to it and took out the household bottle of whisky and the soda syphon. We were not spirit-drinkers; it usually took us a month or more to get through a bottle of whisky and a lot of that went on visitors. But I poured out a good comforting one for myself, and another for Mairead. The ringing of the telephone had stopped now and I could hear that Mairead was talking to someone. To be clearly audible her voice would have had to travel out of the kitchen, along a stretch of passage and into the front room, and she would have had to speak up. She wasn't speaking up, she was talking in a quiet voice and a level tone, and I decided not to strain every nerve to hear her. Perhaps it was just someone asking a question about a library book or something. I splashed out some soda water. Then she appeared in the doorway and said, 'It's Brian.'

'What does he want? He's only just been here, hasn't he?'

'He wants to know if you'll talk to him. I said I'd ask.'

I tried to think. Was I willing to talk to Brian, or not? The question seemed to elude me. It slipped about on the surface of my mind, like an orange pip on a plate. I couldn't pick it up. Brian? What could I possibly say to him? What could he possibly say to me? Then I realized that my mind was losing grip. The shock had left me vague. Obviously I would have to confront Brian at some stage.

I went to the telephone. 'Where are you, Brian?' I asked.

'Bargeman's,' he said.

'When d'you want to come round?'

'Now,' he said, 'if that's all right with you. I don't know what I'm going to say to you but I feel we ought to be together.'

What a strange thing to feel, I thought. Why should he feel we ought to be together? My mind was still shocked, half dead, and in addition the whisky was beginning to cradle it into insensibility, but why should Brian think that when I did get back to something like normal I would want to see *him*? Be together with *him*? When if it hadn't been for him Michael would not be . . . I mean Michael would be . . . Michael would be alive. Perhaps even here with me at this actual moment. Or with Heather. Or with Sophy. Did Sophy know about this?

'Have you told Sophy?' I said.

'Have I what?'

'Never mind, it doesn't matter.'

'Look, can I come round, or not?'

'You can't leave the pub, surely?'

'Oh,' he said in a do-be-reasonable-voice, 'leave all that to me. The point is, can *you* put up with seeing *me*?'

Mairead came in. 'Don't let him come round if you don't feel like coping. There'll be time,' she said.

'My darling,' I said, 'you are wonderful.'

'You can't be speaking to me,' Brian said.

'No, I'm not speaking to you,' I said, 'but come round anyway.' And I rang off.

Mairead had made some sandwiches, and brought some in on a tray for herself and me. We sat and munched them, or started to, but were soon satisfied. As soon as we stopped being starvation hungry, food and the idea of food became repulsive, so we just sat together with her hand in mine. I asked about Keira and Moira. Mairead said they had all had a wonderful day and Keira had danced a lot.

Keira had danced and Michael had died. I had made notes for lectures. Life had no pattern, no meaning. *I will show you fear in a handful of dust.*

There was a knock on the door and Mairead went to answer it. She was out of the room for a few minutes and then came in and said Brian was in the kitchen. I asked why he didn't come in to where we were and she said she didn't know. He had just gone into the kitchen and sat down; he seemed under such strain that she didn't think it was worth chasing him up over details. He had said that if I would care to speak to him I would find him there.

I went along the passage and into the kitchen. Brian was sitting at the table. When I came in he pushed his chair back and started to get up, but almost at once he sank back as if he were too exhausted and stayed sitting down, looking up at me helplessly. His expression made me think of an animal piteously waiting to be released from a trap.

'Peter,' he said. His voice made a dry sound like a cork being twisted out of a bottle.

'I'm here, Brian.'

'Peter,' he said again. Then he put his hands over his face. I heard his voice coming muffled through his heavy, strong hands, not dead like Michael's.

'It should never have happened. It was against all the chances. Nobody could have . . .'

He stopped and was silent for a moment, and when he took his hands away I saw that his face was wet and his eyes inflamed.

'Did you see it happen?' I made myself ask him.

'No. It was out on the circuit. But the stewards told me. And I went out . . . afterwards and reconstructed it from the skid marks.' He began to spill out words quickly. 'He was having a duel with this E.R.A. driver. Name of Ferguson. Driving one of those two-litre jobs. They were both after second place. There was a Maserati in the lead and he was out of sight, long gone, a much faster car. Mike was giving Ferguson a real run. Wouldn't let go of him. Eleven hundred against two litres, of course Mike had nothing like the speed but he was driving far better. Wouldn't give an inch on the bends, not one solitary inch, and much faster through the gears. And personally I'll never believe that Ferguson bloke was up to it. He should have surged away from Mike, with all the power he had. But he could never get clear of him. Every time they came past the pits, you could have tied them together with a piece of string. The people in the grand-stand were standing up and cheering, and you don't get that much at Vintage meetings, they're a cool lot. But this was motor-racing. It's what Mike wanted to do and he was doing it. Then they didn't come round on one lap and the announcement came. Race abandoned.'

'Is that what they do when someone gets killed?' I asked.

'The old E.R.A. was always a safe car,' Brian said. He was speaking at an even faster pace now and his eyes were fixed in the one position, as if he were looking at something suspended in mid-air. 'But she needed a good driver. She could be an awkward cow to drive. The steering column was askew, you know, Peter. Set at an angle. It was designed like that . . . to miss the gearbox. She could be a cow to handle, unless you were really used to her. I never was myself. Had a few laps in an E.R.A. on the old mountain circuit at Brooklands but never got used to that off-angle steering. Once I got over the ton I felt nervous. Of course I'm not a racing driver. Mike was a racing driver. I know it must have been Ferguson who made a mistake. But coming into that nasty curve they touched, and instead of bouncing clear they tangled. The K3 was a very stable car. We built her like that and she was like that. But once they got locked in, the heavier car won. The E.R.A. stayed on the road. It was the K3 that flipped over. Landed upside down.'

He stopped. The effect was like switching off a machine in full career. He kept staring in front of him. What was he seeing? What was that air-suspended image? His racing car, his beloved K3, as it was during the last second of my son's life?

Whatever the vision was, it had gone. Brian's fit of hysterical tension had passed. He looked at me, sitting on the other side of the kitchen table in that simple Kingston Road house, and he saw me.

He stood up now and said, 'Peter, is there anything I can do?'

'No,' I said. 'You've done enough already.'

'Don't be like that, Peter. Don't see it like that. Don't hate me.'

'Did I say I hated you?'

He still seemed to want something of me. 'Peter,' he said pleading-ly, 'it was a quick death.'

'They always say that.'

He shook his head. 'Not me. I don't always say it. I've been mixed up with racing drivers for a lot of years, and I've always faced the fact that when they get killed it can be any way. Sometimes very quick, sometimes slow. It's like any other kind of accident. Sometimes a car overturns and catches fire and traps the driver underneath. You can hear him yelling to be pulled clear and you can't get near him. I've seen that. And there was a chap who drew flame into his lungs and they took him to hospital and he didn't die for four months. Mike didn't have anything like that. He was a perfectly fit young fellow and then in less than a second he was dead.'

'Brian, stop talking. Just – stop – talking. It's all I want you to do.'

He started for the door, stopped before he went through it, and said, 'I'll leave you alone.'

'There'll be a time to talk later, Brian,' I said. 'I'll just say one thing now, that I honestly don't hate you.'

'You don't know that,' he said. 'You don't know till you see. You may come to hate me.'

'I may, but I don't think so. Anyway, let's talk some time. Not now.'

'No,' he said. 'Not now, at any rate.'

He went out and began to walk down the path. I got up and went to the front door and called after him, 'Just do one thing for me. Don't tell Mother and Dad. Let me get round to it and tell them in my time.'

He stood there on the path in the almost darkness, just some light falling on him from a street lamp, and looked at me with unbearable sorrow in his eyes. 'Peter,' he said. 'Peter.'

'What?'

'It's in the paper.'

And so it was.

Mairead came into the room. 'I heard the door. He's gone, I suppose?'

'Yes.'

'Did he say anything at all helpful?'

I shrugged. 'I suppose it was helpful for him to come here. But he's still pretty down, naturally. And needless to say, nothing he said made any difference to *me*.'

'No, of course not.' Then she looked at me enquiringly, perhaps wondering how I was going to take the next bit. 'Peter. There's still Heather.'

'I'll ring.'

'No, you won't; you've had enough. I'll ring. I'd have done it while you were with Brian, but I wanted to do it in a different room and the telephone's in here. I'm going to ring her now. You ought to go into another part of the house and think different thoughts. Just let it go.'

'But she's already given you one outburst. If you ring again she'll probably give you another. I'd rather she screamed at me than screamed at someone who's done nothing to deserve it.'

'My darling, I feel very sorry for Heather and I've got enough imagination to know what she must be going through. To have some idea of it, anyway. Her screaming and throwing insults are just cries of agony. I'd be a terrible person if I resented them. If I thought it would help her I'd encourage her to throw that kind of stuff at me for hours together. But I don't want you exhausted and beaten down, after what you've had to take already. You need a night's sleep and you need to have it with me. To soothe you. If I can't do that I can't do anything.'

'All right,' I said.

'It's just to be reassured she's still there and hasn't done anything desperate.' Mairead dialled the number. I made no attempt to move to another room. I was sinking into a weariness so profound that I really doubted my ability to get up from the kitchen chair I had flopped down on. Perhaps I could if my objective was bed, beside Mairead. But not to move for moving's sake, on these leaden legs.

Mairead was speaking. 'I was ringing to ask about Heather. Mairead Leonard. If she doesn't want to be disturbed, please don't. As long as she's all right.'

I couldn't hear what the person at the other end said, but Mairead's face became expressionless, as it generally did when anyone said aggressive or insulting things to her.

'Oh. Well, all Peter and I wanted to establish is that she's not in need of any immediate help. You're there with her, I take it? Thank you. Peter will ring tomorrow.' She spoke the last few words in a tone that suggested a steady forging ahead, as if her voice were having to push its way through a barrage coming from someone else's. Then she hung up the telephone and said, 'I wonder who that was.'

'Man or woman?' I asked.

'Middle-aged woman, rather mannish.'

'That'll be Meg Bolsover. Friend of Heather's who lives quite near by and sees a lot of her. I don't know how much of a real friend she is, but she's taken Heather up and uses her to fill the spaces in her own life. A snob and a bit of a battle-axe.'

'Oh, well,' Mairead said. 'She's there with Heather at the moment, and that's all to the good.'

I nodded, forcing myself to stand up. 'Yes,' I said, 'even the Meg Bolsovers have their uses. For me, now, it's bed.'

'And for me.'

I went up the stairs, very slowly, and Mairead followed a few paces behind, almost as if she were getting ready to catch me if I swayed and fell backward. I must have looked ghastly.

★

After we fell into bed I lay holding Mairead close to me: her warmth and love seemed like a miraculous poultice drawing the grief out of my body, grief that I would otherwise not have been able to survive. I had no hope of sleep, but her nearness and yieldingness drew me into a state that was almost as remote from normal consciousness, a hallucinatory state in which I knew I was in our house, in bed, with my arms around my wife, and yet experiencing other things too, things that came from my shocked mind and racing imagination. It seemed to me that the grief she was drawing out of me was a material substance, a kind of evil syrup, thick and tarry without having the clean astringent smell of tar: rather, it smelt like stagnant water that has been lying many days in a ship's bilges, a dead, heavy, lowering smell, like what one might imagine to be the smell of sadness itself. After a while I asked myself, Where is this syrupy grief going to? It isn't in the bed, it isn't coating Mairead's warm, smooth body, so where is it? Then I imagined it drawn downwards, strained through sheet and mattress and underblanket, forming a dark pool on the floorboards under the bed, lying there deepening and spreading outwards. And the more of it accumulated there, the more my heart pumped out because it was never-ending. And then, without leaving our bed, I had somehow wafted over the roofs and the mile or so of intervening space and was floating down the River Cherwell, following the current down through the Parks, under the Rainbow Bridge, past Parsons' Pleasure, over the rollers, and down into the lower stretch where the river is engineered into two streams. Following the right-hand channel, as boats always do, the bed approached Magdalen and stopped beside Addison's Walk. I got out, leaving Mairead sleeping, and climbed up the bank, to find the calendar had gone back (or forward?) from September to early May, because the grassy plot contained by the oval path was bright with fritillaries. As I marvelled at their delicacy and the gentle lyricism of their colours, I became aware of two figures, a man and a woman, walking among these wild flowers and frequently bending to pick them. Knowing that Magdalen College discourages this practice, I watched, expecting some groundsman to come hurrying over to this couple – who, as they drew nearer, revealed themselves as dumpy and middle-aged – and put a stop to their picking, but they were unmolested as they came towards me through the bright haze of the fritillaries, each carrying a generous bunch. They looked happy enough, but when they came up close to me I recognized them as Heather's parents, the Burrells, and they recognized me too and their faces became set and

−325−

grim. 'Now you know what it's like,' Mrs Burrell said, and old Burrell beside her echoed, 'Ay, he knows what it's like. He was too hard on us, too hard on us all along, but now he knows what it's like,' and the two of them stared at me with sorrowful, accusing eyes. 'You never knew how it hurt me to lose Tom,' Mrs Burrell said, 'and you never knew how it hurt Jim when Phil got . . . Phil got killed.'

'Murdered, he got, murdered, with a hole straight through his neck from one side to t'other,' old Burrell shouted.

'It wasn't any different with Tom,' Mrs Burrell said, 'Tom got murdered too, in an aeroplane. And this man didn't care – he didn't show any pity.'

The two of them had now got up on to the path and as they stood facing me they both, with one accord, tossed down their bunches of fritillaries as if they had no further use for them, as if in some way meeting with me had robbed them of their beauty. They turned and walked away, disappearing round the curve of the path, and feeling utterly nonplussed I stopped and gathered up the two sheaves of flowers. I wanted to take them home for Mairead and the children, but as I held them in the warmth of my hand they wilted, drooped, faded. Standing there in Addison's Walk, sick at heart, ashamed, disappointed, lonely, I began pulling gently at the heads of the flowers to try to give them a fresher appearance, as a woman pulls at a garment that has become creased, but it did nothing for them because they had died, there was no life left in them, they were dead flowers, they were dead, dead.

★

I knew I ought to telephone Heather, but I couldn't face doing it. I have never liked or trusted the telephone, and in particular I have always been very reluctant to handle any of the deeper emotional issues of life by speaking into a plastic mouthpiece to a person who is somewhere else, and whose voice comes back, if at all, drained of colour and individuality by the low-definition medium. Telephones are for enquiring train times or fixing up to see the dentist, not for trying to convey emotional realities. The next morning, which was dull and leaden, I looked at the instrument as it hung on the kitchen wall but made no move to pick it up. Only after Mairead had silently put in front of me the third cup of after-breakfast coffee in a row did I force my feet into action before my brain had time to raise any objection. Shambling to the telephone, lifting it up and dialling the number as mechanically as if I were doing something of absolutely no consequence, I found myself speaking to Heather. Her voice did not sound much different from usual.

'I need to come out and see you.'

'Well, don't!'

'It might be a help.'

'Not to me.'

'But we ought to talk. It could help,' I urged.

'Not today. I shan't see anyone today.'

'Not even me?'

'Least of all you.'

I paused a second. 'Well, can you suggest a day, then?'

'No. There's no day I'll want to see you. I never want to see you again.'

'I'm sorry, but I'm coming this morning,' I said. I knew it was the only thing. I briefly explained the situation to Mairead, who looked up and nodded; she was engaged in settling Keira and Moira down to a session with plasticine and finger-painting. Then I got out the little car and drove to Chinnor. How hard it was, as the house came in sight, to realize that I had once lived there. Of course it looked different now, with all those outbuildings.

The sun had come out now and it was a picture-book autumn day, which only made everything seem worse by driving home the point that nature is indifferent to the sufferings of humanity. One knows this fact perfectly well, yet at times of unhappiness there is always a little extra unhappiness in having it rammed home. As I stood ringing the front doorbell, Heather came round the side of the house, carrying a trug. She was wearing a pair of what I supposed were sunglasses, though if so they must be the kind that are designed to be worn in the brightest possible sun beating on white Alpine snow. They made her eyes totally invisible. The trug had a few weeds in it, and in her other hand she held a small gardening fork. Was this scene-setting? Did she want me to find her setting about the garden like the demure, perfect wife she would have been, if only I had stayed with her? No, no, Heather was not like that. That was my guilt talking. She was clearing up the weeds because to have a weed-choked garden didn't look good when people came to enquire about the riding stable. A more pertinent question, which now arose in my mind, was, Has she started her day's drinking yet? It was barely eleven o'clock: was I in time to catch her sober?

'Heather,' I said, starting towards her.

'Don't come near me, please,' she said politely.

'But we ought to talk.'

'What is there to talk about? If you mean Michael, he's gone and that's all there is to it. He was all we had left and he's gone.' Her voice had a hard, strangled quality.

'But . . . there must be something we could cling to that would help us to comfort one another.'

'Why should there be? You're just afraid of facing the situation as it really is.'

Well, who wouldn't be? I thought. Why shouldn't I be afraid of it? Then she said the thing I had been most afraid of, the one I knew would be coming sooner or later.

'You had your own way and this is the result.'

'You see it as simply as that, do you?'

'Course I do. Why did he get into that fool motor-racing? Because he was hanging around Brian. Why was he hanging around Brian? Because he needed a father and his real father had taken off and gone chasing after his own pleasure.'

I swallowed. 'Heather, if you went to one of those Silverstone meetings, you'd see a lot of young fellows involved in it. Are they all there because their fathers left home? When a young man goes in for any dangerous sport, ski-jumping or mountaineering or anything else, is it always because his father left home?'

'I don't know and I don't care. It's *our* son I'm talking about. If you think there's anything we can say to each other at this stage that's likely to bring any *comfort*,' she underlined the word with her voice, mockingly, 'you must be mad. Why don't you just face it — he was all we'd got left and now he's gone.'

She moved past me as she spoke and went into the house: the door had not been locked. As she passed close to me I got the whiff of gin. How early, I wondered, would I have had to get here to catch her before the first drink? Or did she greet the day with the first one? But then, it was unthinkable that she had spent last night here just on her own, and had woken in an empty house, and got up and dressed by herself, with or without gin. When Mairead had telephoned after Brian had gone she had been answered by someone other than Heather, and I remembered my conjecture that this was probably Meg Bolsover, who had presumably taken over and seen Heather to bed, drunk or sober, it didn't matter. She *couldn't* have been here alone. And what was this weeding business, the trug and the fork? Was she going through the motions, holding herself together? How could I get near enough to help her? I followed her into the house: uninvited, yes, but this was no time for etiquette. We were both in the kitchen, that room I remembered with such agonizing sharpness from the last night I had spent under this roof. I had no right to expect that she would come towards me out of her frozen isolation. But equally I had no right not to make a try for it.

'Look,' I began, 'I know there's no point in trying to talk to you, but I just thought we might—'

'No, there isn't. I don't know why you came to see me. You took our marriage away from me and now you've taken our son away from me. There's nothing else you can take, why don't you go away?'

I was about to answer something, anything – to babble out some string of words that would at any rate represent to her my urgent, deep, terrible need to reach out and touch her, to join hands with her at this moment, if only for this moment, as the two people in the world who knew the dead weight, the mindless blind negative sacrifice of Michael's death – when from the corner of my eye I saw a car draw up at the gate. It was a long, heavy, dark green Bentley saloon, *circa* 1938: Meg Bolsover's car.

I stood still, watching her get out of the car and prepare to come to the door of the house, and as I did so my mind sank into frozen despair and my tongue seemed to swell and become incapable of speech, as if a sadistic dentist had injected Novocaine into it instead of into my gum. That first glance told me what kind of woman this intruder was. In the face of what she represented, I couldn't, just flatly *could not*, go on trying to talk to Heather about what had happened and how we could try and face it together. Meg Bolsover's presence, her thick externality, would squash out of the situation anything that still remained in it of reality, any quickness of life or possibility of response.

I saw her hyperthyroid eyes rest briefly on me as, nearing the house, she looked in at the window. Then she knocked on the door and Heather called, 'Come in, Meg, it isn't locked.'

'Heather,' I moaned softly in one last appeal.

'This woman wishes me well,' she said to me between set teeth. Then the door was opening and Meg Bolsover was in the room, Fair-Isle-jumpered, mackintoshed, brogued, impervious.

'Ready, Heather?' she addressed my ex-wife. 'Just walk out and leave everything, darling. I've told Alec and Wilma to see to the horses; they know all the drill. I've got everything ready for you to have a nice restful stay – you mustn't come back here till you feel completely ready.' Her eyes moved to me. 'Good morning,' she said flatly.

I made some kind of sound. It probably didn't much resemble 'Good morning,' but it filled the punctuation gap.

'Meg Bolsover,' she said. 'I'm doing what I can to tide Heather over.'

'Good of you,' I said. It was a silly answer, but what would have been a sensible answer?

Obviously she knew who I was. She had never seen me before, but finding Heather in the kitchen with a man, staring at him accusingly through her opaque black glasses, Meg must have realized that there was no need of polite introductions.

'You probably gathered that I spent last night here,' she said brusquely. 'Somebody I took to be your new wife rang at about ten o'clock.'

'Yes.'

'There's no point in ringing here from now on for a while. Heather's coming to stay at my house. She'll need to be looked after till she gets on her feet.'

Did she imagine she was giving me information? Or was she just upbraiding me?

'You may as well know,' Heather suddenly said, 'that the hospital have been on to me. Already. Asking how long he's going to be left there.'

'Well, good God, they're in a hurry, aren't they? If they ring again, put them straight on to me, unless you particularly want to handle it yourself.'

'No, I don't. You can handle it, you've handled everything else. But just tell them, when they do take his body away, not to bring him here.'

'Of course not,' I said. 'You won't be here, for one thing.'

'No, and for another thing she ought not to have all that business loaded on to her,' Meg Bolsover intervened, moving definitely on to the attack.

'I agree entirely. I had no intention of letting anybody load—'

'What she needs is a little bit of imaginative sympathy. A little bit of understanding of how she must be feeling.'

'I came out here,' I said desperately, 'because I wanted to try to give her some help.'

'Help from *you*? I don't believe my ears,' Heather said.

'It would help,' Meg Bolsover said to me coldly, 'if you'd make some effort to see the situation as Heather must see it. Put yourself in her place.'

I clutched at my forehead. 'Oh, for God's sake—'

'Men always have a struggle to do that. They find it so difficult to come out of their entrenched male point of view.'

'Look,' I said, distraught, 'I don't see what's male and female about this. We're parents and we've lost our child in a hideous accident. I just . . . I just want to—'

'But there *is* male and female in it. Heather's a mother, and what's more she's a wife who's been left to cope on her own. You must forgive me butting in like this. Heather needs someone to speak up for her.'

I turned and walked out on to the garden path. The day had ripened into warm sunshine, but the air was still damp as the dew

-330-

evaporated, and the cottage garden was sending out a gentle, all-pervading scent, the smell of peace and well-being and the fulfilment of late summer. Down the brick path, through the fragrant air, I walked with my head bent and the agony kicking and jumping inside my chest like a live eel. Walking past Meg Bolsover's big, old-fashioned, consciously superior car with its wide solid wheels and enormous headlamps, so level-headed and useful and well planned, I felt a mad urge to kick it, or, better still, to look round for a stone big enough to smash the windows with. I wanted to yell out, to send my voice echoing down the long village street, to tell everyone in earshot that I had been robbed. If the woman had picked my pocket and stolen a wallet full of money she could have been sent to prison, but the law had no penalty ready for people who stole other people's life-blood, snatched away their last slender chance of salvaging something human and permanent out of the wreck of a relationship. '*She robbed me! She robbed me!*' I wanted to howl, awakening the sleeping Chiltern echoes. '*And she robbed Heather too! That chance was our last!*'

As I drove away, I looked back fleetingly at the house where Michael had grown up and thought suddenly of his room upstairs. I would never see it again now. Was that big chart of 'British Mammals' still on the walls? Unlikely. What would it be? Racing cars? But he would be past that stage. Girls? Well, at twenty-one he would be past ordinary pin-ups: but one special girl? Obsessively photographed, framed, displayed? Was Sophy still his girl-friend? If so, what was she thinking and feeling now? But I would never know, I would never meet her, or her replacement if one existed.

And then it came over me with a cold thrusting pain, what a vast range of things I would never know, now, about Mike. All those things about his growing-up years that he would have revealed, casually, as we chatted together later, all the crises and conflicts he would have been able to mention lightly, humorously, once the pain of them was over. We would never have that easy, chatting, gathering-up time. We would never have anything more. Mike was gone, Mike was gone, Mike was gone, and for some reason I heard in my head, over and over again, Heather's voice, clear as a bell and deadly as frost: *He was all we had left.*

*

My father telephoned on the Monday, mid-morning. 'I didn't want to bother you before. I can't say anything, Peter. You know how shaken up your Mum and I must be feeling. I don't have to say it, do I?'

– 331 –

'No,' I said. 'And thanks.'

'We'd like to send comfort all round. If we only could.'

'I know you would, Dad.'

We were both silent.

'Your mother'd very much appreciate it, Peter,' he said, 'if you could pay us a visit, even if it's only a short one. Just a few minutes.'

'Wouldn't you rather come here? The two of you?'

'Well, we'll do that too, of course, but we don't want to intrude. We can imagine what it must be like for you just now, and for Mairead. If you could just drop by for a few minutes . . . The fact is, your mother's got something she'd like to put to you. A suggestion.'

'A suggestion? Presumably it's something to do with,' I paused, 'the only thing I'm thinking about at present.'

'Well, of course it is, Peter, what d'you take us for? It's something she knows she'll have to bring up now rather than waiting, if she's going to bring it up at all.'

I decided it would be simpler not to speculate and just go round and see them. I went within an hour. They had bought, for their retirement, a bright, comfortable little house in West Street. They had seen no reason to uproot themselves from Oseney where their life had been; and the closeness of Brian, who occasionally flattered his father by asking his advice about something, was another comfort. No one likes to be forgotten.

I drove round. I knocked on the door of the neat little dwelling. Our first moments were wordless. Our feelings found issue in a hug with my mother, a long hard handshake with my father, a speechless communion that gathered in all of us. When we had moved into something like normal conversation, I could see that my mother was eager to make her point without loss of time. Dad looked at her expectantly and she took centre stage; I could see she thought it her duty.

'There's only one thing I specially want to say to you, Peter,' she said. 'Most of the things I ought to say I just can't. There's so many things I feel for you and understand about, but I can't put words to them. They just lie inside my chest like a lead weight. It's as if the whole inside of my chest was made of lead. You know all the things I must be feeling, and Dad too, but we can't say them. And we feel them for everybody who's caught up in this . . . *everybody*, Peter.'

She was silent for a moment. I held her hands tightly and shared the silence with her. It was a form of talk between us. Then, blinking a few times, she forced herself into utterance.

'One thing I do want to put in that you mightn't have thought of, and I have to do it now because it could be too late if I waited to give you time to get over things a bit. I have to bring it up now, when what I'd really like to do is leave you in peace.'

She put her glasses on, which she did when she wanted to concentrate and be very serious. I suppose they helped her to see. Certainly they helped her to think. 'Go ahead, Mum,' I said. 'Bring anything up.'

'You know I was born in Binsey,' she said. I was slightly thrown by this, not seeing at first what it could have to do with the matter in hand, but I had invited her to bring anything up, so I sat patiently and listened.

'I used to be taken to Binsey Church when I was a little girl,' she said. 'We used to go as a family. Of course most people used to go. Everything was different, then, you know, Peter.'

I could see it all: the riverside inn, the spacious communal green, the row of cottages that made up the hamlet of Binsey, the tree-crowned line of Wytham Hill in the background, and my mother in a pretty Sunday frock with a lace collar, in summer with a big shady hat. She would enjoy assembling with the other village families to walk the half-mile along the lane to Binsey Church, its surrounding graveyard bowered in trees, its western front graced by the legendary St Margaret's Well. When she made her first visits there, Queen Victoria was on the throne, motor-cars were unknown on the roads, and the Thames flowed gently between banks enamelled with countless wild flowers. I knew that was a sentimental view to take of that epoch, I knew that those years had their hard, cruel side, I knew that even in Binsey the working hours were unmercifully long, that the picturesque cottages had leaking roofs which the farmer-landlords could not afford to repair; I knew that food was very plain and clothes very coarse. But the picture-book side of it had been there too, and my mother as a young girl had inhabited an England I would never see. I could tell from her face that she was reaching back to that England now.

'I was just thinking, Peter. Have you made any plans about where Michael's going to be . . .'

She was going to say 'buried'. Obviously it was the only word in all the immense vocabulary of the English language that could possibly be slotted into that space. To be buried was the only thing that could happen to Mike now. Cremated first, then buried. That was the modern way. At least the old popular religious objection to cremation had died down. People no longer fiercely argued that the God who made the universe would be unable to find and re-assemble the scattered molecules of a cremated body and bring them back into effective life at the Resurrection. My mother could not actually utter the word, so overcome was she by the pain of having to convey it; but I knew what she was getting at. She wanted a grave to visit. Well, so did I, come to that. She wanted a spot on the earth's surface where she could feel in some symbolic way that Michael was present. Well, so did I.

'You must have thought about it,' she said timidly, hardly daring to set foot on what must be still, so soon after the blow, such terrible ground.

'I haven't really thought about it,' I said. I saw that my father, though silent and taking care not to be seen interfering, was listening intently. 'I suppose if I don't make any particular move and Heather has no strong wishes, it'll go through by the usual routine, and living where we are that means Wolvercote. That says nothing to me – it's not even *in* Wolvercote, which at least is an Anglo-Saxon settlement, though I suppose technically it must be in that parish. It's just a big impersonal plot of what must have been open space in the thirties when the City Council decided it would be a convenient place to put bodies in.'

'Where is . . . he now?' my mother whispered. All this was a great strain on her. She had lowered her head at the point of being unable to say the word 'buried', and my father had put his arm round her, at the same time using his other hand to give her a clean handkerchief. This she had put to her eyes and now looked at me over it, ready to lift it to her eyes again.

'He's in the mortuary at Northampton General Hospital,' I made myself say. 'They'll bring him anywhere we . . . want him.' I want him back, I said inwardly, I want them to bring him *back* as he was when I saw him last.

'There isn't a Vicar at Binsey these days, Peter,' my mother said. 'It's run by the Vicar of St Frideswide's. But they have a few services. About one a month; the St Frideswide's Vicar takes them. I've been to a few, since we gave up the Bargeman's. Never had time free on a Sunday, all through the years. But now, with having my Sundays free, I sometimes go along. I rather like it; it takes me back all those years.'

'She's even got me to go a few times,' my father put in.

'I got right out of the habit, all those years, I forgot about it altogether. But I was surprised when I started going again how it was all there in my memory. Even the first time I went to a service after forty years I found I often knew what was coming next. When the parson spoke one sentence, it seemed to pull the next one up out of my memory.'

'I can just imagine it,' I said.

'Peter,' she said, leaning forward, her eyes urgently seeking mine. 'Have Michael's grave in Binsey Churchyard. It's such a beautiful place. Beautiful and peaceful. It'll be a comfort to think of him being there. I'm sure Heather'll understand. Ring up the Vicar at St

Frideswide's. Or just step round and see him; he lives next door to the church and I know he'll agree to it. There's plenty of space left in that lovely little churchyard – I don't know why, but there is.'

I promised to make enquiries. I liked the idea myself, if 'like' was a word I could possibly use about any of this leaden business. Later that same day I went round to the Vicarage and set the arrangements in motion.

That evening, feeling that I ought not to take such an important step without giving Heather a chance to express an opinion, I tried to get in touch with her. She wasn't at the house, which I expected; no one answered the telephone, so I looked in the directory to find Meg Bolsover's number. It wasn't there. I rang Directory Enquiries, but they wouldn't tell me because she was ex-directory. I was stumped; but the next day's post brought me a terse note, posted at London Airport, in which Meg Bolsover informed me that she owned a farmhouse in Tuscany and was taking Heather there to rest until she was ready for life again. When I had seen her, trug and gardening fork in hand, dark glasses hiding her swollen eyes, she had, I gathered, been holding herself together for a brief spell between two collapses; when the second one came, more or less immediately after I saw her, it had been much more protracted than the first.

I had not taken to Meg Bolsover, but that didn't stop me from being glad that she existed just then, glad that she had a Tuscan farmhouse, glad that she had taken Heather there; glad that even people I didn't like were capable of performing actions that I recognized as necessary, and timely, and a blessing.

*

Funerals are a good custom. The very things that are urged against them by inexperienced, unreflective people – that they are artificial, that they impose routine, that they are nothing like the spontaneous effusion of real grief – are their greatest virtues. If someone you loved very much has been taken from you and you have no idea how you are going to rebuild your life round the huge void left by their going, then what you need is routine, artificiality, a prescribed ritual. All the formalized procedures – the long black cars, the polished wooden box, the flowers, the precise drill-instructions given by the undertaker in that professional manner they have, half kindly and half bossy – must have prevented many a person from going to pieces, especially in our Anglo-Saxon culture which teaches us that the emotions are indecent and have to be hidden away as carefully as the private parts of one's body. In equatorial cultures, it is good manners to show your grief at a death by howling, grinding dust and ashes into your scalp and rolling on the ground – a wise custom, excellent for maintaining psychological health. The Celtic cultures permit – enjoin, rather – the open display of sorrow as long as it follows traditional patterns such as keening. The English had to take over the word from Irish (*caoinim*, I wail); there is no English word for it, simply because the sound of Irish keening is not like any sound that is normally heard in England.

I had these thoughts in the funeral car being driven from our house to St Margaret's Church, Binsey. I liked having them; I deliberately let them run through my head because they pushed sorrow to arm's length. I find words very calming. I like to inform myself about their origins. I suppose that is because I am a don. It's a donnish taste. That car ride would have been a dreadful experience if I hadn't been able to cling to those objective, neutral thoughts about the way human beings express themselves.

And of course it was all held safely within the framework of the funeral, in which everyone had something to do and everything was prepared beforehand. As our *cortège* moved slowly along the lane to Binsey Church I felt glad, then, that it was all so routine, so rehearsed and predictable. The dark clothes, the dark cars, the measured steps, the measured words, took me through it as they have taken so many thousands. Mairead was with me. Once she was certain that Heather, being away in Tuscany having a breakdown, wasn't suddenly going to appear and put a curse on her, she had come to give me the support of her presence; though she never made any pretence that Michael's death could have fallen on her with the force with which it fell on me, she had been fond of him. My parents were there. Some friends of Mike's were there.

I had asked a favour of the parson; I had asked him to read the Burial Service, which is not very long, in its entirety rather than in the heavily cut and truncated form that is usually all the clergy think they can get away with. So it was that we were all sitting in the small church in its pastoral setting of trees and fields, listening to the words:

'All flesh is not the same flesh; but there is one kind of flesh of men, another flesh of beasts, another of fishes, and another of birds. There are also celestial bodies, and bodies terrestrial; but the glory of the celestial is one, and the glory of the terrestrial is another. There is one glory of the sun, and another glory of the moon, and another glory of the stars; for one star differeth from another star in glory. So also is the resurrection of the dead.'

As I heard the words 'bodies terrestrial', I was aware of something unobtrusively going on at the back of the church; I looked round and was in time to see the door open quietly and Brian come in. Letting it shut gently behind him, he sank into the last pew and sat with bowed head. I turned back to giving my attention to the service, but without paying full heed to the range of meaning contained in Corinthians IV, 15. My mind was at least partly occupied with another subject: how, at the instinctual level, was I reacting to Brian's presence? Did I resent his being here? Had I managed to get free from the shadowy aftermath of the idea that Brian had killed Michael? And that, being the killer, it was obscene for him to be present at the communal expression of sorrow at his dying?

During the rest of the service, until the time came for the bearers to hoist up the coffin and all of us to troop out into the open air, I probed stealthily at my feelings on the matter as one might investigate a broken tooth. The answer I came up with, consistently, was that I had no feelings at all. I neither minded, nor didn't mind, Brian's coming to the church. That whole area of my mind seemed to be completely desensitized, something else that made me think of dentistry.

I suppose at any funeral the moment of ultimate bleakness is when the coffin is lowered into the long, steep trench of the grave and they start shovelling earth down on to it. That's when it comes home to you that that particular human story really is over. 'Dust thou art, and to dust thou shalt return.' My parents were standing beside me, my mother the nearer of the two, only a few inches away. On my other side stood Mairead with her hand in mine. If ever a bereaved person at a funeral had all the means of comfort close by, I was that person. I had it good. Even Brian, whose presence might have disturbed my mind in one way or another, had somehow managed to slip away unnoticed; he had got away before the procession came out and was nowhere to be seen. I didn't hear a car drive off; perhaps he had come on foot. Probably he had been waiting at Binsey village, seen the funeral go by and then walked the half-mile to slip into the church after everyone had settled down. I thought of him only briefly. I just stood there and, on an impulse, took a few steps forward and looked down at Michael's coffin just before it disappeared as the soil dropped spadeful by spadeful. Then I stepped back to my place among the others and just looked up at the line of Wytham hills.

As I did so I was reminded suddenly, with no idea where the thought came from, of Heather's brother Tom, shot down while defending England against the Luftwaffe. His body must have been broken like Mike's, as his Spitfire disintegrated in the air. Or perhaps it had been incinerated as the machine hit the ground in a mass of flame. And another image flashed powerfully into my mind: the field of wrecked German aircraft beside the works at Cowley, and the

R.A.F. test pilot throwing that Spitfire about in the clear blue air above it, and Brian and I standing in the roadway, taking in the strange, indelible scene.

If Michael had been a dozen years older, he would in all likelihood have been a fighter pilot in 1940, because he was the type to volunteer and to go successfully through the training. In which case, he would probably have finished up dead like Tom, or like most of the young Germans whose aircraft lay heaped and broken in that Cowley field. Or, if he had survived the battle and, already a veteran, been put on to other duties, he might have been up there on that bright winter morning, twisting and turning in the azure sky. But had that test pilot himself survived the war, taking risks like that every day?

So many had died. It was the fate of young, active, reckless men. What did it matter, in a larger perspective, that my son had survived the war for a decade and then been killed in a racing car? He was with Bettington and Hotchkiss, with Tom, with the young Germans, with all the countless others who had passed out of life before illness or weakness had time to sully them.

The Vicar, at my elbow, spoke to me and recalled me to Binsey Churchyard. I went through the usual motions, thanking him for officiating. He was a decent man and he said the decent things. Then my mother was standing beside me and looking about her,

'This is a beautiful place, isn't it, Peter?'

'I don't think there's anything more beautiful on earth than this kind of English country churchyard,' I said. 'And it's so quiet. That's what finally makes it perfect.'

My mother nodded. 'It'll be a comfort to you, as the years go by. You'll be able to come here any time and think about him a little, and you'll be glad he's in such a special place.'

She didn't say it, but I understood, as clearly as if she had put it into words, that she wanted my father and herself to be laid here in their turn.

*

'How can I help you, darling?' Mairead asked me one night as we settled into bed. 'What would you really find useful and healing? While the pain's new and raw, what would really be a help? Because whatever it is you ought to do it. If it's something that involves me, fine, and if it doesn't, fine. Perhaps solitude would help you. Just say it and we'll set it up. There won't be any difficulties we can't overcome. Even work ones. If you need a spell away, I'll just tell Episcopus College that I'm standing in for you. I'll gather all your students together and talk to them about Irish history. It'll do them good.'

'The fact is,' I said, speaking very softly, my voice close to her ear, 'if I wanted to forget everything else and just concentrate on my own feelings, see the world from that one narrow point of view, I still wouldn't know what to do just now. My feelings are variable. They come and go. If I were to find myself on a Greek island with no one else there except a few fishermen and their families, it might be perfect for six hours. Then my mood would change and I'd need you and the children again. And at other times I'd need my study and piles of books and all the Bishop Gibson stuff laid out. In the magic-wand fairy stories I could have all that – just wish myself into a place and I'd be there. Travel's become faster than it's ever been, but it's not instantaneous yet and it never will be. So, all things considered, I'm better off where I am. Especially as I'm in the place where you are.'

'It doesn't matter about me,' she said. 'I want you to go for what will help you over this terrible business and not think about anything else. I can't quite share it with you. I can feel for you, deeply, desperately, but I can't stand absolutely beside you, on level ground, and share it a hundred per cent, because Michael wasn't the son of both of us. In a twisted sort of way, you could do that better with Heather.'

'Yes. But as you say, it would be twisted. Too much so to help either of us.'

'I agree. You'll have to find some other way of helping each other as the years go by. Because, my darling, this pain won't go away. It's in your bones.'

That's true, I thought. How right she is. You can't run away from your own bones. Soon we slept, and her nearness to me was a blessing of which I was continually aware; yes, even in the depths of sleep I knew I was touching her.

In such ways did Mairead seek to bring me comfort. And she did bring it, just as Keira and Moira did. Just as the earth did, and the rain, and the slanting autumn sunshine. And work, the great anodyne of work. Paradoxically – and then perhaps, if one considered it properly, it wasn't such a paradox after all – I never attended to the duties laid on me by Episcopus College and by the Oxford University Faculty of Modern History so scrupulously and with such far-reaching thoroughness as I did in the couple of months following Michael's death: in other words, for about the whole of the Michaelmas (as I have no option but to call it) Term, 1955.

Lamont was coming to Oxford for almost a week, and I determined to see as much of him as possible. If he had particular friends in Oxford that he was looking forward to seeing, that was another matter, but I was not going to let irrelevant people waste his time with chit-chat that they could exchange with anybody. The man was valuable. I had not seen him for a long time and I was hungry for contact with his mind. Furthermore, he fitted into a small but to me very interesting category: people whose acquaintance I had made at Oxford, who seemed to me the kind of person one would naturally expect to meet at Oxford, and who were no longer actually there. The place seemed natural to them; certain of their most essential attributes seemed only to come into full play when they were frequenting the familiar streets and buildings and open spaces where I had first known them; yet Oxford was not, in some cases had not been for many years, the actual scene of their lives. As Charles Lamb sadly described the row of tall ledgers he had filled with figures during his wage-earning life as a clerk as 'biblia a-biblia', books that were non-books, so this particular layer of my friends seemed to be non-Oxford Oxonians, with a slight air about them of permanent dislocation; 'exile' would be too strong a term for what they suggested, yet there were moments when my mind came near to selecting even that word.

Lamont was due to arrive at Episcopus between twelve and one, a fact that in itself I found slightly surprising when his telephoned message reached me. Living as far north as Yorkshire, I would have expected him to reach Oxford later in the day, but when he arrived and we were having the usual few minutes of more or less nose-rubbing conversation he revealed that he had stayed overnight in London because that morning he had had an appointment to see a publisher. 'I've never had a London publisher before,' he said wonderingly. 'I've put so little energy into promoting what I write – just let it take its chance, which in practice meant firing it off at random to magazines or letting local publishers have it if they come asking me if I have anything. The wrestle for expression seems to leave me so emptied out that I can't start working all over again as a salesman and *entrepreneur* and publicist and all the other things I see poets quite ready to undertake.'

'Well, I don't know about the literary world,' I said, 'but I understand it's quite usual to run into people there who spend about a fifth of their time writing and the other four-fifths drawing attention to what they've written.'

'So I understand,' Lamont said cheerfully. 'Fortunately, I'm such a recluse that I probably have less contact with the literary world even than you do. I was asked to Durham once to read my poetry at the University – that's about as far as my fame seems to have spread. And now, London! It took me the whole train journey here to get my mind round the idea. The man asked me to leave him with enough material to look through and select a volume. Of course I should have to see the selection. I can't have him butchering the stuff just to get the right length.'

'Is it your Euhemerus you've given him?'

'Yes,' Lamont said half-ruefully. 'That's all there is to give him. There isn't anything else. Since I was an undergraduate, the Euhemerus theme has swallowed everything I've produced. It's such a grab-bag. Of course in a way it's hard to think of a subject that the idea of the frontier between human and divine isn't relevant to.'

'Will the figure of Euhemerus the individual be swallowed up too, in the end, and wither away like the state in Marx?'

'It remains to be seen. I don't think so, at present. He's only a presiding figure anyway.'

'Is there any of you in him, as you've presented him?'

'There's something of every man in him.'

'Well,' I said, 'I'll be content with that till we're sitting down by a fire for a real talk.'

'That'll be a pleasure. And it's good of you to invite me.'

Feeling that there was no need of empty politeness, I made the briefest of replies to this. The plain fact was that I considered Lamont to be doing me a favour by being my guest. He had come back into my life at a time when I needed him. Ever since I first met him, and that was fully a quarter of a century ago, he had struck me as having some kind of healing and restoring power that I could not account for. I had never been one of his real friends, but on the other hand he was not a stand-offish man; when we were all young and all living together in the same college, it had been quite easy to spend a certain amount of time in his company, and it always seemed to me that to spend time with Lamont, even a little time, was to feel an extraordinary relief from the pressures that ordinarily weighed down on one's life. It was not that he preached uplift or 'set a good example'. It was more that he seemed to be playing by different rules, that instead of accepting the ordinary herd-values and trying to live up to them he was obeying some other set of commandments, not quite legible from where I was standing, not quite intelligible to my mind, and yet not totally obscure either. There was an otherness about Lamont, as perhaps there is about people who have a very deeply-held religion, and yet one could not imagine its ever degenerating, as religious emotions can do, into fanaticism.

Often I thought back to that morning when we freshmen had found our way up Bax's staircase and stood on the landing outside his door, waiting for the hour to strike when we should knock and go in. A nervous, unprepared, apprehensive bunch we had been for the most part. Only two of us had been relaxed and confident: Knowlton, with his loose-limbed body, his long careless limbs that somehow, without his ever giving a thought to such matters, always managed to arrange themselves in some graceful attitude, Knowlton the *insouciant*, the casual, whose world was so secure that he could afford to be unambitious, who had never had to face a difficulty that he found hard to solve, and who wasn't nervous at the prospect of meeting his tutor because he didn't suppose there was a tutor anywhere in the world whose demands could strike terror in him; and Lamont, who, as I had wonderingly taken note at the time, had, without a trace of pertness or impudence, simply treated Bax as an equal, one cultivated gentleman talking to another who happened to know rather more about the subject they were addressing.

It was not a matter of having the assurance that comes from belonging to a higher social class; I never had the impression that Lamont's social origins were that much 'better', as the world reckons these things, than my own. The sense of equality must have come from within his own character. I remembered now, thinking back on it, that Lamont had mentioned to me, in those early days, that he had always known he was going to devote his best energies to trying to become a poet – known it, that is, ever since he had known that such a thing as poetry existed. Perhaps the sense of dedication, and the discipline it had led him to accept, had burnt out of him any other kind of diffidence, leaving him with a core of self-belief and self-reliance that he knew he had earned by the vigour of that lonely struggle with language.

For my part, I was riddled with anxieties about how I would adapt to Bax, what he would think of me, whether I would be able to learn from him, and so on. It would have seemed flatly incredible to me on that morning, and indeed for some years afterwards, to be told that one day I would consider Bax as a close and trusted friend. Lamont, obviously, could have entertained such thoughts even then, because for him the struggle lay elsewhere. If he had anxieties they would have concerned his relation with the Muse, not with his tutor.

Lamont, predictably, had quietly taken from Oxford what he wanted. The place had at least provided him with the essentials: books, like-minded friends, attractive surroundings, an opportunity to study in more detail the things he felt drawn to study. He had chosen to study history not because it was his main interest but because, as I well remembered his saying on that first morning, 'Poets need information.' Yet from this unambitious beginning he had achieved enough to be at any rate conventionally inconspicuous; his Second was respectable, and on going down he had been able to use it for . . . use it for . . . What exactly *had* Lamont done for a living? I wondered whether it was worth bothering him for that kind of information. Probably not. He had the complexion of an outdoor man, and the address on his letter had indicated a rural setting; was he something to do with farming, or estate management? Probably not, and in any case it would just be a living while he courted his imagination. The one thing that obviously had been a crucial hinge in his life was the spell at sea during the Second World War. The physical work had thickened his frame; the long hours on deck in the North Atlantic had permanently roughened his skin and put that network of fine wrinkles at the corners of his eyes that sailors get from constantly watching the horizon. Before that period, his appearance had had in it a touch of the Shelley: a slight, agile body, high forehead, eyes that always seemed to be seeking to penetrate a veil of distance, though whether it was spatial or imaginative distance one could not tell. Now, in early middle life, his body was strong and solid, and though his eyes still looked to the distance, it seemed to be a human distance, a panorama rich in figures of men, women and animals.

I had booked him in for lunch, and we went and had it as soon as he was installed in his guest room. After the meal I took him back to my study, sat him down and got through the business of handing on all the information he had asked for concerning books and their whereabouts. He absorbed it rapidly and gratefully.

After that he left me for an hour or two, to walk around Oxford and let me clear away a few tasks. He was to come home with me to meet Mairead and have a meal with us.

I wrote a few letters, saw a student who needed guidance about something, and sat down by my gas fire to wait for Lamont's return. The clocks had just recently been put back for winter time, and I was facing the cheerless annual adaptation to the shortened daylight. Only this year it was going to be more cheerless than ever. The summer had finally been extinguished, and this year's summer had been Michael's last one. I needed Lamont's visit. My life had reached a point where I needed to talk about these issues of death, bereavement, immortality, memory and the possibility of a persisting relationship with those who had gone from life, and I needed to talk about them with Lamont. Either him, or someone just like him – and I did not know anyone just like him.

I suppose, looking back, that it was one of those junctures at which many people feel the need to talk to a priest or to some similar person who has been entrusted with the responsibility of acting as intermediary between God and man. In my case, this resource was denied to me by both trivial and serious obstacles. The trivial obstacle was that the Christian ministers with whom I was most conveniently in touch were two in number, neither of whom I would have dreamed of engaging in conversation involving the deeper issues, spiritual, moral, emotional or philosophical, with which my life confronted me. The local vicar of our North Oxford parish struck me simply as an *apparatchik*, reasonably well-intentioned as *apparatchiki* go, but incapable both by nature and training of understanding any deep issue, especially concerning the recesses of human motivation. The other was the College chaplain at Episcopus, Fanshawe, that pale-hued, sandy-haired man who seemed always to be trying to recede into his ecclesiastical background and become invisible and imperceptible. Given the difficult position of any professional exponent of Christianity in a non-Christian society whose chief demand on him is to attend to certain accustomed formalities and otherwise to show good form by not drawing attention to himself, I had considerable sympathy with Fanshawe and quite understood his wish to blend into his background and disappear into the protective colouring of his routine duties and the sheltering complexities of post-Pauline liturgiology, but the thought of seeking contact with him at a crisis of my life was one that moved me only to brief laughter on its way to passing out of my mind altogether.

No, it was Lamont I needed. He struck me as having a total honesty, an unflinching realism, that would not be afraid to confront anything and would have no reason to be afraid of giving his opinion – not afraid of disappointing, or wounding, or seeming inadequate to the task. He had been to the bare, cold places; he had been in the presence of loneliness and death, and the fear that comes from these. And something had come to him that had enabled him to look at these things and not to flinch, and that something had never left him.

*

Mairead, with Keira and Moira to look after and the dinner to start preparing, had asked me not to bring Lamont home too early; in fact she had forbidden me the house altogether till seven o'clock. As we were out of Episcopus shortly after six, the only thing was to go to a pub. We could of course have sat in my study in College and opened a bottle of something, but, apart from the ever-present fear that some fiend might knock on the door with a bit of business I ought to attend to, I had always had a preference for the neutral setting, where neither party in a *tête-à-tête* was singled out as particularly the host or particularly the guest. We accordingly stopped on our way at the Duke of Cambridge in Little Clarendon Street, in those days a diminutive place with just one narrow bar mostly frequented by quiet beer-drinkers; the arrival of five or six of them together would have seriously overcrowded the establishment. Lamont and I easily found ourselves a place on the long settle, our backs to the windows and our faces towards the bar. Talk flowed immediately; we were at ease with one another.

'I see there've been some changes in College,' Lamont said, setting down his tankard after a long appreciative draught. 'I went along to knock on Bax's door but someone else is in there now. I looked round but I couldn't see a name-plate for Bax anywhere, and I didn't want to come back and disturb you again. I suppose he's still in College?'

'He's gone,' I said.

'Gone?'

'Gone from Episcopus, gone from the University, gone from academic life altogether. He's joined Oxfam.'

Sheer surprise kept Lamont silent.

'An emergency decision,' I went on. 'He had to save his life.'

'In what form,' Lamont asked, 'was death threatening him?'

'Prolonged unbearable unhappiness. Intolerable frustration, leading to exhaustion, which he tried to solace with alcohol until the alcohol became a problem in its own right. Disintegration was only a step away. He acted just in time.'

'And you had to watch him while all this developed?'

'I had to stand by and watch him. There was no way I could have intervened.'

'No,' Lamont said slowly, 'I can see that. He wasn't the sort of person in whose life you could intervene. Too independent. Too strong.'

'Yes. But even he wasn't strong enough to fight his way through this one. It drove him to the bottle and the bottle drove him finally over the edge – or was just about to.'

Lamont was silent, thinking. Then he said, 'What was the root cause?'

'He was homosexual,' I said, 'and he didn't know how to fit it into his life and a girl he fell in love with, probably initially because of her boyish physical presence, loved him very much in return but . . .'

'It didn't work, you're going to say?'

'Exactly what happened or failed to happen between them is something I've never been able to imagine, if only because my imagination switches itself off when it approaches the point where I ask it to perceive the two of them in bed. It just goes dead and its lights go out. Did you ever know that girl, by the way – she was around in our time – Geraldine?'

He shook his head. 'Not by name. I might recognize her if I saw her, of course.'

'Well, it doesn't matter. They kept the attempt going for years and years and Bax evidently found himself deeply involved in the relationship. But she'd been coming to see it more and more clearly as impossible and in the end she walked out of his life. It was at a very fateful time, when everybody was having to make very radical decisions.'

'Which particular time was that?'

'The late summer of 1939, when Stalin had just signed his pact with Hitler and everybody knew the war was inevitable. Desperate weeks, loaded with foreboding. I expect you remember.'

Lamont took another pull at his beer. 'How could I ever forget it? Those were the weeks when I decided that if war really did come, I'd have to volunteer to go to sea in the Merchant Navy. I went and joined a ship straight away, before the call-up got to my age group. I thought if I waited till I was actually in the Army it might be very difficult to transfer. But go on about Geraldine.'

'There's nothing more to tell about her, in this connection. Later on she married a friend of mine called Harry Goodenough.'

'Harry Goodenough! I knew him, if it's the same man. A Shakespeare fanatic, wasn't he?'

'The same. They didn't actually get married till after the war. Anyway, Geraldine split from Bax and I don't believe he had a happy moment after that. It extinguished a certain set of hopes in him, and he didn't know what hopes to put in their place.'

'I suppose,' Lamont said, 'he was still trying to deal with his homosexuality by ignoring it and suppressing it.'

'Well, that's the only way our society'll countenance it, after all. If he'd indulged it and let the fact become generally known, the law would have pounced on him as it pounced on Oscar Wilde. If he'd indulged it and kept the matter a secret, sooner or later he'd have been blackmailed, which must be one of the most hideous nightmare experiences you can have. What could he do? It seems to me he's been very realistic in finally recognizing the fact that as a homosexual who wants to avoid giving way to his impulses, he's in just about the worst profession he could be in, an endless parade of temptations. I think he's right to get out. Of course he could have sat tight and waited to see if social attitudes might change and drag legislation after them, as they seem to be doing over capital punishment.'

Lamont, still thoughtful, asked, 'D'you think that could possibly happen?'

'One hears rumours.'

He nodded. 'But I have a feeling they'll stay rumours for a very long time. I'd like the law to take a more humane attitude, but I can't see it coming in our lifetime. A pity, though. Decriminalization would have lifted all that load of agony off a man like Bax, and I can't see that it would do the fabric of society much harm.'

'Of course not. Society can't stamp things out just by being punitive, anyway. If it were possible for a homosexual to become heterosexual just by wanting to, Bax would have done it long ago. Well, I'm glad he's taken the plunge and got out. It won't be easy to make that kind of change because he must be over fifty now, but Oxfam needs people, and it needs experienced people just as much as it needs young enthusiasts. He'll do good work and they'll appreciate him. And besides . . .'

'Besides?' Lamont prompted.

'Even if he wasn't going to be a lot of use to them – but he is – I'd still think he was doing the right thing from his own point of view. Anything's better than having to act as tutor to a succession of young males any of whom could unwittingly act as the trigger to feelings he simply hadn't the power to control, and having to sit with them alone in his room for an hour every week. And in the end it broke him. Or could have broken him, if he hadn't had the courage to make a break for a more open landscape. Working for Oxfam won't solve his problems, but it might enable him to find some better way of coping with them, and that's all any of us can ask for.'

'Amen to that,' Lamont said. 'And now, before we move on to your house and begin a new phase of our evening, I give you a toast. To Bax and his fight for positiveness! May he succeed in it, for his own sake and everyone else's!'

We each had our glasses about half full. We chinked them together and drank. The toast was an important one; we meant it to have an effect, in some mysterious way, on the vibrations of the universe.

'Was all this quite recently?' Lamont asked, settling back. 'I mean, when did he go?'

'Just at the end of last term. The term that's just about to start will be my first without him. It'll be an altogether heavier burden to pick up.'

'But surely the College will elect another Fellow in History? There've always been two, haven't there? In our time it was Bax and Gadsby.'

'They will, but not straight away. I'll be expected to try out a number of makeshifts and temps. I think they're doing it partly as a test. If I can hold the fort by myself for a bit, they'll probably give me the senior position and leave it to me to find someone to back me up. I'll have the job of choosing a Junior Fellow and the College will rubber-stamp it.'

'So it'll be a new start for you too, as well as for Bax,' Lamont said. 'A weightier role. Making more decisions. You'll be conscious of having crossed a bridge.'

This was the moment for me to tell him about Michael's death. It was evident that he had not heard the news from any other source: why should he? It would be the first time I had actually related it to anyone. Up to now all the people to whom I had spoken of the bereavement had been people who knew about it already. It would be a liberating experience to make a narrative of it, to stand back from the sequence of events and put them in a neutral order, just the order in which they happened. It might help the dreadful, shattering suffering of it all, which at present was accompanying me everywhere as an incessant ache, so acute as to be almost always in the forefront of my consciousness, to be absorbed into a background of 'experience', that flowing river we all swim along in, and be to that extent tamed and set in order.

So I drew in my breath; then let it out again without speaking. Not for any clearly defined reason: it just seemed to me no longer necessary. I had the sense, sitting there, that Lamont *knew*. Objectively, of course, he knew none of the events that had, concretely, 'happened'. But those events, and my reaction to them, had put my psyche into a certain state that was new to me, and yet identifiable; and what I knew now was that Lamont could perceive that state.

We sat silent for a few moments. Lamont seemed perfectly easy whether to go or stay. I never knew anyone less fidgety.

Finally I said, 'A new start for Bax. A new start for me. I suppose you don't need new starts, Lamont?'

It was strange how natural it seemed to address him always by that one name, his surname. I had known him by it ever since I had first met him. I knew, as a fact, that his first name was Patrick, but he was not Patrick to me, he was Lamont, and I was not going to give him an unfamiliar name just to fit in with social usage. That was how Lamont affected people.

'A new start?' he said musingly. 'The time probably never comes when you can say with certainty that you're beyond the need of them. But I had mine ten years ago and more. I had the new start to end them all. Every molecule of my body, every impulse of my brain, had to start anew.'

'During your seafaring days?' I asked. 'May I hazard a guess that it was something to do with that terrifying experience you once described to me and Garrity, when you were standing on the deck of a ship in the North Atlantic and idly watching the ship behind you in the convoy, and she suddenly started to plough down into the sea?'

'What else?' he said quietly. 'I knew as I stood there, rooted to the spot, just helplessly watching it, that this experience had the power to finish me. I knew I could have a really final breakdown through the shock and terror that this was causing me. We've altered the terminology of these things, you know, but the things are still with us in the same forms they used to have. You can be frightened out of your wits and stay out of them, just as surely as you can die of a broken heart, though neither of them is called that nowadays.'

'But something pulled you back from the brink,' I said, half questioning, half stating.

'It was the instinctive wisdom of my body that pulled me back into life. After a couple of days of not eating, and of course I was doing physical work in the Atlantic air, I just became so hungry that the next time there was a chance of food I got a heaped plate and went at it like a famished wolf. I remember – I shall never forget! – what it was: Irish stew, great lumps of rather fat mutton with mounds of mashed potato and carrots and turnips. The turnips were pounded down to the same consistency as the potatoes, but the carrots were sliced. I just sat there getting it down like a power-shovel. As it hit my stomach the food seemed to be saying to me "Live! Live!". Impulses of energy and of something else I don't quite know what to call – purpose, perhaps; joy, even – were shooting out from my solar plexus into all my limbs, into my brain, into my eyes and ears. I went up on deck. All I could see was all I had ever seen from the deck of a ship in mid-ocean – other ships, crests of foam dotted about on a huge featureless plain of water, mostly the colour of lead, and above it all the colossal sky in which you had to try to read everything. There was absolutely nothing I hadn't seen hundreds of times before. But I also knew that I was seeing it for the first time. It wasn't the view that had changed, it was myself.'

'And you feel that change was a very important one?'

'Not just important,' Lamont said. 'Total. I'd become another person. I hadn't willed myself to – it had just happened. It wasn't anything at all heroic – it was simply survival: survival of a personality in one piece. I'd looked straight at death and felt it was very close. I'd stood and watched the death of an entire crew of men before my eyes. I hadn't seen their individual deaths in detail, but I could imagine every one of them, I could see vividly all the things that must have happened, the water plunging in as they lay still sleeping in their bunks, or tried to scramble up companionways and were simply washed down like tea-leaves in a sink, the officers on the bridge dying a few seconds after the rest, and then the silence as the ship drifted down to the ocean bed, turning in slow circles as she went. My fear became so great that I was on the edge of a complete disorganization, the kind of breakdown in which your limbs just won't obey your brain. For about forty-eight hours I was on the edge of that, and then somehow I got over it. As I say, I think my physical hunger pulled me clear. But I was changed when I came back.'

'Have you written about it?' I asked, feeling that I was probably being fatuous but really wanting Lamont's answer. 'Is any of *Euhemerus* about it, for instance?'

'It's all about it. At bottom, there's no page that's about anything else.'

'You'd put it as strongly as that?' I asked him.

'There's no other way I can put it. A poem about the relationship of the human and the divine is a poem about life itself, about the nature of life, the essence of life, the energies of life. About what form it takes, what form it ought to take, whether it's something out there separate from ourselves or something that flows through us and we share it with gods and animals and birds and fish and plants and radio waves and electric currents. And stones, are they alive? Who carved them and contrived them? Just chance? If so, chance must be a great artist – some stones, just as you find them on a beach, are among the most beautiful things in the world, and beauty's a form of life, surely? Or an invitation to life at least. How could I look at these matters in the same way after that moment on deck, after eating the mutton stew, the moment when I knew I had permission to begin living again after the life had been almost frozen out of me by fear, and then saved by animal instinct? Or by something else that I failed to recognize at the time, and perhaps am searching for to this day, searching in my life and in my poem.'

Lamont sat back. I made no reply. I have never entered the Duke of Cambridge since then without hearing his voice saying some part of the words I heard from him then. I have never since walked down Little Clarendon Street, even in its debauched modern form, without being conscious that it was there, in an unremarkable pub in that unremarkable street, that I once glimpsed the inner spirit of a poet.

Obviously that was a natural break in our conversation; I suggested that we drink up and move on to Kingston Road to meet Mairead, have a meal and move, as Lamont put it, into the second phase of our evening.

When we got to the house, Lamont sprang a surprise. I had noticed that he was portaging a brown paper carrier-bag – this was before the epoch of the universal plastic shopping-bag shouting its advertisements – and from this he now produced gifts for the female members of my family. For Mairead he had a small inlaid wooden box, very elegant – 'I had no idea of your tastes, Mairead, but I never met a

woman who didn't like elegant little boxes of handsome wood' –
which he had bought in advance and carried with him. The children,
whose existence he had only surmised without knowing any details of
sex or age, he had artfully provided for by telephoning Mairead while
out for his stroll round Oxford and getting this information from her.
For the infant Moira, he had bought a doll; conventionally enough, but
his reasoning that just as grown women generally like small elegant
boxes, baby girls like dolls. For Keira, at three, he had known that a
story-book was in order, and a search in the bookshops had unear-
thed a beguiling tale of fanciful adventure called *On Wooden Wings*.

Mairead was pleased, and when Lamont asked if he might go up to
the children's room and set eyes on them as they slept, and leave his
presents beside their pillows, she willingly conducted him up the
stairs, returning a couple of minutes later alone.

'Keira wasn't asleep yet,' she said, sinking down with her glass of
white wine, 'and when she saw him she snapped wide awake of
course. He's nice, isn't he?'

'I've always thought so.'

'Moira's asleep like a rock, but when he gave Keira her book she
asked him to read it to her. He asked me if he could stay up there a bit
and just read to her how it begins. He told her she had to get into bed
and lie down, and he'd start reading. You know how she always makes
bargains, well, she didn't make any this time, she just got on with it
and lay down. He's very good with her. Has he got any children?'

'I've told you, I don't even know if he's got a wife.'

'Oh, yes, I forgot that. I think I found it so incredible I just
couldn't take it in. Fancy knowing somebody as well as you know
Lamont and not even knowing whether they're married. In a curious
way it's as if you didn't care for him.'

'It's not that at all. I value knowing Lamont enormously and I
think a lot about him. I always have done. It's just that – well, talking
to him isn't really like talking to other people.'

'I suppose you're going to tell me it's all on a relentlessly high
intellectual plane. Don't give me that, Leonard. You're as earth-
bound as anybody else when you want to be.'

'So I am and I'm glad of it. But we're talking about Lamont, not
about me. His talk is always so . . . well, selfless, somehow. He seems
to have such a generous flowing-out towards the world, towards life.
He's so deeply involved with just about everything that he never
seems to halt at the boundary line between his own concerns and
those of the world in general . . . I'm not putting this very well.'

'No, you're not,' she said, slicing tomatoes.

'But I'm not going on with it now because what'll happen is that
he'll come down and catch us in the middle of talking about him.'

'If what you say is true, that won't make any difference to him. If he sees all subjects as equal.'

'Well, in a way that is how he sees them. I mean he seems to take them all as one big subject, life, and it doesn't seem to matter whether it's your life or his life or the life of mankind in general, which after all is only a conglomerate of all the lives there ever have been.'

'And the upshot of it all is that you can know him for twenty-five years and at the end of it still not know whether he's married or not.'

'He'll tell me if he wants to.'

'Pfoo! I'm not going to wait for that! I'm not a stultified Oxford intellectual, I've got normal human curiosity.'

At this point Lamont entered and put a stop to that particular exchange. General conversation followed, while we ate the excellent meal that Mairead had cooked for us, and drank the good wine I had taken care to lay on. I wanted nothing to go wrong with this evening, and nothing did go wrong. Except perhaps for Mairead's plan to satisfy her curiosity about Lamont's personal life. That never seemed to arrive on first base. Since I knew her intention, I could tell when she was moving the talk towards a position where she could reach out and take hold of the domestic side of his life, rather as a person in a boat might reach out to grasp the bow or stern rope of another boat and pull it alongside. But somehow it never happened. Whenever her hand was just about to close on the other boat, it would bob away again, impelled on the current of Lamont's interest in some matter that lay outside the sphere of the personal.

It was almost as if he were doing it on purpose. But I don't believe he was. His questions were real ones, his interest totally unfeigned. That mind of his was so stored with energy: with reflections, with comparisons, with subjects he would like to know more about. He was, for instance, immediately interested in Mairead's job, the work she did for the Irish government in translating educational and administrative material. To most people, this would have seemed the ultimate in boring routine jobs, undertaken solely because it was a modestly money-earning activity that could be carried on at home. But not to Lamont. He was at once full of questions. What was this material? Was the need for a translation totally genuine or was it programmatic, undertaken to serve a dogma in the same way that a police-court summons in Wales has to be printed in Welsh as well as English, even though the notion that anyone actually needs the Welsh version is strictly a legal fiction. (Perhaps, after all, it might be a good legal fiction, useful in certain not impossible circumstances.) Did it raise tricky problems? Did modern life, things do with motor vehicles or school examinations, prove difficult in traditional Irish? They probed the question together. The probing drew out of Mairead some of her deeper opinions about Irish political and social attitudes, which I had never drawn out. Why not? Why had these interesting revelations about my wife had to wait for Lamont?

From that, he passed to the Irish language itself, asking her a stream of questions about its origins, history, affiliations, and why it was spelt in such a strange irrational way. At first Mairead gave him the kind of fobbing-off answers she might have given to a child – a clever child, naturally – but as she came to realize that he was seriously interested she turned her full attention towards setting him on the road to understanding.

Not knowing enough to join in, I listened contentedly to the warm, interested tones of her voice as she outlined to him a few principles of Irish morphology, and went on to expound the pre-Christian legends of Maeve and Aillil and how they came from Cruachan ('now Croghan, in County Roscommon') to invade the kingdom of Ulster, and set in place for him the jewels of the Irish legend, Cuchulsinn, Fionn, Oisin, and the lovers Diarmuid and Grianne.

Lamont kept her at it while we drank coffee and cleared away the dishes, and when we went into the sitting-room with wine and glasses, he had still not been recalled to personal topics. I could tell that Mairead was waiting for another opportunity to bring up the topic of Lamont's personal relationships, but I had business of my own first. All this talk of legend and imagination, of the high heroic interpretation of an essentially tragic history, had whetted my appetite for the symbolic and the transcendent. I wanted to hear Lamont read some of his poetry. On the window-seat of this room I had put the things of his I had been able to find during my search of the shelves, and now I handed them to him. I wanted to hear Lamont's voice give expression to the forms shaped by his mind. And I knew Mairead did too, and that she would rein in any merely personal curiosity till the more important rite was performed.

I gave him first the extract we had found in the magazine.

'Ah,' he said, taking it from me and glancing rapidly through it. 'I see this is one of my cantering passages.'

'Cantering?'

'Yes, in a long poem you have to vary the tone a good deal, but I don't just do it at random. I have definite stylistic strategies for different areas of the poem. The cantering bits are where I'm moving fairly fast, with what I hope is a springy tread, from one image to another and then another, building up atmosphere and giving a physical setting to the sort of ideas Euhemerus was having and the physical setting they would most naturally spring from. Then again I have very still passages, where the poem isn't moving forward at all, just standing still or revolving on the one spot; dancing perhaps. Those tend to be formal lyrics. And now and then there are walking passages, which are what they sound like. The poem just moves forward step by step, at a very deliberate pace. That's when it comes very close to a prose idiom, but to keep it from just prose I use a pretty tight decasyllable. That's when the framework is built into place – the ideas that the poem actually rests on.'

'I'd like to hear one of the walking passages,' I said, and Mairead said, 'Me, too. The framework would help me.'

'Well,' Lamont said. He scrabbled in his brown-paper bag. 'I did bring a few sheets, because I knew you'd want to hear some and I thought it would be a good way of singing for my supper. Thank you.' These last two words were addressed to me as I filled his glass with an ample supply of claret. He then went on to make some remark, which I have forgotten, about Ben Jonson and his dependence on wine for the creation of a congenial mood.

Lamont then read us these lines.

> Stories of gods and goddesses are not true.
> Nor untrue. They are metaphors, and so
> they can grasp truth, and hold it up to sight.
>
> To say that Ceres is the harvest-goddess
> is to say that the harvest is divinely given,
> which is true. The golden grain obeys its nature,
> but nature on her own would not bring harvest.
> Nature invented the grasses of the field.
> It was the mind of man that pondered them,
> knelt down and rubbed their heads of meagre seed
> and saw a harvest heavy in its sheaves.
> It was man who saw the harvest in a dream:
> he dreamed a harvest before harvest was,
> the sun-warmed grain, the plumpness and the husk.
> He dreamed the harvest waving on its stalks:
> he dreamed the season and he dreamed the grain,
> and then he dreamed the miller and the loaf.
> He woke from dreams to the grey sky of work.
>
> He dug and ached and waited for the spring
> and groaned his prayers and sheltered from the wind.
> Panting and sweating he coupled with the soil.
> Their mating mounted to its ecstasy
> and earth grew pregnant with the thrust of harvest.
> Earth swelled and ripened. Man had given her seed.
> Not his own seed, and yet it was his own.

It was the seed of his strong joy in making,
the sperm of his lust to know and to invent.
He must create. And she must bring forth harvest.
It was a lust that mocked at continence,
a lust that claimed all virtue for its own:
it was the lust of man to be divine.
Such unions are sacred, not profane.
Such marriages were never made on earth,
only in the heaven of the uplifted mind.

Man dreams the name as he has dreamed the thing.
He names the harvest as a goddess. Now
she is outside him. In her Otherness
she can be worshipped. And worship has to be.
It was man's thought and toil that made the seed
plump out for harvest, but the seed was there.
He must give thanks, or the seed will turn to stones.
Where worship is not, harvest will not be,
for prayer is sustenance, gratitude is life.
And so man dreams a goddess of the harvest.
And if he names the golden harvest Ceres,
why, Ceres is the harvest's golden name.
The corn is Ceres! Ceres is the corn!
Not two, but one! Not one, but everything!

Towards the end of this recital, the door opened softly and Keira, in her nightdress, joined us. She stood quite still until Lamont's voice had ceased for some seconds and he had looked up from his manuscript in such a way as to make it plain that the extract was completed. Then she said, 'Daddy.' She spoke to me but she looked at Lamont.

'What is it, Keira?' I asked, trying to show authoritative impatience, though actually I was glad to see her, as I generally was.

'Can I have a glass of milk?' she asked.

This was a well-tried form of blackmail. Before settling into a deep sleep, she often woke once, for a few minutes, and felt inclined for a little sociability from a grown-up. This need on its own was not always enough to squeeze a visit out of one of us, but a request for milk usually hit a knee-jerk. All parents have a secret fear, usually absurdly mistaken, that their children are not getting enough calcium or protein.

I rose to accompany her to the kitchen and then upstairs, this being the usual bargain and the shortest way of packing her down. After about five minutes I came down to find Lamont and Mairead deep in conversation.

Our talk swept round in wide circles, rose, fell; sometimes, like a fire, it flickered and was for the moment almost extinguished, then leapt up with tall flames as the fuel settled into a fresh position and presented new unconsumed areas. Finally Lamont, declaring that he mustn't outstay his welcome, began to speak of walking back to College. I offered to come with him.

'Do come if you very particularly want to,' he said, 'but there's absolutely no need. I'm fond of walking about alone at night. I find it a good time for thinking. As far as the sentiments are concerned I could have written that poem of Robert Frost's that begins, "I have been one acquainted with the night." D'you happen to know it?'

It happened that Mairead did; I didn't. That started the two of them talking about Robert Frost. I had noticed that Frost often appeals to people who otherwise seldom read poetry; his concreteness, I suppose, and his definite opinions. She and Lamont went on quoting the craggy old New Englander to one another until finally Lamont got to his feet and said, 'I really am going now. Thank you for a wonderful evening.'

We made a few sketchy plans for meeting again during his visit, then the door opened on to the windy street and he was gone. I could either have gone with him or stayed to keep Mairead company and help wash the dishes. I chose the latter course. I don't mind washing dishes if I have had a good meal off them, and I wanted to hear Mairead's thoughts about Lamont.

They turned out to be pretty much as I expected, that is, warmly favourable. And she agreed with me in noticing that carapace of impersonality, as if he would find any subject endlessly interesting except details about himself; he soon came to the end of his interest in *them*. We agreed, as we turned off the lights and went up to our bedroom, that this made Lamont just about the opposite of most people we had ever met.

'I couldn't help noticing,' I said, 'that you never did get an opportunity to ask him whether there's a Mrs Lamont or not.'

'That's what you think,' she said, sitting on the bed and stretching out her legs straight in front of her, one after the other. As she did so she crinkled her toes, enjoying the freedom of releasing them from her shoes.

'Why, you mean you did ask him?'

'Yes, while you were giving Keira that milk.'

'Crafty of you,' I said.

'What's crafty about it?'

'Waiting till I was out of the room. You didn't want me sniggering behind your back at your feminine curiosity.'

'Snigger away. I'm not ashamed of being a woman.'

'I'm glad to hear it,' I said, accompanying the words with an appropriate action to which she appeared to have no objection.

'Well, tell me,' I said a little later.

'Tell you what?'

'When you asked Lamont about Mrs Lamont, yes or no, what did he say?'

'So you're curious, too.'

'Of course I am. Tell me.'

She looked up into my face, and I could not read her expression. 'I asked him if he was married and he said, "Sometimes". '

'He said what?'

' "Sometimes." '

'Just that one word?'

'That one word.'

I considered. 'Perhaps that's what he always says to that question.'

'How can you possibly think that?'

'Well, I've never pretended to read his mind, but that may seem to him the most straightforward answer he can give.'

'What? "Sometimes"? How could that be a straightforward answer to "Are you married"?'

'Well, there are two ways it could be that. It might refer directly to his own situation. Just literally, he might have a lady who comes and goes, or he comes and goes in her life. Or it might be describing how marriage itself seems to him. He might see every human being as deeply alone, sometimes touching just one person they're supremely fond of and uniquely attached to. But he might see that touching as intermittent. Even that kind of marriage, the best kind there is, can't be maintained evenly. It slips away and comes back.'

'Is that what you think he means by it?'

'Question time's over,' I said. 'It's love time now. Come here.'

★

The undergraduates duly came up on the Thursday and Friday, dribbling in until they were all in place by Saturday evening for the first full muster in Hall. The great pounding machine of teaching and learning, with all its complex apparatus of tutorials, lectures, classes, seminars, Faculty meetings, examiners' meetings, *und so weiter*, would be fully engaged from Monday morning. On the Sunday, only the Chaplain would have a full day's work, and of course the scouts and the kitchen staff. Looked at from a certain angle, the University, imagined by some as a calm backwater where reclusive and rather indolent people take shelter from the storms of the outside world and indulge themselves by pursuing arcane research into their private hobbies, appears rather as a damned great factory, most of the time working full blast and just occasionally sinking into an exhausted peace.

On the Sunday, since I was not in the habit of attending Chapel, I had decided to avoid Episcopus altogether and enjoy a last day of domestic peace in Kingston Road. I woke up by slow stages, got up at an easy pace and was in the bathroom, shaving, at half-past nine. I lathered my face contentedly.

At that moment Mairead appeared at the bathroom door and said, 'We have a visitor.'

'A *visitor*?'

'Someone who wants to see you!'

'Well, they'll have to wait. Who on earth comes barging in unannounced at this time on a Sunday morning?'

'It's someone you know.'

'Someone I—? Don't *you* know this person?'

'In a way I do, but we hadn't met till a couple of minutes ago.'

I put down the razor I had just taken up. 'You hadn't . . . Look here, what are you telling me?'

'I'm telling you to come down. The visitor's in the garden. I asked her into the house, but she said she'd rather wait for you out of doors.'

As soon as Mairead said 'she' rather than 'he', I knew immediately who was waiting for me. Don't ask me how I was so certain. I just knew.

'D'you want to talk to her with me?' I asked.

'Not unless you absolutely need me.'

'I can handle it by myself.'

'I'd rather you did, then. The girls are just having their breakfast, and if I'm not in there with them they'll get down from the table and run off somewhere.'

'Right, you go down. I don't suppose this'll take long.'

I tried to speak quietly and with composure, though my appearance must have been against any kind of dignity. There is only one thing a man thickly anointed with shaving cream can look like, and that is a circus clown of the traditional kind. If I had taken a couple of minutes to pick up a lipstick and give myself thick red lips and a red knob-nose, finishing off with little black plus-marks over my eyes, the costume would have been complete, and never mind the baggy trousers.

I stood for a few seconds in front of the mirror, hesitating. Now that I was lathered, ought I to finish the job and shave before confronting Heather? It would mean leaving her alone for a couple of minutes in the garden; but what harm could she come to in the garden? What harm could she *inflict*, for the matter of that? She might put a curse on it. But, I reflected, she might equally do that at a distance. Perhaps there was something rational and sensible that she wanted: perhaps she had a normal, ordinary reason for calling round. Without telephoning? At nine-thirty on a Sunday morning? I must go down, anyway. But not unshaved. Not stubbly and villainous-looking. That would put me at a disadvantage straight away. Or, perhaps I should say, at even more of a disadvantage.

I shaved and went downstairs and out of the back door into the garden. Heather was standing at the far end, beyond the tree where I had rigged up a swing for the girls. She had her back to the house and as I drew near I saw that she was looking at the ducks on the canal. She must have had eyes in the back of her head, though, because she turned round to face me although I was only walking on grass and not making a sound.

'Hello, Heather,' I said. She said nothing.

I wondered what I would do when Keira and Moira came out, as they were almost sure to do in a very few minutes. I supposed I had better speak, to move the situation along a little, but all that came out was, 'Is this a social visit?'

'Yes,' Heather said. 'A social visit.' She spoke in a dead voice that might have been intended to express contempt. But it could also have been simply that she was feeling emotionally dead and there was no other way her voice could have sounded just at that time. How was I to know?

'Won't you sit down?' I asked, still unable to come out with anything that didn't sound fatuous.

'I'm all right standing, thanks.'

'Well, what can I do that'll be any use to you?' I pushed on.

'I want to meet your wife and daughters.'

'You've already met Mairead. She came up and told me. I was shav—'

'I've set eyes on her and I've heard her voice, yes. For that matter, I could hear the children chattering away in the background. None of it really amounts to meeting them. Being *introduced*, I mean.'

'Well, what d'you expect? You turn up without any warning when the household isn't up and ready for the day and the children are still having their breakfast. I don't think it's fair to expect—'

'I know all that. But if I'd had to go through all that business of ringing up and arranging a time to come, I'd never have had the nerve to come at all.'

As Heather made this small confession of weakness, at any rate to the extent of telling me that the visit was an ordeal for her, I shot her an attentive look, taking in the details of her appearance. She was her usual outdoor self with the fresh complexion, the shining well-brushed hair and the tall, straight carriage, but I saw signs of strain in the lines round her mouth and the faintly blue circles that lay like bruises about her eyes. She had not been sleeping deeply. Some unresting compulsion had driven her to this invasion of our space, Mairead's and mine.

'You want to meet Keira and Moira?'

'If those are their names, yes, I do.'

'Didn't you know those were their names? I thought you'd have all that kind of information.'

'Yes, I suppose I had heard their names, but you can't *know* somebody you've never seen.'

'And you want to know them,' I said carefully, trying to get all this laid out step by step, to avoid having surprises sprung on me.

'Yes. What have you got against it?'

'I didn't say I had anything against it.'

'You didn't say it, but you have, haven't you?'

The sun, which had been veiled by a passing isolated cloud, came out very brightly just then and illuminated the scene as if for a studio shot. Heather, her full statuesque beauty scarcely diminished by the maturity that was beginning to gather about it, stood looking at me accusingly, and behind her a pair of dazzling white swans rowed their stately forms past along the waterway, filling my mind suddenly with the thought: *Swans mate for life*.

Had I got anything against Heather's meeting, and getting to know, the two children of Mairead and myself? She would meet them anyway, if she stayed where she was for another few minutes. Obviously the only way to prevent it would be to take Heather by the shoulders and propel her violently out of the garden and into the street, or even backwards into the canal. Equally obviously I was going to do no such thing.

'What's in your mind, Heather?' I asked. 'Why is it suddenly so important to you to meet Keira and Moira? Because it is a matter of meeting them, isn't it? Meeting Mairead can wait, can't it?'

'Yes,' she said. I am not a very intuitive person, but on the rare occasions when I have an intuition that is accurate I know it's accurate. Heather didn't argue, she just agreed with my statement. 'I want to see the children. It came over me last night when I was lying in bed, not sleeping. I was lonely. I don't suppose you ever feel loneliness, nowadays.'

'Everybody's lonely sometimes.'

'I'm lonely most of the time. About the only times I've got away from feeling lonely were the times when I happened to be with Mike, and he's . . .'

She stopped. A mallard, its wings whirring rapidly, came down on the water behind her in a long series of light splashes.

'Those children are partly mine,' Heather said to me. 'They're the children I ought to have had; that gives me a share in them.'

'Is that how you see it?' I felt a fool uttering those words. For Christ's sake, of course that was how she saw it. If she hadn't seen it that way she wouldn't have said it that way.

'How else can I see it? Another woman gets pregnant and has a child. Then she does it again. Two children. How did she get pregnant? Not by lying on her back and thinking about it. No, by joining herself with the body of a man. In the particular case we're talking about,' she could not bring herself to say Mairead's name, 'it was a man she stole from me.'

'Oh, hardly that. I explained to you all along that—'

'You can dress it up as much as you like and cover it over with fancy excuses, but we both know. The sperm that went to the making of those two children was something that belonged to me. It was mine; it should have gone to making children for you and me, not for you and her. So that gives me a right to have some relationship with those girls. A right to have a recognized place of my own in their lives.'

'And you've come here to say that?'

'I've come here to start it off, now, this morning. To meet them and begin the process without waiting any longer. I don't want to come into your house, but I expect you to have the decency to fetch them out into the garden and introduce them to the woman who ought to have been their mother.'

I took a deep breath. 'All right, Heather, but not so fast. Yes, you might have been their mother but in fact Mairead is. You may see that as simply the result of wickedness on my part, but it's there and we can't just sweep it under the carpet. And I'm not going to go into the house now and grab them and bring them straight out to meet you without any consultation with Mairead.'

'Consultation! You deserted me without any consultation, didn't you, and went running after her?'

'If you want to know the truth,' I said, 'I did an enormous amount of consultation before taking that step. I consulted my mind and my body and my memory and my view of what were the possibilities for the future, for both of us. I consulted my conscience, and I also consulted my estimate of what I thought were my own possibilities of maturing into a useful person.'

'Words, just words.'

'And I believe I came to the right decision. Mairead is a wonderful wife to me and I'm profoundly glad I went after her and got her. And because she gives me that standard to live up to, I'm a better husband to her than I was to you.'

'That wouldn't be difficult. Using the excuse of having a war job to go rabbiting around in London.'

I let that go.

'So it's as simple as this,' Heather said in a hard, flat voice. 'I've lost the only child I had by you. Now I've got nobody and I'm lonely. There's a lot of empty space in my life and I want it filled. So I'm here to claim my rights, or some of them. I want your two little girls to get to know me. Nothing special, nothing superheated. Just to get to know me in the way they might get to know an aunt, for instance.'

'What am I supposed to introduce you *as*? My ex-wife?'

'Just introduce me as me. Children don't ask that kind of question. Grown-ups to them are just grown-ups.' She looked past me. 'Where are they now? Will they be coming out?'

'Now look, don't let's rush this,' I said. 'I think your wish to get to know the children is a very natural one. I'm quite sure that you'll meet them in any case, as time goes by. Kids shoot up very quickly, remember how Mike did?' (That was a mistake. Pain shadowed her face and I could have driven a nail into my tongue.) 'Before you know it, they'll be big girls, half grown-up, quite capable of going all over the place on their own, making up their own minds where they want to go and who they want to see. Just at present they're tiny things.'

'That's no reason why they shouldn't set eyes on me. I want them to grow up used to me as a presence in their lives, not a vague threat out in the shadows somewhere.'

I thought of Siobhán and how she had the run of our house exactly as if she were a close relative. But Siobhán was different. That helped to pin-point it in my mind. Siobhán was different in absolutely every way. For one thing, she came out of a background of total, mutually supportive friendship with Mairead. There were no unguessably deep rifts between them, no legacy of pain and resentment and hatred, no doors that had been screwed tight shut and must never, never open.

'I understand your need, Heather,' I said, 'but I don't want us to try to run before we can walk, on this one. Quite apart from everything else, Mairead has rights in the matter. Any decision-making that goes on, I'd want her in it from the very beginning.'

'All right, can she come out and talk about it?'

'Not now, for certain,' I said. 'I'm not going to have her swept along on a tidal wave like that. She got up an hour ago expecting a quiet Sunday morning, and a quiet Sunday morning she shall have.'

'You really look after her, don't you?'

'I do no more than I ought to do. If you want the three of us to meet and discuss things, let's talk on the telephone and set up a place and time. Then we'll be able to prepare our minds for it.'

'Is it such a huge thing to set up?' she asked, and her voice was softer now, almost with a note in it of something like pleading.

'An enormous thing, when you think of all the repercussions and ramifications.'

'I think it's quite simple,' Heather said. 'I'm fond of children and I'd like to be fond of these two.'

'Look, I swear that I'm sympathetic to that wish and I won't put silly, artificial obstacles in the way of your getting to know Keira and Moira. But I won't let you do it at the gallop, on impulse.'

'So you won't let me see them now?'

'Sorry, no,' I said. The fact that they had not appeared by now must be evidence, I thought, that Mairead had found them something sufficiently absorbing to do indoors to be able to hold them there for a while. I wasn't afraid that they would suddenly scurry out. I had time to get Heather clear of the place.

'Is that your absolutely final decision?'

'Absolutely final.'

Heather began to move back along the garden path, which led round the side of the house and ultimately to the street. When she got to the front she stopped, turned and faced me.

'Will you ring me?'

'Yes. This evening.'

'They could come out and see the horses. One of the things I could do in their life would be to bring them into contact with horses and teach them to ride. Girls always like that.'

'A lot of them do, yes.'

'I could make good little horsewomen of them.'

'Heather, you're talking about the future. Even the older of them is only just turned three; the younger's hardly a toddler. If you hoisted either one of them up on to even the smallest pony, the only result would be that they'd be frightened and it would put them off for life.'

'Nonsense, if you talk to anyone from a real equestrian background, you generally find they were around horses from just about the time they were born.'

'Well, don't let's argue about it now. I'll ring you tonight.'

'And you'll have made up your mind by then, won't you?'

'We'll be ready to make up our minds, put it like that.'

I almost pushed her through the gate. As she took the last few steps and got into her car, there was something submissive in the lines of her body that made me feel I would die of grief. It told me, more plainly than words could have done, how sharp her pain was, and how deep her need.

That evening, after discussing the matter, I telephoned Heather and arranged that we would take the children for a drive in the country the next Sunday afternoon, and would call in and have a cup of tea with her. The children would wander about where they could see the horses, and if they showed any particular interest they could be held up to pat and stroke their manes.

Which we did. It was all *gemütlich*, and harmless, and appeared to point towards happier and more fruitful occasions in the future. But one cannot tell much, where deep and complex emotions are concerned, from appearances.

★

'Why aren't you getting ready for school, Keira?' I asked.

'I'm not going to school. I'm having dabs.'

As usual I had to seek illumination from Mairead. 'She means jabs. Dr Hargreaves said he'd look in this morning and do the pair of them. I jumped at it, of course – saves us all that sitting in the waiting-room.'

'The doctor's coming to give us dabs. What are dabs? What do they taste like? Can Moira have one the same as mine? Will mine be bigger because I'm a bigger girl?'

'In your case, my doll,' Mairead told her, 'they'll taste like a lump of sugar.'

'Well,' Keira said triumphantly, 'you can ring him up then, Mummy. You'd better do it now. He's bound to have got up. It's getting-up time even for big people. It was getting-up time for little people hours and hours ago. Hours and hours and hours and hours and hours and hours and—'

'Yes, but why?' I demanded. 'Why should we telephone him?'

'To tell him not to come. We've got lots of lumps of sugar. In the cupboard just behind where you're sitting, Daddy, there's boxes of it. I can go to the cupboard and get the box and take two and I can eat one and give one to Moira and then there'll be no need—'

'I hope you'll do nothing of the sort, young lady,' Mairead said to her severely. 'The very idea. Going to the cupboard and getting out lumps of sugar. That's not the idea *at all*.'

'But you said Dr Hargreaves was going to give me and Moira lumps of sugar. Didn't Mummy say that, Daddy?'

'Support, Leonard, support,' Mairead commanded.

'She didn't say that, no,' I said, lifting Keira on to my knee. 'What the doctor's going to do is take a lump of sugar, one out of our cupboard or one he's brought with him, and put a drop of special medicine on it that's good for little girls. The medicine probably doesn't have a very nice taste so he gives it to you on a lump of sugar, so you can't tell what it tastes of.'

'But I never have medicine. I'm too well to have medicine. I'm so well I can jump right up in the air. I can jump over this table. I can jump over this house. I can jump over a tree. I can jump over the Idle Tower.'

–364–

'How d'you know about the Eiffel Tower?'

'I've got a book with a picture in it.'

'Oh. Well, Dr Hargreaves's medicine isn't only for people who aren't feeling well. There are some medicines that are for people who are very well, to help them to stay like that.'

Keira fell silent, considering this, and in the background Mairead said, 'Good back-up, Leonard. Good bit of follow-through. You're learning.'

It now fell to me to assemble Moira's play-pen, which was dismantled and stacked in the hallway when she retired for the night. When I had made ready the small enclosure, I called to Mairead to tell her I was going down to Episcopus.

'When shall I see you?' she called down. 'This evening some time?'

'No,' I answered. She came into view as I spoke, carrying Moira, and as she drew nearer I was able to stop shouting and just speak normally. 'I'll be back sooner. Today's one of the last when there won't be anything much to do after lunch-time. Nobody's had time to write an essay yet, so I shan't need to have them in and discuss what they've done. This morning I just get them all in, some in batches and a few individually, according to the stage they're at, and start them on the term's work. Give them essay subjects and reading lists and start them going. Proper tutorials won't start till next week. At this stage it's more like winding up a lot of clockwork toys and putting them down on the floor to start moving along.'

'Well, good luck,' Mairead said.

I thanked her and set off. As I walked I reflected that whether she knew it or not, this was quite an appropriate time to wish me good luck. I was, finally, in sole charge of the history teaching at Episcopus from this point on. It had taken Bax an incredibly long time to shake free of the place and his intricate involvement with it. They had not wanted to let him go; about the only person, apart from myself, who had not stood in his way was the President, Mowbray, who with his long experience of the wider world was sympathetic to the kind of direct involvement in action that Bax was now undertaking. He may, of course, have known or guessed something of the hidden springs of motivation that were at work in Bax. I feel certain that Bax wouldn't have told him directly, but I had also come to the conclusion that with his varied background and slowly matured wisdom there wasn't much that Jock Mowbray didn't know or intuit. He was certainly in no mood to stand in Bax's way. Most of the other Fellows were to some extent disgruntled at losing someone as reliable and dug-in as Bax. They didn't trust me to run the history business as effectively as he had, in which they were doubtless justified. Nor did they think me capable of the same good judgement in choosing a junior man to bring on. (We were not yet in the era of women Fellows in men's colleges.) It was difficult for me to see how they reconciled the second mistrust with the first, since I myself was in my Fellowship because Bax had put the weight of his judgement behind me; but they managed it somehow. I countered that one by asking Bax's advice about the candidates for the job, when I had brought it down to a short list.

Involved with this and with that, it was not until the end of the academic year 1954–5 that Bax finally left and went overseas for Oxfam. Since then I had had a year for my younger colleague to bed down in the job, and he had proved thoroughly useful and dependable. The period of trial and error was over, the work-load was allocated, and from now on it was my responsibility to make things work; no looking over my shoulder at Bax, no making allowances for a younger colleague who had to be broken in; this was the real thing. I was on the bridge, and the sea was full of icebergs, as the sea always is.

Surely, I told myself as I walked along, I had it in me, after years of Bax's training, at least to try to be good enough. This determination grew in me as I went briskly towards College in the bright morning sunlight, and when I got to the place and saw all the fresh young faces and thought of the empty young heads crying out to be filled, my mood became positively optimistic, especially as the sun was now bringing out the colour in everything – the sky, the trees, the buildings, the people. Before going up to my room I took a turn round the garden. The gardeners had as usual done their work brilliantly, and the profusion of late flowers was wonderful.

My name was down for lunch; at the end of the previous week I had booked in every day this week, assuming that I would be too busy to leave College in the middle of the day. But now, determined to seize one more chance of a little time in the peace of my home, incited to revolt by the glowing colours and the dramatic sunshine, I telephoned down to the kitchen and told them I would not be there today. Then, hastily – for students were already waiting outside my door – I rang home to tell Mairead I was going to be there at lunch-time. She was out; already engaged in the business of the day, no doubt. Never mind, I would just have to go home unheralded and take pot luck.

As it happened, when I got there Moira was still at the house of Mairead's friend and ally Daphne, a few doors away, and no doubt having her afternoon nap. I told Mairead that on an impulse I had signed off for lunch and would like to have an impromptu meal with her. She caught my mood at once.

'What about eating in the garden?' I suggested. 'There won't be many more days like this before winter arrives. None, perhaps. Let's seize it.'

'You're on. It'll be a bit scrappy; I haven't done any shopping.'

'I'll go out and buy a few things if you like.'

'No, don't spend the time. We'll eat what we've got. This is a moment not to miss.'

I looked at her. 'What makes you say that?'

'I've caught your mood, that's what it is. Go and brush the leaves off the garden table and put a couple of chairs out. I'll do the rest.'

I arranged the chairs at the bottom of the garden, where the canal lapped gently at the bank. The season had passed when the banks were enamelled with bright flowers and the vegetation, mostly grass, nettles and docks, was leathery and lacking in freshness. As against that, the nettles were attracting plenty of butterflies, and in the warm still air electric-blue dragonflies hovered a moment here and there before disappearing into the sheer speed of their flight and reappearing in another spot. A mallard, with its perfectly selected subtly matched colours, swam busily past. The occasional ring in the water hinted at the presence of fish, well-grown after a summer of plenty, rising for insects. Silver and gold willow leaves had begun to fall and were scattered here and there on the water, though on this motionless day there were none falling as I watched now. It was a good moment to be beside the Oxford canal; it seemed like a time when the natural world was happy, inviting me and mine to be happy with it. Was that just a subjective impression, the projection outward of my own sense of harmony, or was I seeing the scene that was really there? But then, I thought from the long habit of self-questioning, what was 'really there'? What did I, what did anybody understand by that phrase?

Mairead had brought out a loaf, cheese, a plate of chopped raw onion, and two of the little bottles of dark, strong beer that Garrity always took with him on his 'expeditions', and with whose help he solicited the Muses. 'This is the only drink we've got in the house,' she said.

'It's exactly the right thing. It's what Garrity always drinks in the open air, and he's a good man and he wishes well to the world. I hope he's sitting in the sun now, up in the mountains over to the east of us somewhere, drinking something he likes and thinking splendid thoughts.'

We drank and Mairead said, 'Well, *you* seem to be thinking splendid thoughts.'

'Well, positive ones, anyway. I go into Episcopus and I start thinking about Bax, now that at last I've succeeded to his command. I decided to try to live up to what he was in his best days, and his best days went on for a long time. And that thought was bracing to me.'

Mairead said, 'Yes, and I'm sure his best days will come back now that he's had the courage to break away from all those frustrations.' She raised her glass. 'I give you, Bax's new life!'

'Bax's new life!' We clinked and drank. 'Not forgetting *my* new life,' I added.

'Yes,' she said. 'I meant that as well.'

We sat there for a while, eating bread and cheese and enjoying the sunshine.

'I feel very strong,' I said.

'Good. I'm glad.' She gave me, unexpectedly, a quite serious look and said, 'This is a good time for you to feel strong.'

'Isn't any time good for that?'

'Yes. But this time is specially good. We may all need strength. I can't be more precise than that, but . . . I feel there are changes coming.'

'Really? What kind of changes?'

'All kinds.'

'That's a bit general, isn't it?'

'Yes. It's going to be a general change.'

I stopped eating now and looked at her attentively. 'How seriously ought I to take this, Mairead?'

'As seriously as you like . . . all the way.'

I have often noticed that women habitually say 'I feel' in situations where men would say 'I think'. This is not a triviality, it is a serious gender difference arising from their dissimilar ways of perceiving experience. I tried now to frame a question that would avoid both 'feel' and 'think'.

'But, darling,' I said, 'what are your grounds for believing in this onset of change? What evidence have you noticed?'

Mairead gave me a smile of a kind she quite often did give me. It seemed to arise from a mixture of compassion, amusement and a tolerant wish to make allowances.

'Oh, darling,' she said, 'I can't give those sort of why-and-where-fore reasons. I've just been getting signals.'

'What kind of signals?'

'A feeling in my skin and hair, mostly.'

I looked hard at her. 'Are you joking?'

'No, some people get physical sensations when the weather's going to change. And some people get them before other kinds of change – when everything that concerns their life is just about to change gear in some way. I'd like to be more rational about it, but I can't.'

I drank the rest of my bottled beer, thoughtfully, and set down the glass. 'Have you had this feeling often?'

'No, not at all often.'

'When was the last time?'

'Before Hiroshima.'

'Well,' I said helplessly. There didn't seem to be anything else I could say. 'Well, I . . .'

'Don't try to say anything. If I'm wrong, we'll soon see when nothing happens.'

But enormous things did happen. Mairead's skin and hair had not lied. Neither at the time of Hiroshima, nor at this time.

★

'They pulled it down?' I asked Mairead.

'They pulled it off its platform and then they smashed it into pieces,' she replied.

'You're sure of this?'

'It was on the radio. I heard it at six o'clock. It'll be time for another news bulletin in about twenty minutes, and then you can hear it again if you don't believe me.'

'Well, obviously I believe you. But we'd better listen for the next announcement. There'll probably be more developments. Unless the Russians have managed to impose some kind of news black-out.'

'I suppose they'll try,' she said. 'But the international news services are bound to be listening to every word that comes out, and when you think how easy it is for anybody with a home-made transmitter to send out a signal, there's bound to be someone on our side of the Iron Curtain picking it up.' I remembered that she had worked in diplomacy and must know all about international communications.

The date was October 23rd. I had spent the day immersed in my work-load at Episcopus, and had come home at about half-past six. If I had gone into Hall for dinner and held speech with the other dons, I would doubtless by this time have been well briefed in the extraordinary – the electrifying! – news that was beginning to come out of Hungary.

For the next couple of weeks I, like many others all over the world, was less like a human being than a pair of ears connected on one side to a shocked and appalled intelligence and on the other to a radio. This was not television material, though most people had sets by that time; the news from Hungary was radio news, developing and changing its outlines from hour to hour. It changed the world as decisively as Hitler's invasion of Poland in 1939 changed the world by plunging it at last into overt war and changing a screaming little dictator from a weird, indefinable, almost shimmering vision of something-out-there – a something that might still have its moments of reasonableness, even of friendliness – into a recognizable, focus-able figure, the Enemy. In the same way, those few days in Hungary changed the more withdrawn and looming figure of Stalin, with his

–369–

flamboyant moustache and his peasant features on which lurked at times a half-smile that could – just conceivably *could* – signify benevolence, into what from then on the world knew him for: the gently smiling madman, whetting his axe-blade as he walks calmly towards the cottage where the family lies sleeping. The world, tense and listening beside a million radio receivers, at last penetrated the mask of Stalin although the man himself was safely in the grave. The Revolution of the Hungarian people against Soviet domination began with a mass demonstration of popular discontent in Budapest, in the course of which a statue of Stalin was pulled to the ground and broken up. Listening in Kingston Road, I had a sense of the blind fury that must have driven on the crowd to this act of self-forgetful defiance. It is, and always has been, usual among tyrants to demand from their victims not merely obedience but also homage. Some of the worst oppressors have been among those who most fiercely insisted on being made into cult figures, like those Roman Emperors who decreed their own apotheosis, commanding that they must be treated as gods and worshipped and that this worship should begin in their own lifetime – a custom carried on by the Emperors of Japan until half-way through our own century. This tradition may be acceptable among orientals who have never known anything but persecution, and perhaps even on the European land-mass among Slavs. (The word 'Slav' is derived from the medieval Latin *sclavus*, a captive, and the association is not likely to have been an accident.) But apply it to a proud, independent nation like the Hungarians, accustomed to an important part on the world stage, with a glorious history and enormous achievements to their credit in all the arts and sciences, and the mixture is a simple explosive. To terrorize and bully such people, to drench them in a propaganda that insults their intelligence, to deliver them into the power of a secret police who devise hideous tortures for them if they are caught doing anything to oppose the *régime* – to treat them so is to wipe your feet on them, to spit in their faces. To make the Hungarians undergo this kind of humiliation while being gazed down at by colossal statues of Stalin, in whose name these indignities and outrages are heaped on them, is to compound wickedness with breath-taking insolence. On 23 October 1956, the anger that burnt in the veins of Hungarians could no longer be held back from action. At least one of the huge, mocking statues of Stalin had to be brought crashing down, so that the citizens could gaze at it as it lay on the ground. And then it had to be broken up with picks and sledgehammers, so that they could contemplate the broken pieces. And then they took to arms to defend themselves against the punishment they knew would be commanded from above. And then the Red Army moved in. And then the gutters ran blood for days.

And all the time I listened to the radio. I would have liked to do something to help them, but there was nothing I could do, so I listened to the radio. Sometimes Mairead listened with me, sometimes she went away and did other things. Sometimes I too had to go away and do other things, because I kept up my work at Episcopus, though during those days I neglected it pretty heavily, as most of us did. This didn't seem like a time for dispassionate academic study, with the immediate present situation dragging at one's attention. It was all so urgent and appalling; it developed so quickly. In two weeks I don't think Mairead and I had a conversation, not an actual conversation as distinct from a routine exchange of words, about anything else.

Needless to say, if I didn't talk much to Mairead during this period, I didn't talk to anyone else at all. I avoided company. I found that the mental pictures that filled my mind were so disturbing as to threaten my mental balance, and certainly I was jumpy and suspicious of anyone who might conceivably express the sort of views that would cause my hatred of the gangsters in the Kremlin to boil out in some overtly aggressive form. I was, in a word, afraid of assaulting somebody. In two weeks I only once went into the Common Room to get a mid-morning cup of coffee, and then, standing next to the table where the newspapers were spread out, I succumbed to curiosity and looked through two or three of them. This wasn't much, but it was enough. They were papers with a wide range of reporting, and they surveyed divers areas of opinion, as newspapers should. Some of the remarks they reported were made by people who supported the Kremlin line, and of course they were to the effect that the people who made the 'disturbances' were reactionaries, right-wing counter-revolutionaries, Fascists in the pay of the Western powers. I think if I had actually encountered anyone who talked in that strain during the days when Hungary was being crucified, murder would have been done, either murder of him by me or murder of me by him if he happened to be the stronger. In any event I would have gone for him. Even to hear the matter discussed by anyone I regarded as an insensitive clot or a frivolous twit – by Manciple, for instance, or Watson – would have been enough to give me an ulcer. Once, as it happened, I was standing in the lodge when Manciple went by in company with some acquaintance of his, and as usual his penetrating voice reached my ears.

I was in the inner part of the lodge, just about to step out into the main archway, where the notice-boards were and which was on the direct trajectory of anyone entering or leaving the College. Seeing Manciple and his companion, I drew back a step or two and waited for them to move away. The other man was obviously leaving

Episcopus and Manciple was staying behind, so they paused for a moment to finish what they were saying. I had to wait till the coast was clear, and meanwhile I heard the last bit of their exchange.

'Khrushchev must be kicking himself,' the other man was saying, 'for blowing the gaff on Stalin like that. The speech last February, I mean.'

He was referring, I understood, to Nikita Khrushchev's speech to the closed session of the 20th Congress of the Communist Party in February of 1956, when he had at last openly said that Stalin had committed 'errors' – Soviet language for crimes and atrocities. I also knew that though this speech had not been made public, the American State Department had got hold of a full text and immediately given it wide publication, thereby sending seismic waves throughout the Soviet Union's Eastern European empire.

'Oh, do you think so?' Manciple said in his 'debating' tone. 'You didn't think they managed to counter it pretty well in that Resolution last June?'

'What was that? I must have missed it.'

'The Kremlin obviously felt under pressure. People – their own people, never mind us – were wondering why, if they'd known for years that Stalin was such a shit, they'd stood back and allowed his cult to go on so long. So they got the Central Committee of the C.P. to pass a Resolution giving Socialist explanations as to why it couldn't have been exploded earlier.'

'What kind of explanations?'

'Oh, you can imagine the sort of guff. The simple mass of the peasant faithful weren't ready yet – they'd been brought up to identify Socialism with kindly old Uncle Joe and they couldn't have accepted being told that he was a bastard, not just like that. The time wasn't ripe. And of course they followed that up by saying that the time was ripe *now*, the moment had come, success was here, the economy was thriving, people could stand the truth and needn't be fed on fairy-stories any more.'

'Did it work, do you know?'

'Well, it may have worked with simple souls in Uzbekistan and places like that, but it doesn't seem to have worked in places where they know anything about the world. The Soviet Union's too big, that's its trouble, and when you add all the satellites, it's simply unmanageable.'

There was a silence and I began to hope it was safe to come out, but then I heard the other man's voice again. He must have been thinking for a moment, and now he said, 'This Suez business. Do you think it'll make any difference?'

Manciple, naturally, was ready for that one too. 'Well, it's been handled pretty crassly, of course. It could hardly have been stage-managed worse. Nasser closes the Suez Canal, which he has no right to do because apart from anything else it means tearing up a treaty. As a reaction to that, Israel invades the Sinai Peninsula. Britain and France then gang up and say to Israel, "That's very bad. If you don't stop attacking Egypt we'll attack her too, and then there'll be a right old Middle Eastern mess." They go ahead and then there is a mess.'

'People are beginning to say there's nothing to choose between Hungary and Egypt.'

'Yes, but that was predictable, wasn't it?' Manciple said easily. 'The people who say that are the ones you'd expect to say it. What they didn't like about the Soviet invasion was that it was so clear-cut. It was a straight case of an imperialist dictator punishing a colony that had tried to get away. As soon as Suez happened, the hard Left seized on it for all they were worth because it blurred the issue. They could point to a set of footprints going the opposite way.'

'Well, I've noticed that myself. You can feel the relief of the young almost like a physical wave. They hadn't liked to see a Socialist country in the villain's role.'

'A country whose propaganda describes it as Socialist, you mean.'

'Yes, I do. They were like a lot of innocent young nuns in a convent who suddenly learn that the Pope's been caught with his hand in the Vatican till. They couldn't believe it, and now they can go back to thinking it's all a slander put out by the capitalist West.'

'A great relief,' Manciple agreed. 'It must have been the happiest day for years in the Kremlin when they heard the news of a *gaffe* like that. Mind you, whatever the young people may say, I fancy the older ones with the responsibilities will start singing a different tune when it sinks into them that the Suez Canal's closed, and that every drop of oil they use is going to have to be carried all the way round the Cape.'

'Oh, yes.'

'Righteous indignation soon dies down when people realize it's hitting their pockets.'

'Too true. Well, see you.'

'See you.'

Manciple now came into the lodge. Walking straight towards his pigeon-hole – he was always keen to see what letters and messages had come to him from the outside world, like a long-term convict – he didn't notice me and I ducked out thankfully. The last thing I wanted, with this tragedy weighing on my soul, was the smooth assurance with which Manciple could explain everything, once it had safely happened and he had tucked the loose ends tidily out of sight. In the case of Hungary they weren't just untidy loose ends of cause-and-effect explanation, they were agonized, severed and bleeding loose ends of people's bodies and minds and lives. So I kept silent and let the waves wash over me, because I wanted to stay sane.

In bed one night, holding Mairead close, I at last opened up. I tried to get at one particular source of the pain I felt.

'There are several layers to it, naturally,' I said. 'Of course there's the political outrage. Stamping out freedom is a wicked thing in itself, and it's an affront to anyone who values freedom for themselves or for anyone else. But underneath that there's the thought of the killing. I've lived through such a lot of mass killing since I've been on this earth. You might almost think I've started to get used to it. There were the big battles of the war, and then at the end of the war there were the revelations about the extermination camps in Germany, and right after that the truth began to come out about the deaths in Stalin's labour camps in the Arctic, and there was always the thought of Hiroshima and Nagasaki, and a lot of the time I managed almost to live as if I hadn't heard of it all because there's probably no other way you *can* live, but this wave of murder is different to me.'

'Because you're different,' she said, stroking me. 'That's what you're going to say, aren't you?'

'Yes, I'm different. When Michael got . . .' I wound myself up again and made myself go at it like a horse coming up to a jump it has refused once, 'when Michael got killed it brought death terribly close to me. I know death now. Death is a recognizable being. Death has a face like an actual person, and a voice like a person, and a way of coming into a room like a person, and a way of sitting down and standing up. Death is an individual acquaintance, not an abstraction. And I fear death. Anyone he's come that close to, must fear him. I don't fear him for myself, I fear him for the people I love. I personally shan't mind dying; what I don't see how to bear is the pain of losing the people I need most.'

She lay very close to me and didn't answer. How could she? After a time we drifted to sleep. But in my sleep I dreamt that I was taking a tube train from Paddington to Oxford Circus, and Death got on at Baker Street and sat beside me. He was dressed in a dark blue suit and looked as if he worked in a bank or something of that kind. 'You're Death,' I said to him.

'Yes, and I'm watching you,' he said.

'Me more than anybody else?' I asked.

'No, I'm watching everybody,' he replied. When the train got to Baker Street he stood up and said, 'I have to change here for Budapest,' and was among the first to get out. When I saw him go down the platform I suddenly realized why I was going to Oxford

Circus. I was going because that is the stop for Broadcasting House, and I was going there to ask if they would let me get to a microphone and tell the world about what was happening in Hungary.

The dream ended just as I was pushing through the heavy swing doors to get into Broadcasting House; it didn't take me so far as getting to a microphone, and I wondered when I woke up what I would have told the world that they didn't know already. And yet, in a curious way, that dream came true. Or perhaps I should say it came true in reverse. On the evening of 4 November Mairead and I had a light, casual meal at home – we had almost given up eating – and afterwards I settled down to listen to the radio as usual. We kept it on all the time in case there was suddenly an announcement. So it happened that I heard the message that came over at four minutes to eight that evening from Free Radio Kossuth in Budapest. The message was addressed to the world and the language used was English. It burnt itself so deeply into my consciousness that I might very well have remembered the words from that day to this, but in fact they are in the history-books and I have no need to rack my memory. The voice said, 'Our time is limited. You all know the facts. There is no need to expand on them. Help Hungary! Help the Hungarian writers, scientists, workers, peasants and intelligentsia. Help! Help! Help!'

The Red Army were already in the streets. Another two days and it was all over. The last radio messages blinked out on that day of November 6th.

On that evening, once again after hours of hanging on the radio news bulletins, and once again after pecking at a scratch meal (when had I last felt any appetite?), I fell at last into some kind of conversation with Mairead. We had been through it all together, in so far as mere onlookers can be said to go through any situation, and now the struggle was over and we had to adjust to what was left: ashes, disillusion, the abrupt halting of a surge for freedom, the hammering back into place of a heavy lid of repression. Was Hungary's last state worse than her first? How could one tell, without being a Hungarian and being there? It was hard to think that the great moments – the mass release of political prisoners, for instance, or the decision of the soldiers to join forces with the people on 29 October, which for a few brief hours seemed to give the rebels a real chance – could ever be cancelled out; something, surely, would remain in the collective psyche, and that something would ferment and grow. But that was speculation, and speculation from a distance. People might well have felt the same about the revolt of the Roman slaves under Spartacus, but its only result was an endless row of crucified bodies along the Appian Way.

'One thing I have to face,' Mairead said, looking at me tenderly but steadily, 'is that although I feel very much as you feel about the whole thing, so that I can stand close to you and go through this experience with you, I can't see it *exactly* as you see it.'

'No?'

'No, my love. Any scene looks a little different when it's seen from different angles.'

'And your angle on this one is different from mine, is it?'

'Well, in a sense it has to be; it can't help being. We both sympathize with the Hungarians as victims of oppression, but our feelings about oppression can't help being different.'

'Why can't they?'

'Because,' she said quietly and unaggressively, 'I belong to a country that has grown used to suffering oppression. You belong to a country that has grown used to inflicting it. My reaction to the spectacle of Hungary must be one of pure sympathy, a shared experience. Your reaction must contain at least a streak of jealousy. There must be a part of you that thinks, Why is it they and not we who are oppressing the Hungarians? Pushing people around is all right when *we* do it.'

I was silent for a few moments and then I said, 'Mairead, my darling, I'm going out and I'm going to walk around for a while. I need to be under the open sky and think a few thoughts, which I can't do as long as I'm fretting about at home, fidgeting from room to room.'

'Of course. I understand perfectly.'

'I shan't be long. To give myself an itinerary I may walk down as far as Episcopus. There's a book I need to get out of the Library, and I could let myself in and just take it and sign for it. The walk there and back will give me a few minutes of solitude and space.'

'You don't have to explain. I'll drink a glass of wine and listen to some music. I won't go to bed till you come back – unless you're very late.'

'I most certainly shan't be very late. I don't want to be away from you *for long*.'

'But you do want to be away from me for a bit, don't you? It's because I've said something you find hard to come to terms with.'

'I won't deny,' I said, 'that what you said has made me want to think quietly. To see if my position needs re-examining. But you must believe me, Mairead – that's one of the essential things you do in my life and I love you even more for it.'

I kissed her and she said, 'I believe you.'

I walked down Kingston Road to Walton Street and then along Little Clarendon Street, and crossed the road and got to Episcopus. The book I wanted from the Library was the fourth volume of

Lescure's edition (Paris, 1863) of *Journal et Mémoires de Mathieu Marais*. I knew the other three volumes pretty well, but had decided I needed to take a leisurely look at his letters, which are all in volume IV. I also had a secret hope that some browsing in the intrigues of seventeenth-century France might calm my mind if I could just focus on them; it had links with my own period in English history, and it would take my mind off the immediate situation.

As I went up the stone steps to the Library door, those steps from which I had picked up the unconscious form of Bax, I reflected that Mairead had put her finger very exactly on an English and an Irish view of Hungary. It had seemed to me a foul insult to stamp out their liberties in the name of Stalinism and then to erect statues of Stalin at which they were supposed to stare through a mist of gratitude. But how must it appear to Mairead that during the nineteenth century and right up to 1921, when Ireland was governed as a province of England and Irish people were instructed to think of themselves as identical with English citizens, except that they were somewhat shabbier and poorer and less likely to be taken seriously – during the whole of that time it had been complacently expected that they would sing the National Anthem at their public gatherings, so that for sixty years they would politely request the Almighty to save Queen Victoria? If that wasn't a Stalinesque insult, I thought as I unlocked the oaken doors, what was?

My business in the Library was soon done. I switched on a minimum of lights; I wanted to get in and out unobtrusively, without drawing attention to myself and having to get into conversation with porters and what-not.

The moon had risen now, a big round autumnal moon. Its light came in at the windows and made it perfectly possible to see one's way about in the silent length of the Library, interspersed with alcoves and tables. To look for a particular book one would have had to switch a light on, and I had done that in order to find Lescure's Marais; but now I had that fourth volume in my hand. It was time to go. I turned to walk down that part of the L-shape whose tall windows faced out on to the garden, and as I went past the windows I paused, as I had done so many hundreds of times before, to look out at the broad tranquil expanse of the lawn, the screen of trees at the far end, and the various dark groupings of shrubs and bushes and flower-beds. But it was the lawn that held my attention: the calm, unshadowed space of immaculately tended grass that always seemed, every day of every year, to be exactly right, neither too long nor too short, a triumph of unhurried human skill and patience amid a world so full of haste and abruptness and the random destructiveness that seems so often to be the dominant force in our society.

I stood motionless looking through the latticed window at the sleeping expanse of level grass: sleeping, or just quietly waiting? And if waiting, then for what? For an apocalypse, or just for time to merge quietly with eternity in a Nirvana where all known places were merged in one great Nonspace, calmly radiant and attentive only to its own sacredness?

And as I stood, the lawn changed. Actually, as I think I knew even in my trance, it stayed the same, but my vision of it changed, so that its nature as a reality changed for me. I knew that. I knew that I had not 'gone out of my mind', 'taken leave of my senses', any of those so revealing phrases we are given to using for moments of changed perception. But as I gazed at the lawn, with no conscious thought except to wonder whether the moonlight was strong enough for me to discern colours or whether the brighter tones were all just silvery-grey, the scene before me began to fill with shapes that reflected the landscape inside my head.

And these were shapes of fear, shapes of chaos and shock and disaster. I saw collapsed buildings and broken machinery. I saw bodies. I saw fleeing human figures, some of them maimed and crawling away. I saw a background of flames and oily smoke. I saw a sky with no birds in it, and here and there a broken tree with no leaves. And conspicuous among it all, in a central position where I could not fail to see it, there protruded – dented and battered but still recognizably the sleek outline I had known – the silver-grey snout of a racing car, Brian's K3 that had turned into Michael's executioner, its colour echoing the impersonal moonlight, the death it had absorbed echoing the deaths I saw being inflicted.

How long I stood there, holding that careful scholarly volume in my hand, staring through the window at my vision of the world and my own life, I have no idea. But it faded, the lawn became once more a moonlit patch of grass, and I let myself out and went down the stairs.

I walked deliberately, my back held straight, my face turned towards as much of my life's landscape as still lay before me, be it narrow or broad; and beyond it to the healing and forgiving darkness that will, in its own good time, gather us all together.